MW00696572

STOLEN DREAMS

STORMS OF NEW ENGLAND, BOOK 3

KARI LEMOR

Follow Your Dreams,
Kari Lemor

RYCON PRESS

STOLEN DREAMS

Can he loosen up enough to let her in?

Control is Alex Storm's middle name. Every aspect of his life is scheduled down to the minute. His routines are part of him, and he cannot deviate. Finding a woman who can put up with his strict organization has been difficult... until Gina blows back into town.

A nomadic life spent with her bohemian mother made Gina Mazelli the definition of a free spirit. Inheriting her grandmother's house requires her to put down temporary roots right next door to the sexiest control freak she's ever known.

Alex hopes helping Gina fix up the house will lead to a quick sale and an end to the explosive chemistry between them. But every day they're together, Gina realizes she wants to create a home, especially if she can convince a certain uptight perfectionist that he's the key to making her dreams come true.

STOLEN DREAMS © 2020 by Kari Lemor

Cover Art by: Karasel

First Electronic Edition: April 2020

ISBN - 978-1-7348335 - 0-8

First Print Edition: April 2020

ISBN - 978-1-7348335-1-5

All rights reserved under the International and Pan-American Copyright Conventions. No part of this book may be reproduced or transmitted in any form or by any means, electronic or mechanical, including photocopying, recording, or by any information storage and retrieval system, without permission in writing from the publisher.

This is a work of fiction. Names, places, characters and incidents are either the product of the author's imagination or are used fictitiously, and any resemblance to any actual persons, living or dead, organizations, events or locales is entirely coincidental.

ACKNOWLEDGMENTS

I am blessed to have so many people in my life to help me.

To my husband and children, for the never-ending support. To the Hoodlums, for buying multiple copies of my books even though I know you don't read romance. Truer friends I could not find! To Brooke, the inspiration for my intelligent, free-spirited computer geek, Gina. To Peggy, who helps keep me sane. You are a blessing to me, my friend! To the Fab Four, who keep me going with our weekly motivational goals. To Emily Harmston, for the most amazing editing job and making every word count. To Kris, for all your suggestions and for being an amazing friend and sounding board. To MA Grant, for providing me with the hard questions so my characters are more real and filled with emotion.

And to the amazing state of New Hampshire. You are my home, and I will always love you!

To my daughter, Emily, who truly understands my strange quirks, because she has so many more of her own.

CHAPTER ONE

*S*he was back.

The bright orange Volkswagen Beetle cruised past as Alexander Storm settled the trash barrel into place at the end of his driveway. The horn beeped, and the tiny car jolted to a stop. A petite ball of energy jumped out, the engine still running. His heart sped up. Damn, he wished it would stop doing that.

Gina Mazelli, in all her bohemian glory, bounced over to him, and he braced for impact.

"Felix!"

She launched herself off the ground and jumped into his arms, wrapping her legs around him. Her greeting hadn't changed in years. The nickname she'd given him when they were kids, born from too many reruns of *The Odd Couple*, didn't make him flinch like it used to. She didn't mean anything by it. From her lips, it was a sort of endearment.

"Hey, Dandelion, welcome back." Holding her tight, he shivered as her lips pressed against his neck.

"Miss me?" she chirped, her arms and legs still wrapped

around him like a monkey. Good thing she was small. Her face was so close he could see every long, thick eyelash. They were dark as pitch, and that was without any make-up. Most of the women he dated wouldn't be caught dead without at least a small amount. Gina didn't need it, though. She never had.

He scrunched up his face and pursed his lips. "Why would I miss you? You're loud and annoying, and you nag at me to do things that are way out of my comfort zone."

She laughed, causing her nose to wrinkle. "You did miss me. And, Felix, let's face it, putting your underwear in your drawer without folding them first is way out of your comfort zone."

"Hey." He dragged her arms from around him and lowered her to the ground. "They fit better that way. And how do you know what's in my underwear drawer?"

"You can't hide anything from me, Alexander Peter Storm. My Cajun blood is strong. I can tell everything about you just from studying your face and actions." Her voice had gotten low and mysterious. She should have been an actress.

"Or you snooped inside my underwear drawer, Gina Takara Mazelli."

Her dark eyes lit up, and she stuck out her tongue as she turned to strut away. Almost a foot shorter than his six foot plus height, she still managed to make her presence known. Maybe it *was* her strange mixture of ancestry. Her mother had been half Cajun and half Japanese. Add in her Italian father, and the combination was unique.

Peeking over her shoulder, she planted her hands on her hips. "Coming?"

"Where?"

"To help me carry my stuff in." So damn presumptuous.

"You didn't even ask. What if I have things to do?"

When she crossed her arms over her chest, it pushed her breasts out even further from the low-cut, tie-dye thing she wore. It was loose and falling off one shoulder, showing way more skin than someone should in March. In New Hampshire. The denim cutoffs also showed a decided lack of respect for the chilly weather, although she wore thick, sweatery socks that went almost as high as the shorts. Flowered Doc Marten's completed the wacky ensemble. Wacky for anyone else. Typical for his Dandelion.

Gina tossed her long, dark waves over her shoulder and strode purposefully toward him, her eyes determined. Grabbing his hand, she pulled. "There's nothing more important than helping me and you know it. Plus, you were just outside, so that means you weren't working."

"I was taking the trash out. And I don't have a coat. It's cold out here, if you hadn't noticed. It is still winter."

Raising her eyes skyward, she sighed. "Picky, picky. It'll be spring in less than two days. We should get ready for it."

He looked at her legs. They were ridiculously long for someone so small. "Like wearing shorts?"

"I had a long drive. They were more comfortable. Now, let's go. I need help." Her voice turned girlish. "Big, strong, manly help that only you can give me."

She was feminine in every single way. Her voice, her movements, her mannerisms, and especially her appearance. Too bad her attitude could use an adjustment at times. Like when she ordered him around.

She pulled again, and his legs started walking. He hadn't told them to do that. They apparently weren't listening. It happened a lot when Gina was around.

When she got to her car, she rolled down the window, then switched hands, so she could grab his through the opening. Getting in, she shut the door.

"Wait, what are you doing? I can walk over there by myself. I know where you're going." There were only three houses on the short street. The two Victorians facing each other belonged to him and his cousin, Greg. The one at the end was Gina's grandmother's, now Gina's.

The car slowly began to move, and Alex quickly kept up. God knows what she'd do if he didn't.

"I just want to make sure you're coming. You know I can't live without you, Felix."

"Could have fooled me," he muttered as they pulled into her driveway. Gina's grandmother had passed away around Thanksgiving, and she hadn't been back since. Before that, it had been maybe a few times a year. Not that he was keeping track. Why would he do that with someone who irritated him as much as she did?

She finally let go of his hand and turned the car off. After hopping out, she rummaged in the back seat, her adorable ass screaming for him to stare. Why did she have this effect on him? She must exude some sort of addictive pheromone. There was no other explanation.

Turning around, she shoved some canvas bags into his arms, then reached for her over-sized purse in the front seat. She skipped up to the wrap-around porch and dug in her bag.

"The keys are in here somewhere." Her head popped back out. She frowned. "I hope I remembered to bring them."

He wasn't the least bit surprised. "I have a set at my house. I can go get them and be right back."

"No, no." Her hands spread apart. Her face froze. "I remember now. I didn't want to forget them, so I put them …" Her eyes roamed the sky as if she could find the answer there. She ran down the stairs, back to her car, and dove in the front seat, her cute ass on display again. A second later, she backed out with a set of keys dangling from her fingers.

"I stuck them in the ashtray. Figured the car was coming here, so the keys would, too."

After opening the door, she walked in a few steps, then stopped. "Why isn't this place covered in six inches of dust? I haven't been here in almost four months." Moving to the hall table, she ran her finger over the surface. It came away with only a small amount of dirt.

"There's dust, see?" Maybe he could get her off that subject. "I can help you clean later, if you want. Let's get you unpacked first."

"Hold on a minute there, buster." She grabbed him by the front of his button down and stared into his eyes. Yeah, she definitely had some magical vibe going on there. "Or should I say duster? You've been cleaning in here, haven't you?"

"It's getting late. We should get your stuff before it's too dark."

"Not so fast, Felix Unger. Admit it. Confess. You can't lie to me. I can read your mind."

"Fine, I did a little cleaning. Only once a month or so. It was the least I could do for your grandmother."

Dropping his shirt, she turned away. Her shoulders rose and fell. "Please tell me you don't still feel guilty. God, it was so long ago."

"I don't know what you're talking about. Let's just get your things, Dandy." *Please let her drop it.*

She whirled back around. Shit, he didn't want to have this conversation. It was bad enough he carried the guilt inside him all the time. No need to rehash his worst decision.

Placing her hands on the side of his face, she kissed his cheek and leaned against him. She still smelled of honeysuckle. Her grandmother's fence had the stuff climbing all over it. Gina had loved to cut it and carry it around. The scent tantalized his nostrils as memories hammered away at his mind. Memories of them close like this. Wearing far fewer clothes. He ran his hands up her arms, then eased her away.

She wouldn't be swayed. She planted her hands on his chest and held him there. Well, he could physically move her if he wanted, but his body was doing that not listening thing again.

"Alex."

Oh, God, he was in trouble. She was calling him by his real name. She stroked her fingers down his face. "We both wanted what happened. You didn't take anything or steal anything from me. You were my best friend, and I wanted you to be my first. I knew you wouldn't be rough or icky. And you weren't. Admit it, we had fun." She tortured him with her impish smile.

His jaw tightened. "I was of legal age and you weren't." It had been amazing.

"You were nineteen. I was seventeen. Not that big of a difference. Besides, you thought I'd already—"

"I know what I thought," he snapped. "It was stupid and insulting. Maybe if *I'd* been more experienced, I would have realized that you weren't."

Her lips twisted into a grin. "With all the places my mother used to drag me to live in, at least I had an idea of what to do. One of us needed to know."

"I had some idea," he defended, heat creeping into his face. "But I wasn't about to ask Erik. He would have kicked my ass and given me a lecture on being responsible. And I never would have heard the end of it from Luke. It was embarrassing enough that my little brother had done it before me."

"So, we discovered together. Go ahead and tell me you didn't enjoy it. I won't believe you."

Alex glared at her. "It was the best sex of my life. There. Is that what you wanted to hear?"

She nodded her head. "Yes, even if it's not true. Thank you for humoring me." She skipped into the front parlor and looked around.

Alex stood still, thinking about what he'd said. It was true. It had been the best sex of his life. She'd lured him into the old tree house in the woods behind both the properties. It had been decked out with pillows, blankets, and candles. Honeysuckle had been spread over every surface. He still couldn't smell the stuff without getting a hard-on.

They'd spent hours kissing and touching, simply exploring what their bodies were capable of, and with his Dandelion, everything was always filled with laughter. She'd teased him unmercifully, and he'd given it right back. It had been the most fun he'd ever had having sex. He hadn't found anything similar since. Of course, when he'd discovered she was a virgin, the fun and games had ended. He'd been horrified. Gina had shrugged it off in her usual way. He'd spent the next nine years feeling guilty, wondering if Mrs. Mazelli knew what he'd taken from her only grandchild, her only living relative. Cleaning her house didn't even begin to repay that debt.

He went outside and brought in her stuff. It seemed never-ending.

"I didn't realize those Bugs could hold so much. Did you bring everything you own?"

"Yup."

The casually spoken word made him stop dead in his tracks. Was she planning on living here for good? "Are you moving in?"

She removed a sheet over the couch in the living room. "Well, for a little while, at least. I figure it will take a few months to go through Nonna's things and get this place in shape enough to sell. There's no sense spending money on an empty apartment while I'm here."

Of course, she was only here temporarily. "Where will you live once you're done? I doubt they'll hold your apartment. Not in New York City."

"No, but my job enables me to work from home." She sat down at the computer he'd lugged in and caressed the keyboard. "The computer firm I freelance for doesn't care where I live. And you know me, I don't stay in one location too long. I'll find some place new. Somewhere I haven't lived before."

He did know her. It was one of the reasons he called her Dandelion. She was like a weed, always popping up where he didn't want her. But like a dandelion gone to seed, when the wind picked up, she'd blow every which way, out of his reach.

"Don't you ever get lonely moving all the time? Having to meet new friends?" He had a few friends he'd been close to for years. They knew him and understood him. He couldn't even imagine trying to find other people with whom he got along so well.

"It's fun meeting new people. And if you get tired of them, you can go find other new friends."

That boggled his mind. His family was here, his friends, his job. He loved this town and the people in it. Maybe not every single one of them, but certainly the majority. Squamscott Falls was where he'd been born and raised. It held great memories for him. He had no reason to leave it.

"Where do you want me to put this duffel bag? Up in your room?" He hefted the large bag that had to weigh a ton.

"Yeah. No sense getting settled in the master bedroom, if I won't be here that long." She picked up a laundry basket filled with clothes and started up the stairs. It had been years since he'd been up here with her. Not since they'd been preteens. Once Gina had developed, Mrs. Mazelli had kept visiting to downstairs. She should have chained Gina to the wall.

As she placed the basket on the bed, he let the duffel fall. She looked around the room, old pictures dotting the surfaces. The smell of honeysuckle and something else … something sweet, drifted over. The scent was driving him crazy. He needed to leave.

"I'll let you get settled. Call me tomorrow if you need anything. I'll be working from home all day."

No reaction. Had she heard him? Didn't matter. He needed to get away from her intoxicating presence. He paused at the door and wished he hadn't. She stared at a picture of her grandmother, her father, and herself when she was about six. It must have been right before he died. Her usual happy expression had disappeared. Her eyes glossed over, and her lip trembled.

Shit, she was crying. He couldn't leave her now. Even at her grandmother's funeral, she'd barely shed a tear. Too busy trying to make sure everyone else was okay. He couldn't remember ever seeing her cry before.

He walked up behind her and touched her shoulders. She turned and moved right into his arms. As she snuggled close, she began to sob.

WHAT THE HELL was wrong with her? She never cried. Well. Almost never. Tears poured from her eyes as Alex held her tight in his arms. As she glanced at the picture of Nonna and Dad, their loss hit her hard. Her family was gone. Okay, not her mom, but the woman didn't even own a phone, so contact with her was sporadic at best. Dad had been gone for years and Nonna for months. Why had it taken until now for her to break down?

"I'm sorry," she mumbled into Alex's shirt as he rubbed his hands up and down her back. It felt so good. His solid chest gave her the support she needed right now. Alex was all lean muscle and intoxicating man smell. She shouldn't be enjoying it as much as she was. "I don't know why I'm suddenly a mess."

His voice tickled her ear. "Must be me. I seem to have a strange effect on women at times."

She chuckled, though she seriously doubted he had any problems with women. The man could give her an orgasm just by walking into the room. After her time here at Thanksgiving, her vibrator had gotten an extra workout.

His warm arms stayed around her as she took a few more seconds to wallow in the pain and loss of the past few months. Heck, the pain of leaving this place many years ago. They'd lived here, on the third floor, until her father had died in a freak accident at the boat yard where he worked. They'd stayed for a while, but Nika Takara Mazelli had never really warmed to Nonna and Poppa. Right before Gina was supposed to start first grade, her mom had packed their bags and started what had been a lifetime of nomadic wandering. It had helped Gina keep her mind off the fact her father wasn't around any longer, and had taught and exposed her to so much. But there were times she missed being in the same place, having someone like Nonna and her dad taking care of her.

Alex didn't say much. He stroked her back and hair, making little sympathetic sounds. It was nice. Then, she took a deep breath. *Time to pull yourself together.*

"Thanks for being my hanky, Felix. It was a little above and beyond, so the sentiment is appreciated." She stepped back and sniffed, looking for the box of tissues Nonna always had in every room. She grabbed a few and mopped up as Alex stood looking vaguely uncomfortable. He ran a hand over his blond hair, styled in the traditional men's cut he always wore. He was so different from most of the geeky or artsy guys she hung around with, but she found him so freakin' sexy, it was pitiful.

"You're excused," she said, tossing her damp tissues in the decorative wastebasket by the dresser. "You've done a few good deeds for the day and won't be needed again until tomorrow. Thanks."

Alex glanced around the room, his face still concerned. Yeah, he knew she didn't blubber like that often. Probably wondering if she was going to have a relapse. Hoping he could escape before she did.

"Can I help you unpack?"

Okay, so maybe not the escape thing. Probably the guilt thing again. When would he get over the fact he took her virginity? She'd taken his as well. They should be even. But goody-two-shoes Alex Storm didn't see things that way.

"I think I can manage to unpack by myself."

"Are you sure? Because I've seen the way you organize things, and it isn't pretty."

Only Alex would think of organizing things as pretty. "I think you just want to get into my underwear drawer. Let's face it, mine is probably way more exciting than yours."

Alex laughed. "Oh, I have no doubt. The offer still stands. I'll have your drawers and closet looking sleek and shipshape in no time."

She was tempted. Not because of the organized closet thing, but because she really didn't want to be by herself in Nonna's house. It wasn't the same without her grandmother here. "I guess if you're having withdrawals from cleaning, I could let you help. Of course, I won't be able to find anything after."

"I can draw a diagram with a list of what's in each drawer, if you want."

Oh, boy, he was serious. His tendency to micromanage everything was so freakin' cute. Her stomach fluttered knowing he was doing it for her. Alex was the sweetest, nicest guy she'd ever known. If only…

No, thoughts like that would only get her in trouble. She was here to clean up the house and get it ready to sell. Alex belonged in this sleepy little town with its small-minded citizens. She didn't. Would she even make it the month or so she'd planned to be here? Maybe if she stayed close to the house and didn't mingle, she'd be fine. With no outside contact, she'd be certifiable by the end, but her pride and dignity would be intact.

"Are these all your clothes?" Alex pointed to the duffel and laundry basket.

"The blue trunk has more, plus my shoes."

Alex nodded and sprinted down the stairs. His footsteps were much slower coming up. He dropped the trunk on the floor with a grunt. "Are they cement shoes, by any chance?"

As she started on the stuff that could be hung in the closet, Alex took the dresser. Every time she came across a pair of panties, of which she had many and most were scraps of lace, she tossed them at him. "More for the underwear drawer."

Alex took it in stride, but his face turned red a few times. He mumbled something about silky dental floss, then folded them neatly and lined them up with the others.

He held up a cropped tank. "Is this a bra? And do you have lots? I'm wondering about putting them in with the underwear or if they need their own drawer."

"Only you, Felix. And no, I don't have many bras. Even though my girls are a nice size, they aren't huge and they're still pretty perky." She cupped her hands around her boobs and lifted. "They don't need to be caged."

Alex dropped his head and groaned. "You are the only woman I could ever see myself discussing this with."

Gina held her shirt out and peered down. "That's because mine are spectacular. Admit it, they are."

Alex shrugged, trying to hide a grin. "They're not bad. Although, I haven't really seen them up close and personal in nine years."

Up close and personal, huh? She shrugged one shoulder off and pulled at her low neckline. "You're welcome to peek."

More color crept up his face as he turned away and stuck his head in the duffel bag. "It's fine."

Gina grinned happily. She loved teasing him. She could get a rise out of him faster than any other guy she'd ever met. She went back to hanging things in the closet, then pulled out some jeans from the laundry basket. Alex knelt on the floor, organizing her pants and shorts. Hmm, this could be fun. She tugged her top further off one shoulder so it hung low, then moved toward him with the jeans.

"Here's some more." She made sure to bend over, so the girls were in plain view. He glanced up to take the pants, and his eyes popped out of his head. Turning her face, she pretended she didn't see him looking. But he did. And if she wasn't mistaken, the front of his pants suddenly pushed out some more.

When she went back to pulling clothes out of her basket, Alex stuffed the jeans she'd given him haphazardly into the drawer. His voice was low, but she was pretty sure he mumbled, "spectacular." Yes, one point for her.

After unpacking, Alex made sure the water, heat, and electricity were all turned back on and working properly. Since he'd apparently checked on the house all winter, there were no problems. They quickly wiped down the kitchen, and since she had no food around, Alex offered to spring for some take-out. They settled on pizza and ate it on the floor in the living room.

"I should give you back the keys to the house." He wiped his mouth with a napkin before continuing. "I'll bring them over in the morning."

"You're welcome here any time, Felix, and you know it. No need to knock or make an appointment." Because he was the type who would always call before coming over, even as a kid. "Mi casa, su casa. Keep the keys. You never know when I'll lock myself out and need a handsome man to come to my rescue."

Alex's lips twisted into a grin. "You aren't exactly the damsel in distress type."

"No, I'm not." She shrugged. "But that doesn't mean I don't want you around."

Aside from her crying jag, she enjoyed her time with Alex. But then she always did, even if he acted uncomfortable at times. Usually when she caught him staring at her butt, legs, or boobs. It didn't take much imagination to figure out what was going through his mind. It was the same thing that always went through her mind when he was around. She wanted him desperately.

Alex was too polite and civilized to ever admit that he wanted her, and he was more than likely looking for a woman he could marry. He had that whole *Leave It to Beaver*, Ward and June Cleaver happy family vibe going on. He'd never want someone like her, someone who pushed buttons just to get a laugh. Too bad he wouldn't cut loose enough to have a wild and passionate fling with her. It would be H O T.

She stared at him, her eyes devouring him as he wiped a napkin over his incredibly kissable lips, when a thought came to her. Why couldn't they have a fling? As long as he wasn't currently involved with someone–she'd never poach on another woman's turf–a steamy tryst could help them both. They'd get some wild, steamy sex, and she wouldn't be so bored while she stayed here. The idea had merit.

Alex tipped his head back to down the rest of his water bottle, and his Adam's apple bobbed up and down. Gina squirmed as warmth spread down her stomach and between her legs. She needed to do this. Now all she had to do was somehow convince Alex.

CHAPTER TWO

"Where were you last night, bro?"

Alex pulled the cinnamon rolls out of the oven and set them on the stovetop, before he shot a glance to his younger brother, Lukas.

"Since when do you keep tabs on me?"

"Since never. But I stopped home to change before heading back out, and your car was here. You weren't. On a school night. And the door was unlocked. That isn't like you."

"I left the door unlocked?" Shit. That *wasn't* like him, but Gina had a way of making him forget stuff. Important stuff like locking the door. Not that it mattered in Squamscott Falls, New Hampshire. The little town was hardly the crime metropolis of the universe. But it was something that Alex always did. It was part of his routine.

Luke reached for a cinnamon roll, and Alex slapped him on the side of the head. "Those aren't for you. What are you still doing home, anyway? It's almost nine. Shouldn't you be at work now?" He did keep tabs on his brother. A habit from childhood.

"I was there late the last few nights, so the boss said I

could take my time this morning. We finished the project we were working on. We have a meeting this afternoon to go over the designs."

Luke was an engineer for a firm in Portsmouth who contracted for the military. He worked damn hard at what he did. But he also liked to play hard.

Alex placed the cinnamon rolls on a plate, and Luke scraped his finger over the remnants still in the pan. "Do you plan on eating those all by yourself? You're going to get fat."

Alex glanced down at his trim body. He played enough basketball and ran a few times a week that he wasn't worried. "They aren't for me. And I get plenty of exercise. More than you."

Luke's eyes glinted. "I get a different kind of workout, bro. It's definitely a lot more fun."

Alex cringed, thinking of the kind of activity his brother was talking about. Not that he didn't enjoy that, but he had more discriminating taste in women. Gina's lithe form entered his mind, along with the peek he'd gotten at her spectacular breasts last night. *No, don't go there. Dangerous territory.*

"I assume there was a lucky girl last night. You weren't home when I got back from Gina's later."

Luke smirked. "Her name's Jade. She's only in the area for a week."

"What's the use of dating someone who won't be sticking around?"

"Dating? Sure, you can call it dating if it pleases your sensibilities, but you know I'm not looking for anything longer than a few nights."

Alex sighed. Luke had women falling all over him, wanting him to make a commitment. Alex was no slouch. He had plenty of dates. For some reason, however, he never seemed to get past a few months. They'd go out, have a nice time, get to know each other, and then *wham*. He'd get dumped. Things hadn't connected. Not that he was heartbroken by any one woman, but there must be someone out there who didn't mind his little quirks. A woman who liked his structured, organized lifestyle. It made sense. It was logical. Great, he was starting to sound like Spock.

"One of these days, Luke, someone's going to snag you on the end of their line."

"Not if I can help it. I know all the tricks to wriggling off."

Alex put plastic wrap over the rolls, then grabbed the grocery bags on the table.

"Where are you going? Aren't those groceries for us? I'm starving."

"There's cereal in the pantry. You know how to pour yourself a bowl. These are for Gina. She got home yesterday and doesn't have any food in her house."

"Figures," Luke muttered. "You do more for her than me."

"She's trying to go through her grandmother's things. That's a lot of work. I'm heading over now to see what she needs. I'll be back in a little while since I have a meeting with a prospective new client at one."

"Hope it's for something big. Help pay off the mortgage."

"What do you care? It's my mortgage. You only pay rent, and not a ton of rent I might add."

"Well, Mom and Dad gave you a bargain on the house, didn't they? And can't I want big things for my brother?"

Alex sighed. "Sure, Luke. It's nice that you want me to be successful. This meeting is for a new medical building over in Stratham. If I get it, it could be a big deal for my career. I might be able to stop designing smaller things, like additions and houses."

"Good luck. You're the best architect I know."

"I'm probably the only architect you know, but I'll take

the compliment. Now I need to get these to Gina before they're totally cold."

Luke glanced at his watch. "You actually expect her to be awake at this hour."

"Maybe the smell of the cinnamon will wake her up. I promised to help her get organized in cleaning the house."

"She came to the right guy, then."

Alex pushed his way out the back door, yelling for Luke to lock up when he left, then strolled over to Gina's. He let himself in with his key. After setting the rolls on the table, he started putting the groceries away. It wasn't long before he heard soft footsteps on the back stairway. "Oh, my God, tell me the smell of cinnamon rolls is not just in my dreams."

"No dream, Dandelion." Alex looked up to smile, but his mouth froze in place. Talk about a dream. She wore a snug white tank top that was almost see through and nothing on her legs. *Please let her have on underwear, or I just might die right here.*

Gina stretched and her shirt rode up. Yes, underwear, though he recognized one of the silky string things he'd seen yesterday. Not much to the imagination. He ducked his head and dug through another grocery bag. The front of his pants would be a dead give-away as to his thoughts. Thoughts he should not be having.

Gina moved to the table and bent over to smell the rolls, her rounded cheeks pushed out for his viewing pleasure. Alex tried not to look. He really did. But he had to put the milk in the fridge, and she was standing right there. His pants grew even tighter.

"I can have one of these, right?"

Alex pulled a few more things from the bags. "No, I brought them over merely to torture you with the delicious aroma. I thought it might get you out of bed before the crack of noon."

Swiveling around, Gina crossed her arms over her chest. Big mistake. Those spectacular breasts were even more prominently displayed. Her nipples poked against the thin fabric of her top. He forced his gaze to her grinning face.

"You'll know what real torture is, if I don't get one."

Alex tipped his head to one side. "Help yourself. I also bought milk, if you want something to drink."

Gina already had a roll in her mouth. "That'll have to do until I can get some tea."

He reached into the bottom of the bag and pulled out a box. "Like this?"

"Jasmine tea! You remembered. You are the absolute best ever."

She finished chewing the bite of roll and flew at him. Couldn't she ever do anything halfway? He dropped the tea on the counter, just in time to catch her in his arms. She grabbed his face and pressed her lips to his. Holy shit. She tasted of cinnamon and sugar. Before he could analyze her other flavors, she pulled away.

"Felix, I might start to like the way you spoil me and end up staying. Then, where would you be?"

In heaven. No, hell. Damn, he didn't know. That was the worst part. He liked to know what was happening and where things were going. With Gina, he was lucky if his head didn't spin off his shoulders. She made him that dizzy.

"I thought you said you'd only torture me if you didn't get a cinnamon roll."

Her arms still draped over his shoulders. "You're just too much fun to play with."

"Like a cat with a mouse. Thanks, Dandelion. Go eat your roll while I make you a cup of tea." He disentangled himself from her arms and walked to the stove. As he filled the kettle with water and put it on the heat, he breathed in deeply through his nose and out through his mouth. Gina's groans made him turn around. She sat at the table, licking icing from her fingers.

Fuck. How fast could he help her fix up this house and leave again? Not that she'd asked him to. She simply expected it. And he couldn't say no. Not with her. That's how he'd found himself in the position they'd been in nine years ago in the tree house.

"Aren't you going to have some, too? Or did you make yourself another batch at home?"

The kettle whistled. He poured water in a mug, then dunked the teabag inside. "Here you go. Enjoy." He sat across from her and picked up a roll. Why was he watching her? He should go home and get some work done. Plenty to do. But he'd promised he'd help her figure out what needed to be done in the house, and he never reneged on a promised.

Her hair was wild this morning, spiraling in waves down her back. He loved how she'd casually tuck it behind her ear. Or how she enjoyed every minute of life. Sipping her tea as if it was her last cup. Everything she did was as if life would end tomorrow.

After finishing his roll, he dug in the bag for the notebook he'd bought and pulled the pen from his shirt pocket.

"I got this to help us get you started."

As she glanced at him, devouring her third cinnamon roll, her eyes softened, and she licked crumbs from her lips. "A notebook? For me? Oh, Felix, you always buy me the nicest things."

He glared back, not sure if she was serious or simply teasing him. He was a big boy. He could take both. "I thought we could spend some time today going through the house. Take stock of what's in each room, what definitely needs to be fixed or replaced, and what might be nice to change but isn't necessary for selling the house."

Gina reached across the table and rested her hand on his.

21

Pull it away. It'll scorch you. He didn't. He couldn't get past this control she had over him.

"Thank you for helping me. I know I didn't exactly ask, but I appreciate your doing this. You're my hero."

And she was his kryptonite.

Somehow, he found the strength to move his hand and turn to the first page. "I got a five-subject notebook, because I thought it might help us keep things straight. We can split the house by floor for each subject. There are three floors, plus the basement and the turret room. I know the turret room is only one small room, but your grandmother stored lots of her stuff up there. It'll take a while to go through."

"You've obviously thought this through."

He shrugged. "It's just common sense to divide the house into sections. We'll take notes, and it'll be easier to find them if we need them later. Unless you wanted to organize this a different way."

Gina got up and walked around the table toward him. *Shit, don't touch me.* His mind would be muddled with her too close. Not that she paid attention to his thoughts. She slid her arms around his shoulders from behind. The honeysuckle smell infiltrated his brain, and his cock went right into action, all the blood rushing there hoping for fulfillment. Just another disappointment. Her hands slid down his chest, and some demented part of his mind wanted them to keep going. To touch the aroused part of him that still remembered her. They didn't. They stopped just short of where he wanted them.

Damn it, no. He didn't need her confusing him.

"You're the king of organization, Felix," she purred in his ear. "I'm a mere slave to your talent."

Her breath on his neck made him think of other talents he wanted to use. Ones that had been dormant lately.

"Why don't you sit, and we can do a little preliminary outlining on this?"

"I'd rather look over your shoulder."

"Don't you trust me?" He didn't trust himself with her draped over him.

"I'd trust you with my life. I just like looking over your shoulder. You get all prickly when I'm close like this, and it turns me on."

Her deep, sultry tones turned him on. Her soft body against his back. "Glad you're getting something out of it."

"You're not?"

She stood straighter and tilted her head to stare at his face. She pressed his cheek against her chest, and he actually groaned. God Almighty, did she know what she was doing to him? Probably.

"I can't concentrate when you do that."

One of her hands slid into his hair while the other caressed down his chest. He was going to explode any minute.

"What do you need to concentrate on?"

Focus man! You're losing it. "We need to start making lists. I only have a few hours this morning to help you. I have to meet with a client right after lunch."

"Okay, I'll move out of your way." She stood behind him again, her hands still draped over his shoulders. He lifted his hand to grab the pen, and his arm brushed hers.

"You're hardly out of my way, Dandelion. I can't write with your hands there. I'll never be able to read it later to make sense of these notes."

"Can't have that now, can we?" Her tone was teasing, but she slinked away to sit back in her chair. Not before she nipped his ear with her teeth. Seriously, she wanted him to go insane. It must be her grand scheme.

He put pen to paper to label the first page. She actually smirked at his shaking hands.

～

GINA RUBBED a bit more of the honeysuckle cream into the skin on her neck and arms. Alex might pretend he was immune, but she knew better. His body grew stiff, and he started his deep breathing exercises whenever he got too close to her. She loved that she had that effect on him. Of course, the effect he had on her wasn't exactly tame either. She spent more time clenching her legs together to keep the throbbing at bay than anything else. This morning at breakfast, when his mouth was mere centimeters from her chest, she'd had this huge desire to pull her top down and have him lick her nipples.

Alex would have keeled over. The man was so uptight and proper. Even nine years ago, when they'd first made love, he'd been skittish and hesitant. She'd been the one to initiate everything. Kissing he'd been good at, having practiced with a number of girlfriends over the years. The Storm boys had always been sought after as dates. Alex, however, had been too good and proper to go any further.

They'd started merely kissing, Gina saying he was going back to college in Pennsylvania soon, and she'd miss him. The kissing had moved on to touching and light tickling. They'd explored and slowly removed their clothes, daring each other to take off just one more thing. But after hours of touching and exploring, they'd finally gotten to the good part. The part neither had been to before.

Not that Gina hadn't witnessed it a time or two, or more. Her mother had dragged her from one commune to another. She'd spent time in other bohemian settlements, a nudist colony, and other free-spirited communities. The people they lived with had very little in the way of inhibition. It certainly hadn't been a free-for-all orgy, but sex in the corners of rooms or under the shade of a tree had been par for the course. As she got older, she'd paid more attention to what was happening.

Alex would never understand that type of life. He'd grown up with Molly and Pete Storm as parents. They were good people with a loving home and strong parenting skills. They'd never bring their children to an open-air concert where smoking pot and drinking homemade wine was the norm. They brought their children to church each week and insisted they be home by curfew every night. She sometimes wondered what she'd be like if she'd spent more time with Nonna. Her grandmother had been like the Storms, all good and moral. Not that Gina considered herself amoral, but she certainly didn't have the hang-ups that Alex did.

The front door creaked open. "Hey, Dandelion, you decent?"

When Alex had left this morning, after spending a few hours making list after list, he said he'd be back after his appointment and maybe she could actually get dressed. Yeah, her snug top and flimsy panties had sent him spinning. The way she liked him best. It made her feel powerful and sexy.

"As decent as I'll ever get," she called back. She walked down the hall to greet him. He still wore the khakis and button down from this morning. Standing in the foyer, he clutched the five-subject notebook in his hands. He looked up cautiously and physically relaxed when he saw she was dressed. His eyes narrowed when he looked closer.

She wore a pair of paisley print leggings tucked into ankle-length, high-heeled boots. Her dark-colored top was loose and long sleeved, but very sheer. It had a deep slit in front that tied together with a ribbon. She usually wore it with a tank top underneath, but since Alex was coming over,

25

she wanted to shock him yet again. Although he'd known her long enough, she doubted much she did shocked him anymore.

"How did your meeting go? Did you wow them with your amazing architectural skills?"

Alex's cheeks actually got pink. "I hope so. I sketched out a few possible designs. They seemed impressed, but I won't know for sure for another week. I'm up against two other architects, and the others have more experience with commercial buildings."

She stepped closer and reached up. "A kiss for luck then."

Her lips met his, and she nearly swooned they felt so good. She'd given him a quick peck yesterday, but today she wanted to linger a little bit. Alex didn't protest. A good sign. His eyes closed, and she kept hers open to see what he did. His face relaxed as his lips responded to hers. *Yes. More. Take more. You never know when it will end.*

He tasted of coffee and sin. The sin must be in his *mind,* because it certainly wasn't in his actions. Unless she could keep them going on this course. It had worked once before. Her tongue came out to play and skimmed along his mouth. He opened for her, and Gina almost died of pleasure. Nothing had ever tasted as good as Alex Storm.

The notebook dropped as Alex's hands surrounded her waist. He startled, but Gina pulled his head closer again and whispered, "You still need more luck."

No argument. Hallelujah. She ran her fingers through his short hair as their mouths possessed each other. Pulling her tighter, he lifted so her feet left the floor. His hands now held her ass, holding her against his obvious erection. She wrapped her legs around him, remembering how many times she'd greeted him like this. It was the first time he'd responded this way. Usually, he peeled her off and moved away. *Please don't let him do that now.*

He'd come to his senses soon, no doubt. *Live in the moment. Take what you can get.* Her arms slid further around his neck to cling tighter and help ease the weight he carried. He adjusted her again, and she froze. Was he done with their play?

No. One hand slipped under her top and skimmed her back. Mmm, yes. It felt like heaven. His fingers were rough, and her skin tingled with the contact. The computer geeks she knew never did any kind of work to form calluses. Alex might be an architect and design using computers, but he also was altruistic and helped when local businesses or homes needed a hand with some minor construction. He wasn't afraid to get dirty. Unfortunately, not the kind of dirty she had in mind.

His lips slid from her mouth to her neck, and she groaned when he nipped one spot at the curve of her shoulder.

"You're going to be the death of me, Dandy." He shuddered, but still held her close.

"If you don't get the job after this, then it's not my fault. I did what I could." She grinned and tightened her legs around him. "Unless you want more luck."

He eyed the tie that had come undone and now exposed some of her chest. He wanted her. No doubt there. But if she pushed, she'd most likely push him out the door. She didn't want to do that.

"Not sure I can handle more of your kind of luck."

"Probably not. It'd be fun to try, though." After kissing his sinful lips one more time, she slid down his length feeling his arousal. What would he do? Brush it off or run out the door? He definitely wouldn't want to talk about the kiss. That wasn't Alex's style.

He bent over and picked up the notebook, then turned away, inhaling deeply. It was his way of getting himself in control. She'd seen him do it far too often with her. Was she the only one? Or did all his girlfriends get him excited to the point he needed to calm down? She hated to think she wasn't special, but maybe she wasn't.

When he turned around, he seemed calmer. To an extent. His pants still tented in the front. She'd offer to help alleviate it, but it was Alex. He'd never go for it. She still had work to do there.

"So, let's go over each floor and start making a list of what your priorities are. We need to put them in order of importance, then we can start looking at supplies we'll need to get the work done."

"My first priority is to get all my computers set up and working. And I'll need a big table to put them on. I looked through the house today. Nonna doesn't have anything the right size or height. We need to go to the store and buy one."

Alex glanced at his watch. "It's four-thirty. You want to go furniture shopping now? Tomorrow's Saturday. We could go then."

"I want to go now. I don't need a real piece of furniture. A portable folding table will do. One of the long ones. Where can we get one of those?"

Alex cocked his head. "The hardware store."

"Then, let's go."

Alex stared at her, or more specifically her chest.

"See something you like?" The ends were still untied showing her cleavage and maybe a little more.

"What's not to like? But it's not just the tie. That material is see-through. You're quite clearly on display."

"You don't have any claim on them. What do you care?"

Alex's jaw tightened, and his face hardened. "You're right. I don't. Let's go." He turned away, looking like a little boy who'd just been scolded.

She reached out and grabbed his arm. "Fine. I won't embarrass you. I'll go change."

He sighed and took her arms. "You don't embarrass me, Gina. I just thought—never mind, we'll just go."

Looking down, she grinned. "I suppose I should at least put a tank top under this. We can't have all the men staring at me. Their wives or girlfriends would be totally jealous of how amazing I am. And you'd have to beat the single guys off with a stick. That might slow us down."

Alex chuckled and pulled her in for a hug. It felt so much nicer because he'd done it on his own. That didn't happen all too often. He kissed her cheek, then released her.

"You really are one of a kind."

"I know." She skipped up the stairs. One of a kind. Sure. What would it take for her to convince him to invest in an original?

CHAPTER THREE

"*A*re you seriously wearing that?" Gina stopped short when she entered Alex's kitchen the next day.

Looking down at his outfit, he shrugged. "What's wrong with it?"

Gina sighed, shaking her head. "You're wearing khaki pants and a peach button down shirt. And they're totally starched and ironed."

"I didn't put starch on them."

"But you did iron them."

"Ironing is not a bad thing."

"It is when you're going to a rock concert. None of the typical Ammunition fans will have perfectly creased trousers with a pastel oxford." She pointed to his loafers. "Or those. Go change."

"I'm not going to see Ammunition. I'm going to see my sister, Sara. The fact she's opening for a rock band is irrelevant. I'm pretty sure my parents said they were leaving once Sara was done."

"Your parents are in their fifties. They have an excuse not

to stay. You're what, twenty-eight? No excuse. Plus, didn't you say Sara was coming out to do a duet with Bullet Ryker during Ammunition's show? You can't miss that."

Alex crossed his arms over his chest and glared at her. She ran her tongue over her top teeth and immediately saw his eyes change to a darker blue. Damn, the control she had over him. Too bad it only worked so far.

"Fine, I'll change. But I don't know what you expect me to have that's much different from this."

Turning, he walked down the hallway. She followed and bounced up the stairs behind him. "You're right. I better help you find something, or you could come down even worse."

He pivoted on the stairs, and she plowed into him, her face only slightly above his belt line. Oh, another few inches south. The tingles started between her legs. Why did he have to turn her on so much? She looked up innocently and smiled.

"I don't want you to feel out of place, Felix. It's kind of crappy when you do."

Alex continued on and entered the master bedroom, Gina right behind.

"When have you ever felt out of place, Dandelion? You seem comfortable anywhere you go." He opened up a dresser drawer.

She leaned against the door frame and checked out the room. "I may seem comfortable, but admit it, I stick out anywhere I go. Especially in this buttoned-up little town."

"What's wrong with this town? Most people are friendly enough."

"Sure, if your name is Storm. I could never live here, being so different from everyone else and marching to my own beat."

He froze and looked at her, his eyes sympathetic. Oh, no,

she didn't need any pity. Not from Mr. Perfect himself. She pushed away from the door and went to the closet. "So, you have the big bedroom now, huh? Nice."

"It felt weird at first. It was always my parents' room. But I like that it has its own bathroom. Luke still lives here, and he's a slob. I try and avoid the hall bathroom, if at all possible."

Gina snorted. "I bet you still clean it."

"Well." Alex wrinkled his face. "Not every day. Only if the stench rolls out into the hallway."

"So, once a week?"

Alex only glared and skimmed through his drawers. "What exactly should I be wearing? A polo shirt, maybe? I have one in black. That's kind of badass, right?"

Gina almost fell over laughing. "Oh, Felix. You do amuse me."

More glaring.

"You need something worn, something not in pristine condition. Do you have any old clothes, jeans?"

"Of course, I own jeans. The stuff in that smaller dresser has clothes that I wear when I'm doing construction or other dirty work. Most of it's in pretty bad shape, though."

"I'll be the judge of that." She dug into the drawer and started pulling out shirts and jeans. After she checked for concert worthiness, she stuffed them back in. Alex stood behind her fishing them back out and refolding them. The little sighing noises he made were hysterical.

"These jeans are perfect." They were well worn and would most likely hug his slim hips and waist. She couldn't wait to see him in them. Opening another drawer, she looked for a shirt.

Holding up the jeans, he frowned. "These are practically falling apart. They have rips in them."

Gina rolled her eyes. "That's the whole point, Felix.

Besides, it's only two small rips on the thigh. It's not like your man parts will be showing. Get a grip. How about this for a shirt?" She held up a black t-shirt with an advertisement for a local auto body shop called Bump and Grind.

One side of his lip curled up, then he looked skyward. His shoulders rose and fell as he nodded. "Whatever."

"Yay!" She clapped and jumped up and down in a very bad imitation of a cheerleader. Not that she ever knew what being one of those was like. She'd moved around too much to actually belong to any team or squad, even if she'd wanted to hang around with cliquey teenagers.

"Let's get you dressed." Stepping over to Alex, she started unbuttoning his shirt. He stared at her like she was decorating his body with war paint. *Keep him occupied with conversation, and maybe he'll ignore your hands.*

"Who else from your family is going to this concert tonight?"

"My parents, as I told you. Some of my cousins. Luke is bringing some bimbo he met last week."

"How do you know she's a bimbo?" She slapped his fingers away as he tried to undo the other buttons. The small brushes against his skin felt nice.

When she pulled the sides of his shirt open, he shrugged it off. "Luke won't go out with anyone unless they're as easy as he is. No commitments for him. It's kind of his mantra."

"You don't approve."

"He can do what he wants. I just think the purpose of dating is to find someone compatible you can spend the rest of your life with."

She frowned. That would never be her with him. "So, no hanky panky until you find the one."

"I never said that. I've had sex with more than just you, Dandelion. But I don't take it lightly."

She pressed her fingers against his chest and swirled

33

them through the light hair that crossed his pectorals. She'd really love to follow the happy trail down past his navel. Pipe dream.

"Maybe you should try it a few times. It could be wild and fun…with the right girl."

"Stop that." His hands grasped hers and stilled her actions.

The hands stopped, but her fingers continued to move. "Admit it, Felix, it feels damn good. I dare you to deny it."

Closing his eyes, he inhaled deeply but didn't pull her hands away. She slid her hands over his shoulders then around his neck. His eyes were still closed. *Take advantage, now.*

When she pressed her lips to his, he groaned, pulling her in close and lifting her up so their mouths were more in alignment. God damn, but he tasted like ambrosia. Yesterday's kiss had awoken an addiction she thought had been dormant. She opened her mouth and slid her tongue along his lips. Another groan, then his tongue tangled with hers.

"Alex, are you here?" The voice of Molly Storm broke them apart faster than a spray of cold water. Luckily, it came from downstairs.

Alex took a deep breath, then yelled, "Be down in a minute, Mom."

"Take your time. I know we're early, but your mother insisted we come now." Pete Storm didn't sound the least put out. Gina admired the relationship those two had. It was a beautiful thing. Rare, but beautiful.

"Finish getting dressed. I'll go talk to them." She ran her hands down his chest one last time, her own breath unsteady.

Alex looked at the clothes dumped on his bed. "Are you sure this will fit in with what you're wearing?"

Gina glanced at her short denim skirt and stretchy long-sleeved top. She hated to even admit it was a pair of black, footless dance tights with the crotch cut out for her head. The waist band fit around her rib cage perfectly. She'd known a few New York City ballerinas who wore them like this for warm ups. She liked the look and topped it with accessories. Today, she had a loosely woven crocheted vest and several long necklaces. Alex stared at her top now. Was he embarrassed again, like he'd been yesterday when they'd gone to the store? At least she'd put something over it. She didn't usually walk around with the girls on display. Only if she wanted to get a rise out of someone. Alex was the easiest for that.

Finally, he reached out and took hold of one of her necklaces. He slid it up, and she realized he was fixing it so the clasp was in the back. He did this again with her other necklaces.

"Am I proper now?"

He peered at her legs. She wasn't wearing anything too crazy. Thigh high socks with lace trim and knee-high boots with killer heels.

"There's nothing about you that's even remotely proper. But you'll do for now. Thanks for the fashion lesson."

She ran to his closet and pulled out worn work boots and a faded denim jacket. "Trade the loafers for these shit kickers and wear this on top. Then, you'll be rockin' the look."

Alex's smile was comical. "Just what I was hoping for."

Gina skipped down the stairs and found Molly and Pete sitting in the kitchen with Dunkin Donuts' cups in front of them.

"Alex will be right down. I had to keep him from looking like he'd walked out of a yacht club. I think we got it all sorted out."

Molly and Pete stood, giving her big hugs. She'd almost

forgotten what that was like. There were a lot of touchy feely people in New York City, but the touching was usually sexual in nature and the feeling was for pleasure only. This was like home.

"Your outfit is adorable, Gina," Molly said, her smile genuine as always. "You always look like you belong in some little fairy kingdom. I wish I could carry off those clothes."

"I bet you could. You still have a smokin' hot body." Molly Storm was average height and weight and had the cutest blonde pixie haircut to frame her adorable face. She and her husband both wore jeans and casual shirts tonight. Alex must have been a throwback to some former uptight relative.

"Did you hear that, Pete? She says I have a smokin' hot body. Maybe I'll get lucky tonight and pick up some young roadie."

Pete smiled indulgently at his wife. "Why? So you can mother him to death and start making lists of all the things he needs to do to become successful in life?"

Molly put her hands on her hips. "I don't...well, okay, maybe I do a little. But I'm sure my children appreciate it."

"Of course we do, Mom," Alex piped in as he entered the kitchen. Damn, he looked hot. She'd called it when she thought the jeans would fit nicely. He sidled up to her and whispered, "What do we appreciate?"

Molly rolled her eyes. "None of that. Are you ready? I told Luci we'd be over shortly." Pete's brother Nikolas, lived next door with his wife, Luci, their son, Greg, and Greg's son, Ryan. "We'll ride with her and Nik, so we can leave early. Figured you young kids might like to stay for the whole concert."

"I guess I'll have to, since Gina is a huge Ammunition fan. I'm ready. Sorry for the delay. Gina was helping me pick something out. Apparently, my choice of clothes wasn't appropriate for a rock concert. Who knew there were dress regulations for these things?"

"Are we driving alone?" Gina asked. "We're going to Worcester, right?" An hour or so alone with Alex in a car. She was delirious thinking of all the ways she could torment him.

"Greg is coming with us." Alex grabbed his keys from the hook by the door. "Ryan's only eight, and Ammunition is pretty hard-core rock, so he got a sitter. Sofie and Leah are meeting us there. They had dinner in Worcester with some old friends first. Kevin is bringing his work partner, Mitch, but I think Amy has classes. And Nathaniel ... Well, he has a few other things on his mind right now."

Gina loved all the Storm cousins and was looking forward to seeing some of them tonight.

"What about Erik and his wife? Is it too far from Maine for them to come? I know they have the kids."

"They were planning on it, but Tessa wasn't feeling too great, so they canceled." Molly frowned. "They might try and get to the one in Portland next weekend."

Alex touched her shoulder. "Tessa is pregnant, and Erik's been a bit overprotective of her since they found out."

Molly placed her hand on her heart. "Tessa was in a terrible car accident at the beginning of the year and was seriously injured. She almost lost the baby, so Erik has been pampering her a bit."

"Understandable," Pete said. "The man's just looking out for his family."

Gina had only met Tessa at Thanksgiving, but she'd liked the quiet woman very much. Erik's deep feelings for her were apparent. She looked over at Alex, in his tight t-shirt and snug jeans. He slipped on his denim jacket, and his muscles flexed and hardened. He was such a good man. And sexy as hell. He wanted to find the right woman, his own perfect June Cleaver, so he could have a marriage like his older brother and his parents.

Too bad she didn't fit the bill. Not even close.

～

"Your sister is amazing!" yelled Gina as Sara left the stage. The crowd was going wild. Pride welled up inside Alex knowing his baby sister, Sagey, as he and his brothers called her, was responsible.

"Yes, she is." He had to lean down to talk in Gina's ear, the noise was so loud in the cavernous arena. "She's done her duet. Think we could go now?"

"And miss the rest of the concert? No way. They probably won't play much longer. They've already been out here for a few hours."

He sighed, but smiled back at her. She'd been having a ball. Watching Gina's animated face as the music played and the singers belted out the lyrics, had been amusing. She put so much energy into everything she did. It reminded him of Erik's two kids, Matty and Kiki. Those two were high energy and could wear him out in no time.

Looking around, he nodded to his cousins, who all sat in the same area, thanks to free tickets from Sara. A private area to the side, slightly higher than the floor seats. Sofie, Leah, Gina, and even Greg bounced to the rhythm as Ammunition started on their next song. Luke stood off to the side with his date wrapped around him. Kevin, who was a cop in Portsmouth, was a bit more sedate. He and Mitch had gone to the Police Academy at the same time and managed to get partnered together. They'd been friends since they were kids. They both kept watchful eyes out. He didn't blame them. The crowd was far from tame.

Alex clenched his teeth as Greg pulled Gina in close and

said something in her ear. She threw her head back laughing, then touched his chest with both hands. It shouldn't matter to him. Greg was single and so was Gina. He certainly didn't have any claim on her. Nor did he want any claim on her. She was a good friend, but she'd be a nightmare as a girlfriend. At least, for him. She already had his ordered life unraveling, and she'd only been back a few days. Greg was welcome to her. Maybe he could take over. As a firefighter/paramedic, he worked a few days on and a few days off. That gave him time to help her fix her house. Except Greg had an eight-year-old son, who usually took up his off time. Crap. He was stuck with her.

The band played a few mores songs, left, then ran back on for an encore. Finally, they departed for good, and Alex could hear again. He shrugged his denim jacket on and checked for his wallet, phone, and keys.

"Sara said we could go backstage and meet the band," Sofie squealed, jumping up and down. "She said to meet TJ near the left side of the stage. He'll bring us back. Are you all coming?"

Everyone nodded, and Alex sighed. *Suck it up, party pooper, and let everyone have their fun.* He'd heard that more than a few times in the past. He might as well tell himself this time, so he didn't have to hear it from someone else.

TJ waited by the gate with a security guard, looking about as thrilled as Alex felt. Made him like the guy even more. Which was good since he was marrying Alex's sister. He was also the reason Sara had only done the New England shows on this leg of the tour.

Growing up as the son of the rock world's two biggest superstars should have made True Jam 'TJ' Bannister a total rock and roller, but the death of his sister by a drug overdose when TJ was barely eighteen had caused the man to rethink his life. Alex was only guessing at this, but he'd done enough surfing online to get the gist of when TJ had left the lime-light. Now, he owned a bookstore/coffeeshop on Cape Cod and wrote songs on the side. Sara would laugh at that description since James True, TJ's alter ego, had won numerous awards for his composing. Alex only cared that Sara loved him, and he treated her well.

"Sara's excited you all came to see her. She was also extremely nervous. Wasn't sure what your parents would think about her stage costume. She doesn't really have much say in them."

"I take it you don't approve," Alex asked, seeing TJ's sour expression.

TJ lifted one eyebrow. "Oh, I approve, just not for the world to see."

Alex faked a smile and looked around the back hallway they were in. He didn't like the idea of what TJ had insinu-ated with his baby sister. They were engaged, though, so he had to get over it at some point. When they stopped at a set of double doors, TJ knocked twice, then three times. It opened, and another security guard peeked out.

"They're all with me. Family."

"Family," Gina squealed softly, gripping Alex's arm. "That means I'm related to Abe Bannister and Celia Munez. So cool."

What would she think if she ever met them? They were sure to be around during the wedding in May, if she was still here. "You're not family. You're extra baggage. Be nice to me. I could have you tossed out."

Gina pouted, looking as feminine as ever. "You're an old fart. Let me have my fun for today."

"You've had more than enough fun for a lifetime."

Gina's eyes lit up. "Never."

Sara trotted over to them and gave hugs all around.

"Thanks so much for coming tonight. It means the world to me."

"Of course," and "We loved it," filled the air as everyone assured her she was great. And she had been. Alex could never deny his sister's talent.

"Tell me the truth," Sara directed at him and Luke. "Did Mom flip out over my outfit? I wanted to put a long sweater over it, but the stage is like eight hundred degrees once you start singing and moving around."

"Not even a word," Luke assured her, his bleach blond date clinging to his arm. Sara's outfit was demure compared to what this one, Jade, was wearing.

"She liked what I was wearing tonight," Gina said, "and what you have on is very similar."

Sara wore a leather skirt, short like Gina's and covered in chains. Her thigh high boots also had four-inch heels. The only difference was that she wore only a leather vest with nothing under it. He could totally picture Gina wearing this, but understood why TJ didn't want Sara wearing it in public.

Sara went around the room and introduced the members of Ammunition and her back up band. A bar was set up in the corner, and people already milled around or sat on couches drinking and talking. Sofie and Leah seemed intimidated but thrilled to meet the famous musicians, while Gina threw herself into getting to know them with her usual gusto.

"I wanted to ask if you do plans for additions," TJ said coming to stand near Alex.

"Sure." He nodded. "But your house is huge already. What kind of addition could you possibly want?" TJ owned prime real estate on the beach in Hyannis.

"I was thinking of building a recording studio for Sara in the basement. Figured it might keep her closer to home while still living her dreams of singing. I could also use it to lay down demos for the songs I write."

"I could do that." While they talked about details, Alex kept his eye on everyone. Kevin and Mitch chatted with the security guard, while the others moved through the room. Several of the band members made it a point to chat and flirt with Gina. Not that he could blame them. She was a pint-sized dynamo and the most dazzling woman in the room. Her gorgeous eyes, wild hair, and curvaceous figure drew men to her like flies to honey. Her eclectic clothes fit right in with the stage outfits they all wore. He fidgeted in his jean and t-shirt, but had to admit he'd have felt totally out of place if he'd come in his original outfit.

A few people offered them drinks, but he only accepted soda. It was an hour's drive home, and he had no desire to be pulled over for a DUI. TJ kept to bottled water. Sara had admitted he'd had a drug and alcohol addiction years ago but kept totally clean now. Must be why he didn't like Sara being on the road with this band of party boys.

Sara came over to keep TJ company, and Alex went to get another soda. Gina was already there leaning over the bar.

"I'd like a Slow Comfortable Screw Against the Wall." Her breathy voice made his pants tighter. He wasn't the only one affected. The bartender couldn't keep his eyes off her clingy top. The lead singer of the band, Bullet Ryker, walked up behind her. He placed his hands on the bar on either side of her and nuzzled her neck.

"I'd be happy to screw you against the wall, babe. Slow or fast."

Gina laughed and looked at him with those mystical eyes. "I'll bet you would."

Ryker turned Gina around and pressed closer. "Let me buy you that drink."

Her lips pursed. "The drinks are free."

"So am I right now. But I can get busy with you." His hands skimmed up her legs and dipped under her skirt as he ground his hips into hers.

Red flared across Alex's vision as he stalked over to them.

"Having fun?"

"We were until you showed up." Ryker sneered, then eyed Gina. "Maybe we should head to my dressing room. It's not so crowded."

Alex's heart thumped loudly. Would Gina go with him? She was a grown woman. He had no control over her. Granted, if she went, he might have to pound Ryker into the ground.

He kept his eyes on the singer, not wanting to see Gina's excitement at the thought of having sex with a superstar.

"That's such a sweet offer, but I'm afraid I'll have to pass. My friend, Alex here is my ride home."

Ryker leaned closer, rubbing against her again. Alex's teeth ground together hard enough to crack.

"I can give you a ride anywhere you like, babe. A wild ride."

Gina pushed at him and slipped away, still grinning. "So tempting, Bullet. Not tonight. You really did have a great show. I'm glad I got to see it."

Alex finally let out the breath he hadn't realized he was holding. Sara moved up next to him. "TJ and I are leaving now, so I wanted to say goodbye. I think the others are ready to go, too."

He hugged his sister. "Thanks for the tickets, Sage. You're amazing, you know. I love you."

"Love you, too, Alex."

Sara hugged Gina, then went around to the rest of the family. As they all exited together, Alex whispered to Gina, "Are you sure you didn't want to catch a ride with Ryker?

Sounded like you two would have some fun. That's what you wanted, wasn't it?"

"Don't be such a downer, Felix." She slipped her hand around his arm and pressed her face to it. Why did she have to be so freakin' adorable?

It took about fifteen minutes to get to the car park, and Gina snuggled closer to him along the way. She hadn't brought a coat, and he finally took his off and handed it to her. She tried to object, but he waved her off. She shrugged it on, then wrapped her arms around his waist as they walked.

"I need to keep you warm now."

Heat suffused his entire body just thinking about Ryker touching her. Once in his silver Volvo, Greg plopped on the back seat and shut his eyes. "I have to work tomorrow morning, so I hope you don't mind if I just crash. Gina will keep you awake."

Gina grinned at him as he started the car and pulled out of the lot. The ride home was quiet, except for the speakers playing Sara's CD that Gina had bought. She played it low and hummed along, moving her body to the beat.

By the time they got home, Alex was wound so tight he thought he might come apart. He wanted to blast Gina for her actions tonight, but he'd never do it in front of his cousin, asleep or not. Plus, he didn't have any claim on her, as she'd so recently pointed out. But shit, he hated to see her pawed all over the place. In places that he wanted to touch. Had touched once upon a time.

Greg jumped out when he pulled in the driveway and ran across the street with a "thanks." Gina took the time to get her CD, and Alex had her door open before she could get it.

"In a hurry to get rid of me, Felix?"

"I'll walk you home."

"You don't have to do that. My house is right there. If you really feel protective, you can watch until I put the lights on."

Alex took her arm and started walking. "I'll walk you over. I need to get my coat anyway."

She started to take it off, but Alex tugged it back on and grunted. Shit, he was acting like a caveman. It wasn't something he'd ever dealt with before. At her door, she unlocked it and stepped inside. He pushed his way in, turning on a few lights, then checked the downstairs rooms.

"Expecting someone to be here waiting for me? I think Bullet was able to find a replacement easily enough." She slipped his jacket off and rested against the archway, holding it out.

"Thanks." He took it, but didn't move. He should. Go home and leave her alone. The images of Ryker slipping his hands under Gina's skirt and grinding against her taunted him. It shouldn't bother him so much, but it did. The kisses she'd given him the past few days and her fingers crawling over his chest played through his mind. The images wouldn't go away. He wanted more. Obviously, so did she. Why not give it to her?

Letting the coat drop from his hand, he pushed her so her back was to the archway. "You said you wanted a slow comfortable screw against the wall."

He leaned closer and stuck his nose into her hair. Fuckin' honeysuckle. It would haunt him for the rest of his life. Growing hard, he brushed against her, so she could feel what she did to him.

Gina's eyes opened wide. "You know that's a drink, right, Felix? I was hardly asking for someone to screw me right out in the open."

"You want something though, don't you?"

"I want you."

Shit.

He slammed his mouth against hers and grabbed her head to pull her even closer. She was so tiny he had to bend, so he lifted her and pressed her against the wall to be at his level. She wrapped her legs around him and kissed him back. God in heaven, did she taste like sin. He ground his hips deeper, and she whimpered, setting him off even more. No control. He was on fire, and nothing could extinguish the flames.

Never had he felt such deep desire for anyone before. Or lost it like this either. Sex was something that was nice and pleasant, with someone you respected and had been dating. Nothing like this. It was unbridled and raw. He couldn't get enough of her.

Unbuttoning the one button that held her vest on, he pushed it open. Her gorgeous tits, with their perky nipples, pushed against the thin material. He couldn't resist them, not now. He slid his hand around one and kneaded. She was damn near perfect. He pulled on the stretchy fabric exposing her to his view. Spectacular didn't even begin to describe his view. Round, pert, with dusky nipples that stood at attention, like they were waiting for him. They more than filled his hand. Would they fill his mouth?

He hoisted her higher and ran his tongue over the soft skin, then zeroed in on the tight peak. Her body jerked, and she whimpered. Yes, he needed her moaning for him. Only for him. He pulled on the top again, so he could access both. Closing his mouth around the darker skin, he sucked. Moaning, yes, and he was the cause. He continued, needing to hear her call his name.

"Felix, that feels so good. Oh, God."

His hands slid along her ass as he held her between him and the wall. All he felt was skin. Was she even wearing underwear? Holy fuck, had she gone to the concert commando? Expecting to meet the band and get that screw she had asked for. If she wanted it, he'd give it to her. He skimmed his hands further and discovered the thin silky material she liked to call underwear. It left her ass bare and barely covered the warm center that beckoned to him.

One finger slid inside, and he groaned. Wet and more than ready. Shit. He could slide in now and have the ride of his life. That's what she wanted. Her arms clung to him as a second finger found its way inside.

"Did he get this far when he stuck his hands under your skirt? Were you this ready for him? Or were you saving it all for me?"

Gina stiffened in his arms. "I wouldn't have had sex with any of them. I'm not a slut, you know. I do have some standards."

The room suddenly spun out of control. What the hell was he doing? Sucking Gina's breasts with his fingers inside her? That wasn't him. He didn't do stuff like this. Ever. Heat rushed through him, then cold filled his heart. He wasn't a freakin' animal. He could control himself better than this. And Gina certainly didn't deserve it. God, what was he thinking?

Slowly lowering her to the ground, he backed away. He could barely look at her. Didn't want to see the look of disdain on her face.

"I'm sorry. I'm really sorry, Dandelion." Pivoting, he bolted without a backward glance. He all but ran back to his house and somehow managed to unlock the door with shaking hands. He'd left his jacket on the floor in her living room, but there was no way he'd go back to get it. He wasn't sure he could face her.

He locked up, figuring Luke was out with Jade. He probably wouldn't get back until much later, if not the morning, although typically Luke wasn't a stay the night kind of guy. Images of Gina whimpering as he licked her skin clawed at him, and he shut all the lights off and rushed up the stairs. He didn't even want to put a light on. He was sure his reflection in the mirror would show the beast he'd let loose tonight.

Stripping his clothes off, he left them on the floor. It went against every routine he'd followed his whole life, but he needed to dive into the oblivion of sleep. The clock showed well after two. He should be exhausted, but as he slipped into his bed and tugged the covers over him, he couldn't sleep. His fingers smelled of Gina and damned if he wasn't masochistic enough to keep them close to his face and think of what could have happened.

It was going to be a long night.

CHAPTER FOUR

*D*amn him. He was avoiding her. Or hiding most likely.

Gina placed her tea cup in the sink and rinsed it out. Looked like she would have to be the one to break the silence he'd imposed. It had been four days since the concert, and Alex hadn't been around, called, or even texted once. Damn him and his moral dilemmas. They'd been smoking hot together, and he had to go all prim and proper on her.

She slipped her over-sized sweater over her tank top and stuck her feet in her fuzzy boots, making sure the ragged edges of her jeans were tucked inside. Alex should be happy. She was covered from head to toe. She pushed up the over-long sleeve of the dark blue sweater to grab the five-subject notebook Alex had left here and strode to the front door. Something was stuck in the screen, and she grabbed it as she crunched through the few inches of snow that had fallen last night. Spring had arrived several days ago, but that didn't matter in New Hampshire.

Alex's driveway was scraped clean of the white stuff,

unlike her own. Nonna had a shovel somewhere. She probably should find it and clean off the porch and drive. Not to mention her car. If Alex was still talking to her, he would have done it. She was surprised he hadn't pushed past his pride and shoveled her out anyway. He'd always taken care of her, and she liked it. Expected it. Not that she couldn't take care of herself. Her mother hadn't been the maternal type, always looking for a new place to hang out and chill with her weaving or herb garden. Taking care of her daughter hadn't been a huge priority.

Her dad had loved taking care of her, though. He read her stories and tucked her into bed. Made sure she had discipline, but also love and acceptance. Her mother had accepted her. She accepted everyone. She just hadn't taken any time to get to know her daughter. Maybe that's why she'd always loved hanging out with Alex. He'd accepted her, too, and even though they were polar opposites, he'd never put down her quirky ways. He might tease her like heck, but it was never a real criticism. And now maybe she'd lost that. She hoped not.

She slowly walked up his front steps. What kind of reception would she get from him? What she wanted was for Alex to pull her into his arms, kiss her senseless, then throw her on the nearest surface and ravish her. Kind of like he'd started doing on Saturday. Damn, he'd been on fire. And double damn, she'd been right there with him. His lips and fingers had tormented her to the point she thought she might burst. But then he'd stopped. Made some stupid comment about Bullet touching her, and she'd been pissed. Not pissed enough to want to stop.

When he'd asked if he'd made her ready, why hadn't she just said, yes, it was all for him? But the tiny smidgen of propriety in her had pushed her to defend her actions at the concert. Stupid, stupid, stupid.

She stared at the little sign next to the door: *APS Designs, Alexander P. Storm, architect*. She tried the handle, and it opened. It was only four-thirty, still business hours. Heaven forbid Felix close early on a work day.

She tapped quietly on the door as she closed it, then turned right to his office. The front room, which had been the Storm's formal parlor, had been converted into a waiting/meeting area. It still had the old piano and many of the same Victorian couches, but the coffee table held books with Alex's designs in them, and a few models of his buildings sat proudly on end tables. She looked through the small archway into the back parlor, which was now his office and drafting area. He was just hanging up the phone and getting up from his desk. Probably to determine who had entered the house.

"Hi." She tried to smile, but his stern expression kind of dimmed it.

"Hey." He glanced at her for a minute, then looked down.

What the hell did she do now? She hadn't formulated a plan other than coming over here. Alex was the one who organized thoughts and ideas well ahead of time. She usually winged it. Honestly, her wings were feeling a bit clipped today.

She held up the notebook and placed it on the corner of his immaculate desk. "This is yours."

Alex eyed the book, then sat in his rolling desk chair. "Actually, I bought it for you, if you remember. It's to organize your repairs and clean-up projects."

She settled on the edge of the client chair opposite Alex. "You're the only one who'd know how to use it. It's no use to me without you."

An uncomfortable silence filled the air. Alex thumbed the pages of the book, glancing at the flyer she'd tucked in with it. Gazing at his desk, she waited for him to say something else. A calendar blotter sat dead center with a neat row of ceramic pencil holders lined up precisely on his right against the wall. Two of them held pencils, all sharpened and sorted by kind. His drafting pencils maybe. The others held pens, sorted by color, and one had an assortment of scissors, ruler, and staple remover. There was a small table next to those pencil holders that had his landline and a thick, brown leather Daily Planner on it.

"I left my jacket at your house."

Gina looked up, but Alex was staring at the flyer now, turning it over in his hands.

"Oh, sorry. I forgot it. I'll have to bring it back later." She hadn't forgotten it. It smelled like him, so she hadn't wanted to give it up yet.

"What's this?" He held up the flyer.

She shrugged. "I don't know. It was in my door when I left. You didn't get one, too?"

He shook his head. "It's an advertisement for house clean-outs and packing. Maybe you should give them a call."

"I couldn't let anyone else pack up Nonna's stuff. They'd just toss it all or sell it. I need to go through it myself. It's weird that they left me one of these and not you."

"They may have heard through the grapevine that your grandmother died and specifically went to see you."

"Their footprints on the porch indicated they tried to see into the window. Creeps."

Alex dropped the flyer and drummed his fingers on the desk. Back and forth from his thumb to his pinky and back again. Both hands perfectly synchronized. Always the same pattern. It fascinated her.

"They probably just wanted a look at the pretty young thing that moved in."

"You think I'm pretty? I don't remember you ever saying that before."

His face pinched, almost like a grimace. "Obviously, or I wouldn't have been pulling your clothes off and licking you all over after the concert."

She didn't know whether to be pleased that he actually admitted he found her attractive or upset, because he sounded disgusted by the fact. She stood and walked around the desk. He rolled the chair back, until it bumped the small table.

"I'm not going to jump you, Felix. Look, I can't get much more covered than this." She held up her arms where the sleeves draped inches longer than they should. "You can't even see my hands."

Alex checked out the sweater, and a grin finally made its way to his face. "Where'd you get that? It doesn't seem like your usual style."

"An old lady in my apartment building. I helped her with some computer problems, and she knitted it for me. Pretty sure her eyes aren't as good as they used to be, because it's not really my size."

"I don't think it's even my size, and I'm six foot two."

Gina chewed on her bottom lip and sighed. "Please, tell me we aren't going to let what happened Saturday come between us. We've been friends for too long."

She leaned against the desk and stared at him. He didn't have the desk now to drum his fingers on, so his thumbs took over, touching each finger from pointer to pinky and back. Again, both hands together. She couldn't even count how many times she'd seen him do this. One time, she'd asked him about it, and he'd seemed embarrassed. Made some comment about helping him focus. She got that. Her attention span wasn't the best at times, but she'd discovered a number of coping strategies that worked. She and Alex weren't so different in that capacity.

"When we were young, you were the only one I ever felt truly comfortable with. I wasn't sure why. Luke is my age, but he was more interested in playing in the mud or being a daredevil on his bike. And even though he's brilliant, he never actually wanted to talk about anything serious."

"He still doesn't. Maybe someday something will make him grow up."

"Maybe. Sara was only a few years younger, but it was enough that I never felt that same connection with her. She and Sofie and Leah would be playing with their dolls and be in their perfect clothes with their perfect manners."

"I had good manners, too." He sounded hurt.

"Yes, you did. But you were a boy, and you were smart, and you didn't treat me like some stupid girl. You never seemed to care that I wore strange clothes or used different expressions. You challenged me to think and got me wanting to learn more. And you treated me very nice, like a lady."

Alex stared at his fingers that were still tapping out a beat. "I didn't treat you that way a few days ago."

Gina leaned closer but didn't touch him. "It wasn't anything I didn't want. You have to understand that, Alex. I trust you. You'd never hurt me."

He glanced at her once, then rose and moved toward the window. He shoved his hands into his black dress slacks and remained silent, again. Damn, she was doing all the work here.

Sitting in his desk chair, she spun around a few times before stopping and focusing back on him. "I never understood why you put up with me following you around like a little puppy."

Alex shifted and rested against the window sill. His body posture had relaxed.

"For the same reasons you just said, Dandelion. You were intelligent, even if you hadn't done typical schooling. You challenged me, too. You always asked these bizarre questions, but it made me go look up the answer. Because of that, I learned so many things I never would have known otherwise."

"I loved that you always got me the answer. It might take you a week or more, but you always did. And the Internet was barely starting then, so you couldn't just Google it. I think that was one of the reasons I got so interested in computers. The possibilities simply astounded me."

Alex smiled with a faraway look in his eyes. "You never cared that I wasn't playing in the mud like other boys, or that I didn't want to ride my bike down a steep hill or jump it over some precarious set-up. You liked walking through the woods and looking at nature and the patterns that were there. You encouraged me to draw those patterns, which helped me when I was designing houses that would blend in with the scenery."

He looked down at his hands again. "You never told me my neatness and organization were unnatural for a boy, and you never got weirded out by all the stupid shit I did. You always looked at me like I could do no wrong. Like I was some white knight who came to save you."

Had he been trying to live up to that all these years? Is that why he had so much guilt built up? She started to get up, but the sound of the front door opening took their attention. Luke walked in a moment later.

"Hey."

They both returned the greeting.

"Your driveway still isn't shoveled, Gina. I thought Alex would have had that done by now."

Alex frowned and straightened. "I was—"

"How did, uh, Jade like the concert the other night?" she interrupted. No need to heap more guilt on Alex.

A sly smile crept across Luke's face. "Loved it. Loved

meeting the band. She was very grateful I brought her and thanked me very nicely. Several times."

Alex groaned and shook his head.

Luke's grin got bigger. "You know, bro, maybe if you got yourself a good fuck every now and then, you'd loosen up a little."

"Luke." Alex glared at his brother, then tilted his head toward her.

Luke grimaced. "Ooh, sorry, Gina. My bad."

As he left, he threw back over his shoulder, "I'm just saying that a good … screw might chill you out a bit."

"A slow comfortable screw against the wall?"

Gina whipped her head around at Alex's muttered words. She couldn't help the snort that erupted from her. Seems maybe things were getting somewhat back to normal. She walked over to Alex and rested her head against his arm.

"I want to get an alarm system." He'd started to stiffen, then pulled away to stare at her.

"Why do you need an alarm system?"

"I was going through some of the rooms the last few days, and Nonna had a bunch of old newspapers still there. You must have brought them in, because some were after she passed away."

"I might have done that." His innocent look wasn't working.

"Anyway, I read about a few robberies lately. There was a jewelry theft, and one at the bank, and a few of the local stores downtown. We aren't that far from there. I have lots of expensive computer equipment at the house, and it's not just the cost. The programs and all my work are on them. I back them up, but it's not quite the same when you're in the middle of working out a new design. Can you help me? Please?"

Alex moved toward his desk and sat. He pulled out a card

file and flipped through. "I know this guy, John Michaels, who's good. He can do a security system, no problem. I was actually thinking he might be good to help with a few other things at your house. He did some work for Erik up in Maine. I don't mind painting and cleaning, but plumbing isn't really on my list of accomplishments. He doesn't have a lot of overhead, so he's very reasonable."

"If you think he's good, then we'll use him. Now..." She stepped over to him and settled on his lap. He stiffened for only a second, then chuckled and relaxed.

"Since you mentioned redoing the bathroom, I thought you could help me pick out a new toilet and sink for the one off the kitchen."

"Sure, we can take a peek on the internet and see what the best models are, what's available."

She wound her arms around his neck. "No, I wanted to go tonight. You'll come with me, right? I need you, Felix."

He sat up straighter and put his hands on her waist. Damn the big thick sweater.

"You can't just go to the store and say *eeny meeny miny moe*. You have to research these things. Compare them, price them out, and then check which places have the best warranties and customer service."

She placed her face right up next to his until their foreheads touched. "So, you'll come with me?" She stuck her tongue on her top lip, for good measure. She could tell the minute he gave in.

"Fine, let me get changed. I had a meeting today with a client, so I'm a bit dressier than normal."

Before he could push her off his lap, she grasped his face and kissed him. Not too long, but enough for him to remember what it was like. "Thank you, thank you, thank you."

She gave him one more kiss, and this time he actually

responded. His hands pushed on her back, but all that wool got in the way.

"Stupid sweater," he mumbled attempting to get under it. Whistling from the kitchen reminded them Luke was home. Alex stood, holding her tight so she didn't fall.

"I'm going up to change. Be right back."

"Want me to come and help?"

"No. Stay." He pointed at her.

She held up her hands like paws, stuck her tongue out of her mouth, and panted. Alex shook his head and walked away. Getting cozy in his chair, she examined his desk. After a few moments an idea came to her. She rearranged his pens and pencils so they had different colored ring patterns in each one. Pencils on the outside, blue pens on the next ring in, and then red pens on the inside.

Her head flew up at a chuckle from the doorway. Luke stood there grinning. She held her finger to her lips in a shushing sign, and he gave her a thumbs up.

"I love you, Gina," he whispered, then disappeared.

She pulled Alex's planner onto her lap, wishing he was the one who'd said those words. As she flipped through the book, she marveled at Alex's organization. He had everything planned out precisely. Not that she expected anything less from him, but the man actually had 'take out trash' scheduled in at five-fifteen every Thursday night. His mortgage, car payment, and all his bills were written down all the way to... she thumbed through the book...to the end of the year. He'd scheduled his whole flippin' year. Wow, that was efficient. She was lucky if she remembered what she was supposed to do tomorrow.

Maybe she needed to schedule in some time with him, too. Looked like he didn't ignore his planner too much. She turned to this coming Saturday. Nothing much there. Taking a red pen, she wrote at the top KISS GINA. Then she moved ahead three or four weeks. Let's hope it didn't take more than that to get him here. She scribbled MAKE WILD PASSIONATE LOVE TO GINA - ALL DAY LONG.

She giggled as she turned the pages back to today and placed it precisely where it had been. Knowing Alex, he had some radar that told him when something had been moved. Now to see how closely he followed his planner. It was the first time she ever wanted him to not deviate from what was written.

ALEX KICKED the snow off the bottom of his running shoes and wiped his feet on the doormat. Walking into the kitchen, he wiped his feet on the inside mat as well. Saturday was his typical day to wash the kitchen floor, but there was no sense in making more work for himself by dragging in the dirt from his run. The snow from a few days ago had begun to melt with the warmer weather, and the roads were covered in slush.

After pouring a cup of coffee from the pot he'd put on before his run, he strolled down to his office. Weekends he liked to keep free from work, but he'd gotten a call from Medicore, the company he'd done the medical building proposal for, and they'd offered him the job. He still couldn't believe it. This would be a whole new avenue for his work, and he was stoked. Also, a bit apprehensive. Could he live up to the standard they wanted? His work was flawless, he had no doubt of that. Still, he knew he'd need to put in extra time to ensure the building was exactly what they wanted. Next week, he'd meet with the board of directors to go over all the specifications.

He set his cup on his desk, settled in his chair, and drew his planner toward him. Pulling on the post-it note he'd stuck to Friday, he moved it to today. Not much there except — wait, that wasn't his writing.

KISS GINA. Scribbled in red, capital letters across the top. The little minx. She was the only person he knew who'd have the gall to mess with his daily planner.

Kiss Gina. His cock sure liked that idea. His brain had other thoughts. She was dangerous to his libido and his control.

She gave you a kiss for luck, and you got the job. Maybe you should thank her.

Right. His getting the job had nothing to do with Gina's good luck kiss. *You could thank her anyway...with a kiss.* Damn horny libido. Always needed to add its two cents.

He looked down at the planner. She'd written in the kiss at the eight-fifteen slot. He checked his watch, eight-oh-seven. Not much time to make the decision. Certainly not enough time to shower off the stink of his run. It would serve her right if he showed up to kiss her all smelly and dirty.

He took a few sips of his coffee, then he stood. His legs doing that not listening thing again. Although, he hadn't actually told them not to go to Gina's. He *should* tell her he'd gotten the job. She'd be excited for him. Probably dance around and squeal, while those spectacular breasts bounced along, too. Not that they were the reason he'd tell her. She honestly cared about him and his successes. That's what he really loved about Gina, how authentic and kind she was. No lip service to anyone, for any reason.

After placing the cup in the sink, he grabbed the keys to her house and walked over. He let himself in and quietly mounted the stairs. Her bedroom door was open, so he slipped in and simply watched her for a few moments. The clock by her bedside read eight-eleven. The kiss wasn't scheduled until quarter past. Must obey the planner.

Her hair spread around her head in disarray, so he couldn't see her face. He reached a finger and smoothed part of it away. She twitched, and he froze. The kiss should wake her up, nothing else. Moaning softly, she rolled onto her back. Now, *he* stifled a moan. The sheet had slipped lower exposing her torso. She wore a man's sleeveless undershirt, and it was far too large. The neckline and armholes sagged flashing her breasts quite nicely for his view. Had she gotten it from some guy? Why did he care?

Her right nipple peeked out, taunting him. He licked his lips, the desire to suck on her so strong he had to clench his fists to fight it. *It never said the kiss had to be on the mouth.* Shit, it hadn't. But that was just semantics, right? Kisses usually meant mouth.

Sure, but mouth to...something else is also a kiss. Why did his libido have to be so technically accurate? He took a step closer as the clock flipped to eight-fourteen. One minute to decide. Too much pressure. He liked to research his choices and list pros and cons of each one. But with her nipple seeming to tighten just with his gaze, he couldn't think of any cons at all. There must be some. Surely, his brain would come to its senses and rattle off a whole bunch.

Eight-fifteen. Shit, shit, shit. He leaned down, pressing his mouth to the dusky peak. His cock stood up and applauded.

Gina whimpered, and her eyes fluttered. Alex moved and pressed his lips to hers now, as he settled on the edge of the bed.

"Felix?" She reached up to cup his face, her smile angelic. He knew better.

"Morning, Dandelion."

"What are you doing here? Not that I'm complaining about your method of waking me." Her fingers gripped his hair so he couldn't pull away. Did she know where he'd kissed her first?

"I had this note in my planner to kiss you this morning. You wouldn't know anything about that, would you?"

The impish look in her eyes sent desire rocketing straight to his groin. Added to the already alert arousal her naked breasts had caused, he was in some pain.

Her tongue peeked out and brushed against her lips. "Why would I know anything about your planner? What exactly did it say?"

"It just said, 'KISS GINA' in all caps. And red ink."

"Sounds like an important item. When exactly was it scheduled?"

"Eight-fifteen."

Her lips twisted wryly. "How long was it scheduled for?"

Looking up, he recalled the note. "It was in a fifteen minute slot."

"Then, you'd better get moving. You've just wasted a whole minute talking to me."

Before he could argue, she drew his head closer and set her lips against his. He gave in. When it came to his Dandelion, there wasn't much sense in arguing. Plus, it had been in his planner. It was only a kiss. Well, a few kisses. It wouldn't go any further. He could keep it at kissing.

Like you did the other night? Damn, why did the brain choose now to come to life and debate? Fifteen minutes of kissing. That's it. No more. And with the short conversation it would really be less than fifteen.

Gina twisted, and Alex ended up on his back on the bed next to her, their lips still attached. The brain had totally shut down. The libido was taking over, and he didn't give a shit. Her shifting ended with her laying on him, her legs on either side of his hips. When her tongue licked along the seam of his mouth, he opened, accepting her invitation.

As their tongues danced, Alex slid his hands along her back. The thin fabric didn't hide the feel of her lithe body, small yet firm. She curved in at the waist, back out at the hips, and God help him, she was only wearing the dental floss again. No control whatsoever, he gloried in touching her bare skin. His hands caressed her ass, kneading the silky surface. She wiggled in response, her hips grinding into his.

He allowed his hands to roam further north and slide under the shirt that hung off one shoulder. His thumbs glided along her ribs, then skimmed under the curve of her breasts. So full, so real. Gloriously so.

Those nipples, that had called out to him earlier, begged to be touched. This wasn't in the planner, but it should be. Kissing didn't have to be mouth to mouth. He pulled her along his body, his lips nibbling down her neck and along her shoulder. Heaven dangled before his eyes. He tugged harder and soon had one pert nipple right on the tip of his tongue. He licked and—

The sound of a phone broke through the heavy breathing. Gina sat up and shook her head, her hair flying wildly around.

"Oh, crap, I forgot I'd set that."

"Forget it again." He pulled, but she actually resisted.

"I'm sorry, Felix. I have an appointment with my lawyer at the bank." Leaning down, she gave him one more passionate kiss, then hopped off the bed. What? She was being responsible? Now?

"But you scheduled in our time to kiss." Sure, use her naughty deed to get his way.

She pointed to the clock. "It's eight-thirty. Our appointment is up."

That wasn't the only thing up. Pushing himself to sitting,

he adjusted the huge boner he'd gotten with a half-naked Dandelion on his lap.

"Maybe we can finish later. You need to come with me to my appointment. I meant to ask you, but I forgot."

"Why do you need me?" God, he needed *her*, except it was probably better this way. He could get his brain thinking again. It might have to talk the rest of his body down from the ledge.

She leaned on the bed, her chest on full display. That wasn't helping the brain's case. "I always need you, Felix. You don't want them taking advantage of me, do you?"

Like he'd just been doing? Hell, no. An image of Gina in a bank vault pleasuring two old codgers did not sit well. He slid off the bed and tried to steady his feet. Painful.

"When's your appointment? I just went for a run and smell terrible. I'll need to shower."

Gina stepped closer. Not a good idea. His legs didn't retreat, though. Stupid legs. She reached up and hugged him. His hands automatically went around her.

"It's at nine, but it's close. Right down the street. I'd suggest we share a shower, but I'm not sure how clean we'd get."

She kissed his cheek and rubbed against him. "And I think you smell amazing. Totally turned me on back there."

Her gaze swept to the disheveled bed. He had to keep his eyes away, or he'd throw her down and finish what they'd started. *Get in gear, brain. Back to sensible mode, pronto.*

"Go, take your shower. I'll run home, take one, and meet you back here. I'll drive. I'm not sure I could fit my legs into your car."

"Thanks, Felix. You're the best." She kissed his cheek again, then turned toward the bathroom, yanking off her shirt as she went.

Clenching his hands into fists, he gritted his teeth and left her room, trotting down the steps as fast as his erection could handle. At least she'd be fully dressed when they went to the bank. He hoped so, anyway. You never knew with Gina. For now, he needed a quick shower. He'd better make it cold.

CHAPTER FIVE

"Thank you for coming in today, Miss Mazelli."

Clifton Gramercy, the bank manager, shook Gina's hand and indicated one of the chairs in front of his desk.

"Of course, Mr. Gramercy. This is my friend, Alexander Storm."

Gramercy looked uncomfortable as he shook Alex's hand. "Storm, of course, I know the name. There are many of you in town. Mr. Scarsdale should be here any minute."

Alex took the other chair and looked at her oddly. "I thought Wayne Scarsdale retired last year."

"He did. His grandson, Rick, took over his law practice. He's the one who had the copy of Nonna's will."

Alex scowled, but left it at that. Gramercy went off, mumbling something about getting another chair, and she smiled at Alex, touching his hand. The morning had started off with a bang, though the explosion never quite got off the ground. The fact Alex had actually read her memo in his planner, and followed through, thrilled her. She hadn't thought he would. There was hope for him yet.

Of course, it had left them both a little frustrated. She'd turned the shower to cold and had a feeling he might have done the same.

"You look nice today." He eyed her outfit with an approving gaze. A gray maxi skirt with muted stripes and a long-sleeved blouse with flowing sleeves.

"I even wore a bra." She pulled the side of the blouse over to show him the strap. He closed his eyes and shook his head.

At least she was appropriate. He could hardly complain. Well, if they were still in her bed, he might, but certainly not here in the confines of the local bank. Before she could say something else to shake him up, Gramercy returned with her lawyer. Nonna's lawyer.

"Gina, it's nice to see you again," Scarsdale said, then glanced past her. "Alex, I didn't expect to see you here."

Alex shook hands with the lawyer.

At her confused look, Alex supplied, "Rick went to school with my brother, Erik." It didn't seem like that was a good thing. She'd have to ask about it later. "Gina asked me to come along with her, in case there was something she didn't understand."

Actually, she simply wanted his company. Numbers were no problem to her. They were all part of the analytical mind that knew how to create and take apart computer programs. Some of her college professors had called her a genius. It was just how her brain did things.

"Of course. Have a seat," Rick said. He installed himself in the new chair Gramercy had set on the other side of her. "I have the documents showing your inheritance. This is simply a meeting to get your name on your grandmother's bank account, enabling you to take over her funds."

"I do hope you'll continue to use our services, Miss Mazelli," Gramercy said, his greedy gaze roaming over her. Because of her money or because of her? He was only a few years older than Alex, and his interest was apparent. What that interest was, she wasn't sure. Another reason to have Alex here. He was a nice buffer. She'd hate to piss off her lawyer or bank manager, as temporary as they may be.

"I'm not really sure yet. I don't plan on staying here permanently, but it'll be a few months before I have my grandmother's house ready to sell. I'll happily keep the money in here at least until then."

Both men smirked. Were they hoping to get bonuses or more business from her?

"I know a few good companies that do an excellent job of cleaning out houses, if you need help with that. They're very reasonable with their rates, too. I could give them a call for you." Gramercy was already flipping through his Rolodex.

"I couldn't possibly have anyone else go through Nonna's things, but thank you."

This time Scarsdale dug through his pocket for business cards. "I know a great real estate agent. He has contacts with many local businesses that do repairs and updates to old houses like yours. I'd be happy to talk to them for you."

"I think we're all set, gentlemen." Alex sat up straighter in his seat. "Gina and I plan on cleaning out the house, and I've already contacted someone regarding any projects that need doing. We'll keep your offer in mind, if our man doesn't work out. Now, let's get down to the business at hand."

She should be mad that Alex took charge, since she was perfectly capable of taking care of herself. But there was something so beautiful about Alex in full organizational mode that she loved watching. Scarsdale rattled on about some of the provisions of the will, then Gramercy explained the legal documents she needed to sign to get the accounts transferred over. It seemed to take forever. She must have signed her name a few hundred times. Alex sat back and watched, never interfering with this part. When Gramercy showed her the balance of the accounts, however, she almost choked.

"Are you okay?" Alex reached for her hand and squeezed it.

She nodded. "Yeah, I wasn't expecting that amount in Nonna's accounts."

He squeezed again, then smiled. Gramercy handed her a few more documents to sign, and finally, they were out of there. Scarsdale caught her at the door as Alex went out to get the car that he'd parked a block away.

"Gina, I do hope you'll reconsider using one of my guys for your home improvement, or at least for the real estate transaction. I can have them there today to appraise the house for you."

"Thank you, Rick, but I'm not ready for it to be put on the market yet. Alex is helping me with everything else."

He touched her elbow and edged closer. "What's your relationship with Alex Storm?"

"He's a friend. My grandmother's neighbor. He used to help her with the chores that got to be too much as she got older."

"That's all?"

"Yes." Not that she didn't want more with Alex, but she wouldn't start any rumors here in this small town. If he became the subject of gossip. he'd never forgive her. To be hooked up with the likes of her, a bohemian vagabond, would be a nightmare for him.

"In that case, perhaps now that my legal advice is finished, you'd think about going out for a few drinks with me?"

"I'm flattered, Rick, really, but I don't plan on staying around here."

"It doesn't have to be anything permanent. We could go out, have a good time, and enjoy each other's company. I haven't had any complaints yet. What do you say? You'd have fun."

He definitely wasn't the typical lawyer type. His hair was longer, and his clothes more in style with what her artist friends wore in New York. They'd all think he was handsome. He just didn't do it for her. Not after she'd had Alex Storm nibbling on her nips. She wanted him to nibble on more of her. Rick was not in the same class.

"I'm sure I would, and I appreciate the offer. Right now, I have to concentrate on going through Nonna's things. That'll be hard enough."

Looking contrite, he patted her shoulder. "Of course. I'll make sure to keep in touch. You have my card. Please, call me if you have any needs I can fulfill."

Alex pulled up in front of the bank, so she nodded and left. As she got in and they drove away, he frowned.

"You looked awfully cozy with Rick just then. Everything okay?"

"He wanted to make sure I had his number in case I had any needs he could fulfill."

A growling noise came from Alex's mouth, and she almost giggled. Was jealousy the answer? Alex had jumped her after Bullet Ryker put the moves on her. Would he do it again, if she insinuated she might get it on with Rick?

"Yeah, I've got his number, too."

"You don't seem to like him. Any reason? Besides that he wants to have sex with me? Because you shouldn't care about that, since we're only friends."

"Erik didn't really like him. Thought the guy was a bit of a weasel. He went off to school in New York City. I hadn't realized he was back until today."

"Hmm, I felt a New York vibe coming from him. Umm, why are you heading this way?" They'd gone away from their street, toward downtown.

"I thought I'd take you to lunch or maybe brunch since it's only eleven. The Loaf and Ladle has great breakfast sandwiches and soups."

"That sounds wonderful." There he was, taking charge again. The feminist in her should be mad. The little girl who'd had to take care of herself loved it. It was one of the reasons she'd loved being with Nonna. Her grandmother had always taken care of her and shown how much she loved her. Tears welled in her eyes, and she turned her head but couldn't hide the sniff.

As Alex parked in the lot, he took her hand. "What's the matter? What did I say?"

Hurling herself into his arms, she clung to him. It wasn't Nonna, but it was the closest she had. He rubbed her back as she sniffled.

"I was thinking of Nonna, that's all. Sometimes it hits me that she's gone. I don't mean to cry all over you again."

"You can cry on me anytime you like. Any time you need to. Never apologize, Dandy. I'm here for you."

The beautiful thing about Alex was he meant it. He was there if she needed him, and not for sex or for her needs to be fulfilled. He hadn't been *there* for her yet. Maybe soon. She was getting closer.

After holding her close for a few minutes, he eased back, then took her hands again. "Listen, if you need any money to get the house fixed up, I can help you out. I don't want you worrying about that."

He thought she needed money. After seeing the bank account balances, she actually laughed.

"You are so sweet, Felix. It's fine. You don't have to—"

"You can pay me back once you sell the house. I don't want you worrying about how you'll pay for it."

She pulled him in and hugged him tight. "You're so good

to me. But you don't need to worry. Apparently, Nonna was loaded."

"Really?" He scowled. "When I mowed the lawn in high school, she was always a bit stingy."

"Maybe that's why she still has tons. Why I have tons." Damn, she still hadn't accepted Nona's loss. Didn't want to.

"Tons, huh? Maybe you can give me a loan to fix my house, then."

"I'll give you anything you need, Felix." She wanted him to need her. Desperately.

His eyes grew warm, then his jaw got tight. That irksome control was back. "Right now, I need to eat. Someone dragged me away before I had breakfast this morning. I barely even had two sips of coffee."

Getting out of the car, she jogged up the sidewalk as Alex joined her. They approached the door, and she smoothed down her blouse and skirt.

"So, I'm appropriately dressed today?"

He gave her a once over, then reached down and fixed the clasp on her necklace so it was in the back again. His hands rested between her breasts. They didn't stay long, but the feel of them there made her shiver. She'd have to make sure her necklace clasps always moved around front if it got his hands on her willingly.

"I told you, you look nice."

They walked into the shop and found a table by the window. He pulled her chair out for her and she sat. As Alex studied the menu, she studied him. Beyond gorgeous, in a clean-cut sort of way. His manners were impeccable, and he always knew what to say to make her feel better. He ran a successful architectural business and owned his own home. Most importantly, his lips and hands set her on fire. Why the hell wasn't he married? What was wrong with the women in this backwater town that they hadn't stampeded their way through his door? Or was he the one who was picky? She could see him having a list of proper traits for the woman he would marry.

What she wouldn't give to be on top of that list. But as she didn't plan to stick around all that long, it was a moot point. She picked up her menu to study that instead.

GINA STEPPED out of the claw foot tub and scrubbed the towel over her body. As she stepped into her panties, her mind roamed to Alex. They'd had a nice lunch a few days ago, then he'd shown her the building plans for the new project he'd been offered. Pride swelled inside her thinking about how well he'd done. Not that she ever doubted him. His organization and attention to detail was beyond anything she'd ever seen before.

She ran the towel through her hair and crossed the hall. As she pushed open the door, she froze, staring at the hinge. That was it. Perfect. Now, if only she could get it into code.

After sprinting down the stairs, she sat on the stool in front of her computer. She turned on all three screens and within seconds her mind was whirring and creating. If she was right, this was exactly what Alex needed to complete his newest project.

Time stood still as her fingers flew and designs folded and unfolded in her mind. It was always this way when she had a new project. Lost in thought and creation.

"Hey, Dandelion, I just finished my run and had a hankering for Chinese. You up for that?"

Alex's voice barely made a dent in her concentration, though her body went on full alert. Especially the part between her legs. It would only be disappointed again.

She tapped away at a few more keys, then sprang up as he

entered the room. He stood riveted in place, his eyes wide.

"I did it. Felix, you're going to be so happy." She jumped up and down.

His whole body stiffened, and his eyes went to her chest. Oops. Forgot something.

"Why aren't you dressed?" His hands clenched at his sides.

Yup, that's what she forgot. Happened often, unfortunately.

"I was so excited." Grabbing his hand, she pulled. "Look, come here. I did this for you."

"Got naked for me?"

The idea got her insides curling with desire. "Well, I'd do that, too, but, no, look."

She glanced at the clock. After six. "I've been working on this for the last few hours. See what it does? You said you were having some problems getting the hinges to work right on your computer-generated model. I fixed that. Aren't you happy?"

"I'd be happier if you put some clothes on." Was he even breathing?

"No, I have to show you first." He still hadn't moved. "Fine, give me your sweatshirt if you're so prudish." She reached to unzip his hoodie, and he grabbed her hands.

"I just went for a run. I don't have anything on under this."

She plunked her hands on her hips and thrust out her chest. "Which do you want exposed? Your boobies or mine?"

He shrugged out of his sweatshirt and handed it over. She slipped it on, then turned back to the computer, not bothering to zip it.

"It doesn't bother you, walking around naked?"

"My mother and I lived in a few nudist colonies. I'm letting the impurities out." Sounded like a better reason than she forgot she wasn't dressed.

"They seem to be getting into me," he muttered, yet he moved closer as she typed instructions on the keyboard.

"See, here's what I did." She demonstrated the new program and how it could help him. Was he even listening? His erection pushed against her back, making her more aware of him than ever. Focus. Pay attention to the computer.

When she peeked up at him, he was looking at her chest, not the screen.

She swung around on the stool, and his running pants tented right in front of her. Reaching over, she stroked the material. So hard. A strangled sound erupted from Alex's throat.

"If you let me get that swelling down, you might be able to focus on my genius program."

He took a step back, his face a mixture of fear and need. "I, um ..."

Rising, she moved closer. He moved back. And kept moving until Nonna's armless Queen Anne's chair stopped him. She ran her hands up his chest. God, he was gorgeous. Wide shoulders, trim waist, and slim hips. A dusting of light hair covered the nicely defined pectorals and swirled down the center dipping into his waistband. He wasn't bodybuilder muscled, but she'd never gone for that type anyway. She'd mostly dated geeks and artists. Alex was buff compared to them.

"God, you turn me on, Felix. You have the most delicious body." She let her hands wander.

His eyes lowered to her chest, though he kept his hands tightly curled at his sides. "I could say the same to you."

"So, why not enjoy?" He started to object, but she slipped her hands onto the waistband of his pants and pulled down. He backed up again, or tried, but only landed in the chair. She knelt in front of him, admiring the arousal she'd released. Hot damn. Even better than she remembered from nine years ago. He was a man now.

"My, how you've grown, Felix." When she stroked him, he shuddered. The rest of him sat still as stone, his eyes never moving from her hands. "Is this for me?"

A few mangled sounds came from his mouth, but she couldn't understand it. Angling forward, she twirled her tongue over his tip. More groans. He fisted the sides of the chair as she continued to lick him. Holy shit, she was turned on. Please, don't let him stop this. *Please*.

She took his hard length in her mouth and sucked. Her nipples ached, and her hips wiggled in anticipation. Could she keep going? Or would Alex put a halt to it like he'd done after the concert?

"God Almighty, Dandelion, you're gonna kill me. I won't last if you keep doing that."

"What should I do then? You're driving me absolutely crazy, Felix." She ran one hand down her torso and between her legs. "I'm so wet from just seeing you and touching you."

"Fuck. You can't say things like that and expect me to be able to stop."

"I don't want you to stop." She stood and gave him another long stroke, then cupped her breasts, pulling at the nipples. "I need to finish. It's been too long. You need to help me."

He pulled her closer, and she straddled the chair. Shrugging the sweatshirt so it hung on her arms and exposed her chest, she leaned until Alex opened his mouth and sucked on the aching peak. Desire coursed through her, running straight to her core. She rotated her hips, needing more, needing completion.

Reaching down, she stroked him as his hands ran over her ass, and his talented mouth nibbled her into a frenzy. He was so close to her opening, she had to have him. Thank

God, she'd worn a thong. She pulled the fabric aside and wiggled her hips until he filled her opening. Bliss. She still needed more. She sank down until her pelvis met his.

His hands froze. "What are you doing?"

"Please. It's fine. I don't have cooties, and I'm on the pill. Don't make me stop. Shit, Felix, I need this. I need you."

She gyrated her hips, and a low moan came from his throat. His hands roamed her back, and his lips fastened to her nipple again. Thank God. She sifted her fingers through his hair and held him to her chest as she raised and lowered herself. The friction sent waves of pleasure through her body, and her blood boiled. Why did Alex affect her this way? She'd always enjoyed sex, but with him it reached down into her soul. Emotions and feelings she kept hidden away bubbled to the surface and threatened to explode.

The sucking on her breast and the rhythm of their bodies drove her higher and higher, rushing through the waves of desire and need. She grasped his head tightly as she fell off the crest and burst into tiny pieces. Little aftershocks pricked along her nerves, and she twitched, then sagged against him.

Alex grabbed her hips and lifted, then thrust into her again and again, harder and faster, his breathing heavy and strained. He bit her shoulder, then cried out and stiffened. His shoulders relaxed and fell back against the chair.

It wasn't more than a minute before his body tensed under her. No, he wasn't going to start on the guilt trip again. She wouldn't let him. Placing her hands on the side of his face, she stared into his beautiful blue eyes. They were already distancing from her.

"Don't you fuck and run on me, Felix. I'll hunt you down and make you regret it."

He swallowed hard, his Adam's apple bobbing up and down. "I already do."

CHAPTER SIX

*T*ears filled Gina's eyes as Alex said the words. Shit. He'd hurt her. This was why he hadn't wanted a physical relationship. *Liar, you've always wanted to have sex with her, and denying it won't make it so. Why don't you just admit it?*

She turned her face and bit her lip, but not before the pain blasted from the chocolate depths. Double shit. Do something, dickhead. Make her stop crying.

Sliding off him, she stood, pulling his sweatshirt tighter around her. He yanked his pants up, then pulled her close, his arms enclosing her. The cool air swirled around their sweaty bodies, lowering their temperatures. Her semi-naked skin, pressed against his, heated it right back up again.

"Why do I lose control around you, Dandy? Seems every sensible thought in my head flies right out the window." He kept his forehead touching hers, not wanting to lose contact. Leaving would be a better option. Avoid more temptation.

Her eyelashes swept down, hiding her emotions, but the way her arms clung to him, her need was apparent. He scooped her up and lay beside her on the couch. When she nuzzled into his chest, her leg slid in between his. Was she cold? He ran his hand down her body, but the stupid sweatshirt got in the way.

"Why do you always regret being with me? Am I that embarrassing to you?"

"Of course not. I wouldn't be over here all the time if you were."

"Is the sex that bad? You totally rocked my world, but maybe I don't live up to your dream girls."

"No! I mean, yeah, the sex was…yeah. That's not the problem." He liked it too much. That was the problem. Gina was an aphrodisiac, and sex with her simply made him want more. He'd been looking for something with the same effect for nine years. Gina had given it to him yet again. Only Gina.

Was it the same for her? Magical and soul reaching? Or did every guy give her that feeling? His muddled mind recalled her saying she was on the pill. Why? Because she had sex so often? But she'd said it had been a while for her. What did that mean in her world? A few weeks? A month? Or half a year like it had been for him? Was that why it had been so great, because he hadn't had sex in a while?

"So, about my genius program that will solve all your problems."

Gina babbled on about the hinge design she'd worked on. He should be excited that she'd done this for him. It would really help the animation he wanted to do for the board of directors. His mind couldn't move away from what they'd just done. Why was it so mind blowing with her? He'd gotten off with other women, but never as explosively as today. The need was never this strong. There'd been no desire to grab any of them and screw them against the wall, long, slow, or comfortably.

She'd also given him a blow job. Fuck, he got hard again just thinking about it. He'd only had one other woman do that, and it was obvious she hadn't enjoyed it. Gina had stared at his erection like she'd won the lottery. When her hand had disappeared between her legs, it had done him in. He couldn't fight at that point. Even now, he grew harder simply listening to her soft excited voice describe a computer program.

"Thank you for creating that for me. I appreciate it. I'm sure it's perfect." He ran his hand over her leg again, then slid it up to her hip and under the sweatshirt. Totally asking for trouble.

"How grateful are you?" Her hands ran over his chest, then one slipped under his waistband to cup his ass. Her eyes lit up curiously.

Shit. In for a penny, in for a pound. As he plunged his tongue into her mouth, he moved over her. Her legs wrapped around his waist, and heaven opened up right there for him. She pushed his pants down as he sucked on her nipple, then he thrust inside. God in Heaven, this was pure bliss. Her walls clenched around him, and it was all he could do not to screw her senseless.

Her hands pulled on his ass as he pumped in and out, her feet against the back of his legs. He couldn't get enough of her. Touching, tasting, skin to skin, lips to lips, their hips doing a dance so intimate he should be ashamed. They'd never even been on a date. But he couldn't stop. He needed her like he needed air. Needed her to help him reach that pinnacle he'd never quite achieved with anyone else.

Reaching between them, he flicked at her sensitive skin. She arched her back and called out.

"Felix. Oh, God."

He didn't even care that she'd used that nickname. Only that she knew it was him bringing her to the edge and pushing her over. So close. He watched as her head fell back, and her face radiated satisfaction. With a few more thrusts, it was enough to send him over, too. He collapsed on top of her, then lifted onto his elbows. He'd crush her if he wasn't careful. She was so tiny.

As he shifted to his side, she snuggled into him.

"You're so beautiful, Felix. Thank you for making me feel beautiful, too."

"You are beautiful, Dandelion. I don't know how you could think otherwise."

She didn't answer, just sighed and rested against him. Her eyes closed, and her breathing evened out. After two rounds of hot sex, he could pass out, too. But his brain had other plans.

He replayed the sex in his mind, trying to figure out why things between them were so explosive. She was gorgeous and intoxicating, but he'd slept with plenty of beautiful women. More sedate and traditional. They'd date for a while before jumping into bed. Get to know each other and make sure they were compatible. Then, after a few months, they moved to having sex. That's the way it should be done.

Why hadn't any of them made him feel the way Gina made him feel? And why hadn't any of those women stuck around for the long term? Not that Gina ever stuck around either. What the hell was wrong with him?

Closing his eyes, he allowed himself a few minutes of rest. Losing control like that had taken a lot out of him. Couldn't continue to do it. He liked being in control. It's what helped him become successful and have enough money to buy his parents' house, his car, and all the other things he had. There was nothing wrong with being meticulous and organized and having a plan. A dream.

Looking down at Gina's peaceful face, he could feel his dream drifting away. He couldn't allow that. He gently eased away, then covered her with the quilt from the back of the couch. He couldn't let her steal his dream. A successful career with a calm, loving wife and his family all around was exactly what he wanted.

Gina was a nomad, who never stayed in the same place for long. If he allowed her into his heart, she'd only break it when she left. She'd never be happy living in Small Town, New Hampshire, and he refused to be that guy who simply used her for his own enjoyment. He'd never do that to anyone, especially not his Dandelion.

News flash. You just did.

Shit.

He walked out into the early spring night, his sweatshirt still around Gina, and shivered. It served him right. A cold slap in the face was what he deserved after what he'd done. Now, all he had to do was figure out how the hell he'd keep from touching her again. After having her twice today, it wouldn't be easy. It would be damn near impossible.

FIVE-FOURTEEN. One minute until Gina put her plan into action. If Alex ran true to schedule, and he always ran true to schedule, he'd be rolling his trash barrel down to the curb any time now.

She slipped her feet into flip flops and went out the back door. Her barrel didn't have the fancy wheels, but that would make it even better. The warmer weather played along nicely, too. Sunlight still peeked through the trees, keeping the spring chill at bay for now. She took hold of the handle and began to drag.

Oh, Lord, it was heavier than she thought. Of course, she'd been on a cleaning whirlwind the last few days. It couldn't have anything to do with Alex sneaking out on her after they'd had sex. No. Or the fact she hadn't seen or heard from him in the past two days. Since they'd had sex. The best freakin' sex of her life, and he had to pack up and head out on his guilt trip.

She peeked around the corner of her house and waited. Any second now. And…there. Right. On. Time. As usual.

Stage one. Butt first, she wiggled down the driveway, dragging the heavy container. She had on her snuggest, worn jeans and a pale pink camisole. No bra, of course. Maybe it was a little chilly for the top, but hauling the trash down the driveway warmed her up.

She used her peripheral vision to make sure Alex was still on course, and that he'd seen her. Yep, he slowed down, paused, then finished placing his trash in the exact location as every Thursday night.

Stage two. She stumbled on her pathetic footwear and fell, pulling the barrel over at the same time. She landed on her ass and swore. Shit. She'd done too good a job of making it look real. Ouch. Her bottom stung. Could she get Alex to check if she had a bruise? She'd be lucky if he actually came over to help.

Getting on her hands and knees, she started to push up, sneaking a look at the Storm house. Unbelievable. Where had he gone? Had he really seen her fall and gone back in the house? She swallowed as moisture welled in her eyes.

"You okay?"

Her heart raced as she whipped around and fell down again. She held her hand to her chest and stared. "You scared me. I didn't see you come over."

He reached his hand down to her. "Need help getting up?"

Now that her plan had worked, she was pissed. He'd had sex with her and left. With no phone call, text, or even a goodbye when he'd slipped out.

"Maybe I want to be down here. Maybe I like being down here. It's probably where you think I belong anyway, right? With the other trash. The crap that you just throw away when you don't need it anymore. Kind of fits me, don't you think?"

The pain in Alex's expression softened her and made her want to comfort him. Yes, she'd practically jumped him, but he hadn't tried too hard to fight it. He was almost a foot taller than her and she'd guess twice her weight. She wouldn't have been that hard to fend off. It wasn't fair. He could make her madder than anyone, yet also illicit sympathy in seconds.

Kneeling in front of her, he took her hand. "I don't think you're trash, Dandy. You're my friend. You mean a lot to me."

He pulled her to her feet, then bent to pick up the stack of newspapers she'd dumped on top. "You know you should recycle these."

Seriously? What would he do if she punched him in the face? She was very close to that now. She grabbed at a few boxes that were scattered about and stuffed them back in the barrel.

"I mean so much to you, huh? That's how you treat friends. Boinking their brains out, then sneaking out the door once they aren't looking."

Alex turned to where his cousin Greg's son, Ryan, was kicking a ball around his yard with a friend. His eyes narrowed, and he stuck his thumb in the directions of the boys.

"I didn't say it that loud, and they aren't paying any attention to us, anyway." She picked up a few more things, then began to drag the barrel down the rest of the driveway. Why had she bothered? She'd been hoping for at least an apology, but that seemed unlikely now.

"Let me help you with that. It's heavy."

She swatted at the hand that reached for the handle. "I can do it myself, *Alex*." His face fell, but she couldn't be swayed. "You can go do whatever you have written in your planner. I'm sure it's important." When he paused, she continued, "Go ahead, leave. It's what you're good at."

Stupid plan. This is why she needed Alex. He was the one who tallied up the pros and cons of things. Need brilliant computer programs written? Sure, come to her. Plan ahead of time what you want to do? Nah, not her thing.

Alex walked next to her as she dragged the barrel the rest of the way. It seemed lighter. He probably had his hand on the other side helping her along. Altruistic son of a bitch. She never could stay mad at him. She had to try.

Once the barrel was in place, she turned toward Nonna's house, her house. When was she going to get it in her head that Nonna wasn't around any longer? Maybe once she sold the house and moved away permanently.

Permanently. If she sold the house, she wouldn't have an excuse to see Alex. Wait, if? *When* she sold the house. How could she even think of keeping the house? What the hell was there for her in this tiny town?

"I know you're mad, Dandelion. I'm sorry. I didn't mean to hurt you."

Argh, that's what was here for her. Alex and his guilty conscience. Alex and his hot hands and talented lips and gorgeous body. Alex and his meticulous organization and his daily planner. The one he followed to the point of waking her with a kiss. Because it was in his *damn planner*.

She turned to face him, and her heart ached at the look of regret on his face. "Well, you did hurt me. And not because we had sex, but because you walked away without a word. If you keep disappearing every time you touch me, I'm going to get a complex"

He glanced at the boys playing next door and touched her elbow. The chill that ran up her arm had nothing to do with the air temperature or her skimpy shirt.

"Why don't you come over for supper? I put a roast in the crock pot this morning, and it's tender and ready to eat."

She should refuse on principle alone. He only invited her because he didn't want to discuss this out in the open. There was also that assuaging his guilt thing. But the food did sound amazing. All she had in the house was peanut butter and crackers. And jasmine tea.

"Fine." She rolled her eyes and started for his house. He popped open one of the boxes from the trash and deposited all the newspapers into it, then set it next to the barrel. She glared at him.

"What?" He took her elbow and walked alongside her. "This way they'll recycle them instead of throwing them in the landfill. You grew up with all that hippy, go natural, save the Earth stuff. Figured you'd be happy to recycle."

"You're confusing me with my mother. But...thank you. You'll have to come over every Thursday to organize my garbage."

"Until you leave, anyway."

She followed him through the kitchen door. Was that part of his problem? She was leaving. He had said the point of dating was to find someone to spend the rest of your life with. So he'd resist all temptation, until he found his own June Cleaver? Seriously?

The delectable aroma in the kitchen took her mind away from analyzing Alex's sexual habits. For now. She'd probably stew over them more later. Now, she needed to get some food in her stomach.

"Have a seat." Alex opened the cupboard to pull down two plates from the perfectly organized cabinet.

"You don't have to wait on me. I'm capable of getting my own food, if you want to just sit and eat."

"I don't mind, Dandelion." He dished out the food and brought the plates to the table. She dug her fork in and relished the delicious meal. Alex sat across from her, and they ate in silence for a while.

"How come my plate doesn't have any onions on it?"

His expression showed confusion. "You don't like onions. Did you want some?"

He remembered her food preferences. This was why she couldn't stay mad at him. That, and he cooked the most scrumptious food.

"No." She smiled at him. "It's nice that you remember what I like and don't like."

"Does this mean I'm not a total shithead?"

She sighed. "No, not total. I still don't get why you keep running away. I thought we were friends."

"We were a little more than that a few days ago."

She shrugged. "Friends with benefits."

He shot her a glare. "There's no such thing."

"Sure, there is. We're friends who have sex with each other. There's nothing wrong with that."

His eyes narrowed. "Have you had this with a lot of other guys?" His stiff posture told her he hated that idea.

"None, actually. You're the first. Congratulations."

"It can't work. It'll change the way we see each other."

She rested her face in her hand, her elbow on the table. "I don't think it will. Admit it, you've always wanted to boink me. Our first time was just too amazing."

As she leaned back, his eyes grew wide...and guilty. She'd hit it perfectly. "I'll admit it, too, Felix. The mere thought of getting naked with you and doing the nasty gets my juices flowing."

"Oh, God." His head dropped into his hands as he shifted in his seat. "Can you *not* say things like that, please?"

Still so polite, even when he had a boner. "Pants getting too tight?" She looked down at her shirt where the nipples poked out. "See what else happens to me? All your fault. You're too damn sexy."

He peeked at her, then stood and brought his empty plate to the sink. She cleaned up the last of her meal and followed him.

"Can you at least consider it, Felix? Luke thought it was a good idea."

"What did I think was a good idea?" Luke came from the hallway into the kitchen. She hadn't heard the front door open. Too busy picturing Alex's erection and where it would go best.

"Nothing," Alex snapped and stuck the plates in the dishwasher. "There's roast in the crock pot, if you're hungry."

Luke zeroed in on the food, their conversation forgotten. "Always hungry."

As Luke dished out food, she cleaned up the rest of their stuff from the table. Now what did they do? No way Alex would finish their talk in front of his brother.

"Oh, a guy at work recommended that new cop flick. It's cued up on Netflix. Did you guys want to see it, too?"

When she glanced at Alex, he shrugged and cocked his head in question. She didn't really care about the movie, but spending time with Alex was high on her list of favorite things to do.

Luke took his plate and went into the family room, and in seconds, the movie theme floated through the air. Alex took a paper towel, wet it, and wiped the table.

"You said you knew a guy who could help me with my repairs. Will you still contact him? I can always call Rick. He said he has anything I need."

The look he threw her could melt steel. "You don't want anything he has to give you, believe me. I'll call John and get you set up. You staying for the movie?"

"As long as it won't make you uncomfortable. I'd never want to do that."

Alex breathed out a huge sigh, then slung his arm over her shoulder. "Everything you do is uncomfortable for me. Why should that change now? Come on."

Luke took up the recliner, so they sat next to each other on the couch. She tucked her legs under her and leaned against Alex's side. He lifted his arm and stretched it out on the back of the sofa, his fingers brushing her shoulder. As the movie played, she realized how nice this felt. Sitting companionably side by side. Maybe they didn't need sex. They could simply be friends and hang out like this. She could keep her libido under control. No problem.

An hour later, she recanted that thought. Alex's hand had accidentally brushed her breast a few times, sending her nipples into hard peaks. He'd noticed. Well, his cock had noticed, if the bulge in his pants was anything to go by. However, with Luke sitting nearby, there was nothing she could do, short of dragging Alex up to his room. He'd be mortified.

She sat through the rest of the movie, so aware of Alex that her legs ached from clenching them together. Normally, she loved being with him, even with the sexual tension, but now she couldn't wait to get home. Her vibrator was going to get some action tonight.

CHAPTER SEVEN

"Thanks for coming over on such short notice, Sofie. I appreciate it."

Sofia Storm smiled. "No problem, Alex. I'm happy to do it. I always loved this house."

Alex led his cousin into the kitchen where Gina sat with her cup of tea. Sofie was an interior designer and had agreed to help Gina pick out colors and hardware that would maintain the Victorian style of the house yet give it an update.

"Jasmine tea." Gina held up her cup. "Want some?"

Sofie sat across from Gina, her blond hair in such contrast to Gina's dark. He sat next to Gina, knowing he was flirting with danger being so close. When they'd watched the movie together a few nights ago, he'd thought he might explode. She hadn't made any sexual advances, but she hadn't needed to. Her slim, warm body snuggled next to him, and the scent of honeysuckle that always drifted off her had been enough to keep him in a state of arousal.

"I'm all set, thanks. I can't wait to go through the house and see what you want to do. I haven't been in here since I lived next door. That was a lot of years ago."

"Where are you now?"

"Leah and I live in a two-family a few streets over. Right across from the Lincoln School, where she teaches. I do some of my interior designing from the house, although I still need to work a real job, until I can get my business off the ground. If you like what I do for you, make sure to recommend me to others who might need my services."

"Of course I will. Felix, you have the notebook."

Opening the book, he turned to the first section. After showing it to Sofie, and explaining how the book was set up, he pointed out the list of everything that needed fixing versus stuff that could use updating. The front bell rang as they were discussing the projects.

"It's probably John. I'll get it."

He walked to the front of the house and opened the door. John Michaels was almost as tall as him, with dark hair and Mediterranean features. He had a slight accent Alex couldn't quite place, and it wasn't any of his business, so he never asked. John wasn't one to engage in small talk about himself.

"John, come on in. Thanks for coming over, especially on a Saturday."

"No problem. I've been pretty busy during the week with all the spring building projects."

They maneuvered down the hall, and Alex introduced him to the ladies.

"This is Gina Mazelli. Her grandmother left her the house. And this is my cousin, Sofia. Not sure if you've met before."

Sofie's eyes sparkled. "We've met a few times. It's nice to see you again, John."

John just nodded, then looked at Gina, who approached, her hand outstretched.

"Thanks for coming to help. Take off your coat and make

yourself at home. We're just going over the possibilities for each room."

John shrugged off his coat, and Gina's eyes widened. What the hell? John was about his size, nothing special. What was she ogling? He looked at John again. Okay, maybe he was a bit more toned and muscular than him, but he did construction all day. He would be.

Sofie also had her eyes glued to John's physique. Alex sighed. What was wrong with these ladies? You'd think they'd never seen a man before.

"Let's go through each room and take notes on what we think. Are we ready?"

They spent the next hour discussing renovations and simple fixes for each room. There was still a ton of stuff to clean out, but he and Gina could do that piecemeal. The ladies went to the kitchen to get some snacks, while he and John walked around the outside, checking on the repairs that were needed there.

As they finished looking at the lattice work on the front porch, he said, "I'm going to grab a cold drink. You want something?"

John looked up from the small notebook he was scribbling in. "Sure, a soda is fine. I want to check some measurements on that shed in the back first. I'll be in shortly."

After entering the house, Alex walked down to the kitchen. Gina stood by the window, looking out. She was eying John as he examined the shed. He moved closer, and she sighed.

"He'd be a fun ride, huh? Totally hot."

When she turned, her face flushed a deep crimson.

"Oops, sorry, thought you were Sofie."

"Obviously," he grumbled. Was she seriously considering having a go with John? After what they'd done? *You said you didn't want to have those benefits with her. She has to have her needs fulfilled somewhere.*

Why couldn't she have taken a vow of chastity? He hated the thought of his Dandelion having sex with anyone else. She was meant for him. *But you don't want her.*

He froze. He did want her. Maybe not as his dream wife, but he certainly wanted the feeling she gave him when they flirted and touched. Yet he also wanted to respect her and not treat her as anything but the lady she was. Shit, he was screwed. He couldn't have it both ways.

John and Sofie both came back in, and they spent more time on plans. Once they had an order to when things would be done, the two of them left, leaving him and Gina alone.

"Do you really want to have sex with John?" There, he'd asked the question. Not sure he wanted the answer.

"He is gorgeous, Felix, I won't lie. I bet he knows how to make a woman feel good."

He swallowed hard. What do you say to that?

"But," she slinked closer and pressed her hands to his chest, "he's not you. You're the only one who can turn me on by simply walking into the room."

"Right. By walking into a room."

Leaning into him, she ran her hands up to his head. "Yes. This blond hair and angled chin, straight nose, and kissable lips. These broad shoulders…"

As she said each part, she ran her hands over them. He was getting turned on, and she was only naming body parts.

"Your trim waist and slim hips and these long legs that look amazing when you have snug jeans or shorts on. And then when you start talking about lists and details, it practically sends me into an orgasm on the spot."

He put his hands on her shoulders and narrowed his eyes. "Now you're just making fun of me." None of his ex-girlfriends had ever liked how detail-oriented he was. After a while, they all found it tedious and exasperating.

She slid her hands around his waist and sidled as close as possible. "Think about it, Felix, you and me. Slum it a little. You need to have a wild fling in your life before you find your perfect woman and marry her. You can't do it after."

True, he'd never cheat on a woman. Right now, he didn't have anyone special. Except Gina. She was always special. Could he do it? Just have a fling with her?

She rested her head against him. "What we have is good, Felix. Enjoy it while I'm here. I'll be gone soon enough, and you can go back to your boring, scripted sex with a Stepford wife."

Scripted sex wasn't boring, it was comfortable. But that wasn't what he had with Gina.

"Friends with benefits?"

"Really good benefits." She hummed and tugged his shirt from his pants, then slid her hands underneath and caressed his back. God, that was nice.

"We both agree that it's only until you leave."

She shrugged. "Can't very well do it if I'm not around."

"But you're still my friend. I respect you and care for you. You understand that I'm not slumming it with you? I don't ever want you to feel that way."

"I won't." She pulled his head down and kissed him. The guilt was still there, but he pushed it aside. The kiss was too amazing to not simply enjoy it.

He walked her backwards to the counter and lifted her onto it. Widening her legs, she pulled his body between them. No place he'd rather be. Today's shirt was a typical peasant blouse with a stretchy neckline. Shit, he loved her clothes. The accessibility of them was incredible.

"This is just screaming for me to pull at it."

"I think you're right." Her voice was low and husky and

made his cock harden. Inching a finger toward her neck, he slid the top down her shoulders. No bra again. His mouth watered at the spectacular sight. He lowered his mouth and —a knock sounded at the door.

"Are you friggin' kidding me?"

"We could ignore it," Gina suggested, her breathing fast. "I wasn't expecting anyone else today."

The knock sounded again, then the bell.

"I suppose I should get it. Might be Girl Scouts selling cookies." Gina sounded disappointed. Hell, he was, too.

"They sold them a few months ago. I got roped into buying a dozen boxes."

He helped her down from the counter and reluctantly fixed her top. "I'll get rid of whoever it is."

"Can I help you?" Gina asked as they opened the door to a middle-aged man in jeans and a tool belt.

"I left a flyer here a few days ago. I'd heard you were cleaning out the place. I wanted to offer my services. I'm very reasonable, and I work fast."

Her expression showed she was weakening. She was too kindhearted.

"Thank you for the offer, but we're all set with help." Alex began to close the door.

"We'll hold onto the information, in case we end up needing more help," Gina offered. He finished closing the door and leaned against it.

Her eyes grew sensuous, and he reached out for her. As he lowered his head, his planner flashed through his mind.

"Crap. I almost forgot. I have to get a present for my parents. It's their anniversary tomorrow, and we're having dinner at my house. I need to grocery shop, too." How the hell had he not done this already? Gina had taken precedence over almost everything else in his life, making him forget what was important.

A dainty sigh escaped Gina's lips, but she smiled and kissed his cheek. "I'll go with you. Walk in front of me, so I can check out your gorgeous ass and think about what I want to do with it."

~

"Did you have an idea what you wanted to get your parents?" Gina picked up a ceramic vase and turned it over in her hands. They'd gone to downtown Portsmouth and wandered through a few of the fancier shops.

"Not really. I was hoping something would jump out at me."

She stopped and stared at him. "You didn't have this all planned out ahead of time? Their anniversary is tomorrow. Who are you, and what have you done with my Felix?"

Alex slung his arm around her shoulder and tugged her close. "Very funny. The problem is they just moved into a smaller house, so they don't need any more knick knacks or dishes or decorations. I'm hardly about to buy my parents clothes, and gift cards are too impersonal."

"Did they give you any hints about what they want?"

"They don't want anything. They're thrilled to be getting together with all of their children at one time. With both Sara and Erik moved out of town, they don't see them as much."

She patted his arm. "Good thing you'll always be here for them."

He shot her a glare and sighed.

They walked into another shop and looked around. Frowning, Alex shook his head.

"Come on, Felix, think about your parents. What makes them happy? What do they really want?

"Up until recently, I'd say grandkids. But Erik pretty

much cornered the market there. He's got two, now that he adopted Matty and Kiki, and Tessa's expecting another. I think the rest of us are off the hook for a while."

"Grandparents always want more grandkids. I bet Nonna would have liked more."

Alex made a face at her. "Oh, I'm sure you were more than enough for her."

She stuck out her tongue at him.

"They love that Sara's getting married. They always wanted their kids to find the right person and spend the rest of their life happy."

"So, they want to see you and Luke happily married, too?"

Alex shrugged.

She glanced around. "I think Luke might be a lost cause for now, but you…"

Alex narrowed his eyes. "Don't even go there, Dandelion."

"You need a bride. Let's go shopping for one."

"You're crazy."

"Yup, but you love me, anyway."

He got a weird look in his eyes. He didn't love her, not that way, but she didn't need him dwelling on it. Pulling his hand, she dragged him through the store. She tilted her chin at the sales clerk.

"Hmm, how about her? Pretty, well dressed, respectable job."

Alex glared. "She's about forty and wearing a wedding ring."

"Semantics." She dragged him further into the store, scanning the space.

"Anything look good, Felix?"

He stared at her with a grin on his face. "Crazy."

"Ooh, that one's nice. Sweet, innocent, good looking, great shape. She'd be perfect for you…in another six years." Definitely jail bait at this point.

"Why don't I just take out an ad in the paper? List all the qualities I want."

She cocked her head. "You could, but I don't think you'd find one by tomorrow."

"My parents don't expect me to have a fiancée by tomorrow. I think they expect *you* to be there."

"I'm hardly your type." Wouldn't that be amazing, though, if she and Alex announced their engagement? Or not. She needed to stop dreaming about him in her life forever. She was leaving as soon as she got the house done and on the market. The sex was great, but they'd probably kill each other in the course of a month.

They strolled around the store a bit more, then, as they were leaving, she stopped short. Alex plowed into her.

"Hey, put your brake lights on, Dandelion."

Grabbing his arm, she spun him around. A tall, lithe redhead bent over a counter examining a dainty bracelet. Her tailored dress was demure and classy and a soft lilac color. She wore sensible pumps, and her sleek hair was smoothed back into some fancy French twist.

"See? She's perfect for you."

The woman stood and moved away from the counter, heading in their direction. Alex took her arm and pulled.

"No, she's not."

The woman looked up as she neared them, and her eyes opened in recognition. A tiny smile played about her lips.

"Alex? It's nice to see you. How are you?"

Damn, she knew him already. Maybe that was a good thing. They could hook up and— and what? Leave Gina in the dust, just when Alex had finally seemed eager to give the friends-with-benefits thing a try.

"Kristan. I'm fine. How are you?"

Wow, these two were boring. They'd be perfect together.

Kristan pressed a small kiss to Alex's cheek, then stepped

back and looked at her. Alex shifted uncomfortably. Embarrassed by her, maybe? He dropped her arm and shifted away.

"Kristan, this is Gina, Mrs. Mazelli's granddaughter. You remember Mrs. Mazelli from next door? She passed away last year."

Concern appeared on Kristan's face. "Oh, yes, I'm so sorry. She was always nice to me when Alex and I were together."

Kristan asked how Alex's parents were, and Gina took a few minutes to really assess this woman Alex had been with. Long toned legs, perfect teeth, eloquent speech, string of pearls around her neck, tiny waist, and boobs even bigger than the girls. Although looking at how high and pert they were, she assumed they were either fake or the woman wore a very expensive bra. She was going with fake. Had Alex liked that? Had these two been intimate? Why weren't they still seeing each other? Was this lady stupid? If she'd had Alex in her hands, she'd never let him go.

You did have him in your hands. Right, well, that was just sex. Alex didn't want someone like her as his life partner. He'd want this June Cleaver clone, not Gypsy Rose Lee.

"It was nice to meet you, Gina. Maybe I'll see you around town." Kristan's full lips pursed, and she kissed Alex's cheek again.

"Perhaps, but I won't be staying long once I sell my grandmother's house."

Kristan waved, and Alex pulled Gina out of the store and down the street. Her three-inch heels tottered as he moved quickly.

"Hold on there, Felix. I'm going to break an ankle."

He looked down at her worn leather boots with the ripped jeans tucked in. A bit different from the elegant Kristan.

"Sorry, I just didn't need to hang around there."

She faced Alex and clasped his hands. "I don't get it. She's perfect for you. Why'd you break it off with her?"

Pain radiated from his eyes as his mouth tightened. "What makes you think *I* broke it off?"

Leaning back, she crossed her arms over her chest. "Seriously? You're gorgeous, intelligent, nice, polite, have a great job and family. Any woman would be stupid to break it off once they managed to snag your attention."

He glanced away, his shoulders rising and falling as he muttered, "Guess there's a lot of stupid women around here."

As he started walking through the square, she trotted to keep up. Kristan couldn't be too smart, if she'd let Alex get away. His jaw clenched, and his hands fisted at his sides.

She sidled up next to him and slipped her hand around his elbow. "Do you still have a thing for her?"

He stopped short and stared at her oddly. "No, I don't still have a thing for her. I never did. She was nice, and I enjoyed being with her, but we just didn't click. That was her reason for breaking up with *me*. I seem to get a lot of that."

"Some women just like the bad boys. You wait, when they want to get married, they'll be flocking to your side in droves."

He still stared at her, but his eyes focused on her necklace. The clasp was down at the bottom again. She bit her lip to keep from grinning and waited to see how long he could last without fixing it. His hands rubbed against his pants, and he attempted to look away.

"Let's go to a few more stores. There has to be something I can find for my parents." Taking her hand, he started walking. They passed a little wine and cheese boutique, and he paused, glancing in the window.

"In here. I'll get my mother's favorite wine and some cheese to go with it."

"That's a great idea. They'll love it."

They neared the door, but before they went in, Alex took her shoulders and stopped her. He reached out and slid the clasp back up behind her neck.

"I think you're slipping, Felix. You resisted that for a whole three minutes."

He shook his head, put his arm around her shoulder, and pulled her into the store.

CHAPTER EIGHT

"*T*hat dessert was amazing, Gina. Thanks for bringing it."

Alex watched as his mother devoured the last bit of cake on her plate. Gina paused her tickle game with Kiki long enough to nod. "I was happy to, Molly. I haven't made it in a while, so I hope it was good enough."

"That's her third piece, Dandelion," he informed her. "I think it was good enough."

"It's my anniversary. Therefore, I get to have as many pieces as I want."

His dad chuckled. "I'll be the one to hear about it when her pants don't fit tomorrow."

"Don't even go there, Peter Storm. You had far more to eat than I did." His mother playfully slapped her hand in her husband's direction.

Squeals and giggles rang from the corner of the room where Sara, Gina, and Tessa sat, playing with Matty and Kiki.

"What kind of cake was that?" Sara asked. "I don't think I've ever had anything like it."

"It's a kasutera honey cake. Some people call it castella.

My Japanese grandmother, my sobo, taught me to make it. Nonna kept the recipe and helped me make it sometimes when I'd come to visit with my mom."

Her dark eyes grew shiny, and he wanted to wrap his arms around her. She was thinking of her grandmother again. Luckily, Matty knocked over the stack of blocks he'd been building and distracted everyone.

Gina swiped a hand over her eyes and pasted a smile on her face. "Tessa, how've you been feeling?"

His sister-in-law patted the tiny baby bump and her eyes lit up. "I'm fine. I wish Erik would believe me when I tell him that. He's been treating me like glass."

Sara touched Tessa's arm. "He's just worried about you, because he loves you so much."

Erik stood against the door jam, scowling. His knuckles were white on his cane as he glanced at his wife. The love that shown from them was true and clear. Despite their marriage, which was for the sake of the children, and the hardships they'd gone through, Erik and Tessa had found love and happiness. He desperately wanted that someday. The way he was going, it might never happen.

Gina had said lots of women liked bad boys. Guys who were dangerous and treated women poorly. No way he could do that. He'd been raised too well. Except, he hadn't been polite and well-mannered with Gina. Apparently, she liked a bad boy, too.

"You know, Sara, I'm going to be huge for your wedding," Tessa complained as the kids played around them. "Maybe you want to ask someone else to be your Matron of Honor."

"Uh uh. You aren't getting out of it that easily, Tess. The wedding's only six weeks away. You aren't even due until the end of August. The dress we got will definitely hide your belly."

Tessa looked doubtful but didn't argue, something she

rarely did anyway. On the other hand, Erik had said she'd become much more forceful and protective when it came to the children. That mothering instinct kicking in. Molly Storm had it in spades.

"Gina, I'm getting ready to send out the invitations," Sara said. "You'll still be here, right? I want you to come."

Gina shrugged. "I'm not sure. It depends how long it takes to clean and fix up Nonna's house."

"Promise me you'll stay until, at least, after the wedding. Who else will keep Alex in line?"

Gina laughed. "Right, because he's the one who'll be causing problems."

Sara ducked in closer and whispered something in Gina's ear, making her snort. He'd only caught something about organizing. Yeah, his little sister didn't want him interfering with the wedding plans. *Note to self.* Stay in control, and don't try to give suggestions during the wedding.

"Promise?"

Gina nodded. "Yes, I'll stay until the wedding."

Relief, strong and deep, surged inside him. Why, he didn't know. Gina bounced in and out of his life all the time. Why should her leaving be any different this time? And why did he feel good knowing he'd get another six weeks with her?

"Is Bullet Ryker going to be there?" Gina asked.

He almost growled. What was with these women who went nuts for over-grown, sex crazy, party boys? What did they possibly have to offer any woman? Except money and sex appeal. Damn.

"Sorry, Gina. We want to keep the wedding as low key as possible. It'll be bad enough that TJ's parents will be there. He's already asked them not to tell anyone, and we're planning for a few security guards, just in case it gets leaked."

Standing, he stalked into the kitchen where Luke and TJ

chatted away, sneaking a few crumbs of Gina's cake. Erik limped in behind him and frowned.

"They're talking about wedding plans. Can we go do something manly? My dick might shrivel up if I hear any more about pastel colors and flower arrangements."

"Why do you think I'm in here?" TJ replied. "I love your sister, but I'm leaving all those dainty details to her. My idea of a fancy reception is coffee and pastry at the store."

"I'm sure that went over real well with Sage." Luke laughed.

TJ lifted one eyebrow. "Oh, I never suggested that to her. Are you crazy? I like my—" He looked around as if suddenly realizing who he was talking to. After clearing his throat, he continued, "I want Sara to be happy."

"Smart man." Erik grinned. "We want her to be happy, too." There was a veiled threat there, but TJ didn't look too concerned.

"I envy you two," Alex said to his eldest brother and future brother-in-law. "You've both found women you love and who love you back. That's got to feel great."

Both men grinned but remained silent. That was answer enough.

"Maybe you need to find a wife," Luke suggested.

"You sound like Gina. She said that to me when we were shopping for Mom and Dad's anniversary present."

Luke lifted one side of his mouth. "Did she make a recommendation? Or was she offering herself?"

"She pointed out a few unsuitable candidates. Kristan was one of them."

"Kristan?" Erik placed his hand to his throat. "Kristan of the red hair and pearls?"

Man, his love life sucked, and his brothers all knew it. His face warmed as he remembered what he and Gina had done in her living room. And what they'd talked about doing. And what he fantasized about doing.

"She was totally boring, bro," Luke said. "You need someone to liven you up. Have you considered Gina?"

Yes. Maybe not for any length of time, but lately he was beginning to see that he liked having her in his life. Before he could think on that any further, both Erik and Luke broke into laughter.

Luke wiped away a pretend tear. "I can see it now. She'd tie-dye his pastel shirts and he'd put starch in her see-through blouses. Oh, damn, that's hysterical."

He glared at his younger brother. "Let's go play some b-ball."

They all agreed, and as they shuffled out the door and to the driveway, he sidled up to Luke. "Gina didn't even bother thinking of a wife for you. She said you were a lost cause."

Luke grabbed the basketball Erik had retrieved from the shed and swished it through the hoop. "Damn straight. It'll be a cold day in hell before some chick snags me on the end of a wedding ring."

They dribbled the ball and tossed it around, all except Erik who got a pass and was able to shoot without them jumping all over him. He hated that Erik still couldn't walk without the cane, but his brother seemed more adept at getting around, and the pain lines around his eyes weren't so pronounced anymore.

After another three pointer from him, Luke grabbed the rebound. "You're hitting quite a few of these today, Alex. And you seem way more chill. Did you actually take my advice and get laid?"

"Jesus, Luke, you know Alex isn't the kind of guy to just —" Erik stopped mid-sentence and stared at him. His face was on fire. "Alex? You got a new girlfriend you haven't told us about?"

He tried to snatch the ball and dribble away, but his brothers flanked him. He looked to TJ, but the other man simply shook his head and shrugged. He'd get no help there.

"Who's the babe?" Luke smirked, his eyes more than curious.

"I thought you didn't have sex until like the twentieth date," Erik added.

Taking a deep breath, he glanced back at the house. And it was the tenth date not the twentieth. Or at least two months, whichever came first.

Luke got right in his face. "No one's coming to your rescue, so fess up. Who did you—holy shit. Wait. The only one you've been hanging with lately is…" Luke looked at the house, too. "You and Gina doing the nasty?"

Erik narrowed his eyes. "Again?"

"What do you mean again?" Luke sputtered. "You and Gina have shacked up before? Where the hell was I?"

Erik shrugged. "You were probably distracted by football practice. You were captain that year."

Luke's eyes raised in thought. "Captain? My senior year in high school. That was…a long time ago."

Clenching his jaw, Alex glared at Erik. "How the hell did you even know about that?"

"Alex, you wear guilt like a toddler wears peanut butter. Have you started back up with Gina? She isn't planning on staying, you know."

"I know that," he snapped. He hated the fact. "And we haven't started anything. Well, not exactly."

"So the two of you haven't banged each other lately?" Luke never could call it anything that wasn't crude.

"We haven't—I mean, we have, but only once— I guess technically it was twice. But we aren't going to—although, she did suggest we —oh, just shut the fuck up, Luke. I won't have you insulting Gina. What we do is no one's damn business."

"I never said anything bad about her." Luke held up his hands. "But her taste in guys could be better."

He wanted to pound the smile right off Luke's face. Unfortunately, his brother's thoughts too closely echoed his own lately.

Erik stepped in between them and claimed the ball. "You're right. It's none of our business. I happen to like Gina, and just because you two are polar opposites, it doesn't mean you can't have some things in common. I never would have pictured myself with Tessa even a few years ago. Now, I can't imagine my life without her."

"Sara isn't my typical either," TJ said as he moved in to take the ball and restart the game.

Erik shook his head as he threw the ball toward the hoop. "You've always had a thing for Gina."

"I don't have…haven't had a thing for her. We're friends."

"Very good friends. I don't know too many kids who would give up two weeks of their summer vacation to sit inside and keep their friend company."

Alex grabbed the rebound and stared at his brother. "She had the chicken pox and couldn't go outside. I'd had the vaccination, so most likely couldn't get them. Made sense for me to keep her company."

Luke stole the ball and dribbled toward the net. "I remember that. It was the summer before I started first grade. You sat inside watching old reruns the whole time. I couldn't imagine anyone wanting to do that while the weather was great."

Yeah, TV Land had been big back then. It's where they'd first seen *The Odd Couple*, and Gina had started calling him Felix. He'd fixated on how perfect Ward and June Cleaver were in *Leave It To Beaver* and the Nelsons in other fifties shows like *Ozzie and Harriet*. Maybe it was where he'd gotten some of his ideas about what a perfect wife should be. But when you were eight, the sweet personality of June Cleaver was addicting.

"Gina had recently lost her dad and her mom was planning on leaving town. I couldn't just leave her all alone inside with only her grandmother as company. Mrs. Mazelli would have driven her crazy in no time."

"Is that how it eventually happened?" Luke smirked.

Alex bounced the ball off his brother's head and scowled. The conversation got pushed to the back of his mind for the next few hours as they threw the ball around the makeshift court. But once everyone had gone and Gina was the only one left, having stayed to help him clean, he started thinking again. Did he and Gina have any common ground? Certainly, they had great sex. Something he'd been thinking of a lot since she'd mentioned the friends-with-benefits thing.

Walking her to her porch, he waited as she punched in the new security code. She opened the door and walked inside, then turned. He attempted to close the door behind him, but she still held onto it.

When he pressed in to kiss her, she nestled closer, and his hands slid around her back and under her top. He couldn't wait to touch every inch of her. Taste her skin and feast on her gorgeous body.

"I had fun with your family today, Felix. Thanks for asking me to come."

"We can still have more fun. It doesn't have to end here. You talked about friends—"

Her finger on his lips stopped his words. "Not tonight."

"Why not?" Had she changed her mind? No, not when he'd finally accepted having casual sex with her.

"You have an early meeting tomorrow. You need to be perky and bright-eyed."

He narrowed his eyes. "How do you know about my meeting?"

"I peeked at your planner. Don't look at me that way, Felix. It's sitting on your desk open for anyone to see. If you stayed over, we'd be up all night long."

"We wouldn't have to be. We could—"

She shook her head, her wild hair floating around her shoulders. "If you stayed, I'd want to ride you all night long. Believe me, there wouldn't be much sleep. Then *I'd* feel guilty. It's not an emotion I do well, Felix."

The vision that swirled through his mind, a naked Gina gyrating on top of him, caused his already growing erection to turn to concrete. Shit, this wouldn't end pretty.

She wrapped her arms around his neck and kissed him, short but steamy. "I promise to make it up to you later. Show up after work tomorrow, and we'll have…dinner."

The way she'd said *dinner* left him with no doubts what they'd be eating. After a deep inhale, he exerted every ounce of control he had to turn and walk out the door.

Why did this have to be the first time Gina was the sensible one?

"Knock, knock."

Alex peeked inside the front door, calling out to Gina. She'd texted that dinner would be ready at six. It was just that now.

"Who's there?" she called back in her sultry voice. Was he really getting something to eat or were they going straight to dessert? He'd forgo food to get another taste of his Dandelion. It had been almost a week since she'd jumped on him and taken a ride, and a few days since he'd agreed to do the friends-with-benefits thing. Did she realize he'd agreed? He went back over the conversation making sure he'd been clear.

"It's Alex."

"Alex who?"

She chuckled at her silly joke. Too bad he wasn't witty enough to come up with a decent response. Luke would have something sexy and ribald right on the tip of his tongue. The only thing he wanted there was Gina.

He stopped in the kitchen doorway and stared. Holy shit. Gina was cooking, and he didn't mean on the stove. Her outfit wasn't her usual funky loose bohemian thing. This was some knit material that skimmed and clung to every curve. The skirt went down to her knees but showed off her gorgeous ass and mile-long legs. The tank style top showcased her breasts nicely. Not that they ever needed any help.

The color was anything but subdued. It wasn't quite neon, but the pink emphasized the olive tone of her skin. At least half a dozen long, jeweled chains dangled around her neck, and a paisley print scarf trimmed her slim waist. A pair of spiked heels accentuated the ensemble.

"Wow. You didn't tell me this was a fancy occasion. I would have dressed up more."

Gina turned, resting her hip against the table she was setting. Her eyes traveled up and down his body. Did he meet with her approval? Khakis and a button down. He sighed. Maybe he needed to diversify his wardrobe a bit.

She sauntered over and slid her hands up to his shoulders.

"Hi, there, handsome. Hope you're hungry."

He pulled her near, inhaling her intoxicating fragrance. "The honeysuckle haven't even blossomed yet. How do you still smell like that?"

Her eyes twinkled. "I have my secrets. I noticed it has a habit of getting you wound up. I like winding you up."

"I've noticed. Any particular reason."

She sidled even closer, pressing her delectable figure tight against his. Her hips swayed, and he groaned, his arousal making itself known.

"That's one reason. Plus, you're so darn adorable when you're turned on but trying to stay cool."

He couldn't help but chuckle. She really was something. He leaned to kiss her, but she backed away and smirked.

"We need to eat dinner first. I didn't slave in this kitchen all afternoon to let it congeal. Have a seat."

"Can I help you with something?"

"Just sit. I've got this." She moved about the kitchen handing him a bottle of wine, then pulled a pan from the oven.

"Want to pour that while I cut us each a piece?"

The aroma of spicy tomatoes filled the air, and Alex's mouth watered. "Is that your grandmother's lasagna?"

Gina slid out two slices and brought the plates over. He quickly poured the wine and picked up his fork before she even sat down. A small bowl of salad rested between them.

"Yes, it's Nonna's recipe. I used to help her make it whenever I came to stay."

He inhaled the scent, but held off eating until she'd dug into her first piece. "I remember. You'd always beg her to let me eat over. You have no idea how much I appreciated that."

Gina delicately took a bite and chewed. "I think I do. It's why I made it tonight. I wanted something that brought you good memories."

Hanging out with Gina and her grandmother were definitely good memories. "Thank you, Dandy."

"Any time, Felix." She dished some of the salad onto her plate, then his.

They ate in silence for a while, though Alex couldn't get

enough of watching her animated face. Once finished, she dabbed her red lips with a napkin and sat back.

"How was your meeting this morning?"

"Great. They like the ideas I have, and we worked out a few of the details that had some kinks in them. I'll be putting in a lot of hours with this, but it's great money. And if I do well, they'll be a fabulous reference for future jobs."

She played with her necklaces. "You'll do a good job."

"How do you know?"

"Because I know you, Felix. You're fastidious with details and can't stand when something isn't perfectly where it should be."

She continued to play with the chains dangling over her breasts, making the clasps move up and down. He clenched his hand around his fork and tried to relocate his eyes. Not happening. The fasteners weren't in the right place, and he knew it. Why did he have such a hard time leaving them alone? Her lips turned up at the corners, and her eyes glimmered. The little minx was doing it on purpose.

Grinning, she flicked at one of the beads laying against her chest. "Something wrong?"

He simply stared, daring her to— what? He didn't know, but he wanted her to take the dare. She never could resist.

Gina stood and took their plates and silverware. He started to rise, but she shook him off with a toss of her head. Once the dishes were in the sink, she returned to her seat.

"Did you save room for dessert?"

He didn't see any cake or pie on the counter. Please, let her idea of dessert be a non-food thing. Her fingers fiddling with her chains drove him absolutely crazy. Maybe he could move things along a bit.

"Come here. I need to fix those clasps once and for all."

"If you say *please*."

"Please, Dandelion."

She got up, but instead of circling the table, she crawled on it and across to him. Fuck. What was she doing? Her hands slid closer, and he pushed his glass of wine to the side, so it didn't get knocked over. Soon, her face was inches from his.

"Can you fix them from here, Felix?"

They draped down and scraped the table. Reaching up, he took his time sliding the clasps to the back of her neck. Before he got the last one done, her head lowered, and she kissed him.

This was what he'd wanted all day. Heck, for quite a few years. Who was he kidding? He'd wanted it ever since he'd had his first taste of her nine years ago. He ran his hand through her hair, then cupped the back of her head. She tasted of spicy tomatoes and salad dressing. He skimmed his hands down her toned arms, then back up to caress her bare shoulders. God, he couldn't believe she was on the table on all fours kissing him. He wanted to flip her on her back and take her right here.

Would she like that? Probably. He wasn't too sure. Table. Hard. Uncomfortable. They'd spill the wine, and he'd hate to get stains on her pink dress. But the thought of thrusting into her almost overrode that concern.

She adjusted her position, and Alex stood, causing her to kneel up so they were face to face. He slid his hands behind her and pulled her tight to his chest. No control now. His hands roamed her back and down to her ass, then cupped and lifted her off the table.

"Is this dessert? It's just about the sweetest thing I've ever tasted."

She shimmied out of his arms, and his stomach dipped in disappointment. Was she getting something out of the fridge? An actual food dessert?

She sashayed to the back stairs and put one foot on the

bottom step. "I thought we could have dessert in a more… intimate location."

She climbed a few more steps, sliding her hands into the waistband of her skirt and skimming it over her hips. Her gorgeous ass swayed from side to side as the garment slipped lower and lower, revealing the golden skin underneath. Oh boy, she was wearing the dental floss again.

He got his feet in motion and followed her up the steps. She'd disappeared around the curved stairs, and as he got to the top, the fabric landed in a heap at his feet. She turned into her bedroom. His feet moved faster.

Stopping in the doorway, he watched her shimmy out of her top. Her back was to him, and he heard the beads click as they knocked together still around her neck. He couldn't move. He was frozen in place, the scene surreal. The shades were drawn, shutting out the light, but a dozen candles littered every surface of the room, mirrors behind them or under them, illuminating their flickering flame. The scent of honeysuckle overwhelmed him, and he wasn't sure he wouldn't orgasm right here on the spot.

She slowly turned, and his breath hitched. The most beautiful sight he'd ever seen. Draped in nothing but lace at the juncture of her thighs, the chains around her neck, and the spike heels. Holy Mother of God. This wasn't anything he'd ever even imagined. Obviously, he needed some work on his fantasies.

"Spectacular."

She looked at her chest and grinned.

"Not just that. All of you. Gina, you are so amazingly gorgeous. What are you doing here with me?"

For a second, a sad expression crossed her face. She stepped toward him and reached out to touch his collar.

"You really have no idea how handsome you are, Felix. How is that even possible?"

He shrugged. "Good looks aren't everything, apparently."

"True." She cocked her head. "It certainly isn't the reason I'm here with you now."

"You want sex."

Her hand traced the shell of his ear, then down his neck to the opening of his shirt. "I can have *sex* with anyone. What I have with you, Felix, is mind-blowing emotions swirling through me like a hurricane. No one else makes me feel this way."

Was she telling the truth...or just stroking his ego? He'd felt that way, but figured she'd be a bit more lackadaisical about sex. Considering her upbringing.

"Well, I'm ready to have my mind blown again. You mentioned something about dessert." He ran his fingers down the necklaces attempting to cop a feel. Sometimes, the teenage boy never grew up. "I love the chains."

He lifted them a bit, and the backs of his hands caressed the perfect skin underneath. Her nipples tightened, and he flicked his fingers over them as they traveled down.

"I think you're a little overdressed for this party, Felix. Maybe I can help you with that."

"Mmm, I'd like that. As long as I don't have to stop touching."

She took her time unbuttoning his shirt and sliding it off his shoulders. With his shirt gone, he could pull her close and feel her against his chest. As he skimmed his hands up and down her back, he squeezed her cheeks, pressing her even closer.

She made quick work of unfastening his pants and pushing them down his legs as he kicked off his shoes.

He backed her up to the bed and began kissing his way down her neck to her chest. Moving the beads aside, he licked her taut nipples, then traveled lower to nip at her navel. Destination ahead. He pushed her lightly, urging her to sit on the bed. When he pulled the dental floss off her hips and down her legs, he kissed her there. Then spread her legs further and...stopped.

"You have a tattoo." He caressed the skin next to the trimmed triangle of hair. So close to where he wanted to be.

"Don't stop now. Please."

"Why do you have this?"

"It's a cat."

"It's Felix the Cat."

CHAPTER NINE

*D*amn, Gina hadn't wanted him to notice that. Maybe she should have pushed *him* on the bed. But no, she'd been greedy and wanted his tongue licking her downtown, sending her spiraling into oblivion. Now she had some explaining to do.

"It's just a cat." Like he'd buy that.

Stroking her skin, he traced the outline of the ink. "Are you saying this has nothing to do with me?"

She scooted back on the bed and settled on her elbows. "Why would it have anything to do with you?"

"You call me Felix, and this is Felix the Cat. You don't see the relationship?"

Get out of this one. "I call you Felix, because you're like Felix Unger of the Odd Couple. This is a cat."

Alex bit his lip, but she still saw the smirk he couldn't hide. "Okay, if you say so."

He studied her hip. Was he going to insist it was about him again? She could hardly tell him she'd put it there to remind her of her first time. The most amazing time. Maybe it hadn't been the steamiest or the most innovative sex, but it certainly had been the time that had evoked the most emotions. The time that had meant the most to her.

His face tensed, and she stroked his cheek. He frowned. "I'm not sure I like someone else being down here, with you and no clothes for how long it must have taken to do this."

She ruffled his hair. "He was tattooing, not screwing."

Alex sighed. "I guess."

He pressed his lips to her leg again and winked. "You don't mind, then, if I taste a little bit of this pussy … um cat, I mean."

She giggled. Real mature.

After kissing the inside of her thigh again, his tongue moved and hit exactly where she'd wanted it. When it flicked, she arched off the bed and grabbed his head.

"Oh, shit, yes."

His mouth and tongue tasted and explored and his fingers slid inside. She was about to burst apart. Nothing more than garbled sounds came out.

Reaching up, he kneaded her breasts, pinching the tight buds in the center. Her body jolted, a tiny scream erupting from her.

"Felix."

He stood, leaving his fingers inside wiggling back and forth, then leaned forward nibbling on her ear. His erection pushed to take the place of his fingers. Her head arched back, and her mouth opened, but no sound came out.

When he remained still for a few moments, she thought she'd have to tell him what to do. He stared at her face, a smile lighting his own.

"You're so expressive. It always gives you away. What you're thinking."

She wrapped her legs around his waist. "Really? What am I thinking right now?"

Doubtful he could read her that deeply. Know how badly

she wanted him to stay with her always and never let her go. How she'd do anything for him.

"You're thinking I'd better get things moving."

Of course, he'd think she only wanted him for the sex. It was what she'd told him. What she'd always tell him. She didn't belong in his nicely organized world. He might put up with her for short periods of time, but she wasn't the type he'd want hanging out with him on a permanent basis. No sense adding to his guilt with her feelings.

"Damn straight." Let him think he was right. Alex was brilliant and successful, but too often still had doubts that circled him like crows.

As he thrust in deeper, she shoved her own doubts to the back of her mind. She wanted every second with Alex to be ingrained in her memory. Gripping his back, she ran her hands over his tight ass with the rhythm that would send her flying any second. *Hang on. Enjoy the sensations rushing through you.* His skin against hers caused flames to flicker to life and grow into an inferno.

Soon, she exploded, lights dancing across her vision. Alex concentrated intently, just like he did everything. Moments later, he shuddered and collapsed on top of her. He rolled to his side taking her with him. Her nerves tingled from her release. Being in his arms was all she'd ever wanted.

"For all that's holy, Dandy. What you do to me. I don't understand it. Don't know why it's so much better than anything else."

She thrilled at his words, wishing she could answer him. Wishing he would figure it out for himself. Wishing he could bend enough from his structured, meticulous life to accept her into it.

≈

"Are you slumming it today, Felix?" Gina asked as she eyed his worn, ripped jeans that hugged his lean figure and the ragged sweatshirt clinging to his wide shoulders. "Or did you dress up for me?"

Alex shuffled from foot to foot as he hovered on her front porch. "I just wanted to let you know I was here. I'm going to see about fixing that loose shutter next to your bedroom window."

He walked toward that side of the house, and she followed him. She'd follow him anywhere.

"How do you know it's loose? It looks fine." She stared at the shutter, trying to figure out how he could tell it needed fixing.

"You didn't hear it banging against the side of the house the last few nights?" His face flushed, and he positioned Nonna's old wooden ladder against the house. He still got embarrassed that they'd slept together. Two nights in a row. And he'd actually stayed the whole night, even though he'd been gone early enough to shower and be in his office by eight. He'd kissed her cheek both mornings before he left. It had been the sweetest thing ever.

"The only thing I heard banging was the headboard of the bed as you rocked my world."

She ran her hand over his back, and he turned, so she stepped into his arms. They closed around her quickly, no hesitation. Nice. She tilted her head up for a kiss.

He pressed his lips to hers briefly, then eased back. "Greg and Ryan are out playing ball in the yard."

She rolled her eyes at him. "They're on the other side of the house. They can't see us here. What are you afraid of?"

Staring at her, he swallowed. "Honestly? You. I'm afraid if I touch you, I won't want to stop, and then I won't get the shutter fixed. It's going to be dark in less than an hour, and the next few days I'm really busy with work. I won't have time to do it then."

"Why can't it wait until the weekend?" She wrapped her hands around his neck. How cool was his admission he was afraid of losing control with her? Alex was control.

"It'll bug me and keep me awake. I have a few important meetings this week for the new medical building. I need to be in prime shape."

Unzipping his hoodie, she ran her fingers down his chest. "Seems like prime shape to me. And if you expect to hear it, that means you plan on staying over again."

His gaze went sideways, while his lips straightened. "Oh, uh…yeah, well, I mean, I wouldn't want you to be kept awake either."

When she brushed against him, his breath hitched. "I don't mind if you stay over. I kind of like having you there. You could hang out all day, and I wouldn't complain."

He ran his hand down her back and over her ass. "I don't think I'd get much work done with you around, Dandelion."

"If you wore these all the time I wouldn't either. Something about you in worn jeans just flips my switch."

"I think everything pretty much flips your switch."

She pressed her lips to his neck, and his pulse jumped. "Everything about you, Felix."

He allowed the contact for a few minutes, his own hands and lips doing some cursory exploring, but then pulled her away. Reluctantly?

"Let me fix this shutter, and we can eat. I've got a pork roast in the oven with some scalloped potatoes. They'll be ready in about twenty minutes. I don't want them overcooked."

Easing back, she grinned. "No, we certainly wouldn't want the food overcooked."

"If you have things to finish in the house, I'll come get you when I'm done." He reached down for the screwdriver and hammer at his feet, stuck them in his back pockets, and placed his foot on the first rung.

She stepped back and crossed her arms over her chest, rubbing her sleeves. It was getting a little chilly, and she only wore a light blouse. "I think I'll just supervise. It is my house, after all. Have to make sure you do the job right."

He glared, but continued to scale the ladder.

"And the sight of you in those jeans…Whoa…I may need to have dessert before dinner tonight. Screw the overcooked meal."

Alex climbed a few more rungs and called down, "Dinner first."

A sassy remark hung on the tip of her tongue, but the material clinging to his ass robbed her of speech. Those long, runner's legs did something to her. Maybe she *should* go in the house, otherwise she'd be tempted to climb up after him and jump him on the ladder. That could be interesting, though maybe not so safe.

"Felix, I'll—"

A loud crack shattered the air, and the rung under Alex's right foot snapped in half.

"Alex!"

His foot swung in midair, and he tried to place it on another rung, but the ladder unbalanced and careened to the right. Her scream sliced the air as he fell.

The ladder clattered to the ground next to him. She rushed over and only began breathing again when she heard him groan. He was alive.

"Don't move. I'll get someone."

Reaching out, he grabbed her arm. "No, I'm—" He pushed to sit up, but his wrist gave out, and he bit off another moan.

She took off toward the other side of the house. Relief

surged through her when she spotted Greg and Ryan running in her direction.

"I need your help."

Greg's speed picked up, his eyes full of concern. "What happened? I heard you yell."

"Alex fell off the ladder. He's hurt."

Greg pulled his phone from his pocket as they rounded the corner. Alex sat up rubbing his wrist.

"I told you not to move," she chided him. "What if you'd broken your neck or your back?"

"I'm fine. You didn't need to call the paramedics. Put that phone away, Greg. I swear, if you call for an ambulance, I'll have to clock you one."

Greg shoved the phone back and knelt near his cousin. "If you have any injuries that need an ambulance, I'll call one whether you want one or not. What hurts?"

"Besides my pride?" Alex grimaced. "I should have checked the ladder better. It seemed sturdy enough, but some of the rungs must have been rotted through."

Greg looked at her. "How far up was he?"

"I'm right here, you know, and I'm not unconscious."

Greg glared at him. "I'm aware of that, but Gina probably has a better idea of how high up you were, since she was down here."

"He was almost at the second-story window."

Greg began running his hands over Alex's arms, and he winced as his right wrist was probed.

"Yeah, that hurts. The right ankle's throbbing, too."

Greg did an exam of both Alex's legs and ran his fingers down his spine and neck. "Did you hit your head when you fell?"

"No, I put my hand out, which was probably stupid. I need this to draw up plans for work." Alex tried to flex his wrist, and his face tightened up in pain.

"Are you sure he doesn't have a concussion," she asked, understanding now the guilt Alex always felt.

"Nah," Greg laughed. "His head's too hard. It doesn't look like you broke anything, but I'd still suggest a trip to the hospital for x-rays, just to be safe."

"I don't need to go to the hospital. You said nothing's broken, so I'll wrap them up, and I'll be fine in a few days."

"I said I didn't *think* anything was broken. I'm not a doctor, and I don't have x-ray vision. A sprain can be as bad or worse, definitely more painful, than a break. You need to get a medical professional to look at you. I can call an ambulance, if you want, or get my truck and bring you myself. Gina, would you mind staying with Ryan while I'm gone?"

"I can take him, Greg." It was her fault he'd fallen. Greg shouldn't have to waste his time sitting around at the Emergency Room. "Thanks for coming over so quick."

"Dandy, I'll be—"

"Don't even argue with me, Felix Unger. I'm taking you to the Emergency Room, or Greg is calling an ambulance, and you can go in that. Either way, you're going. Let me get my keys."

"Not your car," he yelled after her. "I'll never fit in it. Get my keys. They're hanging on the hook by the door."

Greg stood. "I'll get the keys and bring the car over. Gina, why don't you put some shoes on and grab a coat? It'll be cold once the sun goes down. Ryan, sit here with Alex and make sure he doesn't try and get up without one of us helping him."

Her face heated. How could she not remember she had no shoes on? She started toward the house, then stopped and pointed her finger at Alex. "Sit. Stay." See how he liked it.

He merely glared. Once in the house, she slipped on a pair of canvas sneakers, grabbed a sweatshirt and trotted back out again. After closing the door, she set the alarms. Greg already had the car backed into her driveway.

"Are you sure you don't want me to come with you? I don't mind."

They both gathered where Alex stood, leaning on Ryan. The boy looked pleased to be helping. Alex wore a huge scowl on his face as they got him to the car and settled him inside.

"Call or text and let us know what happens," Greg asked as she got behind the wheel and adjusted the seat about a foot forward. Damn, he was tall.

When she put the car into gear, Alex held up his hand and pressed the button to lower the window. "I have food in the oven at my house. Can you go turn it off?"

Leave it to Alex to remember something like that. She would have burned the house down. Greg gave a thumbs up. Again, Alex indicated she should wait.

"Actually, why don't you two eat the dinner? A little payback for coming over to help. Leave the dishes, and I'll get them later."

"I think we'll take you up on that. Mom and Dad went looking at those Fifty-five Plus Community houses your folks live in, so we were on our own for supper tonight. I will clean up, though. Now, go and get checked. And don't let him give the hospital staff a hard time, Gina. Make sure he follows orders, huh?"

Slowly, she drove down the street toward the hospital. Follow orders. Alex was all about following certain rules, but the ones she really wanted him to obey weren't the ones in his rule book.

"I'm fine, Dandelion. Stop hovering."

Alex hobbled into the kitchen and sighed. His friggin' foot throbbed, and trying to hold the crutches with his sprained wrist hurt like hell. He glanced around. The place was neat as ever. Greg must have cleaned up after he and Ryan ate. At least, he wouldn't have to do that.

Gina entered behind him and closed the door.

"I'm not hovering. I'm trying to help. It's my fault you fell, so I need to make sure you're all right."

"It wasn't your fault." He checked the clock. Just after nine. It had taken far too long at the Emergency Room. The place hadn't been that crowded, but between exams, x-rays, and the two million pages of information they needed, it had been longer than he'd wanted to spend, only to have them tell him his wrist and ankle were not broken, only sprained.

"I should call Greg and let him know I'm fine."

"You're not fine, Felix. You've got two sprains that need to be iced and elevated every few hours. They gave us enough pain killers and anti-inflammatories for tonight, but I'll need to run to the pharmacy tomorrow morning to get this prescription filled."

He sat at the kitchen table and lifted his hand to rest there. Gina bustled around, pulling a cold pack from the freezer.

"See, it's elevated. Happy?"

She pressed the cold pack to his wrist. "No." Her expression was one he hated seeing on her. And he recognized the emotion right away. Guilt.

"Dandelion, this isn't your fault, so stop blaming yourself. I should have checked the ladder more carefully to make sure it was safe. If anyone's to blame, it's me. Hand me my phone, please."

Gina dug through her purse for his phone, and he pressed the numbers for his cousin. Greg picked up right away.

"I just saw your car get back. What's the verdict?"

"I'm fine." Gina glared at him, so he added, "They're just sprains. They'll be better soon enough. Thanks for cleaning up the kitchen."

"Thanks for dinner. It was great. We may invite ourselves over more, now that we know how good your cooking is. Especially if my folks are moving out."

"Any time, Greg. I'll talk to you soon."

"Wait. I took a look at the ladder that broke. It wasn't rotted wood."

"No?"

"The bottom of the rung was sawed through most of the way. The next two also were like that."

What was he saying? Someone had meant to hurt him? Or Gina? "Are you sure? I don't know how that would have happened."

"Just telling you what I observed, Alex. That house was empty for a while before Gina came back. Could be someone was fooling around in the garage during that time."

"Maybe. Thanks. I'll keep an eye out."

"Sure. Let me know if you need anything."

"I'll be okay. I've got my little mother hovering nearby."

Greg laughed. "I'm not sure she sees herself in a maternal position with you, but it's good she's there. See ya."

Hanging up the phone, he placed it on the table.

"Everything okay?"

"Yup, they loved my cooking so much I'll have dinner guests for the next few weeks." No way he'd tell her about the ladder. That would only add more guilt. Guilt sucked.

Her eyes narrowed. "Well, they'll have to eat my cooking, since you're not in any shape to stand around and fix food for people."

"How many times do I have to tell you I'm fine?"

"Maybe when you aren't on crutches anymore, and you can use your hand. Can I get you anything?"

He hated to have her wait on him, but he truly felt like crap. Every muscle ached from the fall. Luckily, the drugs they'd given him at the hospital were starting to kick in.

"I am kind of hungry."

Popping up, she dug in the fridge. "There's leftover roast and potatoes. Can I nuke some of it for you?"

"Yes, please." He was too tired to argue that he could get it himself. "Is there enough for both of us? You must be starving, too."

She nodded and spent the next few minutes hustling and heating up plates. He almost fell asleep as he ate, but Gina kept up a running dialogue of what she wanted to do to the house, and he managed to keep his eyes open long enough to listen.

"Thanks, Dandelion. I think I'm gonna head up and crash now. Those pain killers have kicked in, and I'm not sure I can stay awake much longer."

"I'll help you upstairs."

He glared at her as he pulled his crutches closer.

Her hands planted on her shapely hips. "Have you ever tried to climb stairs with crutches? Let me tell you, it isn't easy."

"I'm sure I'll manage."

Shifting the crutches under his arms, he moved toward the back stairs. As soon as he tried to go up the first step, he realized exactly what Gina meant. And with his bum wrist, it would be nearly impossible. He glanced over his shoulder to where she stood with an I-told-you-so grin on her face, her arms crossed over her chest.

He took a deep breath. "Do you have any suggestions? Other than me sitting on the stairs and crawling up them?"

She walked closer and placed his crutches against the wall, then slipped under his right arm and placed her hand around his back.

"Hold on to the banister with your left hand and lean on me. I'll help you upstairs."

They got up without too much trouble, and she lowered him to the bed like a damn invalid.

"I'll go get your crutches. Why don't you get undressed while I do?"

He attempted to toe off his shoes, but his right ankle was weakened, so he needed to use his hand. And he could only use his left. He wanted to scream. Why hadn't he checked the friggin' ladder before climbing it? Stupid. He'd been too preoccupied with getting away from Gina, so he didn't shove her against the side of the house and take her right there. She made him crazy at times.

His shoes off, he started on his shirt buttons. Again, not an easy task with only one useful hand. He never realized how many things you needed both hands for. By the time Gina returned, placed the crutches by the headboard, and tossed a few cold packs on the bed, he'd barely managed half of them. She knelt in front of him and did the rest. He allowed it, only because his head was fuzzy. The Vicodin was definitely kicking in.

Pulling the shirt off his shoulders, she tossed it behind her.

"Hey…"

She rolled her eyes. "I'll pick it up later, after I've got you in bed."

"I'm not two. I can put myself to bed."

She didn't answer, simply unbuttoned his jeans, then pushed him back on the bed. Clutching the pants by the hem, she got those off in no time. His head was fucked up if he was just lying here, letting her. He needed to get up, brush his teeth, and take a shower.

Before he could muster up the energy, Gina pulled the

sheets from under him and attempted to coax him further up on the bed.

"I'm fine. You can go home, Dandy."

"Sure," she said, then adjusted his covers once he'd gotten himself up to the pillows. He closed his eyes and felt himself drifting off. She tucked a pillow under his ankle and another under his wrist and added the ice packs.

"These need to stay elevated."

"Thanks. For all the help."

"Paying you back for keeping me company when I had the chicken pox."

Chuckling, he adjusted the covers. "I was thinking about that the other day. All the shows we started watching."

She tipped her head and squinted. "It's where you got your perfect wife complex. June Cleaver, Marion Cunningham, Harriet Nelson."

"And when you started calling me Felix."

She wrinkled her nose. "You know I say it with love."

"Yeah, I do. I appreciate your help tonight."

"Happy to do it." Her voice sounded soft and sad. When he didn't hear her leave, he cracked one eye open. She sat on the chair in the corner, folding his clothes and placing them on top of the hamper. His shoes were even set near the closet.

"What are you doing, Dandelion? Go home."

"What if you need something in the middle of the night? I'll just hang out here for a while."

No energy to argue with her right now. "If you're going to stay, you might as well get comfortable." He drew the comforter back.

"I don't want to accidentally bump you."

"I'm hurt on the right, so come stay on my left. And don't argue with me. Just do it. Like you said, if I need anything, you'll be here to get it for me."

"Okay, if you're sure." She slipped her blouse off, then skimmed her pants over her hips.

"Get one of my shirts to sleep in. The middle drawer of my dresser has some comfortable ones." A naked Gina in bed would not be conducive to a good night's rest. Hopefully, she'd pick something thick and flannel.

The sound of her rifling through his dresser kept him alert, especially when her amazing ass was bent over it. At least her underwear today had slightly more fabric than her typical string ones. The sight of her naked back and the beautiful toned muscles made him think of all sorts of things he wanted to do once she got in bed. She turned, and he groaned at the Bump and Grind t-shirt she'd picked. Leave it to Dandelion.

After a few minutes in the bathroom, she shut off the lights, then slid in beside him. Way on the other side.

"Night, Dandy." Was she mad at him? Rarely did she have nothing to say.

"Night."

"You okay? You're awfully quiet."

"I don't want to disturb you. You should be resting. I'm sorry you got hurt."

Alex reached for her hand and tugged her closer. "I'll rest a lot easier if I know you're close. And stop feeling guilty."

"Okay." She adjusted in the bed and kissed his cheek.

He wanted more than that, but it wouldn't be tonight. As he drifted off, he realized that she'd be here next to him when he woke up in the morning. That thought was far more pleasant than he'd ever thought it would be.

CHAPTER TEN

*G*ina snuggled deeper into the covers as the incessant noise buzzed next to her. Alex mumbled in his sleep, and she realized it was his alarm. Why was he not jumping up and shutting it off?

The memory of him falling off the ladder jolted her awake, and she stretched over and slapped at the offending device. The noise stopped, but Alex slept on. Something to do with the painkillers she'd given him somewhere past midnight last night. She'd run into Luke in the kitchen. That hadn't been too embarrassing. Alex's t-shirt had certainly covered enough, but she wasn't in the habit of sleeping over at men's houses. Especially ones who still lived with a family member.

"Hey, Gina. You guys bunking here tonight for a change?" Luke had grinned, and she'd flushed all over. Obviously, he was aware Alex had stayed at her place a few nights in a row. Not that Luke could say anything. The man had a revolving door where women were concerned, although Alex said he never brought them here for sex. Probably afraid the staid brother would burst a blood vessel or something.

"Alex fell off my ladder, and we spent a few hours at the Emergency Room," she'd said as she got new cold packs out of the freezer.

Luke's face paled. "Is he okay?"

She'd filled him in on his brother's injuries and the treatment. "He'll need help getting dressed and with work. I figured it'd be easier if I were here."

"Thanks. Let me know if I can do anything. I'm right down the hall."

"He doesn't even want my help." She chuckled. "I doubt he'd want yours."

"Yeah, big brother is kind of touchy about how things are done. Appreciate you taking care of him."

She hadn't needed to do much, except get him more medication and ice during the night. And stay close to him. That was the easy part. Being close to Alex was something she'd wanted her whole life. It wasn't something she could have forever, so she'd take what she could get for now.

Running ran her hand over his chest, she twirled her fingers in the smattering of hair between his pectorals. A satisfied moan drifted from his mouth, but he stayed asleep. Probably needed it. He worked too hard most of the time. Could she loosen him up and get him to play and take more time for Alex, the man?

Yet one of the things she loved about him was his dedication to everything and everyone who meant something to him. It was nice to be included in that list. Unfortunately, it was how he'd gotten hurt. His job was important to him, but so was his family.

His job. He'd said something about meetings this week he needed to be in prime shape for. Had he mentioned what time? Sleeping more would be good for him.

As silently as possible, she eased out of bed. There was one place she could find out this information. His planner.

In his office, she sat at his desk. The planner was already turned to today. Of course. And he had a meeting first thing in Stratham. Guess she'd better wake him up.

"Morning."

Luke stood in the doorway, a cup of coffee in his hand.

"Hey. Checking to see what he has planned for today."

Luke frowned. "Maybe he should take a day to recover."

"This is Alex we're talking about. You seriously think something as minor as a few sprained limbs would keep him from doing his job?"

"No, not Alex. Where is he? Do you need help with anything?"

"He's still asleep." At Luke's raised eyebrow, she continued, "I think the pain pills knocked him out good. He'll most likely need help in the shower and getting dressed."

Luke made a face. "I'll help if you really need me, but honestly you're probably a better person for that job."

"Thanks."

Luke glanced at his watch. "I'll be here for another half hour. There's coffee already made, if he needs something more than you in the shower to wake him up. If he does, I may have to disown him."

Carefully, she placed the planner back on the desk in its position and marched past Luke shaking her head. His laugh echoed up the front stairs. Alex still lay sprawled on his bed, the covers now tossed aside. God, the man was gorgeous. Tall, lean muscles, long legs dusted with blond hair that matched the stuff on his arms. Arms that were heavenly when they held her. Why couldn't she be what he wanted in his life? A perfect little woman, who was perfect for his image and lifestyle. That would never happen.

Sitting next to him on the bed, she kissed his perfect lips. His eyes stayed closed, but his mouth woke up and joined in.

When his hand surrounded her waist, she knew he was awake enough to talk to.

"You have a meeting this morning, Felix."

His eyes popped open. "Shit, what time is it? I need to get up." He struggled to sit, and she hated that his face contorted in pain. The doctor had said he'd probably be sore from more than the sprains this morning. He'd hit the ground pretty hard yesterday. That scene was not one she wanted to relive. It had taken a few years from her life.

"You've got time for a shower and coffee, but it may take longer with the sprains."

"I'll be fine."

"You're getting to be a broken record with the I'll-be-fines. Take some more pain killers, so it doesn't hurt so much."

"Are you kidding? That's what knocked me out last night. This meeting is important to this project. I can't be falling asleep in it."

She reached for the anti-inflammatories and handed him a bottle of water. "At least, take these to keep the swelling down. What do you want to wear today? I'll get it from your closet."

"Dark gray suit, a white shirt, and the burgundy paisley tie. My black shoes." No argument insisting he could do it himself. He must be hurting. Or worried that it would take him too long.

As she dug in his closet for the prescribed outfit, he leaned on his crutches and shuffled to the bathroom.

"I don't know how Erik used these for so long. They're a pain in the ass."

"I don't think he had a choice, Felix."

Alex's expression darkened. Thinking about how his brother was still reliant on a cane, most likely.

After setting his suit on the bed, she followed him into the bathroom. He glared at her.

"I need a few minutes in here privately, Dandelion, if you don't mind."

She rolled her eyes. "Let me turn the shower on, so the water gets hot. I'll check back in a few minutes to make sure you don't fall."

He merely sighed, so she adjusted the water, then closed the door most of the way. To hear him in case he fell. Underwear and socks were also something he'd need, so she rifled his drawers and tossed those on the bed beside his suit.

"Make sure you get dark gray socks," Alex called out to her. Heaven forbid his socks didn't match his suit.

"Yes, master. Any specific color you want for underwear?" He only had white.

"You're hysterical, you know that, Dandy?"

The toilet flushed, and the water ran, so she moved back to the door. "You ready for me?"

"I can—"

Something clattered, and she rushed through the door. Alex was plastered against the side of the shower stall, shampoo bottle and soap on the floor.

"You can what? Do it yourself? Yeah, looks like it."

"Okay, maybe I need a little help opening the shampoo."

She picked up the shampoo and poured some into his outstretched hand. He leaned further against the wall, so he could run his hand through his hair. It would take all day doing it this way. She stripped off the t-shirt, slithered out of her underwear, and stepped in beside him.

"Don't fight me on this, Felix. You'll miss your meeting if you keep up at this pace." That got him to shut up.

Okay, feelings off, enter nurse mode. *Ignore the hunky naked man in the shower.* Well, ignore that he's naked and starting to get a boner. She soaped up her hands, then went to work getting him clean and shiny. She didn't know if the moans coming from his mouth were due to discomfort of his injuries or growing arousal. When he was done, she stepped out, grabbed a towel, and let him lean on her while he got out.

"Let me dry you off a bit, so you don't slip." She wanted to explore his body as she did this, but knew it was her responsibility to get him to his meeting. After running the towel over him quickly, she rubbed it over his hair.

"I'll let you shave, while I take my own shower."

His eyes glanced in her direction as she soaped up and lathered shampoo through her hair. The clear glass didn't hide anything. Not his tight ass as he bent over to rinse the shaving cream off or his flexing muscles trying to hold himself up on one foot.

"Knock it off. We don't have time for you," he muttered. "I have a meeting, and I can't afford to be late."

What was he talking about? She almost broke out laughing when she realized he was addressing his erection, which was quite impressive. The mirror showed his clenched jaw and stern face. And here she'd thought he was being so good not sneaking peeks at her. He didn't need to. Her reflection had been on glorious display her whole shower.

With her back to him as much as she could, she rinsed off. No sense getting him into a worse condition. Not that she wouldn't help him relieve it, but today she had to be the responsible one. She didn't want him to ever regret what they'd had the past week.

"I'm going to start getting dressed."

Alex hobbled into the bedroom while she toweled off. A few minutes later, she joined him, squeezing her hair with the terry cloth. He'd already donned his pants, socks, and shirt. The buttons all still needed to be done up.

The towel slipped around her middle, so she secured it as

best she could, then finished the fasteners. The wrap he'd had on his ankle was discarded on the bed. She picked it up and knelt by his feet.

"Let me wrap this for you. It needs some support."

"I might not be able to get my shoe on," he complained.

She didn't wait for his consent. She slipped his sock off, wrapped the ankle, then pulled the sock back on. His shoe was a tie kind, so she stretched the laces out and eased it on his foot, then tied it loosely.

"See, all set."

He wasn't looking at his shoe. His gaze zeroed in on her cleavage exposed by the small towel she'd wrapped around her. Maybe more than her cleavage. She peered down to where her tattoo winked out at them.

Get the temptation out of his way. Standing, she took the comb from his dresser and ran it through her tangled waves. The towel dropped as she tugged on an especially nasty snarl.

Alex's groan drifted across the room, and she spun.

"Are you all right?"

His eyes opened wider. Okay. Naked wasn't the way to get him ready on time.

"You're going to kill me, Dandy. You know, sometimes I don't even care."

"You'll care, if you miss this meeting." She rifled through his dresser. She plucked out another t-shirt and some drawstring shorts and slipped them on. "Come on. Luke made coffee, and I'll bet you have some breakfast pastry stashed somewhere."

She carried his crutches as he limped down the stairs. Luke got up from the table, concern on his face.

"Should you be moving around?"

"They're just sprains," Alex growled. "I'm fine, and wish everyone would stop treating me like an invalid. Now, I know how Erik feels."

As Alex slid into his seat, Luke placed a full cup on the table and said, "Except his injuries won't heal. Be grateful you'll get better and have someone to help you around. Not everyone does."

Alex sighed and held his hand out to Gina. She clasped it and took the seat next to him. "I am grateful. I'm sorry if I haven't shown it."

"You're allowed to be grouchy when you're hurt."

Luke snorted. "What's his excuse for the rest of the time?"

Alex remained quiet and sipped his coffee. Luke rinsed his cup in the sink and headed for the door. "Great outfit, by the way, Gina. I personally like your skin-tight or see-through stuff, but somehow stiff and baggy works for you, too."

Alex glared at his brother, and she could tell he was bothered by the remark. Because Luke liked her sheer clothes, or because he had the gall to notice her at all? Alex didn't want her permanently, but he didn't want anyone ogling her either. Yeah, totally fair.

Luke left, and Alex finished his coffee. Taking his keys from the hook by the cabinets, she shook them.

"Let's go, so you aren't late. I'm not sure where we're going."

"I can drive. You don't need to come." He settled his crutches under his arms.

"Actually, the doctor said you shouldn't drive for a few days, at least. The pain in your ankle could cause you to lose control of the gas or brake pedal. I promise I won't come in and embarrass you."

Alex followed her out and locked the door behind them. Even injured, he still had his routine. Once Alex was in the passenger seat, she got behind the wheel and started the vehicle. "For the next few days, I'm your personal chauffeur. I'll drive you anywhere."

He cleared his throat. "I have a feeling you'll drive me crazy."

Driving him crazy was something she liked doing, but she didn't think Alex was talking about the same kind of crazy she was.

~

ALEX PEERED at Gina as she coughed and waved her hand in front of her face.

"The dust in here is horrible. We should open a window." Gina pulled a stack of books from a box in the turret room of her grandmother's house. Her house. Alex had to remind himself it was her house. Not that it mattered. She'd be gone as soon as it sold. She wasn't planning to stay.

"Yes, we should open a window," he repeated but didn't move from his seat in the middle of the room.

Glancing over, she started to say something, then stopped, got up, and opened the window.

"Can't overtax the ankle or wrist, Dandelion. How many times have you told me that?" She'd been bugging him to take it easy the last few days. This was how he got her back for all the nagging. It was a gorgeous day, and he'd much rather be working on the outside of the house, but she'd insisted he should leave that to John. Not emasculating at all.

"Glad you're finally listening. Here. Will you go through this box and see what's in there?"

The label on the outside of the box said *books*. What did she expect to find? He opened the top and sorted through. "Looks like some old college textbooks on Physics and Geology."

"Poppa's. He loved anything to do with science."

"Did you want to keep them?"

Her expression was torn, but she shook her head. "I can't

keep everything just because it reminds me of my family. Put them in the donate pile."

After sliding them toward the side of the room, he dove back into the box. Gina's cry had him rushing to her side, screw the ache in his ankle. She held out an old shoe box stuffed with tissue paper.

"What is it?" He knelt on the floor next to her and peeked inside.

"Jewelry. Tons of it. I didn't know Nonna had this." She unwrapped one item. A huge emerald ring surrounded by diamonds. He reached for it and examined it closely.

"It looks real. You never saw her wear this?"

Gina shook her head. "Nonna wasn't one for fancy stuff. I wonder if it was her mother's or maybe Poppa's mother. Some of the stuff in this room is ancient. God knows if Nonna ever went through any of it."

They spent the next half hour unwrapping and checking out the items. Rings, necklaces, bracelets, and pendants, all covered it a variety of precious gems.

"We should probably take it to a jewelry store and get it appraised. You'll want to get it insured, if you don't plan to sell it."

Her eyes widened. "I couldn't sell Nonna's jewelry. But we should have someone look at it. It could be fake."

"I'll put it by the door. We don't want to lose it in all this mess."

They continued sorting through the millions of boxes, but Gina kept stopping to study and examine things. He didn't mind. It was nice seeing her so focused and absorbed. The small pile of things she wanted to keep grew. Mostly photos and albums, but there were also bits of nostalgic clothing she thought could be integrated into her eclectic wardrobe, letters from one of her relatives to another, legal documents regarding the house, and a stack of bonds that

Alex suspected were worth a good deal of money. He made sure to keep those apart, so they didn't get misplaced.

"Oh, Alex."

The sad tone of her voice, along with his real name, drew him immediately to her. She had a small fancy box that held pictures. He sat down next to her on the floor.

"More pictures of old relatives?"

"No, me and my mom and my dad." She spoke so low he could barely hear her. The pictures were grainy, but it was clear enough who was in them.

"This was my sixth birthday. Nonna made me a huge chocolate cake, and my dad took me to the movies. We didn't get to go that much, because my mom didn't like them."

"I remember your mom didn't want you watching TV or listening to the radio either. She hated that we spent your two weeks of chicken pox checking out reruns of old shows."

Nestling against him, she flipped through more pictures. "She was never into technology of any kind. She hates what I do, but I think I was drawn to it because I never saw much when I was young. Especially after my dad died."

She grew heavy against his side and sniffed. Was she crying? The picture now in her hands was of her riding on her dad's shoulders, laughing. He remembered Mr. Mazelli. He'd always been super nice to all the kids, and he'd loved Gina so much.

"Remember the year he got all the neighborhood kids to decorate the two huge pine trees in the front yard at Christmas time?"

"I do. And all the *neighborhood kids* were basically you and your brothers and Greg and Leah. I think Sofie and Sara were too little still."

Alex patted her shoulder. "You were a neighborhood kid back then, too."

"Thanks. I remember I got to go to the store with my dad

and pick out a bunch of the ornaments. He said he wanted the tree to be exactly the way I wanted it."

"And one tree was between your yard and mine. And the other was between your yard and Greg's. So it seemed like you got them both."

"I know. My dad told me they gave us all sorts of Christmas magic and made sure Santa would find us. That was my last Christmas with him."

Gina sucked in a deep breath, and a sob escaped when she let it back out. He hugged her close and kissed her hair. It had been a long time since her dad had died, but since he'd never lost a parent, he had no idea how long the pain lasted, or if it ever went away.

"I really miss him. And Poppa and now Nonna. I have no one, Alex. Why do I have no one?"

"Oh, Dandy, you've got people. Your mom's still alive."

Her eyes snapped up to his and narrowed. "I haven't spoken with her since I told her Nonna died. She didn't care or even bother to come see me and make sure I'm all right."

Sliding one hand through her waves, he framed her face. "Well, you've got me, then. And my family. They all love you. I bet they'd adopt you, if you wanted. You could be my sister."

That got her laughing. He was never so happy to see someone smile before. Dandelion was not meant to be sad.

"I'm not really into the incest thing, and I don't think I could quit you cold turkey." Her hands crept up his chest and twined around his neck. Since she was this close anyway, he might as well take advantage. Not of her. Never of her. Only the situation.

Their lips met, and the electricity he always felt with her surged through him. She recharged his batteries and brightened his life. Why couldn't he find someone like this, who would actually stick around? The thought sobered him, and he eased back.

"You okay now, or do I have to suck on your neck and give you a hickey?"

Gina giggled. God, he loved when he got her laughing, especially after a somber moment like the one they'd just had.

"Why don't we stop for today? We'll never get this whole place sorted in one try. We'll drag down the stuff we know is being given away, set aside the stuff to be tossed until we get a dumpster here, and store the items you don't want to lose in a safe spot."

They schlepped the donation stuff down the stairs and stored the bonds and jewelry in Gina's room. She picked up a brooch and turned it around in her hands.

"Do you think we could take this to a jeweler today and have them look at it?"

"Today? Tomorrow is Easter, and I've got my whole family coming over for dinner. I need to get the house cleaned and the spare rooms ready for Sara and Erik and their crew."

"Please, Felix." She sidled up to him and pressed her sultry body against his. "I'll help you clean and do the rooms. I'll even do *you*, if you're a very good boy."

Shit. Why did she have to talk to him like that? "What does 'very good' entail?"

"It's easy. Just come to the jewelry store with me. I did say 'please.'"

"Yes, you did." Why could he never refuse her anything? Good thing she wasn't hanging around. If he ever managed to get someone to marry him, he couldn't imagine any wife accepting Gina jumping all over him, even just as friends.

She fingered his hair, and her lips nibbled on his neck. He didn't need any more convincing.

"We can go. But you owe me. Cleaning and...more."

"I like the *more* part. We can do that now, if you want

payment up front." She lowered her hand to his crotch and rubbed. God. He hated to do it, but he removed her hand.

"Not now. Tonight. And tomorrow we need to be good and sleep in our own beds. We'll have extra guests, who don't need to see Uncle Alex having his own slumber party."

Gina rubbed her gorgeous chest against him and pouted. "Tonight, then. Although, I don't think we'll be doing all that much sleeping."

No, they never did when they were together.

CHAPTER ELEVEN

"Ooh, look at all the shiny baubles." Gina glanced into the glass cases as they walked through Hofstetter Jewelers. Expensive jewelry had never been her thing. She'd rather have a string of flowers tucked in her hair, but she had to admit it was pretty.

"We're here to get the brooch appraised, if they have time." Alex shook his head. "You might have to make an appointment for something like that. We probably should have called."

She stopped herself from rolling her eyes. The organizational side of Alex never stopped. But he'd come with her, so she wouldn't complain.

"The place is empty, Felix."

He took in the room and sighed. "Fine, let's get this done." He approached the counter, where a young woman wiped down the case. She looked up and smiled.

"Hi, may I help you? I'm Tabby."

"Hi, Tabby," he said in the deep, charming tone that always sent thrills through her. Tabby was apparently having the same reaction. Flipping her long blond hair behind her shoulder, she straightened so her chest was on display.

"We were wondering if there was someone here who could look at a piece of jewelry and tell us if it's real."

Tabby looked behind him, and Gina moved closer. The woman's smile dimmed, but only slightly. Gina removed the brooch from her purse and unwrapped the tissue paper around it.

"It's beautiful. Mr. Hofstetter is in the back room. Let me get him for you."

The woman strolled behind the counter to the door near the back and poked her head in, then turned around, an invitation in her eyes. It wasn't aimed at her though. Jealousy niggled away at her. She needed to remind herself she was the one rocking Alex's world, not this chick.

A large, burly man with a neatly trimmed beard ambled out.

"I'm Charles Hofstetter." He held out his hand, and Alex took it.

"Alex Storm, and this is Gina Mazelli. We were wondering if you could look at a piece of jewelry and tell us about it."

When she held out the piece, Hofstetter reached for it. "Mazelli, you say? Any relation to Antonia Mazelli?"

"Her granddaughter. This was her jewelry."

Hofstetter eyed her strangely, then gave a sly smile. "Your grandmother was a lovely woman. I was so sorry to hear of her passing."

"Thank you. So, the brooch, is it real? There's lots of diamonds on there."

The jeweler examined the piece and frowned a few times. "It's a beautiful replica, but I'm afraid these aren't real diamonds or jewels. Do you have more of this?"

She nodded. "There was a whole box. I'd never seen it

before, so wasn't sure if it was my grandmother's or another relative further back. The house has been in the family for a while."

"It isn't worth much, but it's gorgeous workmanship. I often have customers looking for pieces like this at a fraction of what it cost for the real jewels. If the rest of what you have is of similar quality, I could give you a decent price for them."

The brooch sparkled in the afternoon sun, and she shook her head. "Thanks, but I want to keep them. They were Nonna's."

The brooch was passed back, but Hofstetter wasn't satisfied. "Are you sure, my dear? I don't remember your grandmother buying this. In fact, it looks fairly old and outdated. I'd think a young woman like yourself might want something a bit more in vogue. I'd be happy to take it and the others off your hands."

Maybe they weren't Nonna's and maybe they were. It didn't matter. They belonged with the house, and so she'd keep them. Except she wasn't keeping the house. Did that make sense? Why was she suddenly questioning whether she should sell the house? Because Alex lived next door? Alex who liked his June Cleaver clones and appropriately dressed women with excellent manners and good behavior? No, she couldn't live next door to him and whatever perfect woman he ended up choosing.

A hand clasped her shoulder, and she welcomed the comforting touch. He always knew when she needed it.

"Thank you for your time, Mr. Hofstetter," Alex said and shook the man's hand.

Wandering away, she gazed at some engagement rings in the center display until Alex joined her.

"You okay?"

She smiled to reassure him. "What kind of ring would you pick out, if you were buying an engagement ring?"

"I'm not buying an engagement ring, Dandy."

"I know you're not buying one, but I asked what if you were? Pretend you met the woman of your dreams in her sensible heels and pearls, and she had a matching planner fetish. Which ring would you buy her?"

"I don't have a planner fetish."

"Well, you are very attached to yours. Don't think I didn't notice you often add things in after you do them, if they weren't already there."

His face hardened. "Sometimes, it comes in handy knowing when something occurred. That's the only reason I do it."

"Mmmhmm. So which ring?"

His gaze roamed over the assortment, and his eyebrows knit in thought. "That one probably. Or any in that row."

They were all diamond solitaires. Every one. Nothing but a band and diamond. No extra etching on the band or scattering of smaller jewels on the sides.

"Boring. Seriously?"

"What's wrong with them. It's a traditional engagement ring."

"They have no soul, Felix."

"Since when is a ring supposed to have soul?" His face scrunched up in confusion.

"It's for the *person* who owns your soul. The person who makes you so crazy you could never live without them. The missing piece to your puzzle. It has to have soul."

"I don't think I'm missing a piece of my puzzle, Dandy. But you may be missing something. Like a few screws."

How could he not understand what she was saying? Finding the perfect woman and getting married was high on his list, but he didn't seem to know what he was looking for. The perfect wife had specific features and characteristics. He wouldn't find it looking that way.

"So which ring would you pick?" he asked, glancing further down the case.

She studied his face. Why was he asking? Highly unlikely he was thinking of her. Probably just wanting to know how her mind worked. He always said she was an enigma.

One ring called to her, and she stepped near where it set.

"That one." The center stone was an emerald. It was flanked by a scattering of smaller diamonds in a cluster on each side. The band had a fancy, deep gold vine pattern all the way around.

"Is that even an engagement ring? I think you're supposed to have a diamond and spend two month's salary on it. This one doesn't cost that much. And it looks like something a fairy or sprite would wear."

"You're hopeless, Felix."

"I'm just saying, I don't think most women would want a ring like that."

A sigh escaped, before she could stop it. She wheeled around and headed out of the store. "I'm not most women."

Catching up, he flung his arm over her shoulder. "I actually kind of like that about you."

The warmth of his arm settled over her as his words sank in. He liked that she was different, but that still didn't mean he wanted her for the one to get that boring diamond solitaire.

"How's the house coming along, Gina?" Molly Storm asked as they were finishing up Easter dinner.

Alex cocked his head to study the face of the bohemian at his side. She'd known his family her whole life, but for some reason she wasn't her usual bright, upbeat self today.

"We're getting there," she answered. "There's so much in

the house I didn't even realize she had. It'll take a while to clean it all up."

His mother's eyes turned sympathetic. "It must be difficult going through all your grandmother's things."

"It is. Alex is helping, though."

Setting his hand on her thigh, he squeezed. Her hand found his and returned the gesture.

His mother glanced their way, and a mischievous smile curved her lips. What was that for? She couldn't possibly be matchmaking with him and Gina. They were polar opposites. Or had Luke tattled and mentioned he'd slept at Gina's this past week? Not sure his mom would be smiling at that. Her morals were fairly old-fashioned. They still had to hide the fact Sara and TJ were bunking in the same room tonight, and it was only a month until they got married. And she couldn't possibly imagine that Sara was staying in a separate bedroom while living at TJ's.

"Luci said Sofie was excited about helping with some of the internal fixes. Is there a lot to do?"

"Well, Nonna hadn't updated much in the past thirty years. I'm still not sure exactly what I should do before I put the house on the market. It'll cost money to remodel, but then I'd get a higher price. Honestly, I don't care that much about the money."

Running through the list of repairs in his head, Alex ruminated about a few of the ones outside. He'd checked the ladder that had broken, and Greg was right, it had been tampered with. There were a few other tools in the old garage that didn't look right either. Had some kids been sneaking in from the woods that abutted the back side of the property? Maybe they should put an alarm system on the garage, as well.

"That was wonderful, Alex," his dad said, scooting his chair back. "It's nice that your mother doesn't have to do all the work anymore, especially now that Sara isn't around to help her."

"Hey, I helped, too," Luke whined. All heads turned, and his crooked grin came out. "Peeling potatoes is helping."

"You can all come down the Cape next holiday," Sara invited, rising and collecting plates. "TJ has a huge house with plenty of room to stay. I'd be happy to cook."

"*We* have a huge house and would be happy to host," TJ added, his arm around Sara. His sister's face turned pink, her lips twisting into a grin. Thank God, she was happy. Otherwise, he'd have to give her future husband a black eye, like the one Luke had given TJ when they'd first met. And the one he'd gotten, too, in the scuffle of miscommunication. Didn't look like it would be needed, though.

Erik attempted to pick up some plates one-handed, but a few forks fell on the floor. Matty scrambled off his chair and retrieved them. The smile his brother gave his son was mixed, both gratitude and pain. He knew Erik still hated that he couldn't do everything he used to be able to.

"How's the physical therapy coming along, Erik," their dad asked as the men all grabbed plates and bowls and schlepped them to the kitchen.

"I finished a few weeks ago," he said, carefully lowering his load to the counter. Matty helped push them further on the counter and got a pat on the head from Erik.

"You're done? Like forever?" Luke questioned, his gaze moving to the cane clutched tightly in their eldest brother's hand.

"This is as good as it gets, little brother." His expression was resigned, then Tessa moved up behind him, and his face lightened. Leaning down to kiss the top of her head, he added, "Good thing I have a wife who doesn't seem to mind."

The interaction between Erik and Tessa was heartwarming to see. They hadn't been in love when they'd gotten married. He didn't think so, anyway. They'd done it to get custody of the kids. But love had grown between them, and it was a beautiful thing.

"Why don't you boys go throw a ball around outside?" their dad suggested, taking Kiki from Tessa's arms. Leave it to their dad to still think of them as boys. "I've got the little ones, and we've got big plans for those blocks you brought."

"You don't have to take them," Tessa said, sidling up close to Erik. "They can—"

"No, you go chat about wedding plans with the ladies. I'm not interested in that, but I'm not sure I can keep up with these young bucks on the court, either. Building blocks are just about my speed."

"TJ." Luke stuck his head into the dining room, "We're heading out for some b-ball. Are you available, or do they need you to discuss flowers and dresses for the wedding?"

TJ's gaze swiveled to Sara, who chuckled and rolled her eyes.

"Go," she said, and the relief on his face was palpable as he leaned down and kissed her tenderly. He patted their dad on his way to the kitchen in thanks.

Once outside, they split into two teams and began passing the ball around.

"So, are you still technically in the military, Erik?" Luke asked, tossing the ball to TJ.

Erik strode shakily toward the net and caught the rebound. "Now that PT is done, I'll get my official Honorable Discharge. I still get my VA benefits."

"Will you need them?" he questioned. "You get insurance through your job at The Boat House, right?" Erik was a chef at a local restaurant up in Maine, where he, Tess, and the kids lived.

"I do, but it's always good to have a back-up. Plus, we can still use the counseling services at the VA clinic."

Luke tilted his head as he dribbled the ball. "You're going to counseling? Or is Tessa?"

Tessa had been a foster child, and Alex suspected she'd had a tough life. Once she'd moved next door to their grandparents in Maine in her early teens, Sara and the cousins had befriended her, but she still rarely spoke when too many people were around. Erik and the kids had been good for her, though. She seemed more confident lately, at least around them.

"It's mostly for me," Erik said, his jaw taut. "Having a little PTSD from my time overseas. Counseling has helped. Tessa goes with me, so she knows what to do if I get...um, have an episode."

"Do you have these often?" Luke's face seemed paler. Serious for their fun-loving brother.

Erik shrugged. "I've been able to deal with them better. Certain things still set me off. Fireworks, violent movies, that sort of stuff."

Nodding his head, Luke said, "Good to know. We'll make note for your wedding, TJ. No fireworks, no alcohol."

"We don't plan to have a dry wedding," TJ noted. "I can handle being around it. On the other hand, if we did, my father might not come. That could be a good thing." His eyes twinkled. "May have to rethink this."

After an hour of throwing the ball around, Erik leaned against the shed. "I'm done. This getting old thing sucks."

"'Cause thirty's so old," Alex said.

"I'm still up for more." Luke dribbled a few times. "Maybe we could get one of the ladies to join us. I'd love to see Gina bouncing around on the court. That cute little skirt she has on would give us quite a show."

"No shows for you." He grit his teeth at the thought of Luke watching Gina's anything bounce around. "Keep your eyes in your head around her."

"I'd never poach, bro. You got nothing to worry about. Plus, it seems like all her shows are for you. I'm assuming you got one in the pantry earlier. Like when you were supposed to be getting dessert ready."

"Is that why it took so long?" Erik smirked and tossed the ball in the shed.

Shit. He'd hoped everyone was too busy eating and listening to Matty sing a song he'd learned in school to notice how long they'd been gone. Thinking of what they'd done in the pantry got him hot and hard. Like everything to do with Gina. Luckily, she'd helped fix his problem. That flirty little skirt Luke had commented on had provided easy access. And bless Gina, she was of the mindset the show must go on.

"AND THIS IS MY WEDDING DRESS." Sara scrolled through her phone and held it out for Gina to see. "But this stays here. I don't want TJ to know what it looks like, until I walk down the aisle."

"No worries," she assured her. "I doubt Alex or any of the guys would be that interested. They booked it out of here fast enough."

She had thought of booking it out there, too, but she'd been caught by Molly and hijacked into this little coffee klatch. Not that she minded. Molly and Sara had always been nice to her. And Tessa seemed like a sweetheart, though certainly introverted.

It was kind of surprising to see Erik with someone like her. He was the big man on campus, the popular jock, and heartthrob to endless townie girls. Not that he'd dated them all like Luke, but he'd always gone for the head cheerleader or the prom queen type. It was nice to see him with a down to earth woman like Tessa. Watching them today, and a week ago at the anniversary party, had filled her with envy.

Then, there was Sara and TJ. Another strange match if you threw in TJ's background. But interacting with him recently, she'd never have guessed his parents were super famous, and he'd grown up in that lifestyle. The love between those two was also obvious and something she longed for. She hadn't always, but losing Nonna had her thinking it wasn't so important for her to travel and get out in the world as much. She'd seen so much already.

Could she live in a small town like this? Would she ever be accepted, or would people always judge her and criticize her choices as they'd done when she was growing up?

"These are the bridesmaid dresses," Sara continued, flipping through her phone.

"Who's in the wedding?" Gina asked, glancing at the pictures. The dresses were surprisingly sedate and classy. No big bows or flowers, and the color was soft. She could totally see Alex's friend Kristan, of the sensible heels and pearls, looking fabulous in it. Her, not so much. Good thing she wasn't in the wedding.

"Tessa's my Matron of Honor."

Tessa rolled her eyes and patted her belly. "Whale of Honor would be more like it."

"You'll be gorgeous. My cousins, Sofie, Leah, and Amy are also bridesmaids. You remember them, right?"

"Sure," Gina nodded. "Sofie's been helping me renovate the house." Leah, Greg, and Sofie were siblings and had lived next door growing up. Amy was Nathaniel and Kevin's sister and a good deal younger. Since their parents, Kris and Anna, didn't live on the same street, they hadn't interacted as much, but they'd met numerous times.

"And my friend from the coffee shop, Darcy is going to be in it. You'll like her. She marches to her own beat."

"Another rebel. Yay. And the guys?"

"TJ's friend, Jim, is his best man. All my brothers, of course. And we needed to even it out, so we asked Nathaniel. He's been doing some legal work for TJ, in regard to his house and business. I've partnered him up with Darcy. It should be fun to watch."

Darcy marched to her own drum, huh? Nathaniel, as she remembered, was starchier than Alex, and by his own choice. The organized part of Alex was simply part of his personality.

"We tried not to make it too big, but when you have a good-sized family, it's hard." Sara swiped her phone off.

"I won't have any difficulty then, if I ever get there."

"Same here." Tessa smiled shyly. "I had Sara, and Erik had Alex. No one else."

"But you have all of us now, Tessa," Molly chimed in with her huge accepting smile. "And we've always thought of you as family, Gina."

"Thanks. Alex said that, too."

"As family, perhaps you'd like to help us out next weekend with the Youth Center." Molly picked up a notepad from the table behind her.

"The Youth Center?"

"Yes, you've been there before when you were kids. They had some damage to one of the large rooms from some broken water pipes. Lots of the townsfolk are getting together to work on fixing it up and even putting on an addition. Alex drew up the plans for it."

"TJ's donating books to the center, and I'm coming up to help as well," Sara said.

Molly pushed herself off the couch and tidied the already spotless coffee table. "Luci, Anna, and I will be providing food for the crew."

"Well, if you want me to write a program, sure, I'm your

man, but not sure how handy I am with a hammer. Or with the people of this town." The last words she said under her breath.

"Everyone in this town loved your grandmother," Molly assured her.

"Yes, they did love her." *Not sure they loved me quite as much.*

Sara stood. "Mom, I'm going to get those boxes from your car."

"I'll give you a hand," Molly said, then paused and patted Gina's shoulder on her way out. "We love you, but we understand if you have too much to do. Just know you're always welcome."

"Erik and I are coming down." Tessa shifted in her seat, gazing at her shyly. "I said I'd watch all the kids of the volunteers. You can always help me." Did she really want help, or was she only being nice?

"Not sure I want to be inspected by the town. I always seem to be found lacking."

"I get that. I grew up in foster homes and never had decent clothes. I was a total freak. I still feel that way, but the Storms never cared. I'm cautious about what I wear now. I don't ever want to embarrass Erik."

The woman was gorgeous, with her long, wavy, brown hair and cute maternity outfit. Doubtful Erik was embarrassed.

"I don't think he cares what you're wearing. I've seen the way he looks at you. Like he'd slay dragons in order to be with you and keep you safe. The man's totally in love."

Pink tinted Tessa's cheeks. "I wish I was a bit braver and could get away with some of the adorable outfits you wear."

Looking down at the flirty skirt and loose flowing top, she smiled. "I started wearing stuff like this because my mom dragged me all over the country with her hippy, free-love friends. But I grew to like the eclectic style. It's my own and kind of a screw-you to anyone who is uptight and judgy."

Tessa's sympathetic expression made her want to confide in her. "It doesn't mean it doesn't hurt when people make fun of me or talk behind my back. It would be nice to be accepted for who I am. Me, myself, and I, you know, and not be expected to fill some weird stereotypical mold of a perfect young lady."

"I wish I could say *screw you* to those who were mean to me." Tessa's gaze flitted around, her tight mouth revealing how much past hurts still haunted her.

"You've got the Storms now, Tessa."

"I do." Her eyes perked up. "Being in their circle really helps. You've got them, too, especially Alex."

"Alex is a good friend," she admitted.

Tessa tipped her head. "I thought Erik said—"

"Friends with benefits, yeah, but I'm not staying. I'd never fit in here with them. Not permanently."

Reaching out, Tessa patted her hand. "I didn't think so, either. But sometimes miracles happen."

CHAPTER TWELVE

"*A*re you ready to go, Dandy?" Alex called up the stairs, after letting himself into her house. She'd used his birthday as part of her alarm code. Should he be flattered?

"Almost," she yelled back down.

"Remember, we're doing construction work today." If they could get there. They were already running late, though it was completely his fault. Last minute adjustments on his medical building project he couldn't put off.

"You mean the shear blouse and mini skirt won't work? Damn." Her sarcastic voice floated back down. But he'd detected a little hurt there, too. *Back off and let her be who she is. Don't try and change her.*

Footsteps echoed down the stairs, and he looked up. Flannel shirt, cut off carpenter pants, crazy patterned knee highs, and her flowered Doc Martens.

"Do I pass inspection?" She twirled as she got to the bottom.

His lips twitched. "Could be worse. You'll do."

"We kind of match," she said, gazing at his plaid flannel shirt. Hers was similar. And familiar.

Narrowing his eyes, he said, "I used to have a shirt just like that. Old, worn, and had a stain on the…" Yup, beige paint stain on the shoulder.

Her head tilted as her hands planted on her hips. "It was in a bag in the back of your closet in your old room. Figured it would work for today."

"What were you doing in the back of my closet?"

Her eyes twinkled mysteriously. "I wanted to see if the notes were still there. Remember we used to write down stuff we thought was important and stick it in that hole in the wall. You drew pictures, and I invented things. We made wishes."

Memories returned of them sitting together with flashlights, planning how successful they'd be. "We figured they'd be worth millions when we were rich and famous. Not sure how well that worked. Did you find them?"

Her lips curled up in a smile, but she remained silent.

"Are you ready?"

"Yep, but I need a hammer."

"Were you planning to use one?"

"I have this cool little hook here." She indicated the tab on her cut off pants. "For a hammer."

"I thought you were helping my mom with the food."

"I should stay away from the food. I've been eating a little too well lately with all your cooking. I won't fit in my clothes soon." Patting her hips, she frowned.

What was she worried about? Every pound she had was perfect and gorgeous. If he thought too much about them, he'd be hard as a rock soon.

"Let's go."

As she skipped out the door, he watched her cute behind wiggle. Better not think about that while he was doing construction today, or he could cut off something important.

She leaned against the porch railing, her arms crossed

over her chest, waiting for him as he locked up. Suddenly, her eyes flew wide, and the railing tipped backwards. Her arms shot out. Shit. Grabbing for her hand, Alex pulled, but her weight propelled him forward. They both crashed against the sagging wood and tumbled over.

Pain lanced through his back as he twisted to keep Gina from taking the brunt of the fall. Luckily, the bushes near the porch hadn't been trimmed lately and were thick enough to cushion them. They rolled onto the grass, Gina sprawled on top of him.

"Holy crap, are you all right, Felix?" Her eyes were anxious.

"I will be, as soon as you get your knee out of my groin." It didn't hurt. It was starting to get excited with the proximity.

"Oh." She rolled to the side and sat. "What the heck happened?"

Grunting, he pushed himself up, then hauled her to her feet. His sprained ankle and wrist twinged. "The railing gave way. I thought John and I checked that a few weeks ago. It didn't seem like it needed replacing." Had they totally misjudged the shape of it?

"We should go. We can take care of the railing later." Her voice was shaky, and she held her side.

"Are you hurt, or did it just scare you?"

Taking a deep breath, she pursed her lips. "Don't you know by now nothing scares me?"

It was good that one of them had no fear. His feelings for her scared the shit out of him most of the time.

They climbed in his car and soon entered the parking lot of the Youth Center. Quite a few cars had already pulled in with more arriving behind them. Excellent. He'd been one of the main people to get this started. If they had a place for teens to go and do fun stuff, maybe they could keep them off the streets and out of trouble. Bored kids created bad situations. Even in Squamscott Falls, New Hampshire.

"I'm so glad you came, Gina." His mom gave her a hug, then his aunts, Luci and Anna. "Alex, your father and uncles are inside getting the wires ready."

Peter Storm and his brothers, Kris and Nick, owned Storm Electric and had volunteered their services for this project. Kris' son and Alex's cousin, Nathaniel had managed to talk quite a few people into donating money. Those he or Luke hadn't managed to talk into physically helping, anyway. It was definitely a community effort. Another reason he loved living in this small town. People helped each other.

"John and I organized this event, so we need to get people started," Alex said. "The first step is framing the walls. We got the concrete poured last week. Why don't you say hi to anyone you know, while I check who's here already?"

Gina's smile dimmed as she said, "Yes, I'll just skip on over and get reacquainted with all my old friends."

As he set off to find John, Gina wandered over to the playground where Tessa and Erik stood watching their kids. Wouldn't it be nice to have that kind of happy family? Glancing around, he noticed several women he'd dated getting their areas set up. Maybe he needed to try harder with one of them. If any of them would even want to date him again. Edele Farmer was one he'd dated in high school and still so pretty. Unfortunately, she was married and had four kids. Too bad. She'd been a great kisser. Not that they'd done much more. Gina had been the one to initiate him into the big time.

John was all set up with blueprints, sitting next to the list of who was working in what area. Thank God for his mom and her lists.

"Are we ready to get this show on the road?"

John nodded. "They just dropped off the lumber, and I got Greg, Kevin, and Mitch prepping the area."

"Excellent. Hey, didn't we check the front porch railing on Gina's house?

"Yeah, it was fine. Why?"

"It broke this morning when Gina leaned against it."

John's expression turned dark. "Did she get hurt?"

"We both ended up in the bushes. A little banged up but fine." He had a definite bruise forming on his back, and he'd need to be careful with his wrist today. Luckily, he'd grabbed Gina with the good one.

"There's no way her weight could have caused that. She's too little. I'll take a look on Monday."

"Thanks. I should have done that when it happened, but we were already running late to get here. Let me make sure the rest of the people are in their areas, and I'll be back to help with the framing."

Passing his mom and aunts, Alex snitched a donut, then checked inside to see Mitch's sister, Macy, and his cousins, Sofie, Leah, and Amy all geared up with paint rollers to brighten up the inside of the existing rooms. With Sofie's eye for color and style, she'd have this place looking better in no time.

The youth group from the church was already busy cleaning the playground, Ryan among them. The older kids helped pull out the rusted parts of the chain link fence, while the Rotary Club members installed a new one.

As he spoke with the kids from the local Vocational School, and thanked them for the prep work they'd done in their classes, he kept his eye on Gina. She'd been with Tessa when he'd passed the grassy area the kids were playing on, but now she picked up the two by fours they were using for framing and carried them to the work site. God, she was amazing. Her tiny frame still managed to haul lumber with the big boys.

"The bathroom by the office has a new sturdy lock." Luke walked behind him carrying supplies. "If you're as fast as you were at Easter, maybe no one will miss you."

Whipping his head around, he glared at his brother. "I have no idea what you're talking about."

Luke simply laughed and walked away toward where John and his crew constructed the sides of the new frame. Better get back to work himself.

A few hours later, he was tired and sweaty, but they'd gotten the walls up and were working on the roof. With so many hands, it had been faster than he'd expected. Like an old-fashioned barn raising.

His gaze roamed the area looking for Gina. She'd flitted from group to group, wherever help was needed. Surprisingly, she'd been adept at swinging a hammer, painting the walls inside, and even screwing in drywall in the revamped office. And her math skills when they'd been measuring and cutting angles were fast.

Wherever she was, though, many of the high school boys followed. Her flirtatious and friendly manner didn't help. It only lured them deeper, like a siren at sea.

They weren't the only ones. He needed to keep his mind on the job and not on what they could do once it was finished. Having her here today had been fun. He couldn't deny it. It was a whole different side to her he'd never seen. Her personality still bubbled over with exuberance, but usually they were alone or with his family. Today, they were surrounded by dozens of other people. She still outshone all of them, outworked all of them. Nothing was out of her wheelhouse. She gave everything her best shot.

Could she ever settle down in a place like this? Would she be happy here? More than a few people gave her clothes a curious look, but screw them. At least, nothing was see-through today, and she actually wore a bra. He only knew because he'd felt it when she'd hugged him earlier. He certainly hadn't copped a feel.

"GINA, do you have a minute to help watch the kids?" Tessa bit her lip, her hand on her stomach. "I need to use the ladies' room. Again."

"Of course, go ahead. Take your time." Gina perused the kids running around the grass and frowned. How had Tessa kept track of them all day? There were only a half dozen left, and her anxiety rose. But Tessa had other helpers earlier, she had no one.

"All right, everyone, over here. We're playing Leap Frog. Get in line!"

Matty tipped his head. "What's Leap Frog?"

"I'll show you." Ryan had finished with the playground clean up and had come over. "Crouch down into a ball, and I'll jump over you. Like a frog."

"Daddy and I caught a frog in the lake." Matty jumped up and down.

Scooping up Kiki, Gina moved her in front of Matty and put her on the ground, then did a quick hop over her. "Now, Matty, you get to hop over her, and Ryan will hop over you and Kiki."

The kids all got in a line and settled on the grass. When they'd all leaped over everyone, and it was the little girl's turn, Gina picked her up and helped her jump over the rest. Kiki giggled and squealed.

When she was done, the child raised her arms up in the universal sign she wanted to be picked up. Happily. Not that she'd had much experience with kids, but the innocence and exuberance of them seemed to bring joy. As soon as she was up, Kiki snuggled onto her shoulder and shoved her thumb in her mouth. Her eyes started to flutter closed. Damn, this was sweet. Ryan and the other kids continued the game without her assistance.

"You look good with her there." Molly Storm's warm voice floated her way as she deposited a plate of sandwiches and cookies on the nearby picnic table.

"She feels good. I never really thought much about kids. I mean, I like them, but having my own...it's not like I had a good—" Her gaze shot up at what she was about to say. "I mean..."

"It's okay, sweetie. Every mother is different in how they express love. They all have different abilities and weaknesses."

"Your kids are so lucky, you know that? You have great abilities and no weaknesses."

The smile on Molly's face was pure pride. "Thank you. I'm not sure they'd all agree with you on the no weaknesses thing, but I'm fortunate. They've all been wonderful children. It was easy to love them."

Rocking Kiki felt so right. But holding a child for a few minutes was not raising one. Swaying back and forth with her hips in a figure eight rhythm, Gina thought about her own mother. No doubt she'd loved her, but that maternal instinct had never seemed to kick in. Especially when it had been needed. Nonna had been the one to provide that type of love, and Gina had stayed away too long from her in recent years. Because she'd never felt like she quite belonged here.

Today hadn't been so bad. Most people had been nice, even if they'd stared at her outfit critically. It certainly wasn't what most of the women wore.

"Hey, Gina, thanks for all the help with the sheet rock

inside." Greg nodded to his aunt, then wiped his hands on his olive-green cargo pants, watching the kids playing.

"It was fun." And so was holding this now sleeping child, despite the baby's foot resting right where the broken railing had scraped her ribs. A quick adjustment to the other side eased the ache a bit.

"How's Alex holding up with the sprains? I didn't see him slowing down at all today."

"After the one-week mark, he refused to use the crutches anymore. He's being a brave little soldier, but the ankle and wrist still ache. He can't fool me."

Molly rolled her eyes. "Alex never did like to stay inactive."

"Dad!" Ryan rushed toward his father and jumped. Greg braced himself and caught the flying child.

"Did you get the playground all cleaned up, kiddo?"

"We did, and even Mrs. C.C. helped us."

Greg smirked and shook his head.

Looking at Ryan, she asked, "Who's this Mrs. C.C.?"

"Mrs. Cabrera-Cassidy." Ryan's eyes sparkled. "She teaches fourth grade. She's so cool and is the best teacher ever. I want to have her when I'm in fourth grade." After the rushed speech, Ryan raced off to a woman with dark hair approaching one of the younger kids.

"Ryan has a bit of a crush on her. She lives across the street from the ball park, where he has Little League." Greg's gaze never left the pretty lady, either.

"Just Ryan?" Her own grin slipped out.

Greg shook his head. "She's married with a kid."

Probably the little girl she was picking up, who was maybe three-ish.

"Actually," Molly interrupted, her voice low. "She's now divorced. She's going back to just Ali Cabrera. Leah works at the same school and says Ali's bastard husband left her right after their daughter's first birthday."

"He is a bastard." Greg's face tightened, though he never stopped staring at where Ryan had gone. "What kind of man deserts his kid?"

Glancing from Molly to Greg to Ryan. and the young woman and little girl he was chatting with, she thought about her own upbringing. Her dad had died, so he didn't really have a choice in leaving her. But often she still got mad at him for doing so. She'd loved him so much. Moving around the country with her mother had seemed exciting at first, but recently those memories didn't stand out as much as the ones she had of hanging here with Nonna and the Storms.

"I'm going to grab Ryan and get some food into him before I leave. I need a short nap. Twelve-hour shift tonight." Greg nodded at them and walked toward his son, who was still hanging with the teacher.

"Oh, thank you, Gina." Tessa rushed back and sighed. "This bladder thing is getting inconvenient." She patted her baby belly and smiled. Maybe not that much of an inconvenience.

"I'll hold Kiki for a bit, if you want to check on the other children." No way she'd admit how much she was enjoying holding the baby. Ideas started forming in her head. Ideas she'd never had before. Ones she shouldn't be having with no man in her life. No permanent man, that is.

Erik approached, relying heavily on his cane. He leaned in to kiss his wife. "How are you holding up? Do you need to sit and rest?"

Tessa frowned. "I'm fine. What about you? Have you been on your feet too long?"

She chuckled when he produced a matching frown. "I'm

not dead. Even if I can't climb a ladder, I can still pound a hammer."

Tessa smirked and touched her stomach. "Obviously."

"I'd still feel better if you sat down for a bit. Did you ask my mom about Thursday yet?"

Molly tipped her head. "Thursday. I'm working until five. Did you need me for something?"

Erik shifted. "We've got an appointment with a specialist in Boston. Figured it would be easier to leave the kids here than with a babysitter in Maine. But don't worry, we'll figure something out."

"Is something wrong?" Molly's expression grew concerned.

Tessa gazed skyward. "Ever since my accident, Erik has been a wreck about this baby. I agreed to see this doctor and have an advance ultrasound done simply to keep him from flipping out. I'm sure we can find someone to keep an eye on the kids, or we can bring them with us."

"I can do it." Gina rubbed the sleeping baby's back. "No sense in Molly taking a day off work when I'm available. If you trust me to watch them." Too many people thought she was too offbeat and wacky to be responsible.

"Are you sure it's not a problem?" Tessa asked. "I know you've got the house project going on."

"Most of what I'm doing is going through Nonna's things. Alex and John are doing the repair work. I'm sure I can use his house to watch them, since mine's a bit beat up at the moment."

"That's very kind of you to offer, Gina," Molly said, her lips twitching. What was the cause of that? "I'm sure if Alex doesn't have an appointment, he can help you with the children, too. He loves his niece and nephew."

"That's settled, then." Erik nodded. "Thanks, Gina. Appreciate it. We'll drop the kids off by ten."

"Yes, thank you. Now, I'll take Kiki and put her in the carriage." Tessa held her arms out for the little girl. "I knew she'd fall asleep at some point."

Reluctantly, she handed the child over to her mother, but managed to kiss her head before letting go.

Tessa smiled and whispered, "It's magical, isn't it?"

It was. No sense dwelling on it now.

"Since you've got these rug rats all under control, I'll go see who else needs some help."

The inside rooms had all been painted, and a few of the rooms that had needed new walls had the sheetrock up and ready for spackling. She could do that. Better check with Alex first, so his organization didn't crumble.

"Hey, there, pretty lady."

As she turned, Rick Scarsdale walked right up to her. Like, in her space, and she had a very small personal bubble. Taking a step back, she smiled at him. "Hey, Rick. I didn't know you were working on this project, too."

"Oh, sure. My grandfather donated money to buy some of the building supplies. I thought I'd stop by and make sure his money was well invested."

"So, you aren't actually swinging a hammer or lifting a paintbrush?" Big surprise.

He glanced at his manicured nails. "I'm a lawyer. I don't do dirty."

"That's too bad. I like a little dirt on my men." Like Alex, who was currently on the roof, his snug jeans giving her ideas. He glanced her way and frowned.

Wrong thing to say. Rick's arm snaked over her shoulder to pull her closer. "I know plenty of ways to get down and dirty without actually lifting a paintbrush. Though it could include some drilling, if you know what I mean."

Tilting her head, she glared. Was this guy for real?

"What do you say? We could head to your place and bang out a few things before anyone even knows we're gone."

"Sorry. I promised to help out here today. This community building is important for the people of this town."

"Of course, it is. It's important to me, too. But if we go back to your place, I could go over your grandmother's portfolio and find ways you could help this community without lifting a finger."

She might have believed him, if his hand hadn't slipped over her pants to grope her ass.

"I'm sorry—"

"Hey, Rick," Alex interrupted, his mouth tight across his face. She hadn't noticed him descend the ladder. "What brings you here?" His gaze focused on Rick's hand, which swiftly retreated. Good thing, since she was about to jab him with her elbow.

"Just checking on what Grampa's money was buying."

"Not Gina. I don't think she's for sale."

Rick crossed his arms, his expression smug. "You'd be surprised what money can buy."

"I'll have to figure that out, since Nonna had a ton of it." She addressed Alex, who was still scowling. "I was going to help them tape and spackle the walls inside. Does that meet with your plans?"

Rick threw her a seductive look, then winked before walking away. Alex followed the man's retreat.

Sidling close, she snuggled into his arm and pressed a kiss to his neck. "You're cute when you're jealous."

His head whipped around, his mouth puckered. "I'm not jealous."

She leaned past him to stare at Rick, and Alex's arm wrapped around her back.

"Okay, maybe a little jealous, but that guy's a slime. I don't like him hanging all over you. Pawing at you."

Standing on her toes, she slid her hands over his shoulders. "No worries. You're the only guy I let paw at me, Felix."

Looking around first, he lowered his head and kissed her, quick and with purpose. What that purpose was, she didn't know. Certainly not to stake a claim on her, since he just as swiftly let her go.

"What are you working on next?"

"I said I was planning to tape and spackle. Didn't you hear me? Or were you too busy dissecting Rick in your mind?"

"Dissecting would be too good for him," Alex muttered.

Her smile couldn't be stopped. "So bloodthirsty. It's kind of a turn on, Felix."

He narrowed his eyes. "How do I turn you off, then? Especially around the teen boys. John and I have had to corral them too many times today, because they keep wanting to work where you are."

"This might keep them away." She pressed her body against his and kissed him passionately. "You've got to let them know I'm taken."

As she walked away, she glanced over her shoulder. "Unless I'm not, and then it shouldn't matter to you."

CHAPTER THIRTEEN

*A*lex peeked at the broken railing as he escorted Gina up her front porch stairs. The crack in the wood sure didn't look like it had rotted naturally. First, her grandmother's ladder and now the porch railing. He'd mention it to John, and they'd have to go over everything again.

"Are you coming in?" Gina hovered in her doorway, hand on her hip, big grin on her face.

"I need to take a shower. I'm filthy."

Her eyebrow rose. "That's what I was hoping for. We could share."

"Your master bathroom is torn apart right now. All you have is the half bath downstairs or the claw foot tub."

She crooked her finger in his direction. Damn, but she held some power over him. "I'm a bit sore from falling earlier and the very different muscles I used today. I need a good soak in the tub, and you need to scrub my back."

He and Gina in a tub together. Clean would not be their main goal. But that claw foot tub was huge. They might be able to manage.

"Okay, let me grab a snack first. All I've had to eat was a tiny sandwich, and that was almost five hours ago."

"Great." Gina jumped up and down, then bounced toward the front stairs. "Take whatever I have in the kitchen. I'm going to start the water."

There wasn't much there, since he typically cooked for her at his house. He found and chomped down a few granola bars, then headed upstairs. Her offbeat singing drifted from the bathroom across the hallway from her room. When he opened the door, he stopped at the sight.

The tub was filled to the brim with bubbles.

"A bubble bath?"

"Bubbles are fun and relaxing." She shucked her shorts, then pulled off her socks.

Relaxing wasn't exactly a word he'd ever use about Gina, but fun was her middle name.

As he unbuttoned and removed his shirt, she got started on hers. The two flannels dropped on the floor together, and he reached for the snap on his pants. When he saw the huge bruise on her side, he stopped.

"Is that from falling earlier?" The skin hadn't broken, but it was discolored from under her arm to the lower part of her ribcage. "Why didn't you tell me before we left? We should have put some ice on it when it first happened."

"We were running late, and I know how crabby you get when you're late for something. Besides, it's fine. It doesn't hurt that much. The tub will make it feel better."

Kneeling beside her, he examined the skin that had been damaged and scraped. Pulling her near, he kissed the bruise, then stood and stroked her face. "I'm so sorry, Dandy. I thought that porch railing was safe, but I messed up."

Kissing him back, she smiled. "It's an old house. No need to feel guilty. But if you want to make it up to me, you can rub my shoulders. I may have done a bit more than I'm used to today."

"No problem. I can do a massage."

Within seconds, they were both undressed and immersed in the hot water. After a moment of getting adjusted to the temperature, he settled back and Gina leaned against him.

"Oh, this is heaven. Thanks for being a great pillow, Felix."

Yup, heaven. Gina's trim body rubbing against his. Nothing better. And she was right. The hot water helped ease the tension and aches in his muscles. Surprisingly, sitting here doing nothing but soaking in the water was all he wanted.

Except he owed her a massage. Lifting his hands, he rested them on her shoulders and gently kneaded, working out the knots in her muscles.

"Mmm, that's out of this world." Her hands scraped bubbles off the top of the water and pulled them to cover her breasts. Good, they were always a bit too tempting.

"You did a great job today, Dandelion. Thanks for all your help. You're quite the Jack of all trades, aren't you?"

"I pick things up fast. Can't let any man get the better of me." She eased away and turned around. Her face was covered in a bubble beard, her eyes flashing mischief.

"Silly girl."

"How would you look with a beard?" She scooped up more bubbles and patted his cheeks. "Very Santa Claus. Only not as fat."

Wiping the bubbles off his face, he laughed. "Ho, ho, ho."

"How about a hat to go with this distinguished beard?" She added more bubbles on her head as a hat and horns, then some covering her shoulders. "Do you like my new gown and bonnet, darling?"

"They're beautiful, you nut. I thought you wanted to relax in the tub."

"Relax and fun, I said. That was the fun part. Now, I can relax. The bubbles won't last all that long, anyway. I needed to use them while they were still fresh."

Everything about Gina was fresh and fun.

"Do you remember the last time we had a bath together?"

"What?" He stiffened. "I've never had a bath with you before. You must be thinking of someone else." That thought alone had him clenching his teeth.

"Sure, we did. I think I was only about four at the time, but Erik had fallen and broke his arm, and your mom needed to take him to the hospital. I think Luke and Sara had gone to Luci's, but Nonna offered to watch you, since you were already over here."

"Okay, I vaguely remember Erik breaking his arm. Wait, did we get covered in mud?"

She nodded her head. "Yup, we turned the hose on in the backyard and thought we were helping Poppa water the garden. I ended up slipping in the dirt, and you came in after me to help."

"You pulled me down into the mud, if I remember correctly."

"I did not." Her head whipped around, but the mischief in her eyes belied her denial.

"Maybe not on purpose, but you pulled on my hand—"

"To help me get up."

"And I slid right into the green bean plants. Your grandmother was horrified at how filthy we were."

"Yup, and she didn't think your mom needed any more stress, so she threw us both in the tub and washed your clothes."

"And you made bubble beards then, too."

Turning around, she rested against him again. He

wrapped his arms around her, then tipped his head back on the edge of the tub, allowing the water to ease the aches in his muscles.

Gina remained quiet and still. Had she fallen asleep? She'd certainly worked hard today. Harder than many of the guys there who typically did physical work. She was used to sitting at a computer for her job.

The job that had her traveling all over. She didn't even work for one company but contracted out whenever and wherever the wind brought her. How long before the wind blew her away from him again? Just like the dandelion seeds he'd nicknamed her after. It was coming, though he didn't know when. He'd prepared for it and made sure to tell himself often enough that she wasn't staying. Why, then, did something like relaxing in a tub together make him want things he knew he couldn't have?

"Oh, we're babysitting for Matty and Kiki on Thursday."

"What? How did this happen?"

"Tessa and Erik asked your mom, but she had to work." Her shoulders rose and fell. "I didn't want her to have to take a day off, so I said I'd do it."

"You, not us?"

"Well, I have to do it at your place, considering my house is torn apart in spots. It's probably not safe for little kids. Especially Kiki, since she does that put-everything-in-her-mouth thing."

"I suppose my house is a better place for them, but I have an appointment on Thursday for a possible new client."

Her head bobbed from side to side against his chest. "I'll keep them so quiet you won't even know we're there. Don't worry."

Oh, he'd worry, but he supposed he could send them upstairs in one of the extra bedrooms while he met with his clients.

"What's up with Tessa and Erik needing a sitter?"

"Some medical test in Boston."

As he jerked up straighter, his heart raced. Erik had almost lost his wife and baby a few months ago. "Is there something wrong?"

"Yeah."

His mouth dried up, and his lungs stopped. "What?"

"Erik is a worrywart, and his wife is humoring him, so he doesn't lose it. Something about the accident she was in a few months ago and Tessa's condition affecting the development of the baby. She says everything is fine, but I wonder if she's nervous, too. They are a very cute couple. I like Tessa."

"Yeah, she's great." His shoulders relaxed at Gina's words. "It's a good thing. That they found each other. And they have the two kids and now another one on the way."

"Mmm," Gina hummed. "Wonderful."

Holding her here, skin to skin, was pretty wonderful, too. As much as he loved caressing every inch of her body and kissing and making love to her, he had to admit this was damn nice, too.

"Thanks for watching the kids today." Erik dropped a diaper bag on the floor in Alex's foyer as Tessa carried Kiki in. Matty straggled behind, his shoe laces undone.

"I'm happy to do it." Gina held her arms out for the little girl. "I'll take her, if you want to get Matty's laces." Holding her was getting to be addictive.

Once Tessa handed over Kiki, she held her stomach to bend over. Erik stopped her. "I'll do it."

But Alex frowned at the cane his brother held and knelt down quickly. "Let me get those ties for you, Matty."

"Oh, I'm so sorry, I should have just tied them myself." She'd been too busy getting her baby fill.

Tessa grinned. "Don't worry. I know what it's like. When the kids first got here, I rarely put Kiki down. She helps me stay calm when there are people around."

Gina kissed the toddler's head. "I don't mind being around people, but I'm beginning to think I like babies even better."

Alex threw her a curious look, then clapped his brother on the back. "Don't worry about the kids while you're gone. We'll take good care of them."

Erik's face tightened. "It's not these kids I'm worried about."

"We'll be fine." Tessa patted her belly, her face stoic. "The diaper bag should have everything in it you need. Kiki usually takes a nap after lunch. Matty, too, if he's not too worked up."

Erik tousled Matty's hair. "Be good for Uncle Alex and Auntie Gina, okay?"

Auntie Gina? So cool. If only it were true. She held the little girl for her father to kiss and then her mom. Matty got kisses next.

"We should be back by three at the latest. I'm not sure how long these things take. Or how long we'll have to wait. It is Boston. Hopefully, we can beat the rush hour traffic back here."

Alex hugged Tessa and shook Erik's hand. "Drive carefully."

Erik glared at his younger brother. "I know how to drive."

Once they were gone, she hefted Kiki higher on her hip and took Matty's hand. "You can go run off and play with your planner, Felix, if you need to. I've got the kids."

No way she wanted him complaining they were a bother.

Picking up the diaper bag, he walked into the living room

and placed it on the couch. "I took down those wooden blocks from upstairs, Matty. You and Kiki liked playing with them last time you were here."

"I love blocks," Matty squealed. "Kiki, too. Thank you."

Placing the little girl on the floor next to the bag of blocks, she shooed Alex away. "We're all set here."

He glanced around the room and stared at the kids, already digging into the blocks and stacking them. "Okay, if you're sure. I would like to go over my notes and portfolio one more time before the Belfiores get here. Word is they're very picky and have already passed on half a dozen architects."

"We'll be quiet as little mice. Right, kids?"

Matty made a little squeaking noise, which made Kiki laugh. Alex laughed, too, then left the room. This shouldn't be too hard.

After about the four millionth time of stacking the blocks, and Kiki knocking them down, she decided maybe another activity was needed. Digging in the diaper bag, she pulled out some children's books.

"How about a few stories?" Still sitting on the floor, she propped herself up against the couch and pulled Kiki into her lap. Matty settled against her hip. Wow, so sweet. She could get used to this.

"Which book do you want first?" A half dozen books had been stuffed in the bag.

"Kiki's favorite is that one." Matty pointed to a board book with animals on the front. "Read hers first, and then that one is mine." He pointed to one with a popular cartoon character on it.

Her heart melted at the thoughtful boy allowing his sister to have first choice. Could she ever be a good enough parent to raise children like this? Molly Storm would have helpful hints at being a great parent, but it wasn't like she'd be hanging around here long enough to pick up pointers. Staying in Squamscott Falls wasn't something she'd be likely to do, unless she married a local. And since Alex would be with his perfect prize wife, he wouldn't be in the running. Would she ever get over him? There was no denying how she felt, no matter how much she tried.

The animal book wasn't one she needed much concentration for. It had a picture of an animal with the noise that critter made. Both kids took turns oinking and mooing and quacking. She did her own interpretations that had Matty and Kiki giggling with delight.

After a few more books, the front door opened with a stiff knock, and Alex's voice floated toward them.

"Mr. and Mrs. Belfiore. It's wonderful to meet you. Come on into my office. Can I get you a cup of coffee or tea before we start?"

"No, thank you." A deep voice clipped out quickly. "We'd like to see what you have for us."

As the voices drifted away, she scooped up Kiki and tapped Matty on the head. "Let's move into the kitchen, so we don't disturb Uncle Alex with his clients."

Matty touched his forefinger to his lips as they tiptoed from the living room, through the dining room and into the kitchen. Placing Kiki in the high chair Alex had pulled out of the pantry closet, she told Matty to climb on up to a regular chair.

"Uncle Alex made some macaroni and cheese last night, knowing you'd be here today. How about I heat some of that up for both of you?"

Matty nodded vigorously. "We love mac and cheese. Daddy makes it for us real good."

"From the box?" That was how her mother made the dish, when she was allowed to have it. She'd add peas and spinach to it. That had never made it more appetizing.

"No, Daddy say he like it to scratch. He don't let mama do any stuff from boxes either."

"To scratch? Oh, from scratch." Duh, Erik was a chef at a restaurant. Of course, he wouldn't make box food. He and Alex were alike in that respect.

She handed Kiki a plastic baby book to keep her busy while she got the food ready. Matty was easy enough to keep busy. The kid chattered like a magpie. If you asked him a question, he was happy to answer. And answer. And answer.

"What are some things you do at preschool, Matty?"

That would do it. His recitation of what his teacher did, the other kids' names, and what he was learning took the entire lunch time. He still had food on his plate when Kiki was finished eating hers.

"Sounds like school is lots of fun. How about you finish up that good food that Uncle Alex made, and we can maybe play a quick game before I put Kiki in for her nap." No sense mentioning she'd try to put him down, too.

After wetting a face cloth, she made quick work of cleaning up the little girl, then lifted her from her high chair to clean that up, too. Good thing she'd worn jeans and a T-shirt, instead of one of her fancy blouses. Matty's hands were equally in need of washing.

"Okay, now let's see how quiet—" Crap, where was Kiki? The little girl toddled down the hallway toward Alex's office.

"Kiki, no. Come back here," she whisper yelled. No good. Racing after her, she rounded the corner as the toddler squealed. Right in the doorway to the office.

Scooping her up, she apologized. "I'm so sorry. She got away from me when I was wiping Matty up."

The boy strode in behind her, his hands held high to show they were clean. Alex's anxious expression told her she was in trouble. Shit. She'd promised him and screwed up.

"I'm sorry," she said again, backing out of his office into

his meeting room, her chest tight.

"Why, hello there, young man." The client, a gentleman probably a bit older than Molly and Pete Storm, ambled over to Matty, his hand extended.

"Oh, isn't he adorable, Stuart?" The woman also stood and patted Matty on the head. "Such beautiful curls. Our Bobby had curls like that when he was little."

"Are these yours?" Mr. Belfiore asked, waving his hand at her and the children.

"Ah, this is Gina. And these two are my niece and nephew. My brother and his wife had an appointment in Boston today, so we said we'd watch them. I'm sorry, I—"

"No need to apologize, son." Mr. Belfiore shook one of Matty's extended hands. "Children are what keep us young. It's why we wanted our house a certain way. So our children and grandchildren can come visit us and be comfortable."

"Where are you building?" She wasn't sure if Alex wanted her to simply take the kids and leave, but this couple seemed enamored with Kiki and Matty.

Mrs. Belfiore held her hands out to take Kiki. If it would help Alex, she'd give her up. "We have a large lot in Rye across from the ocean. Alex, here, has some good ideas. Would you like to see them?"

Moving in further to the room, she glanced at Alex, who shrugged and tapped the sketches he had on his desk.

"Oh, this is nice. I like how the kitchen opens up to the living room and how the dining room has easy access to the kitchen, yet still has its own cozy nook."

"We liked that, too. Still unsure about the family room off to the side." Mr. Belfiore frowned.

Studying the design, she pictured it in her head. "What if you put the master bedroom on the first floor, over here where the family room is, and use that space to have a family room on the second floor. Then, you could add a large balcony for the family to use that would extend the family room outside. While it's nice to have the ocean view from the master bedroom, if you plan on having the family with you a lot, then they could enjoy the view also."

Mrs. Belfiore's head snapped toward her. "That's brilliant. You've obviously taught your wife a little about designing houses, Mr. Storm. I love that idea. Can you do it?"

Alex's eyebrows knit together, and he bent over the sketches. "I'd have to skim a bit off the bedroom to make space for the walk-in closet and master bath you want, but it should still be a good size room. And as long as no one builds anything across the street, you'd still have a small view of the ocean."

"Perfect. Get it done. When can you have blueprints made up?" Mr. Belfiore picked up Matty and bounced him high, making the boy laugh.

The expression on Alex's face was priceless. Surprise crossed with elation. His smile couldn't get much bigger. "You'd like to hire me to draft this?"

The Belfiores exchanged a look and nodded. "Yes. We've got a contractor ready to start as soon as you get him the drawings."

Pulling his planner across his desk, Alex flipped a few pages, then back again, scribbling on several of them. "I'm in the middle of another huge project, but I should be able to get initial drawings to you within a week or two. Have your contractor contact me, so we can get started with ordering material. Here are a few of my business cards for anyone you feel needs them."

"Give us a few more, dear." Mrs. Belfiore smiled as she kissed Kiki's head. "We have some friends who are looking for someone like you to design a beach home. Maybe your wife would have some fine ideas for them, as well."

Alex's gaze swept her way, then back to his clients as he

finished up the meeting. The couple cooed and chatted with the children for another minute, then left.

As Alex stared at his departing clients, she stepped closer and ran her hand down his arm. "I'm sorry Kiki got away from me."

One of his eyebrows lifted as he regarded her. "You're sorry?"

"Are you mad?" She couldn't read his mood.

"They didn't seem all that interested in my designs until you and the kids crashed the party. They certainly weren't ready to sign me."

So, he was happy they'd burst in? She could go with that. "I guess you owe me big time then, huh? What do I get?"

Leaning in, he kissed her. Softly, gently, sweetly. "Thank you, Dandy. I'll have to show you my appreciation better, once the kids are gone."

Shivers ran through her. Even after almost a month of having sex with Alex, the thought of being with him that way got her worked up. "I'll hold you to it."

"I like any way you hold me. Now, where are we with the kiddos? They've eaten?"

"Yes, Uncle Alex's mac and cheese was almost as good as their Daddy's."

"Almost?" he growled humorously, reaching out crooked fingers toward Matty. "What do you mean almost?" Matty squealed and ran down the hall, his uncle in pursuit.

God, he'd be such a great dad. Shifting the tired girl in her arms, she wondered who the lucky mom would be.

"Felix, I'm going to change Kiki's diaper, then try and put her upstairs for a nap. If you haven't gotten Matty too worked up, you could try getting him to rest, too."

Alex poked his head into the hallway from the dining room, Matty hanging upside down over his shoulder. "Got it."

Upstairs, she changed the diaper, placed Kiki on Alex's bed, and rubbed the girl's back. Her little head kept popping up to make sure she hadn't left.

"I'm still here, sweetie. Are you used to having your mommy here with you? Or maybe you miss being in your crib, safe and sound?" Maybe the child was nervous on the big bed.

Rearranging the pillows, so a few of them formed a border on one side, she rested next to Kiki on the other side, still rubbing her back. Soon, the little girl was asleep, her mouth still vigorously sucking her thumb.

Gina twisted her head at a sound at the door. Alex stood there with a sleepy looking Matty. He lay the child on the other side of the pillows, then placed himself on the edge of the bed, keeping Matty from being near the side. Good thing he had a King-sized bed or they wouldn't all fit. As it was, it was a cozy scene.

Mrs. Belfiore called her Alex's wife, and he hadn't corrected her. Alex had also been in close-the-deal mode and had basically ignored the mistake. Would he ever set them straight, or would he let them continue thinking she and Alex were married?

A soft snore had her chuckling. It was a busy day for Uncle Alex, too. Perhaps, the anxiety of dealing with new exacting clients and the excitement of signing them had taken its toll. She should probably get up and tidy up the kids' toys and wash the dishes. Alex hated having anything sitting in his sink for more than twelve seconds. She'd counted.

But resting here on this bed, with two beautiful children in between her and Alex wasn't something that happened often. It would probably never happen again. And certainly not with children of their own. She might as well enjoy it now.

CHAPTER FOURTEEN

*M*AKE WILD PASSIONATE LOVE TO GINA - ALL DAY LONG

Alex stared at the red capital letters scrawled across his planner. Shaking his head, he grinned. Gina. The woman was too much. Had she done this recently or when she'd scribbled the kiss message for him almost a month ago? Did it really matter?

The question was ... would he follow his planner? He had for the kiss. But that had taken a fifteen-minute slot. This was scratched all the way down the entire day. Could he afford to take a whole day off work?

It was Saturday. Technically, he shouldn't be working, but he'd just signed a new client on Thursday. The BelFiores. Gina had been instrumental in getting him that account. He liked to think his designs had something to do with it, too, but there wasn't a doubt the couple had become more interested once Gina busted in with the kids. Her idea to switch the master bedroom and family room had closed the deal for him. The least he could do was spend some time with her. To thank her.

As he looked out the window, rain pelted the glass and obscured his usually clear view of Gina's house. He was getting used to calling it hers now. Was she even up yet? It was barely eight, and she liked to sleep late on weekends. Heck, she liked to sleep late most days, but often John was showing up early to do some of the renovations. Alex had been making sure she was up and dressed before he came back here for work, because he hated the idea of her wandering around the house in a skimpy tank top and dental floss underwear in front of the man.

The rain definitely put a crimp in the plans he'd had for some of the outdoor work on her house, so why not go over and follow his planner? No reason came to mind. And he had to return the board games she'd brought over on Thursday, when they watched Erik's kids.

Good excuse. Between the planner and his impeccable manners, he had no qualms about spending the day with her.

As he packed up the games, some breakfast supplies, and headed for the back door, Luke wandered into the kitchen, squinting at him.

"Twister? Chutes and Ladders? What's up with those?"

"Gina brought them over the other day, when we watched Matty and Kiki. She'd found them in one of her grandmother's closets."

Luke's eyebrow rose. "And she wants them back? Or are you planning to have a little game of Naked Twister?"

Naked Twister? Was that a thing? Heat rose to his face at the thought of Gina with left foot blue and right hand red. Not a line of thought he should pursue while in his brother's presence.

"Have you played that?"

Luke smirked. "Not since college."

Was he upset or happy he hadn't had the same experiences as Luke? Didn't matter. Maybe he could make up for some of them today.

"I've uh, got some work to do on Gina's house. I'll be there most of the day."

"So if I need you, I'll just pop over?"

What? No. *No.* Not with what he had in mind for the day. His heart raced, and he blurted, "Why would you need me? And you can call first. You know, so you don't have to go out in the rain."

"I can give you a hand with some of the work. Help you out."

Luke hadn't ever offered to help on Gina's house. Why today? "I think I'm all set. I, um, it's not that much. I've got it."

"God, Alex." Luke laughed. "I don't plan on interrupting your day with Gina. I've got my own plans. Maybe not that different from yours. Go. Have fun. Make me proud."

Throwing his brother a look, Alex stalked out of the kitchen and trotted next door. After punching in the code, he let himself in, locked the door behind him, and set the door alarm. If Gina wanted him for the whole day, she'd get him.

In the kitchen, he took out the supplies and started breakfast. Hopefully, the smell of food would wake her up.

Sure enough, as the eggs were ready, and he'd flipped the last pancake, the scuffle of drowsy feet drifted down the back stairs. Surprisingly, Gina had on plaid pajama pants and a sweatshirt with sleeves hanging past her hands. Her hair had its just-woken-up mess of waves hanging in her face. How did she make that look sexy?

"Is that bacon I smell?"

"Yup, and scrambled eggs and pancakes."

"You are beautiful, Felix." Crossing the room, she wrapped her arms around his shoulders and kissed him.

"I could say the same." He glanced at her attire. "This is a different style for you."

"You weren't here to keep me warm last night, so I needed something that covered more of me."

"Sorry. I hadn't seen Josh and Brendan for a few months. It was nice to get together."

"I'm glad you had a good time. Now, what's all this for?" She waved her hand over the table as she sat and reached for a few strips of bacon.

Sitting across from her, he filled his own plate. "I figured you needed some protein to get you through the day."

Her lips pursed and eyes narrowed. "Protein? Why?"

"We've got a busy day, according to my planner." He tried to keep his grin from exploding.

After taking a sip of her tea, she asked, "What does your planner have to do with me?"

"I'm not sure how it got there—" He took his own sip of coffee. "—but apparently, I have to make love to you all day long."

Her head whipped up, and her eyes crinkled as she bit her lip. "Strange."

"It's in red caps, so it must be important."

She lowered her eyes and dug into a pancake. "Yes, important."

They ate in silence, with Gina shooting him glances every now and then. She couldn't keep the excitement from spilling out. She'd been this way playing with Erik's kids, too. Seeing how good she was with children had surprised him, despite knowing she had that playful side to her. But she was a natural. She seemed to know just what to do to keep them occupied and happy. He also couldn't help but notice how much she'd loved cuddling Kiki and accepting hugs from Matty. When Gina had warbled out a kid's song, Matty had gazed at her like she was a princess in a fairy tale. The boy hadn't minded the off-key tune or the mistaken lyrics.

"So, what exactly did you have planned?" Gina licked a drop of maple syrup off her finger.

Taking her hand, he pulled her finger through the sticky substance on her plate, then sucked on it. "Mm, you taste delicious. Don't move."

He grabbed the dishes and utensils and set them in the sink. It killed him not to rinse them off, but Gina's tongue dancing across her lips was a stronger pull. When he returned to the table, she stood, sliding her hands up his torso. Oh, yeah, he liked that. He'd like it even more without the fabric between them.

"This is definitely in the way." Her top fell to the floor, and he inhaled deeply at her luminous body displayed. "I'll never get tired of seeing this."

"Turnabout's fair play." Her husky voice touched something inside him as she ran her hands under his T-shirt and stripped it off.

"You know, I really should be working on the plans for the BelFiores."

"I'll help get you motivated. Later."

Pulling her closer, he devoured her lips as his hands caressed her back, shoulders, waist, breasts. She joined in with her own exploration, and soon he had her on the table, her pajama pants tossed near their shirts. It didn't take long for her to get her hands inside his pants and push them down.

Seeing his Dandelion laid before him brought out that caveman in him again. With her long legs wrapped around his waist, he lowered his mouth and feasted.

AFTER WIPING OFF THE TABLE, Alex tossed the paper towel in

the trash and rested against the counter, watching Gina put the last lunch dish in the dishwasher.

"What's next?"

Hands on her hips, she cocked her head. "It's your planner. You tell me."

"I might need a short reprieve. How about we play cards for a bit?"

Gina's eyes lit up. "I like it. I'll get the deck of cards."

She flounced off into the family room, and he sighed. The woman had inordinate amounts of energy. After they'd christened her kitchen table, they'd taken a shower together to get rid of the sticky syrup they'd somehow gotten on them. It had taken a while for them to get fully clean with all the distractions. Then, they'd spent some time on her computer playing a few games. Surprisingly, they liked many of the same ones. And she knew way more shortcuts than him.

When she'd beaten him to the final goal, she'd taunted him until he'd chased her through the room and up the stairs. They'd never made it all the way to the second floor. Thinking of what they'd done on the stairs had him getting hard again. He shook his head and followed her into the family room, where she sat crossed legged on the carpet.

"Come here, and get ready for me to beat the pants off you."

He sat across from her. "What are we playing?"

Her eyes gleamed, and her lips twitched. "Strip poker."

His head sagged against the couch, but he smiled. Seeing her naked never got old. "Are we using poker chips?"

"Nope, just playing Draw. Whoever has the better hand wins that round."

"Does the winner get to decide what the loser loses?"

Her laugh echoed through the room. "No, we'll be nice. The loser can decide what to take off."

"Is that why you put on a few layers after we finished our shower this morning? You knew we'd be playing this?"

Holding her hand to her chest, she faked an innocent expression. "How could you even think I'd be that devious? It's chilly with the rain today."

"Deal the cards, Dandy."

She did, and he examined his hand. Three hearts, a club, and a diamond. No other pairs or consecutive numbers. He threw down the non-hearts and put the hearts he did have in numerical order.

"You want two?" Gina smiled up at him.

"That's how many I put down, yes."

Gina discarded one card, then dealt him two from the deck. She gave herself the next one on top. Looking at his cards, he attempted to keep his face neutral. Damn, nothing here. Too bad they weren't playing a bluffing game. He might have a chance.

"What do you have?" she asked, chewing her lip.

He let out a disgusting grunt and put his hand on the rug in front of him. "Nothing. King high."

Her body shimmied, and she actually clapped. "I thought for sure you'd get this one. I only have a pair of twos."

"But you only put down one card. What were you hoping for?"

Pointing to her cards, she counted off. "Two, three, four, and five. I was hoping for an Ace or six, but I got another two."

Her cards weren't in numerical order, so he reached over and rearranged them. There.

Her lips twitched. "You know this hand is over, and putting them in order doesn't matter at this point, right?"

"Yeah. Give me the cards so I can shuffle them."

"First, you need to strip something off."

"Fine." He unclipped his watch, slid it off his wrist, and tossed it to the carpet.

Her tongue touched her top lip. "Ooh, I'm getting excited already."

Snatching the cards, he shuffled, then dealt the next hand. He won with three Queens, then sat back as she took off one of her shoes.

Both their shoes and socks followed as they each won and lost the next few rounds. Staring at his lousy cards in this newest deal, he imagined Gina shrugging off her shirt. God, he sure did like her without clothes. You'd think he'd had enough with all they'd done today, but he was realizing she had so much energy and exuberance, it wasn't something he'd tire of quickly.

"Read 'em and weep. A straight." Her cards were from four to eight, but again, she hadn't put them numerically.

Reaching over, he ordered the cards, shaking his head. "Why don't you ever put them in order?"

"I don't need to. Now, off with something."

He started unbuttoning his shirt, and she grinned. Taking his time, he made a show of slipping the buttons through the holes and then slowly shrugged it off his shoulders. Her gaze stayed plastered to his med-section, a tiny smile on her face.

The next hand was his. Gina played with the sleeves of her flannel shirt, which covered a tank top. Too bad she couldn't take off both. Instead, she popped the snap on her jeans. Seriously? The little minx turned away and shimmied the jeans down her legs, giving him the same slow burn he'd just given her. No way he'd complain. It was like his own burlesque show. And she had on the dental floss today. He swallowed hard, clenching his hands into fists to keep from reaching for her.

Once the jeans were off, she tossed them aside and slunk back to the floor. Picking up the cards, she shuffled then dealt. They'd had a few rounds this morning, but her little striptease had started him on his way to being ready again.

The next hand, she lost her outer shirt. Then, his pants. Her tank top. They faced each other in only his briefs and her piece of string.

His phone vibrated. Who the hell was texting him now? Grabbing his phone as Gina shuffled, he swiped the screen. Luke.

— *Playing Naked Twister yet?*—

— *No, cards.*—

— *Strip poker?*—

Alex sent a smiley emoji.

— *I'm so proud. Who's winning?*—

— *Pretty sure we both are. Now go away!*—

— *Send pics.*—

Damn brother. He wanted to tell him to go screw, but most likely he already had or planned to soon. Luke never lacked in that area.

— *You wish.*—

— *I do.*—

"Are you done? This is the final round to see who wins." Gina held up the cards and started to deal.

Alex stared at the mostly nude beauty in front of him. He'd already won. "Sorry. It was Luke."

Gina's mouth twisted to the side. "Did he want to play?"

"I'm sure he'd love it. Not happening." He picked up his cards, plucked two without even looking and tossed them down.

Gina dealt him two more, then herself three and actually rearranged her hand.

He glanced at what he'd thrown down. Two Aces. She fanned her cards and laid them down.

"Four Kings. I win." Her voice was low and sultry.

Standing, he pushed down his briefs, kicked them off,

then yanked her against him. They fell onto the couch, skin to skin.

He brushed his lips against her cheek and whispered, "Nope, this win is mine."

GINA STRETCHED LUXURIOUSLY and tossed the covers aside. Yesterday had been amazing. Alex had actually followed his planner and made love to her all day long. Maybe not every second. They'd needed some time in between to recover, after all. But most of her rooms had now been christened. It was a shame she was selling the house. There were so many excellent memories here. Not only of Nonna, but now with her and Alex.

Maybe she should write in his planner more often. Or should she?

Had he only spent the day with her because of what she'd written in his book? Of course, he'd enjoyed it too, no doubt, but would he have ever thought of that himself, if she hadn't given him the push?

Something in the back of her mind wiggled its way out. Something she didn't want to think about. After all, she'd been the one to suggest a friends-with-benefits relationship. Did she still want that? Or did she want more? The idea that all she was to Alex was a body to have sex with stung. It wasn't enough anymore.

Voices rose up the back stairway from the kitchen as she pulled off the tank top she'd worn to bed last night and headed into the shower. John was here. Alex had mentioned them going over the needed repairs again, especially since the railing on the porch had broken. She didn't mind. Originally, she'd wanted the repairs finished fast, so she could sell the house. Now...she wasn't sure what she wanted, but leaving Alex wasn't high on the list.

After a quick shower, she towel-dried her hair and put on jeans and a denim shirt. Alex was never comfortable with most of what she wore, especially with John in the house. But she'd seen John's admiring gaze follow Sofie when she was here. Alex didn't need to worry. Not that he had any claim on her. Unfortunately.

She found them outside looking at the electric panel.

"Okay, try it again." John had his hand near the box as Alex moved a switch.

Sparks flew, and she squealed, jumping back. "That didn't look good."

Alex and John had retreated, too.

"Hey," Alex said, his lips turning into that grin she loved. "Did we wake you? Sorry."

"No, it was time to get up, anyway. What happened?"

"A couple of fuses blew. John and I were trying to figure out why. Half of the first floor doesn't have power at the moment."

John closed the box and shook his head. "I can do simple electric work, but I'm not an electrician."

"I'll call my dad. He won't be working since it's Sunday, so hopefully he can take a look and get things started again."

"I hate to bother him on his day off." She slipped her hand around Alex's elbow and snuggled into him. He smelled like stability and support.

"He won't mind. I think he mentioned Sara was coming up to discuss wedding plans. I'm guessing he'll jump at the chance to get out of the house."

"Okay. Is my stove working? Can I make a cup of tea?"

John nodded. "The rooms in the front of the house are the ones without power."

"Thanks." She pressed a quick kiss to Alex's cheek and skipped inside to have breakfast.

After tea and toast with strawberry jelly, she wiped down the counters and glanced out the window. Pete Storm was here.

Not wanting to disturb them when they had their hands inside an electrical panel, she wandered to the bathroom on the side of the house and gently lifted the window to hear what they had discovered.

"These wires are a total mess." Pete scowled, examining the box. "Some of them are crossed. I'd checked these myself right before Antonia passed away, and they were fine. How they got this way, I'm not sure, but the way they are now, Gina's lucky the whole box didn't blow and start a fire."

"So, you think someone may have tampered with them?" Alex's mouth tightened into a thin line.

Pete shrugged. "I can't say for sure, but it absolutely wasn't an electrician." He chuckled dryly. "Unless he wanted to burn the house down."

John and Alex shot looks at each other. What the heck was going on? Why did they seem so serious suddenly? The house was old and had problems. They were slowly fixing them.

"Dad, there have been a few other suspicious problems with the house."

"Suspicious? What do you mean?"

Yeah, what did he mean? She hadn't seen anything suspicious.

Alex ran his hand through his hair and glanced around. Gina ducked behind the curtain. She had to hear what he said.

"When I fell off the ladder, it wasn't an accident. The rungs weren't just old, they'd been cut."

John nodded. "Alex and I checked the front porch thoroughly. The railings were solid. But then Gina leaned against them, and they gave way."

"When did this happen? You didn't mention it to me." Pete looked concerned.

"It was the day we worked on the Community Center. Gina ended up with a gash on her side that turned all shades of purple and blue."

John crossed his arms. "When I checked the railing after, the wood wasn't rotten. Someone had done something to it."

"Why would anyone want to damage this house?" Pete scrubbed his hand over his face. "It doesn't make sense. Everyone loved Antonia."

Yeah, they'd loved Nonna, but what about her? Too many memories of strangers glaring at her like she was an exhibit in a museum surfaced. Were these incidents coincidental or was someone trying to tell her something? Like she didn't belong here.

"Have you mentioned this to Kevin?"

Alex cocked his head. "I was thinking about it, though he works out of the Portsmouth Police Department, not Squamscott Falls. Not sure what he could do."

"He could tell you if it's worth reporting."

"I guess you're right, Dad. I'll give him a call. I don't want to worry Gina with all this."

She snorted loudly, not caring who heard. The men looked up. She glared at them, then stomped out of the bathroom. In seconds, Alex burst through the front door.

"Dandy, I—"

Her hands fisted on her hips. "You weren't even going to tell me someone's been sabotaging my house?"

"I didn't want to worry you. Cleaning out your grandmother's things has been hard enough on you." He reached for her shoulders, but she twisted out of his grasp.

"I'm stronger than you think. And maybe if I knew, I could have been more vigilant."

Alex again rested his hands on her shoulders. "I'm sorry, Dandelion. I should have told you, but I … I get a little over-protective where you're concerned."

When he pulled her closer, she didn't object. She actually leaned into his warmth. "Do you think someone's trying to tell me something? Like get out of town?"

Alex laughed, though there wasn't much humor in it. "I can't imagine any reason someone would want to hurt you."

She stroked her hand down his cheek. "But you were the one who got hurt on the ladder."

"I was, but no one could have known I'd be the one to use it next. Maybe until we figure this out, it might be a good idea for you to stay at my place."

"Do you really think I'm in danger?"

He smiled and kissed her on the forehead. "I doubt it, but I've kind of gotten used to having you close by. And this way John can finally start refinishing the molding in your bedroom."

"Okay, but I still need to work on my computer during the day."

"As long as John or I are around, it should be fine. It's probably nothing, and we're being paranoid. But I don't want to take any chances."

She was taking a huge chance, being around Alex so much. Chances were her heart would be broken when she finally had to say goodbye.

CHAPTER FIFTEEN

*G*ina followed Alex and Luke into The Granite Grill
and looked around. It had been a cornerstone of
Squamscott Falls for more years than she'd been
alive, but she'd never been here before. Nonna had always
insisted on making home cooked meals, since Gina's mom
wasn't the type. At this time of night, it was a place for the
young crowd to grab a steak and a beer, and maybe shake
their bootie on the tiny dance floor. The large, open room
was all rough beams and wood tables with a mahogany bar
that ran along the back. Huge windows covered the wall that
looked out at the wide deck for customers in warmer
weather. The Squamscott River rushed alongside.

"Hey, Josh and Brendan are here." Alex pointed across the
room. "Let me introduce you."

"I've met them already." Luke's gaze focused near the bar.
"I'll catch up with you later." He sauntered over to two well-
endowed women sitting on bar stools.

"He's not still seeing Jade, then?"

Alex frowned. "She was a flavor of the week. I think he's

gone through a few other flavors since then. No one lasts long with him."

Thankfully, Alex didn't have the same affliction as his brother. However, once her house was finished, she wouldn't be around long either. Depressing thought.

"Josh, Brendan, this is Gina. Mrs. Mazelli's granddaughter."

"I'm Josh." He shook her hand. He was an inch taller than Alex with short dark hair and complexion. "I think I remember meeting you when we were younger. You used to hang out in the neighborhood in the summers, right?"

"Yeah, my mother used to let me stay with Nonna, then. Were you one of the guys who ran with Alex?" She remembered it used to take him away from her.

"Both Josh and Brendan were on the track team with me. We always had to get in shape in late August, so coach wouldn't get on our case."

Brendan was only a few inches taller than she was, with longer dark hair that curled down to his collar, offsetting his paler skin. What he lacked in height, he made up for in muscle mass. Some women would find his body builder physique attractive, but Alex's trim and lean muscles were more her style.

"I remember you, too, and that Alex never let us talk to you. I always wanted to. Glad he's letting his guard down now." Brendan stepped forward, and instead of simply shaking her hand, he lifted it to his mouth and kissed her knuckles. Like she was a damsel in an old romance novel.

The look on Alex's face was priceless. He didn't like his friend making a move on her. Not that he made any move to keep her here.

"Back off, Romeo. She's here with me tonight."

"I thought you said you were only friends." Brendan kept holding her hand.

Stepping closer, she lowered her voice. "Friends with benefits. Apparently, he doesn't want anyone else benefiting right now."

"Doesn't seem quite fair. You let me know when his benefits end and mine can start."

Splotches of pink rose up Alex's neck and into his cheeks. Putting his arm around her, he pulled her close to his side. "Why don't we get something to drink?"

His gaze swept to Brendan again, and she had the feeling his good manners told him to go and get her drink, but he didn't dare leave her here with his friend. Did he not trust her? Or not trust his friend?

"How about I get the drinks, and you catch up with Josh and Brendan? Sam Adams? Or did you want something else today?" It was his favorite beer, and Alex was always consistent.

"Sam's good. Thanks." He dug for his wallet, but she placed her hand on his arm, stopping him.

"Nonna was loaded, remember? I'll get this round."

As she walked to the bar and waited to catch the bartender's attention, she glanced around the room. Luke was between the two women, who seemed enamored of him, laughing and touching. The door opened, and Greg walked in. When he spotted Alex, he headed in that direction.

"What can I get you?" The bartender asked as she wiped the counter down with a rag.

"A Sam Adams and a glass of cabernet, please."

"They have a local Merlot here that is also excellent." The voice came from behind her. When she turned, the redhead who'd spoken moved over a step and picked up a full glass another bartender had just put on the bar. It was the lady from the store. Alex's ex. The woman tipped her head. "Aren't you…?"

"Alex's neighbor." She filled in. "Gina."

"I'm Kristan, if you didn't remember."

She had, but she wouldn't admit how much she hated that this woman was perfect for Alex.

"Nice to see you again." She could do boring small talk, if she needed to.

Kristan's gaze roamed the room and stopped on Alex. "Are you here with him?"

"We walked down together. You know how protective Alex can be of the fairer sex."

Kristan laughed. It was dainty and soft. "If you'd like to have some girl talk instead of sports, you're welcome to come join us. We all went to high school with Alex." She pointed to a group of women at a high top near the back windows.

The bartender returned with her drinks. She threw her some bills and thanked her. Hmm, chatting with people who knew Alex but weren't related to him. Could be interesting.

"Actually, if you don't mind, I'd love that. Let me give Alex his drink, and I'll come visit for a little while. Thanks"

Strolling back, she greeted Greg as she handed Alex his beer. "I'm going to have a drink with those ladies over there. You can do without me for a bit, right?"

"What? Why?" She could tell when he realized who it was. "Kristan?"

"She invited me, and I could use a little less testosterone at the moment."

The men all looked in that direction, and both Josh and Brendan smirked. Not sure what that was about, but most likely she'd find out soon.

Making her way across the room, the women ahead of her smiled. Was she letting herself in for a beat down of smug opinions and condescension?

"Hello, ladies. Thanks for having me."

"Gina, this is Cara, Hannah, Ashley, and Kelsey. We were all in high school together and still try and get together when we can." Kristan's smile was pleasant and seemed real. She must have already told them who she was, since she didn't explain.

"It's nice to meet you."

They all smiled and greeted her. Nothing fake so far, but maybe they were pros and knew how to hide it. Being one of the accepted crowd hadn't been a usual occurrence to her. And this crew all looked like a combination of Barbie dolls and June Cleaver.

Hannah took a sip of her wine and gave Gina a once over. *Here it comes*. She wasn't good enough for them.

"I love your outfit. You have the perfect figure to wear that kind of a one-piece romper dress. I've tried them before, and my proportions never quite fit."

Heat crawled up her neck at the compliment. Not what she expected. She'd gone for more conventional tonight, though that wasn't saying much, since she typically was highly unconventional. The navy blue, floral pattern dress was short sleeved and buttoned up the front. But it had a culotte bottom that hit mid-thigh. Not too short but still flirty, especially with her three-inch wedge heels.

"Thanks. I've had it for a few years. I'm surprised it still fits, the way Alex has been feeding me."

"You live next door to him, right?" Kelsey asked.

"My grandmother did. She recently passed away. I've been getting her house cleaned up and renovated, so I can sell it. Alex, in all his organizational wisdom, has been helping me. That includes food, luckily."

"He is a great cook, I have to admit." Cara smiled, then sipped her wine. "That's one of the things I miss about dating him. You never went hungry."

"You dated Alex?" Both Kristan and Cara?

Ashley chuckled. "We all dated Alex at some point or another."

Looking around, her heart raced, and her smile tightened. "Really?" What was wrong with these women? They'd had Alex and hadn't held on to him? She knew Kristan had dumped him.

"Yeah." Hannah sighed as she stared across the room at the subject of their conversation. "He's so good looking."

Alex looked over and gave a tight smile, then lifted his chin. Definitely worried what they were chatting about.

"And really nice," Cara added.

Ashley grinned. "And successful at his job."

"But…?" She needed to know what had kept these women from continuing their relationships, even though it certainly benefited her now.

They all sat back, either rolling their eyes or chuckling.

"First date." Kristan cocked her head. "Coffee and a peck on the cheek."

"Check." They answered together.

"Second date." Hannah piped in with this one. "Dinner and a movie. Full mouth kiss, but less than ten seconds."

"No tongue." Kelsey said. They all nodded.

Ashley leaned forward. "Third date. A picnic or something casual."

"We went ice skating, since it was winter." Hannah played with her napkin. "And this kiss lasted at least a minute."

"But not longer, even if you pushed for it."

Gina set down her glass. "Alex is a true gentleman." Even though he hadn't been with her, she felt she needed to defend his actions.

"A little too much so."

"Yeah, and even when we finally had sex…which he didn't even consider until about date twelve—"

"I didn't get sex until our twentieth date. Maybe because my mom was his Chemistry teacher."

"He tried so hard to be textbook, but it lost something in the translation."

"It's not that it was bad, but his repertoire is limited."

"Missionary all the way, even when I tried to encourage something different."

"He wanted to be so tender and considerate of your feelings, but there was no passion."

They took turns talking about their dates and having sex with Alex. And while Gina was usually free and easy when discussing sex, for some reason she didn't like that these women all had carnal knowledge of him. That had never bothered her before. Why now?

"Gina?" Ashley looked curiously at her.

"I'm sorry, what?" Her mind had wandered far from this room.

"We were wondering which date you were on. If you're dating him, that is. Alex can be an excellent friend, too, and easily avoid any of that sexual chemistry stuff, if he wants."

None of the above.

"I would guess we aren't dating, then." She needed a sip of wine. Darn, her glass was almost empty. "Not if those are the criteria."

"Seriously?" Hannah asked. "Because the look he gave Brendan when he kissed your hand was lethal. No nooky between you?"

Her face heated, which was stupid because she'd been talking about sex for more years than she'd been having it. Why was she getting embarrassed now?

"Plenty of sex. But none of the dates you mentioned."

"Wow."

"Really?"

"Are you kidding me?"

Cara raised her glass to the waitress, then moved her finger in a circle in the air. "But still missionary, right? Alex in control?"

She shook her head. "First time, I pushed him in a chair and jumped on." *Lie*, the first time was in a tree house, but these ladies didn't need to know every little detail of her past.

Their eyes opened as wide as their mouths. She decided to have a little fun with them.

"The pantry during Easter dinner, the kitchen table, his couch, the stairs, even his desk."

"Whoa, whoa—" Kristan held up her hands. "—his sacred desk? There's no way. He wouldn't even let me near the thing."

Gina shrugged. "You just have to hit him at the right time. In the right outfit."

That had been amazing. She'd sauntered into his office near closing time, but he was on the phone with what she assumed was a contractor. She'd toed off her shoes, perched against his desk, and proceeded to stroke his crotch with her foot. With her other foot, she'd rolled the chair closer, causing her short skirt to fall across her hips, exposing the fact she was commando.

He'd cleared his throat and stammered, "Uh, something's come up. I'll call you tomorrow."

He'd been up all right. And ready to perform. Of course, he'd sanitized the surface of his desk once they were done. She'd leaned over his shoulder the whole time, making him aware of her presence.

"So, either Alex has changed, big time," Kelsey said. "Or you got a hold of some magical love potion that he's fallen prey to."

Gina only shrugged. She honestly couldn't say what had made Alex take the plunge with her. Perhaps it was the honeysuckle. But she'd never share that with these ladies. They might try and win him back.

"No love potion that I know of. But he's been very attentive in a variety of ways."

"I could have done with the lackluster sex positions, if it weren't for some of his...odd behavior." Cara wrinkled her nose.

Kelsey nodded. "The straw wrappers. Oh, my God. He honestly couldn't sit at a table if I'd crinkled one."

"Yep, he had to press it neatly, then fold exactly in half and then half again."

"Then, half again. And he'd do it with my wrapper, too."

Gina kind of thought it was cute he did this. Did these women seriously ditch Alex because he liked to fold straw wrappers?

"How about the no walking on a crack thing?" Kristan accepted the new drink the waitress had delivered.

"Oh, God, yes. Taking a walk with him on any kind of sidewalk was painful. He tried to do it without you noticing, but if you actually watched his feet, he'd take a smaller step or larger one, so he didn't step in the wrong place."

Gina sampled her wine, then set the glass down. "Step on a crack, and you break your mother's back. Alex loves his mother."

The others chuckled.

"Did you notice he always starts a set of stairs with his right foot?"

"Or that he washes his hands to a count of eight?"

"He does lots of things to a count of eight. Like rubbing your back or wiping the table."

"And if he does something with one hand, like scratch his leg or tap his fingers, he has to do it with the other, too."

"Lining up the salt and pepper shakers, so they are exactly in the middle of the table."

"Straightening pictures that I didn't even realize were crooked."

Gina's head went back and forth like she was watching a ping pong match as she listened to them bullet point Alex's quirks.

"I love to make sure my necklaces have the clasp showing. It actually makes him twitch, and he has to fix them so they're in the back." She fiddled with the long chain she wore. "And when he does, he always cops a feel."

"You sly lady." Kelsey raised her glass.

"All of those quirks are what makes him Alex. I think they're adorable."

Hanna's eyebrows drew together. "After a while, they can drive you crazy. You must not have known him that long."

"I've known him since we were babies. We lived next door to each other until I was six, then hung around together every summer and any other time I visited my grandmother. I'm well aware of his idiosyncrasies."

Ashley held up both hands. "Like his planner. It's unbelievable how much he depends on that thing."

"He can't live without it." Kristan nodded.

"If he deviates from it, he almost has a nervous breakdown."

"Or he has to erase what was there, and rewrite the new activity so it's accurate."

"That's true," Gina admitted. "And he adds something in if it wasn't there. But he follows it to the letter."

She leaned in closer, gazing at all the women. "What you have to understand is how to use that to your advantage. You need to get creative. If you write in it what *you* want to happen…it will happen."

Again, their eyes and mouths opened wide.

～

"WHAT DO you think they're saying about you?"

Alex whipped his head to look at Brendan. "What makes you think they're talking about me? It's probably girl talk."

Josh snorted. "Dude, you dated every one of them. You think they aren't comparing notes."

"You dated all of those women?" Greg eyes him skeptically. "Recently?"

"No, over the last seven or eight years. I went to high school with all of them, and they all still live in town."

"And now Gina's chatting with them." Brendan laughed. "Wish I was a fly on their table."

"Not me." Josh scowled. "I don't want to know about Alex's sex life. Thank you."

Greg cocked his head as he checked out the women. "Have they all...I mean, I know you like to take your time in a relationship. Did you...?"

"Yes." It wasn't so much admitting he'd had sex with all of them, it was the fact they all, except Gina, had dumped him. And Gina would do that as soon as her house was done. No guy wanted to admit chicks didn't hang around long. He been friend zoned too many times. *After* he'd dated them. Which was somehow worse.

"So, they're discussing your manhood and how you measure up." Brendan smirked.

"Why don't we discuss that new gym you opened up instead?" Yup, change the subject to something on Brendan's turf. He loved talking about himself. "I hear you've been getting lots of new members."

Brendan nodded. "I'm pretty pumped about it. I've got three new instructors that I think will bring in even more people. This new chick, Lynn, does meditation and yoga, and her in a yoga outfit alone will get guys lining up around the block."

Greg asked a question about what kind of equipment they

had, but Alex tuned out. His gaze never left Gina chatting with the band of ex-girlfriends. What were they talking about? Every now and then, one of them, or a few of them, would look in his direction and smile. There didn't seem to be any malice in their glance, but there was too much laughing for him to be comfortable.

The waitress made another trip to get them more drinks. That was Gina's third glass of wine. He didn't remember her ever having more than two. Of course, they always had better things to do than drink.

His own beer was still half full. He took a sip and continued eying Gina. God, she was pure poetry. Every movement, every expression on her face, every smile aimed at one of the people she was with. Staring at her had become a favorite pastime.

The ladies across from her raised their heads and focused on something behind her. Rick Scarsdale. What the hell did he want? Stupid question. Maybe he'd put the moves on one of the other women at the table. They were all beautiful and nice.

His hand landed on Gina's shoulder. She turned her megawatt smile toward him, and Alex wanted to run across the room and rip him away.

"Hey, Alex. You with us, buddy?" Josh clapped his shoulder and shook it. "You can take your eyes off her for a minute or two. I don't think she's going to run away."

"You never know." He apologized to his friends and noticed Greg wasn't with them. "Where did my cousin go?"

Brendan shook his head. "He left a few minutes ago to chat with some friends on the deck. He said goodbye to you, but you were too busy staring at your benefits partner."

Rick's hand slipped to Gina's hip and started to inch lower.

"Yeah, okay. I'll see you both later." As he strode away,

they both chuckled. He didn't care. Rick near Gina was not a good thing. The man wanted to fulfill her needs and was getting a little too handsy for his liking. Not happening. Not if he could help it.

"Hey, ladies. How's everyone tonight?" Facing off with Rick, he stepped between him and Gina. "Rick, getting to know the town again, I see. Have you met everyone here?"

He introduced them all. "Cara, Kristan, Hannah, Kelsey, and Ashley. Not sure if you remember them from high school, as they were in my class, but they're all grown up now. Rick Scarsdale, he was a few years ahead of us. He's a lawyer. Quite a catch." Just not for Gina.

The women all greeted him and said hello. Rick's frown showed he was only interested in Gina. Too bad. Not tonight. Not ever. The guy was too sleazy.

"Did you come over for a reason, Felix?" Gina touched his arm. The electric current that always zapped him did so again.

"Felix?" Ashley asked.

Gina shrugged. "We are such an odd couple, aren't we?"

They all laughed, but before anyone could comment further, he took her hand. "I thought you might like to dance. They're playing our song."

At the pulsating beat, she cocked her head and squinted. "If you say so."

Sliding off the stool, she followed him to the small square near the speakers where one other couple was whirling to the beat.

"I thought you hated fast dancing." Her hips started swaying, arms gracefully slicing the air.

Hauling her hips closer, he matched her swaying with his own. Typically, he wasn't comfortable with fast dancing, but for now, he'd wanted Gina away from Rick.

Her eyes turned seductive. "Okay, I can get into this kind

of dancing." The smile she gave him sent his pulse skyrocketing. And not from the movement.

Fortunately, the song ended, and a slow number came on. Her arms wrapped around his neck, and her warm body snuggled next to his.

"See, I planned it this way." He pulled her closer.

"I like your plans."

Her head settled on his shoulder, and he inhaled her sweet scent. The result was a reaction in his pants that probably shouldn't be happening in public. Luckily, Gina blocked anyone else from noticing.

Pressing his lips into her hair, he whispered her name.

"Mmm," she hummed, lost in the slow music.

"What were you and all your new friends talking about?"

Her head tipped up slightly, but she didn't move away. "Did you think you were the topic of conversation? Not everything revolves around you, Felix."

"No, I, um…just wondered what you had in common with all of them." Besides him.

"You were definitely a common denominator. Don't worry. They all think you're handsome and nice."

"Right? That's why every single one of them broke up with me." Not that he'd had deep feelings for any of them, but his pride had certainly been wounded.

Gina ran her hands over his chest and leaned in to kiss his neck. His own hands skimmed up and down her back, finally resting low on her hips.

"I'm actually glad they all broke up with you. If they hadn't, I wouldn't have had the incredible fun I've had with you the past month."

It had been fun. But being with Gina was never anything else. She drove him crazy at times with her impulsivity and unorthodox ways, though he'd gotten used to it and had adapted as best he could. Adaptation wasn't always an easy thing for him to achieve. All his life he'd struggled with it.

For now, he enjoyed holding Gina in his arms, dancing to the rhythm. When another slow song started, more people poured onto the dance floor. It kind of hid them from view, so he lowered his head and nipped at Gina's ear, then pressed kisses along her jaw.

When she tilted her face toward him, her eyes were warm and dreamy, and a purring sound floated from her mouth. Not wanting to miss an opportunity, he pulled her in and kissed her. Her fingers slid through his hair, grasping his head and holding him in place. Right where he wanted to be.

As he was sliding his tongue between her lips, they were bumped from a couple near them. Damn, he'd almost forgotten they were in public. What the hell had come over him? Holding hands was about the most affection he'd ever allowed himself to show when he wasn't somewhere private. Gina made him lose all sense of himself.

When the song ended, he unwrapped Gina's arms from around his neck and led her out to the deck overlooking the river. He needed to cool down. Greg was still there, and his cousins, Sofie and Leah, had joined their brother. John was with them, too.

They spent the next few hours chatting, he and John about Gina's house and a few other community projects they worked on together. The others talked about the doings of family members and general stuff. Gina had yet another drink. He was milking his second beer.

"I'm going to have to carry you home tonight, Dandelion."

Relaxing into him, she gave him a dreamy smile. The damn honeysuckle scent wafted his way.

"I think I'm going to head out." Greg placed his empty beer bottle on their table. "Ryan has an early baseball game tomorrow."

"Did you walk here?" Leah asked. "We did, too. We'll walk back with you."

"Are you ready to go, Dandy? We can walk back with them."

Her impish expression made him chuckle. "Let me use the ladies' room first."

Sofie and Leah went with her. Alex, Greg, and John settled their tab with the waitress. As he turned to wait for the ladies, Kristan walked past and paused near him.

"Congratulations, Alex."

"What for?" Had Gina mentioned his new contracts?

"You finally found her. I'm really happy for you." Her face showed sincerity.

She didn't wait for a reply. Good thing, because he had no idea what to even say to that. No way she was talking about Gina. Kristan knew exactly how precise and organized he was and how much control he needed to be able to cope every day. Gina made him lose all control. That was something he couldn't allow in his life. Not on a permanent basis.

CHAPTER SIXTEEN

*W*here the heck would Alex hide chocolate?

Gina ran her fingers through her disheveled hair and looked around his kitchen. Yeah, it was barely nine in the morning, but her period was due in the next few days, and she had a major case of PMS. She needed chocolate.

It hadn't helped that Friday night she'd spent an hour chatting with a group of Alex's ex-girlfriends. She'd learned maybe more than she wanted to know. It shouldn't bother her that he'd slept with all of them. Apparently, they'd all been in a steady relationship with him at the time. That was the problem. The steady relationship. The one she didn't have. The one maybe she wanted.

Sure, she and Alex had been routinely having sex for over a month, but never during that time had he referred to her as his girlfriend or significant other. And then there was the whole date order thing his exes had talked about.

"Morning, Dandelion." Alex bounded in from the hallway, most likely having been in his office, and refilled his coffee cup. "You're up early."

His glance slid over her, a grin crossing his face at his white button down she wore. It was an older faded one. She'd made sure. The ones he wore for work were in a separate area of his closet.

"I needed chocolate."

His gaze rose in thought, his lips quirked to the side. "Not sure if I have any. There might be a little chocolate ice cream in the freezer, if Luke didn't finish it off."

"How do you not have emergency chocolate?"

He shrugged. "I didn't realize chocolate was medicinal."

"It is." How could he not know this? Leaning against the counter, she crossed her arms and stared at him. After taking a sip, he narrowed his eyes.

"What's the matter? The chocolate? I can get you some on the way back from my meeting." He glanced at his watch, then took another sip of coffee.

"Why haven't you taken me out on a date yet?"

His eyes got smaller. "A date? Didn't we go to the grill on Friday?"

She had to stop herself from rolling her eyes. "Sure, we walked down with your brother, you hung around with your friends, and I got to chat with all your ex-girlfriends. Then, we walked home in a group."

"Um, we danced. And you're the one who decided to sit with Kristan and friends."

"It was better company than listening to sports talk. So, a date? Or am I only good enough as a bed partner? Someone to have sex with?"

Setting his mug on the table, he planted his hands on his hips. "Isn't that what you wanted? You're the one who suggested the friends-with-benefits thing."

"And the benefits are excellent." She sidled closer and played with his tie. His head bent as he inhaled her scent. She did love that habit of his. "Could we just pretend we're dating? You know, for shits and giggles."

"Why are you all of a sudden interested in dating? What did all my exes say?"

"They simply mentioned you have a routine to your dates. First date, coffee and a peck on the cheek. Second date, dinner and a movie."

He lifted his cup and took a sip. "I'm having coffee with you now."

"It's not a date."

"You want to go out on a date to have coffee?" He looked confused.

"Sure, why not?"

He made a face. "Um, first thought…because you don't drink coffee."

Shaking her head, she sighed. "I don't have to drink coffee. I can get tea or hot chocolate or even a glass of water."

"You want me to take you on a date to get a glass of water?"

"Oh, God, Felix, you don't get it, do you?" Maybe she was starting to understand why some of these women broke up with him. "I simply want to spend time with you…on a date."

After glancing at his watch again, he nodded. "Fine, once I get back from my meeting, I'll check my planner, and we can schedule in a time for us to have *coffee*."

"You have to check your planner to have a cup of coffee?"

He looked at her like she'd suggested he take pole dancing lessons. "Yes, I need my planner. You know I put everything in there."

"For work, sure, but this would be after work time. Can you try and be spontaneous for once in your life, Felix? Just forget the planner, and let's have a coffee date."

"If you really need to know when we can go, I'll get my

planner now. I have to leave in a few minutes for my meeting."

Heat rushed through her. Couldn't he think of her before his damn planner? She stomped in front of him and planted her hands on his chest.

"I swear, if you'd don't do something without that damn planner, I will chuck it in the fireplace and burn it."

Alex had the audacity to snort and shake his head. He took her hands and lowered them, then straightened his tie. "I've got to go now. We can deal with this date thing later. I still don't understand the whole reason you need to have coffee out somewhere with me. Especially since you don't even drink the stuff."

As he exited the room, she stood stone still staring at his back. When the front door shut, she let out a massive exhale. That conversation had not gone the way she'd wanted it to. What had she expected? The ladies had been right. Alex lived and breathed by his planner.

Maneuvering down the hallway, she peeked out the window as his car moved sedately down the driveway. Even after fighting, Alex would never think of speeding. Not that he seemed to realize it had been a fight.

In his office, she sat at his desk and twirled around in his chair, attempting to get her frustration out. Her gaze landed on that irritating brown leather planner aligned perfectly on his desk. Growling, she slapped at it so it fell in the trash can under the nearby table. That felt good.

She should probably go back to her house and let him stew when he saw it there. But John was painting her bedroom this morning, and she didn't feel like making small talk with him.

The planner seemed to call to her as she shifted in Alex's chair. Didn't he see he needed to relax more? Be more spontaneous? Fall in love with her and want her in his life forever? Okay that last one was laughable, considering his preoccupation with control and her being a rolling stone. Didn't stop her from hurting when she thought of a future without Alex in it.

Reaching into the trash, she picked up the book and stared. Hating that Alex loved this thing more than her.

ALEX TUGGED his tie off and shoved it in his pocket as he plopped down at his desk. The meeting had gone great, but he always stressed out at these things. The medical building plans were coming along, and there weren't a ton of changes needed. There was still some work to be done, however. Flipping open the folder he'd brought, he took out the small notepad he'd used to jot down the next meeting time and location. He had two weeks to get the changes done and resubmitted. It shouldn't be a problem. If he recalled correctly, his schedule was mostly this project and the Belfiore's blueprints.

Swiveling in the chair, he reached for his planner and froze when it wasn't there. What the heck? It was always either on his desk or on the table to the right of his desk, if he needed the desk for other work. Then, he put it right back on his desk. Spinning again, he glanced across the room. Not that he expected it to be anywhere else, but it wasn't on his desk. And nowhere else that he could see.

His gaze roamed over his desk and the table again, thinking it would appear. It didn't. Standing, he placed his hands on his hips and turned his head left and right again. He peeked under the desk and table in case something, not sure what, had knocked it off. Nothing. His stomach tightened.

"Gina!" He tried not to sound too panicked, but he kept

staring at his desk where his planner was supposed to be. It still wasn't.

"Gina?" Was she even still here or had she gone back to her house? Except John's truck wasn't in the driveway, and he'd told her not to stay there if someone else wasn't with her. Since when did Gina ever listen to reason?

Soft footsteps sounded on the front stairs, and soon she strolled into his meeting room. His old white dress shirt was the only thing she wore. It had been two hours, and she hadn't gotten dressed yet.

"Were you sleeping?" Her face didn't have the typical exuberance, and she was moving slower as well.

"No."

Her expression remained neutral. Strange. He didn't think she had a neutral gear. Usually, she was bouncing all over the place. All over him.

"Do you know where my planner is?"

One slender shoulder lifted, and her face pulled tighter. "Why are you asking me? It's usually attached to your hip." The snark was heavier in that last sentence.

"No, it's always on my desk. Right here." He pointed to the exact spot he kept it. "Or right here on the table. I never take it off my desk."

One eyebrow lifted. "You took it off when we had sex there."

"Yeah, to wipe down the surface, then I put it back exactly here." He jabbed his finger onto the wood. "Have you seen it?"

Something flashed in her eyes, and his chest tightened.

"You don't need it."

Taking a step forward, he leaned toward her threateningly. "Where is it?"

Her eyes narrowed, and her mouth straightened. "I told you I was going to burn it."

Taking a deep breath in, he clenched his hands. "You'd better be joking." Please, let her be joking. He pushed back the thought of what he'd do if it was true.

She shrugged, the large shirt slipping off her shoulder. He couldn't even admire the silky skin. Tremors ran down his arms.

"You don't need it. Why don't you use your phone, Felix? You can put all your plans in there, and it'd be way more efficient."

The temperature in his body increased.

"I can show you how. It's easy."

"I don't want to use my phone. I need to write things down and see it in print. There are too many things that could go wrong with using my phone. It could break, or the battery could die, or it could get infected with a virus. Then, where would I be?"

"Where everyone else in the world is. You'd survive."

His whole body now shook. His heart raced causing him to need more air. Breath in, breath out. In. Out. It wasn't working. The tremors continued.

Stomping into the living room, he stared at the fireplace. Ashes littered the grate. Were those from the fire he'd made the other day or from his book? Gina hadn't followed, so he walked back into his office where she waited against the door jam.

"Where is it?"

She merely shrugged.

He turned to the desk again, hoping and praying the planner would magically be there. It had to be there. Why the hell wasn't it there? Again and again, his gaze skimmed between the desk and the table, then around to the other surfaces of the room. Where the hell was it?

His fingers began to tingle, and he realized he had his

hands clenched so tight he must have been cutting the circulation off.

When he took in another deep breath, he couldn't seem to get enough air in his lungs. *Try again. You need air.* His arm twitched, jolting him back to the present. The present where his planner was missing.

"Are you okay?"

Gina stood next to him, her expression one of concern.

"No, I'm not okay!" His voice boomed across the room, and she flinched. "Everything I do is in that planner. All my business, my appointments, my whole life."

He looked at his desk again, willing the book to be there. It had to be there. It's where it belonged. On his desk.

"I…I don't know how to…do anything. I live by that thing." The air around him thinned, and his head pounded.

"I know. That's why I got rid of it. Your life is not a book."

Got rid of. The words finally made their way inside his mind. As he ran his hands through his hair, sweat trickled down his face and neck. It was gone. It couldn't be. What the heck would he even do?

He somehow turned toward Gina, though his vision was blurry. "That wasn't yours to get rid of. It was mine!" he roared.

She took a step back, but her face remained passive and tight. How could she?

"You had no right even touching that book. No right at all. What the hell am I supposed to do now?"

Moisture filled his eyes, and he started rocking back and forth. Why couldn't he calm down? His breathing grew heavy and fast, and the room started to spin. As he leaned against his desk, Gina touched his arm.

"Alex, I—"

"No, get the hell out of here! I can't believe you did this. I can't. I can't do this. I can't…I can't…I can't…"

Sweat dripped down his back as the shaking grew worse. His fingers rifled through his hair, pulling it. The pain brought him back slightly to the room, but the empty desk only sent him spiraling into panic again.

He had everything written in the planner for the entire year. Everything. He slumped into his chair and rested his head on the desk. His body still rocked back and forth. The ache in his chest grew until nausea attacked, and he felt like he could vomit.

Oh, God, what was happening? He hadn't had an attack like this in a long time. But it wasn't the first time. Why did he get this way? He hated it. Hated how out of control he got when something wasn't where it should be.

"What am I going to do now?" His weak voice sounded pathetic in his ears.

Get a new planner. Sure, but it would take forever to recreate everything that was in there. And he'd forget so much stuff. All his future appointments. All his past ones. But also the mundane and unimportant, things he still needed to remember and have an accounting of.

Pushing himself to his feet, he paced back and forth, staring around the room, mostly at his desk where the planner should sit. It should be right there. It was always there.

As he bent over the bookcase against the wall, trying to get some air in his lungs, his knees almost buckled.

Then, he saw it. The bottom shelf.

Brown leather. Bound. In between a few of his hardcover architecture books.

His knees hit the floor as he grabbed the item, pulling it from the shelf. Oh, God. Yes, His planner. His body liquefied, and he tumbled to the floor, propping himself up against the wall.

As he opened the book, the tension in him released,

227

seeing it was this year's planner, and everything was intact. The tightness in his chest eased, and he covered his eyes with his palms. The book fell to the floor, but he didn't have the strength to pick it up. His whole body still shook, but he could finally breathe. His racing heart slowed yet still pounded harder than it should.

He dug his fingers into his hair as his other hand wrapped around the leather-bound book. It was several minutes, or possibly longer, before he felt control slowly seeping back in. He was wiped. More exhausted than after a five-mile run.

Why had Gina done that? Had she realized he'd go off the deep end? Looking up, he half expected her to still be there, a witness to his madness. He didn't remember her leaving, but then he'd been fairly out of it.

He did remember screaming at her, though. What he'd said he wasn't quite sure. Nothing nice, most likely. But she'd hidden his planner.

Playing back what he could recall from the scene, he slumped further against the wall. She'd said she burnt the book. Although, had she said that or…who knew?

As the room stopped spinning, and his internal organs started working again, he thought of what had happened. God, what a loser. If he'd only given her time, would she have shown him where the planner was? Instead, he'd totally lost his shit and gone postal.

It took a little more time before he could actually get up and walk. When he got to the kitchen, he hoped Gina would be in there, waiting for him to finish with his hissy fit. No such luck. A quick trip upstairs showed she wasn't there. Not that he blamed her for leaving.

Had she gone back to her house? She only had on his shirt, and she'd been barefoot. Or had he been so out of it she had time to change? Looking out the window, he couldn't see any lights on at her place. Of course, the rain obscured any clear vision he had of it.

When he turned to get a rain coat, he froze. Her house keys sat on the kitchen counter. Had she seriously gone home only to be locked out? Why hadn't she come back?

He knew the answer. He'd been an absolute dickhead to her, and Gina had her pride. She'd rather sit in the rain than come back here, where he made her feel she wasn't wanted.

THE RAIN POURED DOWN SOAKING the lightweight cotton of Alex's shirt. Gina pulled it away from her body as she climbed up the front steps of Nonna's house. Her house. Not much longer. After today, she should probably just sell it *as is* and take what she could get. She didn't need the money.

As she reached for the handle, she remembered her keys were sitting on Alex's kitchen table. The blinking light confirmed the security system was on. Did she really want the police showing up to her sitting here with a now see-though shirt and skimpy undies? Maybe she'd left the back door unlocked. Doubtful, since John had been here earlier, and he was as neurotic as Alex about locking up. She could try.

When she got around back, the rain had lightened up some. Didn't matter since the back door was locked, too. Sitting on the top of the picnic table, she let the moisture seep through her, making her more miserable than she'd already been.

Why had she taunted Alex like that? Yeah, she'd never gotten her chocolate, and her hormones were whacking out. But mostly she'd wanted him to lose some of that iron control he always had. To show she was more important than his damn planner. To see her in a different light. Not just the sexy lady who gave him pleasure whenever he needed it.

Something her grandmother had once said came to mind. *Why buy the cow when you can get the milk for free?* Yeah, well, she was certainly giving Alex plenty of milk.

As she tipped her face up to the sky, tears mixed with the rain sprinkling down. She wasn't one for crying, but why the hell not? She was in love with Alexander P. Storm. There wasn't any doubt in her mind. She loved him inconceivably, irrevocably, and without question. She had for years. Why did she taunt herself with his presence when she knew he'd never in a million years fall for someone like her? Not seriously.

She was addicted. To his strength and control. His quirky humor. His loyalty and love for his family. The way he humored her in all her wacky ideas. And most definitely the passionate way he made love to her. *To her*, but he didn't love her. Not the way he wanted to love the woman of his dreams.

Biting her lip to keep it from trembling, she dropped her head into her hands. The tears came fast and hard, her shoulders bobbing up and down. Nonna always said sometimes women just needed a good cry. This one was a doozy. She let herself mourn. The loss of Nonna, and the loss of Alex.

"Dandelion?"

Damn, his voice was haunting her now.

"You'll get sick if you sit out here too long."

Her head whipped around. No ghost. Alex stood behind her, rain dripping down his face as he pulled off his raincoat.

"What are you doing here?"

"Put this on." He slipped his coat over her shoulders and gathered it together near her chin.

"Why bother? I'm already soaked. If I catch pneumonia, I could die a slow and painful death. Or did you want to do it quickly? I think there's a hatchet in the garage. The rain would wash away most of the blood."

Alex's gaze lowered, and he took a deep breath. Was this where he told her to stay out of his life and never darken his door again?

"I'm sorry."

"Wait? What? *You're* sorry? I'm the one who touched your precious planner."

Closing his eyes, he nodded. When he opened them again, she saw pain. "I found it on the shelf."

"Oh, yeah. I didn't really burn it."

"I should have known you wouldn't."

"I tried to tell you—"

"But I yelled at you. I'm sorry."

Reaching out, she placed her hand on his arm. "Felix. I'm sorry, too. I know how important that planner is to you. I guess I just wanted…"

He placed his hand on top of hers. "You wanted?"

"To be as important in your life as that book."

Stepping toward her, he leaned in until their foreheads pressed together. "You are. I'm sure it didn't feel that way with me having a nervous breakdown."

She couldn't debate that.

When he straightened, he cleared his throat. "I wish I could be different. I don't know why I'm like this. Why I have to have things a certain way. Stuff like this…it just…I guess this is why all those ladies you sat with the other day wanted nothing to do with me."

"I want something to do with you." Taking his hand, she drew him closer.

Alex grinned. "That's because you're crazy."

Crazy for him.

"All those ladies wondered where we were in our dating

order. I figured we weren't dating, since we hadn't gone on any of the typical dates you usually have."

He cupped her face and kissed her. She dragged on him, and he knelt on the seat between her legs. As her arms wrapped around his shoulders, the coat slipped off. His gaze darkened with desire as he stared at her wet shirt.

Placing his hands on her chest, she leaned in. "Can we go on a date?"

As his lips skimmed her cheek, then lowered to her neck, he whispered, "For coffee?"

"Mmm, yes for coffee." Her hands unbuttoned the shirt he wore, which was also soaked, clinging to his firm body.

When he eased back slightly, his gaze raked her figure, now exposed through the sheer fabric. "You know, my typical dates don't include me seeing you naked for quite a while."

"Guess that means I wouldn't be seeing you naked for a while either?"

"That's kind of how it works." Her buttons popped open as his hands roamed.

Excitement danced in her veins as she realized where Alex was going with this. Should she remind him they were out in the open in her backyard? It wasn't as if anyone could see them here. Her garage blocked any view from Greg's house, and who would be walking through the woods in the back on a rainy day like today?

"I still want to go on a date with you." His lips gliding down her throat and over her breasts made her heart race and her thighs clench.

A small reluctant moan escaped his mouth, but he eased away. She clamped her legs together, keeping him where he was.

"How about we start dating tomorrow?"

CHAPTER SEVENTEEN

*A*lex climbed the front steps onto Gina's porch. His palms itched, and he wiped them on the legs of his khaki pants. Should he have worn something different for this date? Less Alex and more the bad boy Gina seemed to like?

No. She said she wanted a typical date with him. He did khaki pants and button-down shirts. It's who he was. If she wanted something different, then she needed to look elsewhere.

After ringing the doorbell, he glanced around the neighborhood. Ryan was out riding his bike in the road, while Aunt Luci sat on the porch reading. With only three houses on the street, it was an ideal place for kids. Almost no traffic, and you knew all your neighbors.

Until Gina sold this house. Hopefully, they'd get a nice family in who would love it the way her grandmother had. Why couldn't Gina love it that way, too? Why did that even matter to him?

The door opened, and Gina stood there, biting her lower lip. Was she nervous? Or simply playing the part of first date?

"Hi, hope I'm not too early." She'd spent the last few nights at her house. Only after he or John had checked for any strange anomalies. He'd still made dinner for her, and left her something to eat tonight, since they were only going out for coffee. But each night he'd gone back to his empty bed, while she slept in hers. Prepping for the sexless date she'd begged for.

"Perfect timing. I just cleaned up, and I'm ready to go."

He held out his arm, and after locking her door and setting the alarm, she took it.

"You look pretty tonight." Better get the typical lines rolling, though she did look pretty. He didn't know a time when his Dandelion ever looked bad. Tonight, she wore white capri pants, one of her famous blouses, and wedge sandals.

"Thanks." She smiled his way. "And you look like Alex."

"I am Alex, so I guess that's good."

"It is from where I'm standing."

So maybe she hadn't wanted the bad boy tonight. That helped ease the nerves twisting in his gut. He didn't know why he was anxious. They'd known each other their whole lives.

After escorting her to his car and getting her settled inside, he took his seat, waved to Ryan, and gently maneuvered down the road.

"Where are we going?" Her hair fluttered in the breeze from the open car window, her honeysuckle scent blowing his way.

"I thought it might be nice to go to Portsmouth and grab a cup of coffee somewhere on the harbor."

Her head tilted. "Somewhere? Are you winging it, or did you have a specific place in mind?"

She knew him too well, which was why this whole first date thing was so weird.

"I have a place in mind, but you'll have to wait until we get there to see what it is."

It took some time to find a parking spot, but finally they were walking down Bow Street, Gina's hand tucked into his. Not exactly what he was used to when he touched her. Surprisingly, she wasn't chattering on in her usual manner.

A little squeeze came from her hand as she gazed up at him. "Are you still mad at me for hiding your planner?"

Is that why she'd been so quiet? Should he make her suffer or let her off the hook? He went for the truth.

"I won't lie and say it didn't throw me for a loop, but I have it back, so I guess all is forgiven."

She stopped in her tracks and faced him. "I'm sorry I did that. Between your exes, no chocolate, and major PMS, I was a little emotional."

"Wish I could use PMS as an excuse." He kept the words soft, but she heard them. She lifted her hand to stroke the side of his face. When she leaned in, he leaned back and shook his finger at her.

"Nope, first date rules apply. Come on, it's right in here." He directed her through the door, and her eyes lit up.

"There's ice cream here, too."

Shrugging, he said, "Yeah, some of the coffee-only shops aren't open at night. This one looks out over the water, which I thought would be nice. I hope you don't mind this is an order-at-the-window place."

"I'm happy to be here on a date with you, Alex."

Alex. Did the fact she called him that mean anything? Or was she trying to be like his other typical dates?

They stared at the menu for a few minutes, then he asked what she wanted.

"Can I get a coffee frappe? A little of the coffee and a little of the ice cream."

"You can get anything you want." Since the weather had

turned nice, and the sun was still out, he ordered a frappe, also. When the order was ready, they moved to seats on the deck with the harbor view.

"Right on the other side of that water is Maine."

Finishing a sip, she nodded. "Nonna would take me up to Kittery at times to get me some new clothes for the summer. My mom wasn't much for shopping for little girls."

"Have you spoken to your mom recently? It's Mother's Day this weekend."

Her expression suddenly closed off as she stared at the water. "I sent her a card a few weeks ago to the last address I had on her. Who knows if she ever got it? I told her I was cleaning out Nonna's house, and she should come get anything she wanted. I doubt I'll hear from her. She was never much for material possessions."

Reaching over, he took her hand and squeezed it. Better to get her on another subject. It was stupid to bring up her mother. Worse that the woman didn't appreciate what an unbelievable gift she had in her daughter.

"What brilliant program are you working on now?"

Her face lit up, and she began to tell him about the work she was doing on a new drafting program inspired by what she'd done for him. Words like discrete optimization, algorithms, functions, and structures flowed from her lips like water. He didn't pretend to understand it all, but he loved her excitement.

When she had outlined a few other projects, he filled her in on the medical building and the Belfiore's new beach home. Once their frappes were finished, he took her hand and they walked toward Prescott Park. The sun had set, but twilight still kept the sky light enough for them to see.

Alex told her about the history of the park, and they stood watching the boats bob up and down on the water.

Gina was an avid listener and asked many questions. Some he couldn't answer.

"I'll have to look that up when I get home. Guess I didn't pay as much attention in history class as I should have."

The smile she gave him warmed him to the core, but she shivered. The night had grown chilly with the setting of the sun.

"Are you cold? We should head back to the car."

Without waiting for her answer, he pulled her close to his shoulder and rubbed his hand up and down her arm. She snuggled in closer with a whispered, "Thanks."

The conversation on the way back to Squamscott Falls was light but comfortable. When he pulled into her driveway, she tilted her head in question. He almost always parked his car in his driveway.

"This is a typical first date. I need to drive you home."

"Ah, okay, I am home."

As they walked to her front door, he clasped her hand, sliding his thumb back and forth across her skin.

"Thanks, Gina, for a lovely time."

Her eyes rolled up, and her lips twisted sideways. "I had a great time, too, Alex."

Leaning down, he kissed her gently on the cheek, then stepped back.

A seductive pout formed on her mouth, and she inched forward. "We don't have to end the night here."

"I'm afraid we do. You wanted a first date. This is what I do on a first date." Undeterred, her mischievous eyes and kissable lips were begging him to make an exception in this case. Parts of him were downright demanding.

He touched her cheek.

"How many dates until we can sleep together?" she asked.

Shrugging, he said, "Ten minimum. Sometime more than a dozen."

She took another step closer. When her hands smoothed along his chest, he almost gave in.

"Seriously, Felix? You never got the urge to simply throw caution to the wind and give into passion?"

It nearly killed him, but he gathered her hands and removed them from his chest. "That was never an issue. Throwing caution anywhere isn't my style. No one's ever made me lose control. Except you, Dandelion."

Some strange expression crossed her face, but he couldn't interpret it. Was she happy about that or upset? After blowing him a kiss, she went inside, leaving him standing on her porch alone.

She'd wanted this first date exactly as he typically did, and he'd enjoyed his time with her, no doubt. But, with Gina, he always wanted more. It wasn't about sex, though he liked that with her, too. But the two of them were oil and water, they could never mix right, no matter how much you shook them up. He'd always known this. So why was it suddenly bothering him so much?

～

GINA STEPPED into the back room at the Loaf and Ladle and looked around. White cloths topped half a dozen round tables with peach and sage colored balloons and streamers floating from a vase in the middle. Thirty women in pretty sundresses or dress slacks and blouses sat chatting around the room.

Glancing at her own outfit, she realized her red sleeveless crocheted top and tie-dyed capri leggings with the spike ankle boots stood out in this crowd. Not that she'd ever minded standing out before, but these people were Alex's family and friends. She didn't want to embarrass him. And why did that matter now, when it never had in the past?

For a few minutes, she stood there, not knowing what she should do. Any of the bridal showers she'd gone to in New York had been at bars or in someone's small apartment. She'd also known most of the people there. Here, she felt like an alien. A few of the ladies stared at her like she was one, too.

"Gina, sweetie." Molly Storm rushed over to greet her. "So glad you came. I would have offered to give you a ride, but we had to be here early to get all the decorations up and ready. Here, let me take that gift."

Gina followed Molly to the long table against the back wall, not knowing what else to do.

"Is there an assignment for where we sit?"

Molly smiled. "Sit anywhere you like. Do you know anyone else here?"

Her gaze roamed the room and zeroed in on the cousins and Erik's wife. Of course, they were in the wedding and probably had jobs during the shower.

"Can I help with anything?" she asked, even though it looked as if it was all set up. Presents on one table, food on another, a row of chairs in front of the gifts with the center one decorated in balloons and crepe paper. A shiny tiara sat on the chair. For the bride. The Storms would definitely be traditional.

"Are you seriously offering?" Tessa asked, walking over with Kiki in her arms. "Because I'm supposed to be running this thing, but can't really do that with the baby dynamo here."

Gina reached out taking the toddler. "I'd be happy to keep her occupied."

Molly grinned and tipped her head. "We didn't invite you here to babysit, but between you and me, we should be able to keep her from being underfoot."

"It's no problem. I had a blast when I watched them a few weeks ago. Where's Matty today?"

Tessa rubbed her swollen belly, her other hand on her lower back. "He's with the men doing manly things."

Molly rolled her eyes. "Which means watching sports and eating too much junk food."

Laughing, Gina looked at Tessa again. "And were all the tests from the hospital okay? I know you said the technician thought everything looked fine, but the radiologist still needed to see them."

"Everything's good, and Erik has finally stopped hovering like a mother hen. To a degree. He's still has this whole over-protective thing going on." She bit her lips and glanced down. "I kind of like it, though."

From what Alex had said, Tessa had been raised in a variety of foster homes, some of them not so great. Even though Gina's mom hadn't been super warm and fuzzy, she'd known she was loved. Plus, she'd had Nonna, who had enough love for a few dozen people.

"Well, let me introduce you around, Gina. I'm sure there are people here who also haven't met my lovely grand-daughter yet."

It was beautiful how Molly loved Kiki, regardless of who her biological parents were.

Over the next fifteen minutes, Gina was introduced to people she'd probably wouldn't remember. Mary and Becca, who worked with TJ. Shelbie something and a few other girls who had gone to high school with Sara. Some people Sara had worked with at the library in Portsmouth.

"She's on her way in," Leah, Sara's cousin and one of the bridesmaids, called out.

"Is it a surprise?" Gina settled in a chair next to Molly and her sisters-in-law, Anna and Luci, as well as Alex's grand-mother, who she'd never called anything other than Gram.

"Not really. We had to get her up here somehow, but we'll all put a show on that she didn't know."

The door opened, and Sara walked in, her face alight with pleasure. Her straight blonde hair was tied up in a high ponytail, and she wore a cute sundress like half of the people here. Maybe it was a Storm uniform.

Everyone called out greetings and congratulations. After giving TJ a quick kiss, Sara was steered to the center chair. TJ stood in the doorway, his expression anxious.

"We're all set, boss. You've done your groomly duty. You can skedaddle." The woman who said this waved her hand, and TJ hurried out.

"Who is that?" Gina leaned over and whispered to Molly.

"Darcy. She works with TJ and is one of the bridesmaids. She's quite a character, isn't she?"

She made Gina seem downright normal. Short, black hair was spiked around her head, and she had half a dozen earrings down each ear. Was that a piercing in her nose, too? The dark make-up surrounding her eyes made her already alluring features stand out even more. She wore black tights with combat boots, a black denim skirt, and some stretchy layered top that fell off one tattooed shoulder. No bra. Gina liked this woman already.

Once Sara was crowned with her sash and tiara, Sofie faced the room and announced, "Everyone grab some food. We'll be getting to the gifts shortly."

"Did you want me to take her now?" Molly offered as they all stood.

"I'll keep her while you get your food. I can get something later. Alex fed me a big breakfast this morning."

Shit. Had she just blabbed that she'd slept over last night? To Alex's mother?

Molly's smile was sweet as she headed to get in line for food. Phew. Maybe she hadn't picked up on that slip. Gina and Alex had slipped as well. They'd gone on their second date last night. Dinner and a movie. It had been great, and he had been a perfect gentleman, opening doors for her, pulling out her chair at the restaurant, holding her hand at the theater.

It was the drive home that had messed up the dating order. They'd stopped at a little pull-out in a remote section of the beach to watch the moon over the waves. Peaceful and gorgeous. But the small kiss, that was only supposed to last ten seconds, ended up being a little bit longer. And there had definitely been tongue involved. There had been a lot of other body parts involved as well.

By the time they got home, they were both so frustrated neither of them mentioned the dating protocol for date number two. Alex had practically dragged her into the house and up the stairs. Pretty sure he'd even forgotten to lock the kitchen door. But after a week of not being together, it had been explosive.

As she lay sprawled over him, swirling her fingers in his chest hair, she'd said, "Maybe we shouldn't date, huh?'

Alex had laughed and rolled her over for round two. There had been no complaints from her.

Molly returned with enough food for an army and an extra plate. "I figured Kiki might be hungry, too. Take whatever you want."

Shifting the little girl to her left knee, Gina put a few things on her plate, then held a fork with some quiche to the child's mouth. Soon, she was gobbling up the rest of the food.

"She does love to eat. I think Erik made a good deal of the food, so it's what she's used to."

Erik had come down, and with his brothers, father, and grandfather, planned to take Matty fishing at their cousin Nathaniel's house on the lake. Alex had confessed he really didn't like fishing. He didn't see the point of catching fish and then releasing them. She had to admit it did seem kind of cruel, but men seemed to love it.

Sara got started opening gifts, and Gina watched as towels and sheets and room decorations littered the table that had held wrapped presents.

"Sara doesn't really need much in the way of kitchen supplies, since TJ already has a huge house. But she'd like to redo the guest rooms and the master bedroom. TJ's decor is all very masculine."

Gina grinned. "So he's okay with lots of pink floral prints?"

"I think she's picking neutral colors for bedspreads and curtains." Molly smiled. "But she wanted more wall art and picture frames to really make the place homey."

Leah handed Sara gifts, while Tessa took the card and recorded the gift and giver. Sofie arranged the items back on the table, and Amy picked up the discarded paper. Darcy had taken the job of town crier, announcing what each gift was and who had graciously given it. She seemed to do a little cheer with each one, making it seem like the best gift yet.

The gifts kept coming, and Gina snuggled Kiki on her shoulder. The little girl plopped her thumb in her mouth and began sucking like it was the end of the world. Soon, she was asleep.

Molly glanced over, her eyes sparkling. But why?

"Will you be there tomorrow, Gina? Alex is having everyone over for a Mother's Day barbecue."

"Oh, I wouldn't want to intrude."

"Nonsense. You know we'd love to have you with us. You're like family."

Giving Molly a tight smile, Gina thought about being in this family. What would it have been like having Molly Storm for a mom? Amazing. It would have been amazing. But then Alex would have been her brother, and that wouldn't work either.

The bridal shower was finishing up, with everyone

moving to take a closer look at the gifts and snacking on some more of the food. These people were all so perfect, in manners and dress and looks.

Tessa rolled a stroller over and gently placed Kiki in it. "Thanks so much. That was a huge help."

It was nothing. Gina hadn't realized how much she really loved children until she'd been with Alex's niece and nephew. Made her wonder about having a few of her own. But who would be the daddy?

What if she made some changes? Little things. Actually combing her hair, wearing a bra, matching her top and bottom, not jumping all over people, and being a bit more sedate in public. She'd done pretty well today. Would it make a difference to Alex?

"Molly?"

The petite blonde turned to her with a genuine smile and cocked her head.

"I was wondering... I don't have anything to wear for Sara's wedding. Would you have some time to go shopping with me and help me find something suitable?"

"Oh, sweetie, I'd love to go. The week before the wedding will be a madhouse, but we could go sometime next week, if you have any time free."

"My work schedule is flexible, so whatever works for you."

Molly leaned in and patted her arm. "You're so good for him. Helps him to loosen up."

Well, if Alex could loosen up a bit for her, she could certainly make an effort to change a bit for him.

CHAPTER EIGHTEEN

"*H*ow about this dress?" Molly held up a spaghetti strap dress in magenta with huge yellow flowers on it.

"It's a little bright, isn't it?" They'd headed out early in the morning to the outlets in Kittery, Maine and had already made their way through a few stores.

"Not for you. You can absolutely carry this off. I think it would be lovely against your olive skin tone. The short skirt would show off your amazing legs."

"I guess I was thinking of something a little different than my usual wardrobe."

"Why? Your clothes are adorable, and they fit your style."

Sliding hangers aside, Gina perused the selection. There had to be something here she could wear. "I just thought I should wear something a bit more…low key. Some of what I wear embarrasses Alex, and I don't want that for Sara's wedding."

She wasn't even officially his date for the wedding since he was *in* the wedding. Her invitation had come separately and addressed to only her.

Molly snorted and shook her head. "What does Alex know about clothes? When he was a little boy, I had the hardest time getting him to wear certain clothes. When the weather got warmer in the spring, it would take me almost a month to get him to start wearing shorts. Then, when the fall came, it was the same deal getting him back into pants."

"Not one for change, huh?" That she already knew about him.

"He wouldn't wear anything with a collar. Not a button-down or a polo shirt. It had to be a t-shirt and it had to be plain. One year I managed to get him to wear shirts with a small stripe across the chest but nothing bigger than an inch."

Yeah, she could see a little Alex tightening his jaw and refusing to wear something he didn't like. "He must have gotten over that since he wears button-downs all the time now. Although, he only buys the ones that are super soft." She wouldn't tell Molly how she knew. That's she'd worn a number of his shirts after they'd had sex.

"Oh, it wasn't only shirts. Shoes. Oh, the trouble I had getting him a new pair. He'd go along fine when we went to the shoe store and try them on, but to actually get him to wear the new pair, that was like pulling teeth. Even though his old shoes were too small. Once he got used to something, it was so difficult for him to change."

"I could see that."

"Don't even get me started on the kind of socks I had to get him. Knee high, white with a colored stripe at the top. They actually stopped making them for a while, and I thought he'd go crazy. When I found some in a little boutique store up in North Conway, I bought twenty-five pairs. Cost me a fortune, but I figured they would last him a while, and I wouldn't have to deal with his little breakdowns."

"Has he had those often? Breakdowns? Like getting really upset to the point he can't breathe, and he starts to shake?"

The sad look in Molly's eyes told the answer. "Yes, unfortunately. Did something happen?"

Should she tell her? It wasn't like Molly didn't already know.

"I...uh...misplaced his planner." Only a tiny lie.

Molly's eyes widened. "His planner? Oh, dear."

"Yeah, and he kind of—"

"Lost it? That planner, it's kind of my fault he's so reliant on it."

"How so?" She shuffled a few more dresses along the rack.

"Once he started having more than one teacher in school, it became quite difficult for him. He'd get so agitated and anxious that he'd forget an assignment or do something wrong."

"That would be Alex."

"I encouraged him to write everything down in one spot. We went shopping and bought a planner that had spaces for all his subjects, plus a full month calendar so he could see it all at once. We made sure it was small enough that he could easily carry it in his backpack. It worked really well, and he stopped having so many meltdowns over his school work. He's been dependent on it ever since."

"Dependent. Yeah, that's an understatement."

"One of his early teachers thought he might be on the Spectrum a bit. She never pursued it since, at the time, he was able to access the curriculum. But he truly can't help being the straight-laced, organized, rule-follower that he is. It's his nature."

They shuffled through a few more racks and each picked out some dresses. Gina went into the dressing room to try them on. The ones Molly had chosen were all things she absolutely loved, while her choices were boring and dull but tasteful.

"Let me see the next one." Molly stood outside the room viewing each dress.

Gina pulled at the jacket on the current one and opened the door. "What do you think? It's got a few different colors."

Molly's tight face gave her opinion. "You look lovely in it. You have a figure that does well in almost anything."

Looking in the mirror, Gina turned left and right, then stared at herself straight on. The pale pink pencil skirt ended an inch or two below her knees. The sleeveless top was a soft buttery yellow. It had a white chanel jacket with black trim. The thick black belt accentuated her trim waste.

It was totally something Alex's perfect woman would wear.

"I'd need to get a pair of sensible black pumps to go with this."

Molly cocked her head. "Are you sure about this one, sweetie?"

"Yes." She nodded her head emphatically. "Alex will like this one." No way he'd be embarrassed by this outfit.

"I think Alex likes you in just about anything." Molly's coy smile told her the woman knew all about what they'd been doing. It wasn't a big secret, since his brothers, Greg, and John all knew they'd been bunking out together lately.

Once Gina got redressed, they ambled over to the shoe department and picked out a nice pair of medium heeled black pumps and a small clutch purse in black and white. She'd have to do something with her hair, though. The long, wild waves didn't exactly go with the rest of the prim and proper outfit.

"How about we grab a bit to eat?" Molly suggested, once they'd paid. "All this shopping has made me hungry."

They tucked their purchases into the car, then got a table at a nearby diner. For a while, they chatted about her house and what kind of work still needed to be done.

"I hope you've had time to go out and have fun, too."

"Of course. I went down to the Granite Grill with Alex and Luke last week. Greg, Leah, and Sofie were also there. Saw some of Alex's friends. Met some of Alex's old girlfriends. Did a little dancing."

Molly did a double take. "You met some of Alex's old girlfriends?"

Nodding, she told Molly about meeting Kristan earlier and how she'd been invited to their table. "They were all very nice and perfect for him. I seriously don't understand why he isn't married to one of them."

"I believe most of *them* ended the relationship."

"That's what Alex said. I don't get it. They mentioned his little quirks, and I guess it bothered them." She wouldn't tell Molly how they dissected his lovemaking skills. There weren't any complaints in that area from her direction.

Reaching over, Molly patted her hand. "I think none of them were the right person for him. He just needs time to realize exactly what he wants."

Was she suggesting Alex would want *her*? Doubtful. Especially since she wasn't planning on staying in Squamscott Falls, and she couldn't see Alex ever leaving. That would be a monumental change, and he didn't handle change so well.

But could she stay here? For Alex? Maybe it was impossible for Alex to change. But she could.

"You've got Gina, right?" Alex asked Greg as the guys from the wedding party got ready to leave for the church. Since the ladies had used his house for their prep, Greg had allowed the men to use his. The church was only minutes away.

"Yes, I'll make sure Gina gets to the wedding. But it's on

you to get her home. I have to work tonight. My folks will have Ryan at their place."

"Hopefully, you can enjoy most of the wedding."

Greg nodded. "I won't be there for the last dance, but I'll at least get the dinner and a bit of the fun."

As Alex jumped in his car, a limo pulled up in front of his house. It would be taking the bride and her wedding party to the church. Looking back at Gina's house, he pulled down the street, wishing he could have brought her himself. It wasn't possible with his groomsmen duties.

TJ and his Best Man, Jim, went to the front of the church, while he, Erik, Luke, and Nathaniel hung around the back waiting for guests to arrive. Soon, the crowds showed up, and they took turns escorting them down the aisle.

Erik had just escorted a crew down when the church door opened again. Luke's eyes crinkled, and his lips curled up.

"I think you should take this one."

The elegant woman standing there gazed around the large entryway. Alex threw Luke a questioning look. Was his brother trying to set him up? But when she rotated, he almost tripped on his jaw.

"Gina?" Holy shit. What in the world? "I didn't recognize you at first. Wow."

Her outfit was classy and proper, and her typical unruly waves had been straightened and set in some kind of elegant twist on the back of her head.

"You approve?" Was she nervous he wouldn't? He *had* harped on her clothes a number of times, but that was mostly because he hadn't wanted anyone else to see her in the skimpy outfits.

"You look lovely. Shall we?" He held out his arm.

She grinned and slipped hers through his. "We shall."

As they walked down the aisle, he took notice of others

staring at her. Better fill her dance card now. "Save every dance for me, okay?"

Her head shook softly. "Already promised one to Greg and one to Ryan. You'll have to get in line."

"Here you go." He squeezed her hand as he stopped at the pew. "I'll see you at the reception. I'll have more time for you, then."

"I look forward to it."

He walked to the back of the church and glanced at Gina again. Even her demeanor was subdued today. Not in a depressed or sad way. Just not her usual self. But that was appropriate for a wedding, right?

More guests showed up and were ushered to their seats. Finally, the only ones left were the parents and bridal party. Luke accompanied Celia Munez to her seat as Abe Bannister walked along behind. Alex had wondered what they'd be wearing since their typical was a bit offbeat. Perhaps TJ had asked them to go traditional, as they fit right in with the rest of the crowd. Except for the length of Abe's hair.

Erik walked their mom down the aisle, and once he and Luke got back, they lined up. Luke first with Amy, then Nathaniel with TJ's employee, Darcy. There was a mismatch, if ever he saw one. Even though Darcy wore the pastel dress Sara had picked out, her shoulder tattoo peeked from the silky material, and a dozen earrings sparkled down her ears like jeweled parentheses. The black make-up surrounding her eyes was heavy and configured in fancy curly-cues that stood out from all the other ladies. Nathaniel's body language spoke loud and clear. His cousin was all about appearances, and he wasn't happy to be paired with Darcy.

Alex lined up behind them with Leah on his arm, and Erik escorted Sofie right in front of Tessa, who walked down on her own as Matron of Honor.

Stepping down the aisle, Alex checked out the guests and

how beautiful the church looked all decked out in ribbons and flowers. Gina sat with Greg and Ryan, looking more prim and proper than he'd ever seen her. What in the world had gotten into her?

The Wedding March started and all rose as Sara walked down the aisle on their dad's arm. She looked stunning and so happy it touched his heart. Her gaze was glued to TJ, standing proud and tall waiting for her. The look on TJ's face let Alex know the man worshiped her. Good, one less thing for him to worry about. As Dad kissed Sara's cheek and handed her off to her soon-to-be husband's loving hands, Alex took a quick peek at Gina again. She was gorgeous, but for some reason it didn't feel right. Maybe, once he got her in his arms on the dance floor, she'd be back to normal. Yeah, that was it.

The wedding was exactly what it should be, and after an electrifying kiss between the bride and groom, they all filed out and headed to cars to trek the few streets over to the Inn at the Falls. It was all within walking distance from the house, but with fancy clothes and a timetable, it was necessary. He wanted to grab Gina to come with him, but he'd been elected to get all the guys to the reception.

Pictures were taken, of the wedding party and then the families, so he didn't have a chance to check on Gina at all. He was in both sets, and she wasn't in any. That thought made him sad. She'd been part of their lives for so long, maybe she should be. But as what? A neighbor? His girlfriend? His lover? Once she sold her house, she'd be none of those.

There was more foolishness as they lined up outside the door to be introduced. Like people didn't already know who everyone was. Then, finally they got to eat. He glared at his sister, when he realized he was at the head table and Gina sat elsewhere. Next to Greg. Funny he'd thought of foisting Gina off on Greg when she'd first come back. Now, he hated the thought of his cousin enjoying his Dandelion's company when he was stuck here, being stared at by the entire crowd.

Gina certainly seemed to be having a good time. Smiling, talking, touching Greg's arm as he whispered something in her ear. That would have to stop. Soon.

Alex barely tasted the food and ate as quickly as he could. Once the first dance was over, and he'd done the obligatory dance with his partner, Leah, he scanned the room looking for Gina.

She was across the way, talking to Gram and Aunt Luci, her hands clasped in front of her, her head tilted a bit, showing interest. A hint of a smile brushed her lips. Like a perfectly polite lady. Not that Gina was ever rude, but her excitement often worked her up and bubbled over. The outfit didn't do her justice.

"Hi, Alex, did you enjoy the meal?" Small talk from Gina?

"It was great." He kissed his grandmother's and aunt's cheeks, then leaned in for a kiss from Gina. Her head twisted, so his lips met her cheek, also. Was she embarrassed by him kissing her? He didn't think so. Pretty sure he'd done it a time or two lately in front of the family. Or had he? PDA wasn't something he typically approved of, but Gina had a way of making it happen anyway.

"Do you mind if I steal Gina away for a dance?"

Gram grinned and waved her hand at the dance floor. Taking Gina's hand, he led her to the middle of the room, where people had started to pair up and sway to the music. Luckily, it was a slow number. Fast dancing wasn't his thing, yet if it meant he'd get some time with Gina, he'd suck it up.

Placing her left hand on his shoulder, her right hand reached for his. Hmm, Gina usually wrapped her arms around his neck and snuggled close. What was up with her today? Clasping her hand, he held it near his chest and began to move his feet in his bad imitation of a waltz. She followed along beautifully, but kept some space between their bodies. Had she been taken over by an alien entity? One with Victorian sensibilities?

"The wedding was beautiful, wasn't it?" Gina asked as they swayed to the music. "The weather couldn't have been more perfect."

"It was lovely, and Sara looks radiant. You look great, too. Did you buy this when you went shopping with my mom?" Maybe his mother had helped pick the dress. That might explain things. Though not the inane conversation.

"I did. I'm not sure it was your mom's first choice, but I thought it was perfect for the occasion."

"You look amazing, as always." No way he'd make Gina feel bad about what she was wearing. He'd done it too much in the past and knew it hurt her feelings. Being aware of other's feelings was something on his goals list. And she did look great, just not like the woman he knew.

During the next few slow songs, they chatted on with more small talk. About the wedding and the weather, and again, Alex wondered what had come over her. Not that he minded small talk. He was the king of polite conversation. But with Gina it felt uncomfortable. Unnatural.

Where was his crazy Dandelion? His bohemian wild child? The impetuous, flirty one, not this cardboard cut-out of what she thought a perfect woman would be. What he used to think...until now.

Yeah. Until now. Whoa. Emotions trickled in that started to make him nervous. Serious feelings.

Did Gina think she needed to play the part of his perfect partner? They hadn't made it past the second date in his typical list. Mostly, because he couldn't keep his hands off her. Had she decided she was going to continue with that charade during the wedding?

Alex almost didn't see the point. Even though he was all about being respectable and in control, he wanted to pull Gina closer and nuzzle her neck in the dim lighting of the dance floor. Maybe take her to the coat closet and reenact what they'd done at Easter in the pantry, though it would be more difficult with the longer, straight skirt of this outfit. He wished she'd worn something a little shorter and looser, but women didn't like having their clothing dissed. That he knew.

When the music revved up into a fast number, Gina pulled back. "Excuse me, I need to use the powder room."

He walked her to the edge of the dance floor, then got a beer from the bar. Nathaniel was propped against it, sipping what looked like water.

"Designated driver today?"

His cousin frowned. "No, but I need to be sober, in case Tanner decides to have one of his freak-outs."

They both stared at the little boy playing with Nathaniel's mom, Anna. His cousin's ex had dropped the child off Christmas Eve, stating he was Nathaniel's, even though she'd divorced him thinking she was pregnant with her new husband's kid. The last few months had been more than a bit difficult adjusting to instant fatherhood, especially since the pediatrician thought the child was on the Autism Spectrum.

"How are things going there?"

Nathaniel's lips tightened. "I've gone through three nannies already. Thank God for my mom, but she can't keep coming to my rescue. I need to get a handle on this, but have no idea how to do that."

"Darcy looks like she's getting some good reactions."

In her bridesmaid dress, the dark-haired woman sat on the floor talking to the little boy, who actually seemed like he was acknowledging her.

"Yeah, she does," Nathaniel replied, his voice surprised.

"Maybe she can give me some lessons on how she's managed it. I can't get any kind of positive reaction from him."

"Give it time." Unfortunately, he didn't have any better advice for his cousin.

"Sure. And maybe Gina could give Darcy some lessons on metamorphosis. That's quite a change from her usual style. Did she do that for you?"

At that moment, Gina walked back into the room and scanned the crowd. Her stance and polite smile so opposite of the peppy, sassy sprite he'd always known.

Had she done this for him? He wished he knew.

CHAPTER NINETEEN

$\mathcal{G}$ ina took a deep breath as she entered the reception hall and looked around. People dancing, chatting, laughing, and generally having a great time. Sara and TJ walked around greeting all their guests. Their hands remained tightly locked together as they thanked everyone for coming. In between tables, Sara tipped her head up, and TJ lowered his to sweetly kiss her lips. God, it was beautiful.

In the meantime, Alex kept looking at her as if she had six heads. Oh, his manners had been impeccable, as always, and he'd complimented her appearance a few times, but something had shifted. What the heck had she expected? That'd he'd see her in her June Cleaver costume and fall to his knees, declaring his everlasting love and devotion? Maybe she had. Wished it, anyway.

Most of the guys in the wedding party had loosened their ties, if not removed them entirely, and shucked the coat and rolled up their sleeves. Not Alex. He was still perfectly outfitted in his tuxedo, all done up like he'd been at the beginning of the day.

Her gaze found him across the room at the bar talking to

his cousin, Nathaniel. Suddenly, he looked up and smiled at her. That smile. It could make her give up most anything. Even her eclectic style. She'd certainly tried today.

The music started up another fast song, and Greg appeared at her shoulder.

"Is this our dance?"

A peek at Alex showed him coming their way. No, she couldn't handle another weird interaction right now. Smiling at Greg, she said, "Absolutely."

The beat of the music urged her to really let go, but she still wanted to show Alex she could behave and be worthy of him and his disciplined life. Her hips swayed softly side to side, and her feet did a step-together-step-apart thing she'd seen many of the women doing today. Instead of throwing her arms in the air and twirling around, she kept them moving to the music near her waist. Tame.

"Thank you for giving me a ride here today. I appreciate it." Keep in the polite, well-mannered character she was disguised as today. Not that Greg cared, but Alex was watching them, a scowl on his face. Was he upset she was dancing with someone else, or had she done something to embarrass him again?

"Happy to help out. Don't forget Ryan wanted a dance, too."

"I'll remember. He's such a sweetheart."

"He has the biggest crush on you." Greg grinned, taking her hand and twirling her around.

"If he were only a few years older, I'd be crushing right back."

Greg was such a great guy and single. Why couldn't she have fallen for someone like him instead of Mr. Control himself, Alex Storm? It didn't matter that he had a kid, and he never seemed to mind her mischievous ways and creative wardrobe.

Not today, though. Today, she was dressed to the hilt in proper wedding attire and impeccable manners. More than a few people had commented on her choice of outfit and her hair. Nothing bad, of course. Just that it was different.

The song ended, and Greg pulled her in for a hug. "Thanks. It's almost time for me to head out, but I had to make sure to get my dance in with you. Once I hit up my sisters, then I'll have filled my quota for the night."

What a guy. He'd danced earlier with his mom, both his aunts Molly and Anna, as well as his grandmother. As she glanced around, she saw Alex doing the same thing. This family was so perfect. And she absolutely didn't fit in.

Ryan wandered by, Matty following behind like a puppy, and Gina waved them over.

"When do I get my dance?"

"Um." Ryan looked behind him, unsure.

"We can all do a group dance. Would you like that, Matty?"

The small boy bounced up and down and grabbed her hand as she took Ryan's. They bobbed to the beat in a circle, singing along to the lyrics. Kids were great. Maybe she could have some one day. Would Alex be the dad? Doubtful.

When the music ended, the DJ announced he was taking a break, but there was a special surprise. Celia and Abe, TJ's parents walked to the small stage and picked up microphones.

"My son isn't the only one who can compose music, and Celia and I also have a bit of talent in the singing area—" Everyone laughed. "—so we put together a little song to celebrate the love these two kids have for each other."

Abe picked at a guitar as he and Celia belted out a tune of love and acceptance between two people who came from different worlds. It was meant to describe Sara and TJ, but Gina couldn't help think of her relationship with Alex. Her gaze wandered to him, where he stood with his mom. What was he thinking? About his sister and her new husband? Or did he even see the similarities to their own relationship?

The music sent her thoughts spinning, then thunderous applause echoed through the room as the bride and groom embraced the singers. She'd gotten lost in the song.

"That was nice." Alex's deep voice drifted from behind her. She hadn't noticed him walking across the room.

"It was. I'm so happy for Sara. Glad she found someone like TJ who loves her to distraction. Glad she can look beyond all he's gone through in the past and focus on the future."

"Me, too. They deserve happiness."

Everyone did. But not everyone got it.

For the next hour, she and Alex danced and chatted with his friends and relatives. They nibbled on wedding cake and had some champagne to toast the lovely couple.

All that time, Gina kept her proper persona in place. It wasn't working, however. Alex treated her graciously, but there were no sly touches along her arm or hidden kisses to her neck or ear. No hand creeping along her thigh as they sat next to each other at the table.

The only conclusion she could come to was that Alex truly wasn't interested in her any longer. With all the sex they'd had, maybe Alex had finally gotten her out of his system. Too bad she'd never get him out of hers.

A few people had bugged out early, as had Greg, but there was still a little more time before the reception ended. Alex had volunteered to help get the centerpieces, gifts, and other paraphernalia back to the house, so she'd figured she would stay and help, too. But now, she definitely wasn't in the mood. Acting like a proper lady, in manner and dress, was so damn boring. She could feel herself wilting from keeping the act going all day.

There was no way she'd be able to do this all the time. It seemed to be what Alex wanted, but if they ever managed to get together, the strain of this much control, of trying to be something she wasn't, would be unbearable. One day, she'd see loathing in his eyes, because she was too wacky and wild and had embarrassed him too often. Better to end things now.

Steering him to the hallway, she took one last look his way. Could she pack up her stuff and be gone tonight? Rick had said he'd take care of everything. She should just let him and cut her losses.

"I can't do this anymore, Alex."

His head cocked to the side. "Can't do what?"

She waved her hand between them. "This. Us. Trying to be what you want. I hate it and won't do it anymore."

"Who asked you to? I never said you had to wear a boring dress and act all proper. I never told you to change."

"Didn't you? All the times you'd groan or get mad at something I did. Something out of the ordinary. Something risky for you."

"Seems like I've been doing a lot of risky stuff I normally wouldn't do lately. With you."

"Yeah, and you can't stand it. You've never even mentioned to your family that we've been dating, because basically we aren't. We're only having sex."

His face turned red as his head whipped around, checking to see who was nearby.

"See, you still get concerned that someone will overhear what I'm saying. I can't be your dirty little secret anymore, Alex."

Hands on hips, he frowned. "You're hardly a secret. Pretty sure my brothers have figured out what we've been doing, not to mention anyone else who's been close to us lately."

Sure, because of her behavior and not his. "Right, but

you've still never introduced me as a girlfriend. Or any kind of significant other. Like you're ashamed of me. I thought I could change for you, Alex, but looks like I can't. I know I was the one to suggest it, but I'm tired of being just the girl you have sex with."

His face darkened, and he looked about to respond.

"I was wrong, and you were right," she jumped in. "Friends with benefits doesn't work out. Especially when one of you is in love with the other."

Alex's expression was unreadable as he stood there, stunned.

"I'm going to pack my things and head out tonight. I'll make arrangements with someone to clean out the rest of the house."

"Wait. What?" It was like he'd woken up from a fog. "What do you mean head out tonight? As in, you're going away? Back to New York?"

"Yeah, and this time I won't have any place to come back to, so you'll be rid of me for good."

He shook his head vigorously, his eyes intense. "But I don't want to be rid of you. I don't understand where this is coming from. When have I ever given you that idea?"

"You haven't, Felix, because you're too nice of a guy. But I can't be around you when you finally choose your perfect, proper wife. I want you to be happy, but it would kill me to see you with someone else."

"Gina, I..." He was searching for the right thing to say. She knew this look well.

Shaking her head, she gestured behind him. "I think your mom needs you. Go ahead and finish celebrating with your family. I'll walk home. It's only a few blocks."

Alex turned to look at the reception room, then stared back at her, conflicted. He'd promised to help clean up, and he never broke a promise.

Reaching out, she patted his arm and kissed him on the cheek. "Be happy, Alex."

Pivoting on her sensible heels, she walked out of the hall and outside. After a deep breath, she squeezed her eyes shut to keep the tears at bay. *Don't fall apart now*. Her lip quivered, and her feet started to move. She wouldn't look back to see if Alex followed. When the door behind her didn't open, she knew he hadn't. Why would he? He'd had a few months of fabulous sex…and it had been incredible…but it was time for him to move on. Obviously, he knew it.

Walking quickly towards her house, she let the pain choke her as the tears poured down her face.

～

"Where was Gina going, Alex?"

His mom stood in the doorway of the reception hall, her gaze following Gina out the door.

"Um, I uh…" *should run after her*. But he'd promised to help get everything back to the house. And he couldn't leave Sara's wedding in the middle. Well, it was close to the end, but he was in the wedding party, for cripe's sake. He had to stay until the end. Right? That's the way it was done.

His mother's brows came together as she approached. "Is everything all right?"

She could always read him too well. It had been great when he was a kid and had a hard time explaining his frustration about something. His mom had been his biggest ally, finding solutions to all the challenges he faced or helping him to find them.

"I don't know, Mom. Seems like everything just blew up. I'm not sure exactly what happened."

"Did it have anything to do with why Gina picked out that dress for the wedding today?"

"Why did she?" He stared at his mom, hoping she'd shed some light on the situation. "You went with her. Did she say anything?"

"Only that she didn't want to embarrass you. She cares about your feelings, honey."

She did. She loved him. That's what she'd just said. And had shown it in so many ways, though he'd been too stupid to pick up on it. Even when she wanted to let loose and flout her eccentric ways, she'd always shifted gears and made it seem like she had made the decision to do what he wanted.

Today, she'd made the ultimate sacrifice and turned herself into a perfect clone of all his ex-girlfriends. Oh, God, while he appreciated it, it didn't work for him. Watching her today, all prim and proper, he realized that wasn't what he loved about her.

Love. Yeah, he did love her. How had he missed this until now? What a dumbass. The feelings he had for Gina went back years. Since they'd first made love. He'd been searching for someone to bring him back there, when she was right in front of him all this time.

He'd made her feel she had to change to be accepted and loved by him, yet all this time she had never wanted him to be anything else. His idiosyncrasies had never been a subject of debate with her. Except maybe his planner, but that had been about him giving the freakin' book more importance than her. There had never been a time where she'd complained about his need for structure. She might have teased him, but it had never been anything negative. In her kitchen, she'd said, *"...when you start talking about lists and details, it practically sends me into an orgasm on the spot."* He'd thought she was kidding, but maybe she hadn't been.

Memories of them through the years, as well as the past few months, floated through his mind. The Teen Center. Babysitting. Going with her to the bank. Playing computer games. How well she got along with his family. Sleeping next to her many nights, even if they hadn't had sex.

And the sex…God, that had been the most amazing thing ever. It had never been anything like that with another woman. Never. Not even close. His blood got pumping with her simply sitting next to him watching a movie or eating a meal. His awareness of her was off the charts.

"I'm in love with Gina." There, he'd finally said it, out loud.

"You've always been in love with her, sweetie, ever since you were little." The smile on his mom's face made him nervous.

"You never said anything."

Shrugging, she squeezed his arm. "It wasn't up to me to decide if you wanted her. You're very different. But that's not always a bad thing. They say opposites attract. They also complement each other. You provide what the other doesn't have. Together, you're complete."

Complete. Yes, how had he not seen it? Seen why she was the only one who fit? Suddenly, it all fell into place. Gina completed him. Like a puzzle.

The words she'd said when they'd gone to the jewelry store and looked at engagement rings rang in his head. *It's for the person who owns your soul. The person who makes you so crazy you could never live without them. The missing piece to your puzzle.*

"She's the missing piece to my puzzle."

His mom laughed. "I guess you could put it that way."

His heart dropped and nausea threatened. "But she's leaving. Getting the house ready to sell."

Mom tipped her head. "Is she? When was the last time she mentioned leaving?"

He looked toward the door. "A few minutes ago when we got in that fight. She planned to pack and leave tonight."

A hand touched his arm, bringing him back to the present, where his mother gave him an odd look. "Have you ever asked her to stay?"

What?

"No. Damn it, no. I'm…I'm an idiot. I need to…" His gaze went back to where his sister was saying goodbye to her guests.

"There are enough people here to get everything tidied and back home. You have something more important to do."

"God, I love you, Mom. You're the best."

Then, he ran out the door. She'd gotten a good head start, but he wasn't wearing heels. Running at top speed, he thought about what he'd say when he caught up with her. Would she listen, or had he left it too late?

At the beginning of their street, he finally saw her. Head down, hurrying along in her sensible heels. That's why she'd gotten so far. Her shoes weren't five inches high.

"Gina!"

Her head whipped around, but she didn't slow down. Good thing he ran almost daily. He caught up to her soon and slowed his pace to match hers.

"Gina, look at me."

Her head shook from side to side, and little sniffles wafted his way. She was crying. Shit. This was all his fault.

Reaching for her arm, he managed to stop her retreat. "Gina, I'm sorry. Please, listen to me."

"No, Alex, you have nothing to be sorry about." She pulled out of his grip and kept moving toward the house. "You can't help the way you feel. I'm not mad at you."

As she trudged onto the porch, he stepped in front of her. "You have no idea how I feel."

Her sad eyes nearly killed him. When she pushed him aside to open the door, he had no power against her. He needed to get her to listen to him.

Closing the door softly behind him, he followed her as she climbed up the stairs, her shoes now in her hand. His eyes took in her gorgeous behind as it swayed from side to side in the tight skirt.

Get your head back in the game. You can't lose her.

"I don't want you to change for me, Dandelion. I like the way you are." They paused in the doorway of her bedroom. Her arms crossed over her chest.

"Sure, you say that now, but it'll be a different story once you get sick of having sex with me."

Peeling off her jacket, she took a hanger from the closet and hung it up. Had he begun to rub off on her, or was she still in her perfect partner role?

"Please, Alex, leave me alone. Don't make this any harder. I said goodbye at the wedding. I don't need to rehash this whole thing. It's over, and it'll be easier for me if we don't prolong it any more than we have to."

"It can't be over, Gina. I want you in my life. I love you."

Her eyes widened at his admission. "You love—" Something clattered on the floor above them. They both looked up.

Hauling her in for a quick kiss, he instructed, "Stay here. Let me check this out. Don't go anywhere. And no packing."

When he turned to go, she was right behind him. "You seriously think I'm going to sit here like a scared little rabbit? Dream on, Felix."

"That's the Dandelion I know and love. But seriously, stay."

"Not happening."

She started up the stairs after him. At the third floor, they paused and listened. The turret room.

"Why don't you go back down and be ready to call the police?" he whispered.

Her lips turned down, and her eyes narrowed. "It's probably a squirrel who found a way in. We can handle it."

The door was ajar, and Alex eased it open. Dim light filtered through the crack, and he shoved Gina behind him as he saw what was there.

"Alex, what's going on?" Her hands pushed at his back, and he sidestepped to keep her away.

While he forced her back, she looped around, tussling with him.

"Gina, get out of here. Go!"

Her face tightened as she gaped behind him. "Mr. Gramercy, Mr. Hofstetter? What the heck are you doing in my attic?"

The men spun around, fear and anger in their gaze. Alex gave Gina another push.

"Go!"

"Alex!" Her eyes went wide. Pain exploded through his skull and everything went black.

CHAPTER TWENTY

"*A*lex!" Gina screamed as Rick Scarsdale appeared from behind a large dresser and hit him on the back of the head with a long piece of wood. Alex's body jerked, and he slipped to the floor.

"Alex." *Oh, God, let him be all right.* She lunged toward him but arms wrapped around her from behind and tore her away.

"Let me go, you big jerk. I have to see if he's okay."

"I don't care if he's okay," Rick growled in her ear. "You shouldn't have come up here."

Clif Gramercy's gaze searched the room, then fell to Alex lying still on the floor. "You weren't supposed to be back for another hour or so. The whole damn street was supposed to be at that wedding. We would have been out of here by then."

"Except we haven't found what we need yet." Hofstetter continued to dig through the boxes piled against the wall.

"What are you doing here? What are you looking for?" As she struggled against Rick's grip, she glanced at Alex again. Eyes closed, unmoving. Was that blood by his head? *Please let him be okay. Please.*

Rick was strong. He dragged her, fighting and kicking, across the room and threw her against a tall trunk, so she lay flat over the top. His erection pressed against her back. Alex had been right about him being a sleaze. The guy got turned on by hurting people. Her heart raced as she struggled against his hold.

"You need to shut up and let us think." Rick pulled a scarf from a nearby bag and wrapped it tight around her hands. This wasn't good. What the hell were they doing here? And how could she help Alex?

Alex, who only minutes before said he loved her. Had he meant it, or was he only trying to keep her from leaving? It didn't matter now, since it didn't look like she was going anywhere. How did she get these men to take off and leave her to care for Alex?

"Whatever you want, take it and go." Her damn voice trembled. Where was that fearless woman who would try anything?

"I know what I want." Rick wiggled against her again, letting her know exactly what he meant. "Something you've been denying me since I asked."

Rick's fingers touched her knee and crawled up her leg. She struggled harder, but he only pressed her further into the trunk, his body at her back.

"Stop it, you pervert. Leave me alone." His weight cut off her air supply, making her lightheaded.

"Cut it out, Scarsdale," Hofstetter snapped, tossing items across the room as he searched. "We need to find the stuff."

"I'm finding plenty right here." Rick's left hand slid up her other leg. "If we can't locate the bonds, I'm taking it out of her hide."

"That's enough." Gramercy shoved Rick. He wasn't on top of her anymore. "Help us look."

Gina fell to the floor and crawled toward Alex, her nerves twitching with anxiety.

"Sure, as soon as I make sure she won't run away."

Pulling her up, Rick tossed her toward a wooden chair and yanked her hands behind her back, retying the scarf to the slats. The fabric cut into her wrists as she resisted. Before he joined the others, he reached around her from behind and fondled her chest.

"Pig." She struggled harder.

Rick grabbed her chin and bent down in front of her. "Oh, baby, you'll be singing a different tune, once I can fully concentrate on you."

"Where are they?" Hofstetter yelled, throwing one of her grandfather's text books across the room. "She must know. She brought one of the pieces into the store to be appraised."

"Jewelry? You're looking for the jewelry that was up here?"

"Yes, where is it?" Gramercy stepped closer, his shoulders stiff and tense.

"I thought you said it was fake." Think. How could she get these men to leave her alone so she could help Alex?

"I wasn't about to tell you it was worth a small fortune. Or that it was stolen."

"Why would you steal jewelry? You own a jewelry store."

Hofstetter glared at her. "My profit on the jewels is considerably less than I'd like it to be, so I faked the theft and collected the insurance money. Now, I can sell the real jewels and have a nice little retirement. On a tropical island."

Her heart pounded like thunder. Could she stall long enough for Luke to get back? Would he even notice what was going on next door? These men obviously hadn't parked on the street, and he probably thought she and Alex were making up after their fight and leave them alone. Oh, God.

Gina labored to keep her breaths even. "How did you even get in here? I had an expensive alarm system installed."

Rick dug clothes out of a bag. "I did some electrical work in high school and college. It took a while, but I managed."

"It would have been easier on you if you'd simply used the people I recommended to clean out your house." Gramercy scowled. "We could have gotten the jewels and bonds and left you alone."

As she wiggled her hands attempting to loosen them, she tried to keep them occupied.

"Bonds, too? Where did they come from?"

"The bank, of course. That string of robberies last fall after your grandmother died."

"You did it? How do Rick and this house fit in?"

Rick puffed out his chest. "I'm the lawyer for both of them, as well as your grandmother. I've got all sorts of information available to me. When Gramercy and Hoffstetter found themselves in dire straits, I simply suggested a little subterfuge. Since I knew this house would be sitting empty until all the legal stuff was finalized, it seemed fitting to hide the stash here, until it wasn't so hot anymore." He was actually bragging at how clever he was.

He turned toward her and scowled. "I never expected you to personally clean the place out and stay here as long as you have."

She glared at him. "You know if you leave right now, no one will know you were here. You could take the money you got from the insurance and leave the country."

Hofstetter folded his arms over his chest. "Hardly enough for us to share. That's why we need the jewels and bonds. Now, where are they?"

"I don't know. Please, just leave, and I won't tell anyone you were here."

"Do you really think we're that dumb?" Rick crouched down in front of her, his hands traveling up her legs again. Her stomach revolted. Maybe she'd puke on him.

"You brought one to Hofstetter's. You know where the jewels are. Maybe you need a little motivation to tell us."

Rick raised his hand, and she braced for impact.

"No," Gramercy yelled. "Let's try something else." He moved over to Alex and kicked hard at his side.

A groan erupted form Alex's mouth. He was alive. But for how long? Rick smirked and joined the banker, letting his foot fly. "We can certainly hurt him plenty. Tell us where the jewels are."

Rick aimed another kick into Alex's stomach, flipping him over onto his back. Another moan drifted her way.

"Stop, please!"

Tears rolled down her cheeks as a black hole opened up inside her chest. *Alex.* "Don't hurt him. I'll tell you."

"Where?" Hofstetter stalked over to her.

Should she tell them they were all in the closet in her bedroom? Or somewhere else, so they'd get out of here fast?

Sweat trickled down her back. "I put them in Nonna's safe deposit box at the bank."

Rick glared at Gramercy. "They were there all this time, and you could have gotten them."

The banker hissed back. "I can't get into someone's box unless I have a key. Where's the key?"

Nonna's box had nothing in it. Everything had been removed months ago. "My purse, down by the front door. Take it and go." That should buy her some time.

Hofstetter pointed at Rick. "Go, get her purse and check while we deal with him." The jeweler stared at Alex.

Once Rick ran out of the room, the two other men dragged Alex across the floor and set him by the wall.

"What are you going to do?" Her hands still struggled against the scarf, but it wasn't any looser.

"Tie him to the wall, so he can't go running to the cops when we leave...if he wakes up." Gramercy's smile was evil. How had she not picked up on that when she'd first met him?

They ripped an old pair of slacks and used the torn fabric to tie Alex's hand to the metal radiator. They were finishing up when Rick ran back in, out of breath, holding up her key ring.

He tossed them to Gramercy and stalked over to Alex. He kicked him again, laughing as he did. Bastard. Her stomach tightened at the damage they'd done to the man she loved.

"Which one is it?" Hofstetter hovered nearby, anxiety written all over his face.

"Right here. Box 427," Gramercy said. "I might be able to get in there tonight with a good enough excuse to the security guard. But you'd both better be ready to get out of town by morning, in case this goes belly up."

"Great." Hofstetter scurried about piling boxes and covering them with bags of old clothes. "Help me set things up. We need to get rid of any evidence. A great big fire should do it."

Tremors infiltrated Gina's entire body, and she couldn't breathe. Was she evidence? More likely a witness. These were business men from this small community. Certainly, they wouldn't kill her. But they'd injured Alex and committed robbery. Why not murder?

"You don't need to burn my house and kill us. If you leave now, you can get away, and it will only be robbery."

"True." Gramercy cocked his head. "But if you go up with the house, no one will even know we were involved, and we won't have law enforcement after us."

"You don't think they'll notice we were tied up?"

Gramercy shrugged. "The fabric should burn up, so there

won't be anything but ash. They'll think the fire started because of all this junk."

"We tried to warn you away nicely." Rick sneered at her. "The ladder, the porch railing, even the electrical malfunction. You should have taken the hint that you weren't wanted here and left it all for me to take care of. Then, you'd have the money from the sale of the house and still be alive."

All three of them pulled out lighters and set the flame to some of the fabric. The flames caught the old fabric, then started on the books under it. Shit, how would she get out of this now? And what about Alex? Perhaps being unconscious was better, so he wasn't aware of burning alive. The shaking grew worse, her heart about to pound out of her chest.

The banker and jeweler took one last look, then started down the stairs. Rick stood in front of her, grinning.

"It's too bad you didn't take me up on my offer. None of this would have happened. And let me tell you, you would have enjoyed it."

Leaning down, he grabbed her chin and kissed her. When he attempted to stick his tongue in her mouth, she bit it. Rearing back, he hauled off and slapped her. The sting on her cheek was nothing compared to the pain of seeing Alex out cold on the floor, knowing they might not make it out of here.

With the smoke circling the room, Rick laughed and ran down the stairs. His footsteps echoed back, and Gina's eyes watered. The heat from the flames smothered her. She pushed with her feet to scoot the chair away from the fire and closer to Alex.

"Alex! Alex! You need to wake up." Coughs racked her frame as she inhaled the thickening smoke. Seriously, how could this be happening? One minute Alex was declaring his love and the next they're both about to die. Life wasn't fair.

≈

A BASS DRUM pounded in Alex's head as loud as an entire marching band. Holy hell. As he attempted to hold his head, his hands stopped their journey. They were stuck together. The place reeked of smoke, and something crackled nearby.

When he pried his eyes open, they began to burn. Smoke filled the room, and his vision watered. Red and orange flames licked the curtains surrounding the windows, as well as several stacks of boxes. By the looks of them, they'd been on fire for a while now. How did his hands get tied together? What was he tied to? What had happened? The last thing he remembered was…turning his back on Gramercy and Hofstetter. What the fuck had they been doing in Gina's attic?

Gina? Another cough racked his body, the smoke filling his lungs with every breath. Squinting through the thick air, he focused on the room. Sweat poured down his back.

As he shifted to get a better position, pain shot through his abdomen. The room spun. *God, don't let me black out now.* He had to find Gina.

A weak cough drifted toward him, and he aimed his gaze in that direction. Gina was slumped in a chair in the middle of the room. Her arms were bent backward at a weird angle, almost like they were…tied together behind her. Shit.

"Gina." His raspy voice barely made any noise. "Gina."

She stirred but didn't lift her head. Flames roared nearby, and chills broke out on his skin, his heart racing in his chest. Would he have to sit here and watch the woman he loved be consumed by fire?

Pulling against the bonds that held his hands, he lowered his mouth to the fabric, attempting to get the knot undone. It gave a bit, but he still couldn't get his hands out. Trying again, he tugged on the knot with his teeth, coughs interrupting his attempts. Each cough sent daggers of pain through his torso. After a few more tries, the fabric loosened. Again and again he tore at the tether, and finally his hands wiggled enough to come free.

Nausea swelled in him as the room tilted, and agony lanced through his midsection. How had that happened? He thought he'd been hit on the head.

Crawling across the floor where the smoke was thinner, he managed to get to Gina. As he'd thought, her hands were tied behind her back and to the rungs of the chair. With his eyes watering, his fingers slipped, and it took several attempts before he got the fabric undone. The heat had ramped up. It slammed into them in waves, making the room undulate.

"Gina, sweetie, wake up." He pulled her down near him. The towering dresser doused in flames began to topple, and he dragged her away just as it fell. It missed them by a few inches, but the cinders flew onto their clothes. Alex brushed them away before they could burn through.

As he pulled her to the door, he scanned her body, searching for any sign she was still with him. But he wasn't a damn doctor. How could he tell?

Wrapping his arms around her, he grabbed the railing and hauled himself up. Pain ripped through his middle, and his legs gave way. *Push past it. You need to get out of here. Need to save Gina.* Finally, he managed to get vertical and slowly took the steps down, Gina dead weight in his arms.

On the third-floor landing, he rested against the wall to catch his breath, but the smoke had already infiltrated this area, too. How much time did he have before flames engulfed the whole house?

He shifted Gina in his arms again and crept toward the

next set of stairs. The pounding in his head had him seeing stars that wavered in and out. She was such a tiny thing, yet he could barely keep her aloft. Leaning against the side of the staircase, he inched down, feeling for each step.

A loud crash from upstairs echoed through the hallway, shocking him in his concentration. Shit, he needed to get going. When he glanced up, flames licked the top of the stairs. They were moving faster than he was.

His feet plodded down the hallway, past the room he and Gina had made love in so many times. Love. Truly had made love. If she wasn't okay, he didn't know what he'd do. She'd been a part of his life for so long, and he hadn't even been aware of how important her role was.

Last set of stairs. He could do this. But then the walls decided to spin, and darkness closed in. He couldn't pass out now. Taking in a deep breath only caused more coughs to rack his body. He stumbled down the first few steps, and his legs gave out. His ass bumped down a few more before he grabbed the railing and huddled against the side, Gina precariously shifting in his arms. He wouldn't let go.

More coughs and this time a copper taste assaulted his mouth. The front of his shirt was splattered with blood. Shit. Definitely not good. Probably the cause of the pain ripping through him. But Gina hadn't moved or whimpered since he'd untied her. That fear was far worse than any he had for himself.

His head drifted back, and he shook himself as sirens wailed in the distance. Had he fallen asleep sitting here? More likely passed out. But he only had half a set of stairs to go, and he'd be within feet of the front door.

Holding Gina closer, he struggled to his feet, pain burning in his gut. His desire to get her help spurred him on. Red lights flashed through the open front door as he finally stumbled through. Several firefighters in full gear crossed the lawn.

"Help her!" His knees gave out again as he crossed the porch. Two men rushed up and pulled Gina from his arms, taking her over to the lawn. Several more moved past with a large hose.

"Alex!" Greg stood in front of him with full gear. He helped him to his feet and almost carried him down the stairs. "Where are you hurt?"

Shaking his head made the marching band start up again, so he waved his hand toward the woman he loved. "Gina. You need to help her. Please."

Greg looked torn, but when Alex managed a few steps and leaned against the lamppost, his cousin jumped in with the other paramedic working on Gina.

"She's not breathing," the man said, looking to Greg. "No pulse."

No! Alex's lungs dried up, and his heart may have stopped. She had to be okay. He clung to the lamppost as if Gina's life depended on it.

Within seconds, Greg had his hands pumping up and down on her chest, while the other man pulled open a metal box and rifled through supplies.

Damn it, save her. She couldn't die. She was the only woman who could handle him. Deal with him. Love him. He needed her.

Agony consumed him, though from fear for Gina or his injuries, he didn't know.

"Sir, do you know how the fire started?" A police officer stood by him.

"Hofstetter. Gramercy." The world started to spin again. "The bank."

The man's eyes widened, and he stepped away to talk into his radio.

Greg still worked on Gina, and Alex felt his world slipping away.

"Save her. Please."

As he whispered her name, darkness edged his vision and closed in, surrounding him.

CHAPTER TWENTY-ONE

*S*he couldn't breathe. Tightness in her throat choked her. Panic welled up, and Gina struggled to get out of the fog she found herself in. Her head pounded, and something was suffocating her. Where was she?

Her attic. The fire. Rick hitting her before he ran out the door, leaving her alone. Alex. She needed to get Alex out of the fire and smoke.

"Settle down, Ms. Mazelli." A soothing voice tickled her ear. "You've got an ET tube in to help you breathe. But you're safe. You aren't in the fire any longer. You're in the hospital, and you're safe."

Safe. She was safe. But what about Alex?

As she tried to speak, her tongue felt an obstruction in her throat and mouth. Her stomach muscles clenched trying to expel the object. As she reached for it, someone took hold of her hand.

"No, you need to leave that in until the doctor gets here to make sure you're breathing well enough on your own."

Her eyes refused to open, but she needed to see what was going on.

"Can't you help her?" That soft voice sounded familiar. Who was here with her?

"I can't take out the tube until we know she's breathing on her own, and the doctor checks her O2 blood saturation levels. He'll be here soon. We may need to sedate her again, if they aren't high enough."

"What have we got?" A deeper voice chimed in to the discussion, and Gina willed her eyes to open. The female voice was talking medical stuff again. Numbers and levels. Whatever the hell they meant.

She needed to find out about Alex.

"Ms. Mazelli? Gina? We're going to be taking your tube out now. You'll feel a bit of discomfort until we get it out."

Someone took her hand as the thing blocking her throat started to move. God, what the…

Her throat revolted, and she started coughing and gagging, something slimy dripping down her chin. Finally, it was out and she still couldn't breathe. The slimy stuff filled her mouth and dribbled out as she coughed.

"Why can't she breathe on her own now?" That soft voice again.

"Coughing and gagging are a natural reflex after being in all that smoke, and the mucus is a normal reaction to the intrusion."

The hand holding hers tightened, and she squeezed back. One more time, she willed her eyes to open and managed a slit. Dark brown waves cascaded down the back of the woman seated next to her. Then she turned around. Tessa.

"Tess—" the name was interrupted by more coughing and gagging. Gripping the hand, she pulled slightly.

The nurse thrust a spit basin under her chin and stood by with a towel. "You may need this for a while."

Tessa took over holding the basin and pushed the hair back from her face. "Gina, it's okay. You're breathing on your own now." Her voice, so calm and comforting. No wonder she was such a great mom.

But her foggy mind knew there was something else she needed to think about. Alex. What had happened to Alex?

"Alex?" Nothing came out but a choked sound. When she tried to sit up, her ribs ached, and she flopped back down.

"I'm Dr. Pierce. You got quite a bit of smoke in your lungs, Ms. Mazelli. Your throat will be sore for a while until it heals. Luckily, the inside of your lungs weren't too badly damaged. Often, you can get serious burns."

She moved her hand to her sternum and patted, letting out a moan.

"Yes, you've got some severe bruising on your ribs from the CPR. That's an unfortunate side effect, but it's better than the alternative. You weren't breathing when you were brought out of the fire."

"Alex?" she repeated, this time a raspy whisper managed to come out.

Her gaze turned to Tessa, who sat biting her lip, attempting to look anywhere but at her. No, he couldn't be gone. You didn't tell someone you loved them and then die. This wasn't a damn Shakespearean tragedy.

Again, she struggled to sit up, but the nurse shook her head and tapped her shoulders.

"You'll pull out your IV. You need to rest. You've been through quite an ordeal."

"Where's Alex?" She stared at Tessa, who leaned in close and stroked her hair.

"He's having a CT scan right now."

CT Scan. That meant he was alive, at least. Sagging against the bed, she closed her eyes, tears leaking through the lids.

After a moment to compose herself, she opened her eyes

again. Her voice was no louder than a whisper. "Scan? What?"

She could guess at the answer. He'd been hit over the head and kicked in the gut a few times.

"I don't know all the details. Something about internal bleeding. The rest of the family is in the waiting room."

"You're here?" Tessa wasn't her family, so why was she here?

"Everyone was worried about you, too, but here in ICU, only one family member is allowed." At this, Tessa checked that the nurse was near the door discussing something with the doctor, then winked at her. "Being your sister-in-law, I was allowed to stay with you."

Gina squeezed Tessa's hand, her lower lip wobbling. Would that ever come true? Would Alex get better and tell her he loved her again?

The doctor came back over and listened to her chest, then checked her pupils. "We'll be keeping you on oxygen for a while, but no tube, so it will be much more comfortable. You should refrain from talking as your throat and lungs need some time to heal. I'll allow your sister-in-law to remain here with you, as long as you rest and don't get too worked up. The police would also like a statement from you, but I told them that would have to wait a while."

Tessa stood. "Thank you, doctor. She's also worried about the man she was brought in here with. Alex Storm. Some of his family are in the waiting room."

"Feel free to use your phone to stay in touch with them. I'd prefer Ms. Mazelli remain calm. We can provide a sedative if she needs one."

Gina shook her head, which made it start pounding against the back of her eyes. God, she felt like shit. But Alex was possibly bleeding inside, so who was she to complain?

By some miracle, they'd both managed to get out of her house alive.

The doctor walked out, but the nurse came over and handed Tessa a notepad and pen. "If she really needs to ask something, this might work better. Otherwise, her throat won't heal as quickly."

Once the nurse got Gina's IV's adjusted and put the nasal cannula in, she left. Gina motioned for the pad and scribbled on the paper.

How did we get out of the house?

Tessa shrugged. "I don't know exactly what happened, but Greg said Alex carried you out just as they were getting there, then he passed out."

Alex carried her out? How had he gotten untied? He'd been unconscious the last she remembered. The smoke must have gotten to be too much for her.

"We heard all the sirens from the Inn and could smell the smoke. Luke ran most of the way to check where it was, then texted back that your house was on fire."

Hofstetter. Gramercy. Scarsdale.

Tipping her head, Tessa grabbed her phone, and her thumbs flew over the screen. "We knew about the first two but not Scarsdale. Apparently, Alex told someone before he collapsed. They'll get them. Don't worry. You should get some rest. If they get any information about Alex's condition, I'll let you know."

Glancing at the clock on the wall, Gina noted it was after midnight.

Where are your kids?

"Aunt Luci and Anna took them all over to Nathaniel's house. They figured it was easier for everyone to be together to get information out more efficiently. Plus, the house is big, and they can all bunk there until we can get them."

With Tessa's condition, she must be exhausted.

You don't need to stay with me. You need rest.

Tessa smiled warmly. "I'm okay. I wanted to be here for you. I understand what it's like not to have any family. Molly was beside herself that you were hurt, also."

But Alex is her family. She needs to stay with him.

"You don't get it, huh? They all think of you as family, too. I volunteered to be with you." Tessa leaned closer. "I was hoping at some point you *would* be my sister-in-law. I can see how much Alex cares for you. And you love him, right?"

Gina nodded. The tears started falling again. Please, let him be okay. Even if they couldn't be together, she needed Alex to be fine and healthy. She'd give up a life with him if it meant he could live.

Her eyes burned, from the smoke or more tears, who knew? Tessa perched on the edge of the bed and pulled her close. The comfort was perfect, and she wrapped her free arm as best she could around the other woman. Everything would be okay. It had to be.

SHE'S NOT BREATHING. No pulse. Not breathing. Not breathing. Not...

The words rang in Alex's head, along with the image of Gina, dead weight in his arms, taunting him. He hadn't gotten her out fast enough. It was his fault. The flames, the smoke, falling down the stairs, barely holding on to her. Why hadn't she listened when he told her to stay? Why hadn't he grabbed her before she left the wedding reception? He couldn't lose her now. But the memory lingered of her still form lying on the grass as the paramedics tried to pump life back into her. *No pulse. Not breathing.*

"Gina!" His throat was on fire, burning as he called her name.

"Alex, honey, it's okay. We're here."

His mom. Something kept pulling him back to the deep sleep he'd been in, but he needed to wake up.

"Mom?"

"Rest, sweetie. You've just gotten out of surgery. But you'll be fine."

Finally, his eyes opened a crack and took in his location. Small white room, antiseptic smells, beeps from a nearby machine, long tube attached to his arm.

"Surgery?"

"You had some internal bleeding." His dad stood at the foot of his bed, his face lined with worry. "They did a CT scan and managed to pinpoint the bleed. Fortunately, that meant they didn't have to open you all the way up to do exploratory surgery first before they stopped it."

Internal...yeah, his abdomen had hurt. But how? And what did it matter if Gina wasn't around.

Staring across the room, moisture welled in his eyes. He loved her. Truly loved her, but he hadn't been able to save her. That hurt worse than any body part currently did.

His mom held his hand, and he squeezed tight.

"Gina. I couldn't..." His voice cracked, the agony of losing her too great.

His mom's eyes opened wide, and she leaned in closer to push his hair back from his forehead, like she did when he was a kid. "Oh, honey, Gina's okay. Bad smoke inhalation, but Tessa's with her, and she let us know she'll be fine."

"She wasn't breathing. Had no pulse."

His dad cleared his throat. "Yeah, Greg said it was touch and go for a few moments, but they got her started again."

A huge weight lifted from his chest. Gina was alive. She'd be okay. Could he believe that?

"Where is she? I need to see her." He attempted to push

himself up, but nothing seemed to work. His head pounded, and his body ached everywhere.

His mother sent him *the look*. "You just got out of surgery, Alexander Peter Storm."

"I need to see for myself that she's okay. God, I thought I was going to have to watch her—" He stopped himself from stating his fears. His parents didn't need to know exactly how dire things had been.

"She's in ICU." Dad had moved closer. Prepared to help his mom keep him in bed? "I believe that's where the doctor said you'd be going once you were out of recovery."

"When can I go? Where is the doctor?"

Soon enough, he was being wheeled down the hallway and into the elevator, his parents following behind him. As he rolled into the Intensive Care Unit, he held up one hand.

"Gina. I need to see Gina."

"We need to get you settled in your room, Mr. Storm," the nurse admonished.

"Fine. As soon as you do, I'm getting up to go find her."

Mom caught up and patted his arm, looking at the woman. "He's quite concerned about his girlfriend, Gina Mazelli, who was also in the fire."

The nurse nodded and sighed, then asked a few questions at the desk.

"She's three doors down from you. I'll stop, so you can peek in."

They paused, and Alex attempted to rise. The nurse shook her head. "Don't get up."

As she walked into what he assumed was Gina's room, he shifted his head to get a better look. The nurse pushed back a curtain surrounding a bed. Tessa sat in a chair on the far side of the room, holding Gina's hand and pointing out the door.

And Gina, she was the most beautiful thing he'd ever

seen. Her dark eyes in her pale face sought him out, and the smile that crossed her face made his heart melt.

He lifted his hand and tried to croak out her name, but his voice wasn't working. His mom trotted into her room and kissed Gina's cheek, whispering something in her ear. In a minute, she was back.

"All set? You can see she's fine and being well taken care of." The nurse pursed her lips. "We need to get you into your bed and start another round of fluids and blood."

He didn't want to go, but the gurney moved anyway. Tears of relief leaked from the corners of his eyes. Gina's hand rose as he was pushed away, and he wanted to scream for them to let him stay in her room. But now that he'd seen her and knew she was alive, his system seemed ready to shut him down.

Once settled in his room, his dad clapped him on the shoulder, and his mom kissed his cheek.

"Your brothers and sister are waiting to see you. We'll let them get a quick visit, so they can see for themselves you're good, then we'll let you get some rest."

Sister? She'd gotten married tonight. God, that seemed so long ago.

Sara showed up in his doorway with TJ in tow, and she rushed to his side. "You had to upstage my wedding, didn't you?" Her watery smile was nowhere near censure.

Reaching for her hand, he groaned. "Sorry, Sagey. Totally wasn't planned, and you know how much I like things organized ahead of time."

"Oh, Alex, you could have been killed."

TJ stood behind her, one hand running up and down her back in comfort.

"I'm fine, so they tell me. What are you even doing here? You and TJ should be on your honeymoon."

Sara crossed her arms over her chest. "What kind of sister

would I be if I took off on a trip while my brother was fighting for his life in the hospital?"

"I don't think I was that bad."

"You've got a concussion, a few cracked ribs, internal bleeding, not to mention smoke inhalation, and some second degree burns on your hands."

His attempt to shrug only caused pain to shoot across his chest. At his grimace, Sara narrowed her eyes and smirked.

"You'll make me feel all sorts of guilty if you miss your honeymoon."

TJ rested his hands on Sara's shoulders. "Our flight isn't until noon. We were planning to stay in Boston tonight, so we haven't missed anything." His face said otherwise. Alex knew exactly what they were missing.

"You've seen me, and I'm good. Now go. This is your wedding night."

Sara's gaze flittered from him to TJ and back.

"You need to go. I'm getting tired, and Erik and Luke still need to assure themselves I'm not dying."

Nodding, Sara leaned over and kissed his cheek. "I'll keep checking with mom to make sure everything's okay."

Looking at TJ, Alex frowned. "Make sure she doesn't obsess over this. You need to enjoy your honeymoon."

"I'll take care of her. Get some rest."

They weren't gone two minutes, when Luke and Erik walked in.

"What the hell happened?" Erik's voice was gruff, but his expression showed his fear. "How are you feeling?"

"Feel like shit. We walked in on Mr. Hofstetter from the jewelry store and Gramercy from the bank. They were looking for something. Then, the lights went out. When I came to, Gina and I were tied up, and the turret room was on fire."

"Scarsdale was in on it, too." Erik's face darkened.

"Scarsdale? What the fuck? Never trusted that guy."

Luke smirked. "Mostly because he kept putting the moves on Gina."

"What the hell were they doing there?" His heart picked up speed thinking of Scarsdale with Gina.

"Tessa's been talking to Gina. Said they were looking for stolen jewelry and some bonds."

Stolen jewelry and bonds? The robberies from last fall? It was all too much to take in with the disco beat strumming through his brain. Lifting a hand to his head, he winced as he touched the sore spot on the back.

"Take it easy. You've got a concussion, along with a bunch of other stuff." Erik shuffled his feet, uncomfortable. Perhaps remembering when Tessa had been injured earlier this year.

"Tessa is in with Gina? You should take her back to my place, so you don't have to drive all the way back to Maine."

"I'm planning on it. But she insisted on seeing Gina. She didn't want her to be alone when she woke up. Too many damn years of being alone herself." The last was said under Erik's breath. His anger at the pain his wife had suffered for so many years apparent in his eyes.

"Hey, Luke?"

His younger brother had been fairly quiet, which just showed how worried he'd been.

"Yeah, what do you need? Anything?"

"Think you can charm the lady at the tux rental place? Pretty sure mine is toast."

That got a smile on Luke's face. "I'll do my damnedest. Gina's house isn't looking too good either, but they managed to keep the damage to the turret room and part of the third floor."

"Doesn't matter. We're both alive, and she can stay with me."

Erik cleared his throat. "I think you'll be in here a bit longer than Gina will. She didn't have abdominal surgery."

"Do me a favor and make sure she's okay when she goes home. I don't want her staying by herself. Luke, you'll be there, right?"

His younger brother's grin exploded. "Every night. I can even tuck her in bed with a sweet good-night kiss."

Alex growled. "Don't even think about it."

CHAPTER TWENTY-TWO

*T*he lights were low in the ICU, but Gina couldn't sleep. All day long she'd been told to rest, and her body had agreed. In between spitting up disgusting black stuff and talking to the police.

They'd assured her the three men had been picked up and were currently waiting to be arraigned on a number of different crimes. One of them being *attempted* murder. Thank God for Alex.

Her gaze moved to the doorway and the nurses' station outside. No one sat there currently, and she'd taken note of the routine all day, enough to know there might be a few minutes for her to go see Alex.

Earlier, one of the nurses had allowed her to take a short walk down the hall and back, but the curtain had been pulled in front of the bed as they'd walked past his room.

Getting up, she swung her legs over the side of the bed. It took a minute for the room to stop spinning. She picked up the extra hospital gown she'd been given, so her ass didn't hang out when she walked around. Soft, grippy socks helped keep her from slipping on the shiny floor.

At the door, she glanced around to make sure she wouldn't get caught, then walked slowly down the hall to Alex's room. Once inside, she tiptoed over to the bed and stared at the handsome man she loved. His skin was pale, but his face was relaxed in sleep. Sleep she knew he needed and didn't want to disturb. But she desperately wanted to assure herself he would be okay.

Inching closer, she rested on the side of his bed and picked up his hand, the one without the IV. She held it close to her face and felt the warmth on her skin.

"Mmm." His eyes opened, and a smile crossed his lips. "Hey, gorgeous. What are you doing in my neck of the woods?"

Leaning in closer, she pressed her forehead to his. "I've been trying to get over here all day, but those nurses have eyes everywhere." Her throat was still raw and her voice hoarse.

"Apparently, I still have the anesthesia in my blood stream. I think I've been asleep most of the day, or I would have headed over to see you." His voice was scratchy as well.

"You also have that little matter of surgery. Internal bleeding. Concussion. Cracked ribs. I've only got smoke inhalation. And a little soreness from the CPR."

Alex reached up and cupped her face. "Don't even joke about that. God, I was so scared I wouldn't get to you in time. The ties around my hands were so tight and then by the time I got to you, my fingers barely worked."

"But you did it. Then, you carried me down all those stairs. Probably one of the reasons the internal bleeding got bad enough to need surgery."

His eyes narrowed as his thumb stroked her cheek. "I still don't remember how I came to have cracked ribs."

She glanced away, then back to the confused gaze. "They wanted to know where the jewelry and bonds were. Rick couldn't get me to tell him by threatening me, so they started kicking you around."

"And you told them?"

She bit the side of her lip. "Yeah, I told them all the stuff was at the bank in Nonna's safe deposit box."

Alex started to laugh, then squeezed his eyes shut, wincing. "You little minx."

Pulling her face closer, he kissed her cheek, then her forehead. "I'm so, so sorry for all of this. It's all my fault."

She tilted her head. "How is this your fault? You didn't hide the stuff in Nonna's attic."

"When we got into the fight, I shouldn't have let you go. Should have gone after you."

"But you did follow me. If you hadn't, I wouldn't be sitting here now."

"I should have stopped you before you left the reception. Then, you wouldn't have gotten hurt."

"You know, they were behind all the accidents, too. The ladder and porch and the electric panel. All done to scare me and get me to move out faster. The police came to take my statement earlier today. I let them know where the jewels and bonds were. I want those out of my house."

"They talked to me, too, except I couldn't remember anything in between getting clonked on the head and waking up tied to the radiator. At that point, my concentration was on getting untied and getting you out. God, Dandy, I thought I'd have to watch you...and then when I finally got us outside, you weren't breathing."

His voice quivered, eyes filling with tears, agony in his expression. She'd felt that way, too.

She nodded, brushing his hair back from his forehead. "I know. When I woke up, I had no idea how I'd gotten out and was scared to death you were...that something had happened to you."

Alex's face grew stormy. His finger trailed down her cheek. "How did you get this bruise? Is it when I almost dropped you going down the stairs?"

Telling him about Rick would get him all stirred up, but she certainly didn't want to heap more guilt on what he already had.

"Rick got a little fresh, and I bit him. He didn't like it." No way she'd tell him exactly what the pig had done.

"That little…" He was holding his temper in check, but he was furious. Probably not good for his condition. Better calm him down before the nurses yelled at her for stirring things up. She pressed her lips to his, and immediately his body relaxed. When she eased back, he kept hold of her face, staring deeply into her eyes.

"Alex, right before we went upstairs—"

"Yes, I did say it," he interrupted. "I love you, Gina. And I'm sorry it took me so long to finally realize it. You threw me for a loop wearing that boring dress and acting all proper."

"But that's exactly what one of your perfect ladies would wear and how they would act."

"Yeah, and maybe that's what made me understand it wasn't what I wanted, even though I thought it was. I missed your uniqueness and exuberance. Your sassy charm and mischievous nature. I missed the part of you that makes you my Dandelion. Mine."

"You're sure? It's not just great sex?"

His eyebrows rose as he grinned. "Well, there's that, too. But it's never been like that with anyone else. Not even close. You somehow get so deep in my soul it's like you're a part of me, and I can't get you out. Just looking at you makes my emotions explode, and I can't get you close enough. I've been looking for that feeling my whole life. Since the first time we made love."

Which was probably why none of his other girlfriends had wanted to continue their relationship. They hadn't connected to him. Lucky her.

A soft knock on the door had them turning. One of the nurses stood there, an indulgent smile on her face.

"You both should be resting."

Gina nodded, then kissed Alex again. "The doctor said I'll probably be heading home tomorrow. I'll stop in before I go."

Alex grabbed her hand as she stood. "You'll stay at my place. Yours is a mess. I told Luke to take care of you, so don't give him a hard time."

Her lips twitched. "Sure, I'll be a perfect angel."

His eyes narrowed as he laughed. "But if he offers to tuck you in, don't let him."

THE PLACE WAS A MESS. Gina looked around her disaster of a house and sighed. Maybe she shouldn't have come over yet. The taste and smell of smoke was still too ingrained in her system.

Molly had picked her up at the hospital late morning and dropped her off at Alex's. The woman had made a small lunch, then apologized that she needed to get back to work. Afterward, Sofie had stopped by and brought some clothes for her to borrow until Gina's could be washed. They all apparently reeked of smoke.

Now, she stood in her living room, watermarks dripping down the walls and soot everywhere. How the heck did she even deal with this?

"Gina, be careful in here." Greg entered behind her. "We spent all day yesterday boarding up the broken windows and roof, but there still could be weak spots, especially on the upper floors."

Sighing, she pushed her hair back from her face. She'd finally gotten a shower a few hours ago, but she wasn't sure if the smoke smell was gone. "Thanks, Greg. I'm not even sure what I should do."

He took her hand and led her to sit on the bench on the front porch. "Maybe you need to take it easy for a few days. Let others help you. We've already started the process in getting the place cleaned up."

"What do you mean you started the process? What process?"

Sitting next to her, he patted her hand. "I hope you don't mind, but some of the community wanted to give you assistance. Stan Leland showed up yesterday saying your grandmother had an insurance policy through his company. He had his insurance adjuster with him, so they went through the house already and are figuring out what the claim is worth. The town council is pushing him to get the money to you as soon as possible."

Her head jerked up. "What? Why would they do that? It was arson. Don't they normally not pay if it's arson?"

Greg grinned. "Sure, if you burn it down yourself. But you solved the case of a few robberies from last fall. The council didn't like that the town was being looked at as an unsafe place to live. Plus, the payoff Hofstetter and Gramercy got for the jewelry and bonds was huge. Those two put the money in Gramercy's bank, so it can legally be held. And now they have the money back plus the bonds and jewelry."

Confusing thoughts swirled through her head. "Okay, so that's good, I guess."

"And there was a reward for finding both of them. Which will go to you."

"A reward for finding the jewels?"

"And one for return of the bonds."

"Oh, it should go to Alex, too. He was with me when we found them."

Greg peeked at the house, then at her again. "I have a feeling you and Alex will be sharing lots of things in the future."

God, she hoped so. They hadn't had much time to talk since the fire. But could she stay here in this town with him? Would people accept her? Did she care?

"I hope you don't mind, but Luke and I wanted to start the clean up process. I've got some off-shift guys from the firehouse showing up soon. One of them is bringing a dumpster."

"You mean for all the burnt timber and stuff?"

His lips straightened. "I was thinking we should get rid of all the furniture that can't be saved first. That'll give the construction crew more room to work once repairs begin."

"Furniture? I'm sure everything in the attic is toast and maybe the third-floor rooms."

Greg took her hand and squeezed. "Gina, between the smoke and the water, everything is pretty much damaged. That includes all the furniture in the bedrooms and even on the first floor. If it's wood or metal it might be okay, though it will need to be thoroughly cleaned. The rest will either need to be professionally cleaned, which can be expensive, or tossed. You've got to decide what you want done."

She thought for a few minutes about all of Nonna's things. Most of it she'd planned to either donate or toss anyway. Nonna hadn't bought new furniture in longer than Gina had been alive.

"There are a few antique dressers in the bedrooms and some tables that I've always liked, but for the most part, I was planning to get rid of everything before I sold the place."

"I'm sorry, doubtful you'll be able to put this on the

market for a while. If you need anything, you know you can ask me or any of the family. We'd be happy to help."

Yes, they would. The thought brought such a rush to her insides, she felt like skipping. But her ribs still hurt from the CPR, so she'd put that aside for now.

"Thank you for everything, Greg. I don't know what I'd do without your family."

"Well, we all kind of think of you as one of us already."

A car pulled up in front of the house, and Greg excused himself to go inside. Easing off the bench, she walked across the lawn to see who it was.

Aunt Anna got out with her daughter, Amy, and they carried large boxes.

"Hey, sweetie," Anna called out. "I wasn't sure if you'd be up and about yet. How are you feeling?"

"Throat's a bit sore, but otherwise fine."

Amy held up one of the boxes. "We thought we'd take all the dishes and pots and pans and bring them over to our house and run them through the dishwasher. I know they shut the electricity off in your place."

"That's nice. I'm sure I can do them at Alex's, though."

"Of course, you can—" Anna patted her arm, "—but you shouldn't have to when you've got this large family ready to help. I'm sure there'll be plenty of other things to do at Alex's. We'll just take a small bit of that away."

"Thank you very much. I really appreciate the help."

Both Amy and Anna gave her a quick hug, then went inside. When she tried to follow them, Anna shooed her away.

"Go, get some rest. You've had an exciting few days, not to mention the injury."

"I'll just get my laptop." Hopefully, it hadn't been damaged too badly. When she got it back to Alex's, after wiping the soot off, she booted it up and aside from a tiny hiccup, it seemed to work.

All afternoon people stopped in to make sure she was all right or to offer help. She set herself up in Alex's meeting room, so she could see who came and went. So many people. The furniture and carpets were dragged out and tossed in the huge dumpster that now sat next to the porch.

After school got out, Leah, and her friend, Ali Cabrera, showed up with cards their students had made to help her feel better. The crude drawings of Leah's Kindergarten students made her smile, but the lovely well wishes from Ali's fourth graders brought tears to her eyes. The women were going over to start scrubbing down any of the lamps and tables that were staying. They told her she wasn't to worry about anything.

The most surprising visit of the day was from Kristan and her friends, Ashley and Kelsey. They'd grabbed all of Gina's clothes, towels, and bedding the day before and had spent hours washing and drying them. They dropped off several laundry baskets, which she knew weren't hers.

"You didn't have to do this. I'm not sure why you did. I've only met you recently."

Kristan cocked her head. "You'll find that this community helps each other out. What happened to you is horrible, and we'll do whatever is needed to set things right."

Ashley refolded a large comforter, which had been on Gina's bed. The one she and Alex had shared so many times. "We're happy to help, even in this little way we can. Hopefully, you'll stick around and get to know some of us."

"I'd like that, but I'm not sure exactly what my plans are at the moment."

Kristan's knowing smile accented her mischievous eyes. "I'd bet Alex has some plans for you."

Kelsey frowned. "How is he? We heard he had to have surgery after what those bastards did to him."

"He'll be okay, but he'll have some healing to do once he gets home." Home, his home. What was beginning to feel like her home, too. Not a building, but a place. With him.

"Give him our best." Kristan picked up her purse and headed toward the door. "If either of you need anything else, please let us know." She dropped a business card on the table and left, followed by her friends.

Weird. It was all too weird. All these people, checking on her, doing stuff for her. Many of them she'd never even met. The insurance guy had called and told her not to worry about anything. He'd be pushing the claim through as fast as he could. Someone from the town council had called also to see if she needed anything. A group of little old ladies had shown up with food and a handmade quilt, since she'd lost so much.

Of course, Alex had all these things at his place, but most of them didn't even realize she and Alex were an item. They'd shown up at her house, and Greg had sent them this way. They'd all come for her.

Digging back into work helped her settle for a bit, but she knew she had to call her boss and make some arrangements. There was a new project he specifically wanted her for, but she'd need to go to New York to meet with the customer and iron out details before she started. She could be gone a week or more.

At dinnertime, Molly and Pete showed up and shared the meal with her. Luke had grabbed a quick bite and gone to help Greg.

As they ate, she told them about all the people who had visited during the day and all the gifts they'd brought.

"I didn't think any of these people ever liked me."

Molly patted her hand. "Whatever gave you that idea, sweetie?"

"Most people look at me strange when I'm around. I dress and act different from them."

Pete chuckled. "Exactly. I'd guess many of them are envious that you can carry off the clothes you wear and wish they had the guts to do some of the things you do."

She threw them both a doubtful look.

"And if I may be so bold," Pete continued, "you are an extremely beautiful young lady with confidence and poise. It's hard not to look." At his wife's expression, he added, "Except for me, because I have the best wife in the world."

They all laughed and the lightness inside her was precious.

"Honey," Molly said, "Your grandmother was well-loved in this town, and you are her granddaughter. You're part of this town, also."

For the first time, Gina finally believed it. Maybe she did belong here.

CHAPTER TWENTY-THREE

"*N*ow, remember, the doctor said you shouldn't try to do too much at first."

Alex looked at his mother as he sat at the kitchen table. After five days in the hospital, he was ready to be home.

"He also said I shouldn't sit around sedentary all day either. I have to build my stamina back up again." As his mom began to argue, he held up his hand. "I'll make sure not to do more than I can handle. You and Dad don't need to sit around babysitting me."

"I'd feel better if someone were here with you at least the first few days. In case you need something."

Standing, he placed his hands on her shoulders. "Mom, I'll be fine. Luke will be here after work. Greg's across the street, and every other relative we have, except Erik and Sara, is within fifteen minutes of here. You don't need to worry."

His dad laughed. "You should know by now, Alex, telling your mother, any mother, not to worry is futile. Just accept that it comes from a place of love."

His heart squeezed knowing he was so fortunate to have

his parents, his family. He wished Gina were here now, too. The last few days had been hard without her.

"Do you know when Gina is coming home?" Like she read his mind, his mom's smile was warm but concerned.

Home? Did Gina consider this home? That question was one he wanted an answer to, also. She'd visited him in the hospital yesterday, saying she was headed to New York for some business, and she'd be back in a week or so. God, he hoped so. Had the fire been the last straw in keeping her around here? He told her he loved her, and he wanted her to stay. Had it been enough? There wasn't much more he could do. Certainly, he wouldn't force her, even if he wanted to, but he'd make sure she knew how he felt.

"She said she had some business in New York."

"Come on, Molly, let's leave Alex to get some rest." His dad put his arm around her shoulder and stepped toward the door. God bless the man.

"Fine, but if you need anything, you make sure to call us."

"I will, Mom, Dad. Thanks. I love you."

Once they'd left, Alex trudged through the house. Gina's presence filled every room. The milk was on the wrong side of the fridge door. His large and small spoons were mixed together. The colander was in the wrong cabinet.

Up in his room, he could still smell her honeysuckle fragrance. The bed hadn't been properly made. She'd pulled the comforter up over the sheets, but that was about it. Holding the pillow to his face, he breathed in deep. God, he missed her so much already. What if she didn't come back? What if she got caught up in her free-wheeling life in New York and forgot she loved him? He couldn't let that happen, now that he'd figured out she was the one he needed to bring him alive.

For so long, he'd thought the perfect woman was prim and proper and dressed in modest outfits with impeccable manners. Gina had stolen that dream from him. But in its place, she'd provided him with someone who could bring him out of his ultra-controlled world and still function. Barely, but with her by his side, he'd manage.

Moving to the bathroom, he cleaned up the best he could, watching for his incision. After drying off, he reached for his toothbrush and the paste. The tube was squeezed right down the middle, and a bunch of her make-up was scattered in the cabinet. So many reminders of Gina.

When he opened his closet, his heart jumped and raced. Her clothes hung near his inside. They were totally unorganized and mixed in with his, so he reached in to move them about. Then, he stopped. Seeing her shirts and dresses intermingled with his gave him a feeling that she'd definitely be back. They couldn't stay that way forever. It would drive him crazy. But for now, he'd allow it.

After getting dressed, he wandered downstairs and sat at his desk. There was work that needed to be caught up on, but when his clients heard what had happened, they understood that he'd need a few extra days to recoup.

Reaching for a pencil, he chuckled. They were totally in the wrong place. Gina had put all his pens and pencils in some fancy pattern again. Not the first time. The thought made him smile. He'd rearrange them later.

His planner sat on the left corner of his desk, and on the right, where it should be, was a big heart-shaped sticky note with an arrow pointing to it. Silly woman. But at least the book was here.

A tag stuck out of the planner, and he opened it to today's date. In bright pink ink—where she'd gotten that he didn't know—was written ALEX HOME in all caps. Half a dozen hearts floated next to the words. His heart felt like it was floating now, too.

As he flipped through the pages, other notes showed up.

The day of Sara's wedding, in the eight pm time slot, she'd written *'say I love you to Gina'* and later *'rescue Gina from murderous criminals'*. Just the thought of what could have happened had his lungs drying up. They were both fine, and he needed to keep reminding himself of that.

He turned more pages to check what kind of projects or activities he had scheduled. June eighth, ten days from now, had another entry in a rainbow of colors, surrounded by balloons. GINA COMES HOME.

His breath left his chest, the relief so strong he sagged against the chair. It was in his planner, so therefore it was going to happen. Gina knew that more than anyone. The fact she'd written it here meant something. She was coming back.

Nothing else was more important than that, so he got up and wandered through the other rooms. Boxes littered his living room. Stuff from Gina's house that had been cleaned and brought here. His mom had mentioned how over-whelmed Gina had been with the outpouring of support from the community. No surprise to him. It was one of the reasons he loved living here.

Sitting on the couch, he eyed the pile of Gina's things. Bedding, computers, kitchen supplies, lamps, and accessories. Another reminder she was coming back. A small wooden box caught his eye, and he bent to pick it up. He grunted at the twinge in his side as his incision pulled.

The box looked like it would hold jewelry. Did she have a ring in there? One that would give him an idea of what size she wore?

Opening it, he found a few scraps of paper. He shouldn't look, but his curiosity got the better of him, and he pulled out the first one. It was his handwriting, from years and years ago. If he remembered correctly, he'd been about thirteen, a very awkward age, when they'd written these notes. Wishes for the future. They'd tucked them into the hole in the closet upstairs in his old room. Gina mentioned she'd found them, but he'd never asked to see.

I want to be a successful architect and design buildings of great importance. I also want people to stop making fun of me. I wish I could not be so weird and be more like Gina. Everyone likes her, and no one expects her to change.

Oh, God, that brought back some painful memories. He was lucky he'd managed to find a few friends who accepted him. Of course, he'd also suppressed some of his stranger quirks when he was with them. Something he'd never had to hide when he was with Gina.

He pulled out the other slip of paper and opened it. Gina's fancy eleven-year-old cursive decorated the page.

I want to invent a bunch of great things to help everyone in the world. I will invent a machine that makes all people nice to one another, so everyone is friends. And I especially want to invent something that would make Alex like me, so we can get married and live together with tons of kids.

The words blurred across the page. She didn't need to invent anything to do that. He already liked her, had always liked her. And now he was completely head over heels, forever, happily ever after, in love with her.

As for tons of kids, they might have to negotiate on that, though a few wouldn't be bad. Maybe between his straight-as-an-arrow need for control and Gina's flighty, live-in-the-moment attitude, they might have a chance at decent kids who didn't have all these hang ups.

With his mind going a mile a minute, he got up and patrolled the backyard. The day was sunny and beautiful, with the birds chirping and a slight breeze whistling through the trees. Just like another day many years ago.

His feet started walking and before he knew it, he was standing under the old tree house in the woods behind his yard and Gina's. Years of neglect showed in the saggy boards and sloping roof. If they were going to have kids, it would need some work.

The memory of how he and Gina had first made love inside flashed through his head. Honeysuckle grew all around the base of the tree, inundating his senses with the fragrance. An idea formed, and he grinned. In ten days, Gina would be back. Hopefully, that would be enough time.

THE CLOSED SIGN was on the door.

Gina frowned and blinked. It was Monday. Alex wouldn't be closed. Unless he was sick. Really sick. Or had had complications from his surgery. But they'd texted back and forth a few times over the past ten days, and he'd assured her he was recovering nicely, though their messages had been extremely brief.

As she walked up the porch, she saw a scrap of bright pink paper stuck to the door. It had her name on it. *In the office*, it said.

The front door was unlocked, as it usually was during his office hours, so Gina stepped inside, passed through his meeting room, and into his office. Which was empty.

"Felix?"

Nothing. No sound, no movement. Where was he? Should she worry?

Another piece of bright pink paper sat in the middle of his desk. *The Master Bath.*

Okay, strange. It wasn't like Alex to play games.

Once upstairs, she checked the bathroom. The pink paper in here sat next to a bottle of her honeysuckle lotion. Now where had he found that? She'd always hidden it, so he wouldn't realize her secret. The one that turned him on so much.

Only one word on this note. *Apply.* One on the mirror said, *Closet.*

He wanted her to put the lotion on? After five hours in the car, she needed something a little stronger than scented lotion. She quickly stripped, took a fast shower, then rubbed the lotion all over her skin. In only a towel, she went into his bedroom to get something to wear. Most of her clothes were in his closet. Unless he'd moved them.

When she opened the door, another note caught her attention. It was attached to the flirty little top and skirt combination she'd worn at Easter. The one that had him so hot and bothered they'd had a quickie in his pantry closet.

Wear.

Okay. Things were getting interesting, especially coming from Alex. Once dressed, she inspected the room and spied another pink paper on the dresser. It simply said *Kitchen.*

After slipping on her shoes, she made her way down the back stairs into the kitchen, where a beautiful vase of flowers sat on the table next to a pink note. *Picnic Table.*

As she headed out the back door, she noted it was unlocked. Had his concussion knocked out his need for rules and routines?

The picnic table on the back deck had a blanket on top and yet another pink paper. *Bring to the tree house.*

The tree house? The one they'd first made love in? No one had used that tree house in years. What the heck was he up to? Was he well enough to be setting this whole thing up?

The path into the woods was a bit overgrown, but obviously someone had been through here recently, as the undergrowth was flattened enough to walk easily on it. Carrying the blanket, she wondered what this whole thing was about. It also thrilled her that Alex had designed this little game for her. It was creative and fun and exactly the type of thing she loved. Like she loved him. She needed to make sure to tell him a few thousand times now that she was back.

It had been years, but her heart remembered the way to the large tree Pete and Nick Storm had built a house in for their children. Since it bordered her grandmother's yard, she'd been encouraged to use it, also. Though probably not for the activity she and Alex had used it for nine years ago.

As she approached the tree, she stopped short. The sagging boards were gone and fresh lumber replaced them. A metal ladder stood against the side of the tree, tied tightly so it wouldn't slide. On one of the bottom rungs hung a pink sign. The only thing on it was an arrow pointing up. Clear enough.

Tucking the blanket under one arm, she grabbed the rungs and started to climb. This better be worth it. Her three-inch heels weren't the best footwear for this event. She pushed the door open, the hinges soundless as it swung in. Oh, God. Oh, my God.

Every available space was filled with honeysuckle and jar candles. They were tucked into built-in nooks and on the few small tables that littered the floor. The scent was heavenly. Covering the rest of the floor was a big area rug with Alex waiting right in the middle.

"Felix? What on earth...?"

"I see you got my notes. And followed directions." A grin lit up his face.

She let go of the blanket and quickly dropped to the floor next to him. "What are you doing up here? You shouldn't be climbing up here with your injury. And how did you get this all fixed up? You just had surgery."

He took her hand and pulled her close. "The surgery was over two weeks ago. But I actually had John do all the work. He thought I was a little bit crazy."

She had to agree, but then she liked crazy. "What is all this for?" In the corner, there was a bottle of wine and two glasses, as well as a small basket with cheese and crackers in it. Reminiscent of their first time. Was he trying to reenact it? How sweet.

"I missed you so much while you were gone."

Leaning in, she kissed him softly. "I missed you, too."

"So your business is all dealt with, and you're here for good, right?"

She shrugged. He'd said he didn't want her to leave, but nothing else had ever been mentioned. "My house is a burnt-out mess. It won't be anywhere near ready to live in for quite a while."

Another kiss followed as he cupped her face. "I was kind of hoping you'd stay with me. I've gotten used to you messing up my system."

"Don't think I didn't notice you've already rearranged my clothes in your closet." Her laughter echoed through the small space.

His eyes twinkled. "I put them in groups for the different seasons and then according to length. Much easier to find now."

She shivered. "When you talk like that, Felix, you get me all hot and bothered."

His head shook, and his eyes rose skyward. "I love that you humor me. Actually, I love every little thing about you."

"Every little thing? Like when I don't wear a bra out in public?"

Reaching out, he flicked aside the shoulder of her shirt, then groaned. "I absolutely love when you don't wear a bra. The public part only makes me upset, because no one else should ever see you that way."

"You want me exclusively?" Was that too bold to ask? But since when had she ever shied away from asking the tough questions?

His finger tugged on her elastic neckline, then trailed down to circle her nipple. "Exclusively. Fully. Absolutely. Undividedly. Solely. And completely mine." His lips covered hers, and her head spun with the effect.

"Do you have a problem with that?" Easing back, he looked at her, anxiety in his expression.

"Not as long as I get the same exclusivity."

A frown marred his handsome features. "I don't think you have to worry about competing interest."

"Oh, believe me, many women are interested. However, most of them don't have the stamina or perseverance to find out exactly how incredible you are. I'm stubborn that way."

"Thank God." He pulled her into his arms again, and his mouth covered hers. The touch was slow but heated as his hands ran along her neck and down her back. She joined in, touching, caressing, pressing her body against his. No one else ever took her to the places he did. When she was in his arms, she soared through the sky, emotions on high alert, gathering in all the feelings she could at once.

"I love you so much, Dandelion. I'm sorry it took so long to figure out my feelings for you. They've always been there, but I was too stupid to see them."

"I love you, too. I've loved you since I was a kid. How could I not?"

His hand caressed her cheek. "Thank God you're so persistent and finally wore me down. Made me see how much I need you in my life."

His other hand rose, holding a small box with a ring tucked in it. The gold, vined band with emeralds and diamonds she'd pointed out to him two months ago. He'd remembered.

"Oh, I uh…"

"Gina Takara Mazelli, will you do me the honor of being my wife, forever and always?"

Tears slid down her cheeks. Silly. She never cried for sentimental stuff. "Forever and always? That's an awful long time, Felix? Are you sure you can handle that?"

"I want to try. For you, I'd do anything. I'll attempt to be less rigid and more spontaneous. Keep my organizing to a minimum. Maybe even let you put the dishes away once in a while."

That would kill him. No doubt. She rarely put stuff away where it belonged.

Holding out her hand, she allowed Alex to put the ring on her finger. It fit perfectly and looked exactly right. "I don't want you to change anything for me. I fell in love with Felix, my super-organized control freak. Why would I want to turn you into anyone else?"

"You're sure? No one else has ever been able to put up with me."

"You have quirks, Felix, but I love them. They're what make you you."

"So is that a yes?"

She nodded exuberantly, then launched herself into his arms, kissing him madly. "One hundred percent, no exchanges, no returns, yes."

His eyes lit up as he kissed her again, this time passionately, and with so much feeling, her heart exploded, overflowing her entire body, blood stream, and every muscle and nerve. It was what she'd wanted for so long. Alex was hers.

As he stroked his fingers through her hair, he gazed deeply into her eyes. "Thank you, Dandelion, for loving me, agreeing to be my wife, for always keeping me on my toes. I used to have these dreams of a perfect, proper wife. Then you came along and stole them right out from under me. But you replaced them with something better. True and lasting love."

Words she'd wanted to hear forever. "I feel the same way about you. You're all I've ever wanted."

Alex's brows knit together. "I thought I always needed to have control…and it's hard when I don't. I won't lie and say I won't have anxiety attacks again, but you help me feel like it's okay to let go once in a while. No one has ever made me feel as good as you, Dandy. You're the one who owns my soul. The missing piece to my puzzle. You complete me."

He'd remembered everything she'd said that day at the jewelry store. Pulling him down on the carpet, with the smell of honeysuckle all around, life was perfect.

"Now, how about putting that puzzle piece of yours in the right place to make me complete."

TAKE a sneak peek at the next book in the Storms of New England series, BROKEN DREAMS book 4.

BROKEN DREAMS

STORMS OF NEW ENGLAND, BOOK 4

CHAPTER ONE

"*C*ongratulations! It's a boy."

Nathaniel Storm closed his eyes and shook his head before he opened them again. When he did, Helene Castleton-Billingsworth, formerly Helene Castleton-Storm, still stood on his front porch.

"Helene, what are you doing here? It's Christmas Eve. I figured you'd be getting ready for one of your swanky parties with the beautiful people." Not here on the outskirts of tiny little Squamscott Falls, New Hampshire.

She might already be decked out. Her fur trimmed cashmere Burberry coat, the one he'd spent a few months' salary on, covered her outfit. Her blonde hair was swept up in a fancy do, and her feet were shod in the newest Louboutins. Jewels shimmered in her ears and on her hands.

"This is Tanner." She pushed a small boy with a mop of blond curls forward. "He's yours. I need you to take him."

Nathaniel eyed the child and scowled. "What are you trying to pull here, Helene? I'm guessing this is the kid you got knocked up with when you were screwing around with Bryce."

She took in a deep breath and let it out slowly. This was so she didn't lose control. Helene had been all about control. Too bad she hadn't used it to keep Bryce Billingsworth out of her pants when the man had been Nathaniel's law partner.

"We recently had some medical testing done on Tanner and discovered his blood type is O positive."

Nathaniel's blood type was O positive. Was that too common for a child of a Billingsworth? "Lots of people have type O blood, Helene."

"Yes, but I'm type A, and Bryce is AB. It's genetically impossible for Tanner to be Bryce's child."

Shit. He'd wondered about that possibility, but Helene had insisted Bryce was the father. Now what the hell did they do? Share the child?

"What do you want? Child support? Because you can kiss my ass if you think I'm paying you anything when you have millions at your disposal."

Helene's lips pinched, letting him know she disapproved of his language. Or of him. Who knew with the Ice Princess?

"I need you to take him. I can't keep him anymore."

"What do you mean, take him? He's your son." The kid stood quietly next to her, his eyes focused intently on the spinning tires of a Hot Wheels he held.

"Bryce…" She cleared her throat and looked over her shoulder at the limousine parked in front of his house. "Bryce doesn't want to raise another man's child."

"I always knew he was a bastard. Oh yeah, the fact he was sleeping with my wife while we were still married kind of confirms that. But thumbing his nose at a child he's raised for what…three years? That's cold."

"Nathaniel, please. Bryce hasn't spent much time with Tanner due to his work commitments, so he's not attached. I'm giving custody over to you."

The cold-hearted weasel and Helene deserved each other.

"You're giving me custody? *Full* custody?"

Her glacial stare skimmed to the child, then returned as icy as ever. "Yes. Bryce doesn't want him living in our house."

"What kind of mother gives up her son? God, Helene, are you seriously that frozen inside?"

Another peek at the boy standing next to her, then her smiled thawed slightly. "I mean, if you and I were to get—"

"Get back together," he finished for her. "Are you out of your mind? Not in a billion years. You're a lying, cheating tramp, and I'd rather be married to a flea-infested alley cat. I want nothing to do with you."

She shrugged, his words bouncing off the cashmere of her coat. "I didn't think so. Just checking. But the fact remains that I can't have Tanner in the house with Bryce."

"You're not even going to want visitation rights?" He wasn't a family lawyer, but he knew she was screwing her parental rights if she gave the boy up completely. If this child was his, and with Helene's previous deceit, he had reasons to doubt, he'd make sure she never saw him again.

She shook her head, making sure not to upset the expensive coiffure.

"I guess you need to follow the money. That always was your first love." At one time, he'd thought it was him. *Fool me once...*

"Yes, well...here are his things." She stepped aside. Several large suitcases sat behind her, along with a car seat and a box of toys.

Seriously, there was enough for a dozen children. "His things."

Leaning down, she scooped a black and white stuffed dog from the top and handed it to him. "This is his favorite toy. He likes to sleep with it. It can get ugly if he doesn't have it at bedtime."

The child, Tanner, his son, never even looked up. He'd

been standing there without saying a word this whole time. Did he not understand his mother was deserting him? Essentially throwing him away and giving him to some stranger he didn't know? Was he able to hear her words? She'd said something about medical tests.

"Helene, what exactly were you looking for when you had the blood tests done? I assume Bryce wasn't just doubting the kid's paternity now. Is the boy sick?"

Her gaze flittered away, and she squared her shoulders, a fake smile appearing on her perfectly made up lips. She was about to lie to him. Too bad he hadn't noticed those tells earlier. Like before they'd gotten married.

"No, he's perfectly healthy. There are just a few odd behaviors that the doctor wanted to check out. Nothing serious, I'm sure."

Nothing serious. The child—Damn, he had to start thinking of him by his name. Tanner hadn't done anything except stare at the spinning wheels of the car. He was no child psychologist, but he didn't think most kids did that. Tanner was about the same age as his cousin Erik's adopted son, Matty. Matty jumped and yelled and couldn't sit still all that long.

A beep from the limo had Helene pressing her lips together and glancing nervously over her shoulder. "I have to go. We've got a private jet waiting to take us to the Vineyard. Bryce will be quite dismayed if they've started it up, and it wastes too much fuel."

"Yes, let's not waste jet fuel. You're seriously going to walk away from your child? Do you know what this will do to him? Do you even care? I know nothing about him. What am I supposed to feed him? What does he like to do? When does he go to bed? What are his routines?"

"I don't really know, Nathaniel. The nannies took care of all that. I really do have to go."

"Is there a nanny who'd work for me that he's familiar with?" The child needed someone in his corner who knew him.

"It won't matter. You'll see." She bent and stroked the boy's hair. "Be good for your daddy, Tanner." Then she skirted the bags and walked down the porch stairs. As she got to the bottom, she turned and said, "Oh, Dr. Malachite in Boston is his pediatrician. I'm sure he'd be happy to send his medical records to whatever doctor you choose for him. Merry Christmas, Nathaniel."

Nathaniel stood in the doorway until the limo cruised away and the bitter nip in the air woke him from his stupor.

What the hell had just happened? And what in God's name was he supposed to do now? Tanner still stood there with the toy car, unfazed that his mother had left him with a stranger. Left him for good. Holy shit. He had a feeling those words would be repeating over and over for a while.

"Hey, Tanner. Let's get you inside where it's warm, okay?"

He took the boy's hand and led him into the house. Tanner looked around, like he'd only just now realized he wasn't home. Would he start screaming for his mom?

Nathaniel's heart beat triple time, about to pound out of his chest in frustration, anger, and terror. He couldn't do this by himself.

Leading Tanner into his study, he placed him on the large leather chair and handed him the stuffed dog. The child tucked the animal under his arm and started rolling the car along the seat cushion.

Pulling his cell phone out of his pocket, Nathaniel pressed number one on his speed dial. When the call connected, his voice sounded weak and pathetic to his own ears.

"Mom, I need your help."

E

ABOUT THE AUTHOR

Stay in touch with Kari Lemor and find out when her next release or sale is.

Website: https://www.karilemor.com/

Join her reader's Group THE LIT LOUNGE for fun and getting to know her better:

https://www.facebook.com/groups/373521153021256/

Other places to get information on Kari:

- facebook.com/Karilemorauthor
- twitter.com/karilemor
- instagram.com/karilemorauthor
- pinterest.com/karilemor
- bookbub.com/authors/kari-lemor

Made in the USA
Middletown, DE
28 September 2022

11289335R00198